Silver Prairies
A More Perfect Union - Book Three
Pegg Thomas

Spinner of Yarns
PUBLISHING, LLC

S PINNER OF YARNS PUBLISHING
Sault Ste. Marie, Michigan

Copyright @2023 by Pegg Thomas
https://peggthomas.com/
Published in the United States of America
ISBN: 979-8-9866966-0-7
Cover Design using Midjourney.com
Cover Art Copyright by Spinner of Yarns Publishing

Pegg Thomas paints an amazingly realistic portrait of life on a long cattle drive from San Antonio, Texas, to Abilene, Kansas. She brings to life with plush sensory detail the characters' exhausting hardships on the trail, the constant battle with the elements, and the life-and-death dangers that arise when least expected. The tender romance that develops along the journey adds to the richness of the story. Anyone who enjoys historical romance with a western theme will enjoy *Silver Prairies*.

~ Susan Anne Mason
Award-winning author of *Irish Meadows* & other historical romances

If you're looking for a formulaic historical romance, avoid *Silver Prairies*. The author has woven together the history, the setting, and the characters into a delightful tapestry that surprises until the very end. Especially enjoyed the historical points about moving cattle through open country, breaking wild mustangs, and taming the wild hearts of the humans involved. Highly recommended.

~ Donna Schlachter
Author of historical mysteries, including *Kate*.

Thomas is a masterful historical fiction writer and her gift shines through in Silver Prairies. She has a keen ability to paint a scene and touch you with the emotions of the characters, completely drawing you into the story world. It becomes so real, you'll flinch when bullets fly and shed a tear when hearts break. Silver Prairies might be her best story yet.

~ Heather Blanton
USA Today best-selling author of *The Defiance Series*

He was a Southerner like her, but had fought for the "wrong" side. Now both hide scars and the pain of loss. With danger lurking at every turn, and more than their hearts at risk, Silver Prairies is an adventure you don't want to miss!

~ Angela K Couch
Author of *Where Wild Roses Bloom*

Join Pegg's Newsletter
writing updates – sneak peeks – fiber arts updates – personal content
https://www.subscribepage.com/PeggThomas

To the American cowboys and all they accomplished in the short years
they reigned over the prairies.

And to the American cowboys who keep the traditions alive today,
including my son,
Jeff Thomas—horse trainer and team roper.
Jeff on his horse Sackett.

ACKNOWLEDGMENT

Thank you, Ann Tuckerman Lyon, for still being my friend after all
this time. Friends since kindergarten—often parted by miles and
years—it's still a joy to get together and find how much we haven't
changed. *(We will not discuss the outward changes, because they don't
really matter.)* Thanks for letting me bounce story ideas off of you and
for being my advocate on the left coast.

I'm not short ~ she's tall!

PROLOGUE

T HE SLEEPY KANSAS TOWN had no idea what was headed its way. Its old men, women, and children weren't cowering in fear of the unknown, however. Not like what had happened in South Carolina. Not like Benjamin Warley's sisters and their families. The people of Abilene weren't rushing to bury their valuables before Sherman's forces burned everything to the ground.

Ben eased his weight in the saddle, letting his horse rest while he surveyed the false-fronted businesses of Abilene. As pitiful as it was, the town had grown since the first time he'd ridden through in the winter of 'sixty-four. There were more sod homes, one of them so fresh the dirt hadn't yet weathered to gray. Several horses stood hip-shot along the hitching rail in front of the general store. The evening sun glinted off a white cross set atop a sod building at the end of the main street. Small marks of progress.

Raising in his stirrups, Ben squinted at the eastern horizon. He couldn't see it yet, but major changes were headed toward Abilene on iron rails and belching steam. It was thought the railroad would arrive before month's end. With it would come something Ben desperately needed.

Opportunity.

He'd signed on for an extra eighteen months with the Second U.S. Volunteers to escort wagons from Fort Dodge to Fort Lyon up in Colorado. Most of Ben's unit had mustered out at Fort Leavenworth in 'sixty-five. They'd had somewhere else to go or someone waiting for them. Ben had nothing but the clothes on his back, a pistol, and a few essentials bundled into his bedroll. Even the U.S.-branded horse he rode and the McClellan saddle he sat on belonged to the U.S. Cavalry.

But Ben didn't. He'd mustered out five days before at Fort Dodge.

He chirped to the horse to get it moving toward the only building with corrals. He'd promised his sergeant he'd leave the animal at the livery stable. A courier would pick it up on his next ride east and return it to the fort. The animal was older but of good stock, likely Morgan breeding. Ben had tried to purchase it, but suitable cavalry horseflesh was in short supply on the western plains. He'd been lucky to be given the use of it to ride as far as Abilene, the collection of sod buildings being the closest town to Fort Dodge.

A town in its formative beginning where Ben could make a fresh start.

Leaving the horse in the hands of a capable-looking stableboy, Ben entered the saloon. His other reason for heading to Abilene stood behind the bar. A bear of a man polished a glass with a rag, the stub end of a cigar clamped in his teeth.

"Well, now." The man slapped his rag onto the bar. "If it ain't himself, come to me humble establishment." He removed the cigar as a grin split the bristle of red beard covering the lower half of his face.

"Hello, Red."

Several heads swiveled at Red's words, mostly younger men, around Ben's age, but two older fellows with lined faces and graying hair laid down their cards to watch.

Red waved him over to the bar. "What brings ye to Abilene?"

Ben leaned his elbows on the polished wood—a luxury on the almost treeless plain—and nodded to the row of clean glasses. "A drink."

Red's hearty laugh released the rest of the room to return to their previous occupations. As the big man filled a glass of beer, the buzz of conversation once again filled the space between the combination of sod and wooden walls.

Red slid the frothy glass in front of Ben. "There ye be."

After a long pull to clear the Kansas dust from his throat, Ben sighed.

"Now, will ye be tellin' yer old friend"—Red parked his elbows on the bar— "what brings ye to the likes of Abilene?"

"The railroad." Ben tilted his head to the east. "And opportunity."

"I was thinkin' maybe ye'd stay in the army after ye signed up for another stint like ye did."

"No." Ben pushed the glass back and forth between his hands. "I just needed more time to decide what to do."

"Ye won't be high-tailin' it back to South Carolina then?" Red's eyebrows rose.

Ben shook his head. "Never planned to." He met his friend's eyes. "There's nothing left for me back there."

"Yer sisters?" Genuine concern colored the big man's voice.

"They're fine, both of them. Miraculously, neither lost her husband during the war."

"They'll be wantin' to see ye, surely."

Amelia and Pauleen would welcome Ben back, of that he had no doubt, but he wouldn't be a burden to them. They'd kept their lands through the war, but that was it. Their husbands had returned to their wives and children living in makeshift tents, fields untended, crops unplanted, and all the slaves gone. They had enough to do without another mouth to feed. Their letters spoke of hope and determination, but also of deprivation—and no chance of employment for someone like him.

Someone who'd turned his back on the South.

His sisters were forgiving. He was their only surviving brother, after all. But the others? His old neighbors? They'd never understand why he'd done what he had. At times, he barely understood it himself.

Pauleen's husband had visited the Warley homestead, the plantation Ben's brother Peter should have inherited from their father. But Peter had fallen early in the war. Father had succumbed to one of the many diseases that thinned the ranks of the poorly fed and poorly equipped Confederate forces sometime before Ben had been taken prisoner.

"I'm moving on to a new life." His tone was short, final.

Red cocked his head. "Ye even sound different."

Ben had spent the past few years diligently trying to rid himself of his deep Southern drawl. A man in his position—a Galvanized Yankee—had enough things going against him. Losing the accent made life easier.

"While you still sound as Irish as if you'd just stepped off the boat." He grinned to take any sting from his words.

Another hearty laugh followed, and then Red rubbed his whiskered chin. "If ye be lookin' for opportunity, methinks I know just the man ye should be speakin' to." He slapped one meaty hand against the bar. "McCoy!"

A man not much older than Ben rose from a table and joined them.

"Ben Warley, ye need to meet Joseph McCoy." Red waggled a finger between them. "McCoy, ye were spoutin' off about needin' a good man to send south to drum up yer herds." He poked his thumb at Ben. "Here's yer man."

Joseph McCoy wore clothing that hadn't seen hard work. His slicked-back hair exposed a wide forehead, while his face tapered into a narrow, shaved chin. There was intelligence in his brown eyes, and something about his mouth hinted at equal parts determination and good humor. He stuck out his hand, and Ben grasped it in a firm handshake.

"Red recommending you is no small thing." McCoy pointed to an empty table near the door. "Bring your beer, and we'll talk."

Ben followed him and sat. The word *herds* had piqued his interest. If there was one thing Ben knew, it was horses. His father had raised some of the best thoroughbreds in South Carolina.

"So." McCoy rested his hands on the table. "What do you know about cattle?"

The hope that had kindled dropped to the pit of Ben's stomach. "I can tell one end from the other." In truth, his father had kept a small herd on the plantation, but they'd been fat shorthorn cattle, purebreds with bloodlines tracing back to England. Nothing like Ben had seen since coming west.

McCoy chuckled. "That's a start. Can you read and write?"

"I can."

The other man pointed to the stripe down the side of Ben's trousers. "Cavalry?"

Ben nodded.

"Good with horses then?"

"Better than most." It wasn't bragging if it was true, and the truth was, Ben could ride any horse with hair on it. He'd been good before he'd signed the loyalty oath that mustered him into the U.S. Army's cavalry, but in the two-plus years he'd been in the West, he'd polished his skills to a high shine.

"I like a man with confidence in himself." McCoy leaned back in his chair. "Let me tell you what I have in mind."

Two hours later, Ben had agreed to work on a harebrained mission to round up herds of cattle in southern Texas and arrange for men to trail them all the way to the new railhead at Abilene, Kansas. From there, they'd ship on railcars to markets crying for beef. Steers that couldn't fetch more than ten dollars in San Antonio would sell for thirty or even forty dollars in the large cities back east. It might be a crazy scheme, but Joseph McCoy was convinced he could make it work with the right people in place. And the man was a powerful salesman for the idea.

Ben almost believed him, but more importantly, he had the chance he needed to rebuild his life. He'd be paid a regular wage he could draw from the bank in San Antonio, be given a horse of his own with full tack, and travel south in the company of a surveyor named Timothy Hersey, an older Abilene man McCoy had hired to map the route north for the cattle to follow.

That night, Ben stretched out on the bed of the room he'd rented from Red and stared at the roots dangling between the boards holding the sod roof in place. His had been a long fall from the walnut-paneled walls and painted ceiling of his bedroom in South Carolina. He'd always miss the majestic hills and winding creeks of his boyhood home. The greenness of everything. The low singing of the slaves from their quarters drifting through the windows in the evenings. Nostalgia clogged his throat, deepened by the loss of his brother and father. Nothing would bring back the way of life he'd grown up with, but at last, he had something to look forward to.

A chance to make something of himself in the postwar world.

CHAPTER 1

B EN'S STOMACH DROPPED AS he eyed the horses milling in the corral behind the livery. "Is this all you have for sale?"

The dark-haired young man glanced at the animals, then back to Ben and Timothy, a wrinkle of uncertainty on his brow. "Yes, sir. They're quality mounts. Each one is sound, broke to ride, and healthy."

Maybe, but they were a far cry from the tall, leggy thoroughbreds Ben's father had raised. The milling herd in front of him were small animals, some of them marked like Indian ponies, and more than one had a wild eye rolled his way.

Mustangs.

He'd seen plenty of them before. They'd passed herds while on patrol, but he'd never thought he'd be reduced to riding one. When McCoy had promised him a mount of his own as part of the deal, Ben had envisioned something like the cavalry rode. Not these... oversize goats.

"I'll catch you the best of the lot." The stable hand shook out his lariat. "The one I'd choose if it were me. He's well-trained and willing."

"They aren't that bad." Timothy propped one boot against the bottom rung of the corral. "And it seems that's what everyone rides down here." He jerked his head toward the hitching rails along the street, lined with horses of the same size and character as those in the corral.

As the young man approached the herd, several horses darted out of his way, one aiming a kick the boy dodged as if he did it daily. Which he probably did. It was obvious he knew his way around horses. In a calm voice, he crooned to the red roan who remained standing. Head up, neck arched, ears pricked forward, it sported a white star centered on its broad forehead. Without a fuss, the boy looped the lariat over the horse's head and led it to Ben.

Ben offered his hand and let the horse nuzzle it, let it get a good smell of him. Its ears stayed up, interested, curious. "Bring him out." Ben opened the gate, then closed it behind them.

The animal wasn't more than a six-year-old, well-covered in flesh, not a bone showing. Its legs were straight, no bowed tendons, not spavined, the hooves with few chips. Ben ran his hand down a front leg and lifted the hoof. No shoes, but a healthy foot. He repeated the process with each hoof and found nothing amiss. While on the narrow side, its chest was deep, the shoulders strong, the back solid, and the croup sloped for strength. The gelding was no thoroughbred, not even close, but Ben could find no other fault in it.

"He ever been shod?"

"Not that I know of, sir." The boy glanced toward the livery that doubled as a farrier's shop. "I can ask Mr. Hart."

Ben waved his hand dismissively. It didn't really matter. The animal was head and shoulders the best one offered. If he hadn't been shod before, he soon would be, and Ben would deal with it. Most horses got comfortable with shoes without much fuss.

Timothy came over to inspect the animal. "He's a mite on the small side but looks like he could go all day and half the night."

Ben grunted and turned to the boy. "I'll need full tack. Is there a saddlery in town?"

He pointed down the dusty street. "Pablo's shop is that way, turn right at the corner. You can't miss it."

"You'll settle the bill of sale, Timothy?"

"I will, and follow you to the saddlery to settle that one."

On the month-long trip to San Antonio, Ben had ridden Timothy's spare horse, there being no decent horse for sale in Abilene. The man would be taking the animal back to Kansas when he left in the next day or two.

Ben took the rope and led the horse in the direction the boy had indicated. The horse stepped out willingly, leaving its companions in the corral without a fuss. Another good sign. The young man hadn't steered him wrong. Ben had already noticed the roan gelding as one of the best of the bunch, but it never hurt to have someone knowledgeable about the animals confirm his assessment.

The livery probably had used saddles and gear it would have sold him, but if Ben had to start his new life on a pint-sized cowpony, it was going to include new tack. If McCoy wasn't happy about that, well, Ben would deal with it when he returned to Abilene.

If and when that might be.

It remained to be seen whether McCoy's harebrained scheme of driving cattle some six hundred miles to the railhead would work or not. If not, Ben would need to start over—again.

He'd finished picking out his new saddle and tack when Timothy joined him and settled the bill, McCoy having given him the authority for such purchases. He handed Ben the bill of sale on the mustang.

"I don't know about you, but I could use a bath and a haircut and a well-cooked dinner behind my belt." Timothy slapped his lean stomach.

They'd been in San Antonio less than an hour, and Ben was already outfitted for his new job. Almost. He ran a hand down his clothes. "A new suit of clothes wouldn't go amiss."

The other man laughed. "Right you are. A new suit, a bath, a haircut, and a fine meal, then we'll ask around about the local ranchers."

"No sense wasting time."

"Mr. McCoy was firm on that, get the cattle moving as fast—and as many—as possible."

"Do you think I can really do it?" Ben asked. "Can I convince the ranchers to move their cattle that far on the gamble they'll arrive in good shape and get paid a fair price?"

Timothy gripped his shoulder, giving a firm squeeze. "The way I figure it, they've got little choice. Nobody's buying cattle in Texas."

That was true enough. Cattle ran wild in the Texas brush, left unattended by men who'd gone to war—many of whom had never returned. And the ranches still running their own brands were full of cattle without a market. They'd heard the same complaint from every place they'd stopped on the way south.

In the East, the demand for meat was huge. Four years of feeding two armies while farmers and ranchers left their land and animals to be scavenged by those same armies had taken its toll.

The combination of supply and demand gave McCoy's scheme a chance.

A fierceness rose in Ben's spirit that made him pause on the street outside the saddlery. He was tired—bone-weary tired—of failing. He'd failed the South. He'd let down his father, even though he'd died before Ben had been taken prisoner. He'd failed himself by taking the loyalty oath and capitulating to the enemy. He'd even failed to leave the cavalry at the first opportunity.

Ben Warley was sick-to-his-stomach tired of failing.

"I'm going to make this work—or die trying."

"Kenna!"

The shout brought Kenna McCrea to the back door of her father's diner. Her youngest sister, Elva, pelted down the alley, skirts held indecently high, ten-year-old legs pumping in a mad dash for the door. Their red-haired brother Tyree loped behind her with a stick from which dangled a snake longer than one of the boy's arms.

Kenna stepped into the alley as Elva shot through the doorway with a squeal.

"Tyree, when are you going to grow up?" Kenna wrenched the stick from her brother's hand. At fifteen, he looked her square in the eye. He could have kept the stick away from her, but he still submitted to her authority as the eldest sibling. "You know she's terrified of snakes."

"Ah, shucks, sis, it's dead as could be."

Kenna shook the stick and its heavy snake at him. "It doesn't matter. She's afraid, and you're too old to be causing such a ruckus." She looked down the alley. "Why aren't you at the livery?"

Tyree shrugged and retreated a step. "I'm going right back."

She thrust the stick at him. "Take this with you. And if Mr. Hart gives you a dressing down, it's no more than you deserve." She dusted off her hands as he trotted back down the alley. Honestly, that one lacked the brains God had given the snakes he so loved to hunt.

The way he carried on with those snakes, as if they hadn't moved into San Antonio to escape them and the other dangers of living on the prairie.

Kenna entered the back of the diner.

Pa slapped two thick steaks on the hot griddle, the sizzle and pop releasing a tantalizing aroma, and shot her a look. "Better calm the wee lassie." He pointed to the staircase leading to their living quarters above the diner. "The lunch crowd is starting to arrive. I need you both down here."

"Yes, Pa." Kenna followed the weeping to the bedroom she shared with Elva and Vanora. "Sweetheart, you know Tyree would never let a snake hurt you." She gathered her trembling sister in a hug. "He's just being a boy."

Except he wasn't. At fifteen, Tyree was nearly a man grown and needed to start acting like one. He was three years older than Kenna had been when she'd had to step into Ma's shoes and take over the family.

"He's awful," Elva muttered into Kenna's apron between hiccups.

"He can be, but he's still our brother. And deep down, he loves you as much as I do." She lifted her sister's tear-stained face and wiped it with the edge of her apron. "Pa needs us now. Vanora is serving lunch already. Come on."

"Okay." But Elva had to dry a few more tears before they entered the kitchen.

Vanora burst through the swinging doors that separated the kitchen from the dining room, a high flush on her twelve-year-old cheeks. "Pa, we got a stranger out front. Says he wants his steak rare."

"Rare, aye." Pa pulled another slab of meat from the crate at his elbow and slapped it on the griddle. "Kenna, you take over in the dining room."

Pa didn't like the younger girls around strangers. Some of the cowboys who drifted in were a rough lot, but Kenna could handle them. If things got bad, Pa would quell the fracas with a cast iron skillet, and a few regulars were usually on hand to help him toss a rowdy one into the street.

It wasn't a drunk cowboy that had Vanora in a flutter. Kenna spotted the stranger right away, seated by himself at the corner table, sporting clean clothing and newly shaven face. A hat that looked brand new was hooked on the back of an empty chair. His grooming and erect posture were the only things that set him apart. Even seated, he appeared to be of average height and had brown hair and brown eyes. He was the kind of fellow who would go unnoticed in a crowd.

Perhaps that was why he took such care of his clothing and grooming.

Kenna approached with the coffeepot. "Coffee, mister?"

He held out his cup. "Please."

His voice wasn't ordinary at all. Just one word, but deep as the gorges she'd loved to play in as a child. And the accent? He wasn't a Texan, and although tanned, not nearly dark enough to be Mexican.

"Cream or sugar?"

He shook his head.

With no excuse to linger, she filled a few more cups at the other tables and returned to the kitchen.

Pa glanced up before handing her two plates loaded with steaks, potatoes, and a helping of greens. "Will he be a problem?"

"Seems harmless enough. Well-dressed and groomed. Maybe he's a drummer passing through."

Pa grunted and turned back to the stove.

"If he is,"—Vanora paused at the wash basin, water dripping from her hands—"might we look over his wares, Pa?"

"We dinna need anything, lassie." Pa's lingering Scottish burr thickened his speech.

Vanora sighed dramatically, earning her a brief stare from their father. Likely the girl hankered for some new hair ribbons or a fancy bit of lace. She was at that age.

"Those steaks willna fill a man if you dinna get them to the table," Pa said.

Kenna whirled and pushed through the doors to the dining room. It was a day much like all the others. They worked hard, her family. Pa and the girls in the diner, both brothers hired out to the livery stable. It was a good life and one she was happy in.

Far better than when Pa had been a sheepherder and they'd followed the flock, living out of a wagon—a hard life that had taken Ma in the end. Anything would be better than that.

A younger girl had taken Ben's order and scampered through a set of swinging doors into the room beyond, the clatter of pans and delicious aromas marking it as the kitchen.

Ben's stomach growled long and low. It wasn't that they hadn't eaten on the trail. They had, but neither he nor Timothy could claim any talent at cooking. Hardtack and jerky constituted the bulk of their diet, with an occasional jackrabbit or prairie chicken adding fresh if poorly roasted meat at times. They'd had bread if they could purchase it from a rancher's wife. As a result, his belt notched a hole tighter than when they'd left Abilene a month prior.

They'd have made better time if they'd pushed it, but Timothy had stopped them at key places to build mounds to guide the herds—should they manage to gather any—on the trail north. If Ben never saw a shovel again, it would be too soon. He rubbed his callused hands against the new material of his trousers.

Once his stomach was satisfied, he'd make inquiries about the ranchers who might have enough cattle to form a herd to drive north. McCoy had envisioned herds of two to three thousand head. He and Timothy had seen cattle since entering Texas and riding its length south, but nothing to compare with those kinds of numbers.

A woman appeared through the swinging doors, coffeepot in hand. She approached, raked him with an assessing eye, then offered him coffee. Red hair escaped the pins trying to contain its waves, a straight nose dusted with freckles, and blue-gray eyes that seemed older than the rest of her. She left to fill more cups and then disappeared into the kitchen as the bells over the front door jingled.

Timothy entered, as well turned out as Ben, obviously having taken advantage of the hotel's bathhouse and a barber. Although he hadn't shaved, his beard was neatly trimmed. He joined Ben at the table.

"Glad we arrived in time to clean up and get lunch." The older man settled into a chair, adding his new hat to the chair that held Ben's. "If it's half as good as it smells, you'll need to roll me back out the door." He rested both palms on the table. "I'd say we look the part of enterprising businessmen now, don't you?"

They'd shopped at the local mercantile and registered at the best hotel. McCoy was picking up the check for the whole operation, so they'd gotten separate rooms. The idea was to look prosperous.

McCoy had stressed that money attracted money, so they needed to look and act the part.

The young woman approached with Ben's plate of food, took Timothy's order, and disappeared into the kitchen with an eye-catching swish of her skirts.

"Now, now"—Timothy tilted his head toward the swinging doors—"none of that. We have business to attend." His grin creased the corners of his eyes.

Ben sliced through his steak and filled his mouth. The flavor would have weakened his knees had he been standing. He closed his eyes for a moment and could almost see Lucy standing in the doorway of the kitchen back home, hair hidden beneath a swath of calico, smile wide at his appreciation of her cooking. Of all their people on the plantation, he missed Lucy the most.

When the young woman reappeared with Timothy's plate, she flashed a smile that took in both of them before heading to a newly occupied table and taking the order there. She was lovely, no doubt, but as Timothy said, they had business to attend.

And there was that other thing.

Texas had sided with the South. A Southern woman wouldn't look twice at a Galvanized Yankee. She'd be more likely to spit on his boots.

CHAPTER 2

B EN COULDN'T REMEMBER THE last time he'd been so full. He'd never seen the cook behind the swinging doors of the diner, but whoever it was, he or she was worth their weight in gold.

Timothy stretched and groaned as they made their way back into the street. "If we find chuckwagon cooks half as good as that one back there, we'd have more men than cattle heading north."

"You could be right." Ben glanced up and down the street. "Where do you suppose we ought to start?"

"Where the talk is, of course." Timothy headed toward a saloon across the street and down a few buildings.

Even at that early afternoon hour, tinny piano music leaked around the door. They entered the dark interior, blinking to adjust their eyes after the blazing sun they'd left behind.

It was nothing like Red's establishment in Abilene. Instead of sod and a little lumber, the saloon was built of adobe. Instead of a highly polished bar, the wood was worn and grooved and in want of a cleaning. The man behind it was tall, thin, and also in want of a cleaning.

Ben leaned toward Timothy. "I'm not sure this is the right kind of—"

"Help you, gents?" the lean bartender asked.

Timothy headed for the bar and ordered two beers.

Ben didn't think he had room for a beer after their meal, but a man didn't ask for information without at least buying a drink.

Frothy glass in hand, Ben surveyed the room. A small black man banged on the piano keys, a bowler hat on his head. Two tables hosted card games, but the piles of chips by the players said they were friendly games, not serious gambling. Three men stood down the bar from Ben and Timothy. The closest, a bull of a man wearing boots with large roweled spurs, looked them over.

"New in town?" the big guy asked.

"Just this morning," Timothy said. "Came looking for ranchers with cattle to sell."

Several chuckles and a few snorts came in response, but these weren't ranchers. These were ranch hands—cowboys, as they were called locally.

"Mister, I guess it's safe to say that every man who owns a herd hereabouts would gladly sell you half or more if you've got Yankee gold."

Yankee gold. The country had been reunified for more than two years, but healing the breach was slow, even so far from the battlefields and devastation.

Timothy nodded to Ben.

This was what McCoy had hired him to do. Timothy would be leaving soon, returning to Kansas, and Ben would be on his own. Time to prove he could do it. He took a step forward.

"There will be Yankee gold, but not here." He poked his thumb toward the door which faced north. "In Abilene, Kansas."

"Kansas!" The word ricocheted around the room, raised by several voices at once.

"The railhead has reached Abilene by now. The same trains that move people and goods can also move cattle. A lot of cattle. Markets back east are paying in Yankee gold." Ben spread his arms, palms up. "Anyone with a boss looking to drive a herd north, tell him to find Ben Warley at the Menger Hotel."

The room erupted into a buzz of voices. Two of the men playing poker dropped their cards and hurried from the saloon.

Ben pushed his untouched beer toward the big man and followed Timothy outside and across the street.

"I don't know about you, but I could use a nap." Timothy smothered a yawn behind his glove. "Been looking forward to that bed ever since I laid eyes on it."

"Sounds good to me."

"We're going to need our rest." Timothy tilted his head toward the saloon they'd just left. "Word's already spreading."

Men poured from its door, likely earning Ben and Timothy a black mark from the bartender for stealing his patrons. The man should be thinking ahead. Cattle drives would bring money back to San Antonio. A lot of money.

Yankee gold.

The more cattle Ben got pushed north, the more money McCoy would have transferred to the bank in San Antonio. Maybe enough money for Ben to purchase a place of his own. A place to put down roots and start a family. The land was nothing like his native South Carolina, but it had a rugged beauty. It wasn't a bad place to start over. And once Timothy left...

Nobody in San Antonio would know Ben's history.

The supper dishes were washed and put away, the kitchen surfaces wiped down, and Kenna was banking the fire in the huge cook stove as Lloyd and Tyree burst through the back door. Her lanky brothers jostled each other as they skidded to a halt.

"Quiet," she hissed between her teeth, glancing at the staircase. "You know Pa's in bed by now." She planted her fists on her hips. "Where have you been? I'd about given up on the pair of you."

"There's going to be a cattle drive—"

"Maybe a whole bunch of cattle drives—"

"They'll be hiring cowboys—"

"Our age and even younger—"

"Don't even need a horse of our own—"

"Make more money than we could ever imagine making—"

The words tumbled out over the top of each other. Kenna could barely separate the voices enough to pull understanding from them.

She held up her hands. "One at a time, and softly, please."

But it was too late. The heavy tread on the stairs silenced them until Pa reached the kitchen floor.

"What has my sons in such an uproar that they canna be quiet while their wee sisters sleep?" His scowl was visible behind his neatly trimmed salt-and-pepper beard.

Lloyd stepped forward, the oldest brother—the serious one—a younger version of Pa. "The ranchers are organizing cattle drives to take herds to Kansas, to a town called Abilene."

"They say they'll hire anyone who can sit a horse to go with them," Tyree said. "I heard some will be paying thirty dollars a month in Yankee gold."

Pa snugged the belt of his robe, then rubbed the back of his head. "Thirty dollars, you say?"

"That's more than twice what we make at the livery," Lloyd said.

"No, Pa." Kenna pushed past her brothers and clutched Pa's arm. "No. Don't you remember how it was? They were sheep and not cattle, but living out of the wagon, enduring the weather and the... snakes."

Pa's face paled, no doubt the same memory that shadowed Kenna had struck him. Ma bitten by a rattler, struck on the wrist as she bent to pick up a stick for the fire. She'd lingered for more than a day before the poison took her. Then Pa had moved them all into town. He'd bought the diner, and they'd been happy here. Very happy. There was no reason to change anything.

Pa wrapped his arm around Kenna's shoulders and pulled her to his side. "We canna keep them under this roof forever, daughter. A man's got to spread his wings."

"They're just boys." But she couldn't put much conviction into her voice. Hadn't she chastised Tyree for not acting his age earlier that day? She knew they were almost grown men, but that didn't mean they needed to leave San Antonio. It didn't mean they needed to face the dangers of living on the prairie to tend to a bunch of animals they didn't even own.

"May we sign on, Pa?" Lloyd asked.

Silence stretched for an unbearable moment, then Pa cleared his throat. "I canna stop you lads. You're grown enough to do a man's work."

Her brothers exchanged excited looks while Kenna's heart dropped to her feet.

"But"—Pa held up one finger—"I ask that you bring me the names of the ranchers hiring and give me a say in which one you sign on with."

"Yes, Pa." They answered as one.

"There are some men I trust more than others. And some I dinna trust at all." He hugged Kenna closer to his side, maybe needing her comfort as much as she needed his. "I want my lads to ride with the best. And dinna quit your jobs at the livery until you have the other, so up to bed. Morning comes early."

Lloyd and Tyree made a show of creeping up the stairs, careful not to wake Vanora and Elva.

That was how it happened. Everything was normal, moving along as it should, and then everything changed. The promise of a job, the slither of a snake. Kenna could almost hear it, a phantom rattle. And once again, their world was falling apart. She stared at the empty staircase a long time before she turned to her father. "I don't want them to go."

"I know, lass." The lines across his forehead deepened. "But I canna keep you all young and under my roof forever. Lads grow up and move on. Lassies"—he shook her lightly by the shoulder—"find a good man to settle with. You should be thinking on that. What of Wilhelm Oden? He's a well-established man, a widower who needs a mother for his children."

Mr. Oden was more than ten years her senior, and while a nice man in every way, he didn't spark anything in her that whispered of romance. She'd deny it till her dying breath, but in her heart, she wanted more than a ready-made family. She'd gotten that when Ma died. She wanted...she wanted a gallant prince, the kind they wrote about in fairy tales, to sweep her off her feet. He'd keep her somewhere safe where she'd be loved and prized for who she was, not just what she could do.

A fairy tale indeed.

"That time will come," she said. Maybe. Someday. "But for now, you and the girls still need me, even if the lads ride away."

Pa grunted, but neither agreed nor disagreed. He yawned and rubbed his hair, making strands stand up straight. "Morning comes early for us too. Up to bed, lass."

She climbed the stairs ahead of him, wondering if—fearing—it would be the last night they'd all sleep under the same sturdy roof.

They just kept coming. For the past twenty-four hours, ranchers had poured through the hotel lobby like the cattle Ben hoped to gather, driven by the hope of Yankee gold to pay their taxes and save their land. He'd known things were desperate in Texas—everyone knew that—but it was worse than he'd imagined. Worse than anyone outside of Texas could have imagined.

Except for Joseph McCoy. The man must be a visionary.

Timothy would leave in the morning, but Ben's doubts about his role in San Antonio had been put to rest. The ranchers weren't all that different from the plantation owners he'd grown up around, except for so many of them speaking German. Their way of dressing and mannerisms were different, to be sure, but at heart, they were men managing acreage and doing their best to keep their lifestyle intact.

Father's plantation had been modest in size. He'd raised horses, cattle, hogs, corn, and tobacco. By the time the war broke out, he'd owned six adult slaves and four children. Nothing to compare with the huge cotton plantations south and east of them, but it had good land with a stream flowing through it and several acres of hardwood forest. Even with all of that, meeting the tax bill and keeping everyone fed and clothed and living their established lifestyle for another year had been a constant concern.

Ben could relate to the men waiting to speak with him.

A man with a drooping mustache approached. His legs were bowed, but that didn't lessen his height. He was painfully thin, but not from lack of health. Everything about him suggested coiled energy ready to unleash.

"Name's Brinkmann, folks call me Squirrel." There was a German accent to his words, but not nearly as thick as many Ben had heard in San Antonio.

There must be a story to that name, but Ben didn't have time to ask. "Do you have a herd of cattle, Mr. Brinkmann?"

"No, sir. But I've trailed cattle near to Kansas before. I know the route."

"Well, you'll need to speak with the ranchers for hiring on as—"

"I want to work for Mr. McCoy himself."

That made Ben sit straighter and give the fellow a closer look. "You know Joseph McCoy?"

"No, sir, I don't. But I learned a long time ago that you hire on with the man in charge."

Ben tapped his pencil against the ledger on his lap. He had no authority to hire anyone for McCoy, but this Brinkmann fellow could be the answer to a problem that had cropped up from the start—what to do with the small ranchers who couldn't amass enough cattle for their own drive.

Ben's mind whirled. He should speak with Timothy. No. If he was going to be in charge, if he was going to succeed, then he needed to make decisions.

"Mr. Brinkmann—"

"Squirrel."

"Squirrel, there's the problem of the small ranchers, those who can only muster a few hundred head." Ben glanced at his ledger. "There are several who would need to band together to make a two-thousand head herd like McCoy wants. If you can organize that, come back to me with the numbers, and we'll talk."

"I can do that."

"I have a list of names—"

"I know who to talk to." Squirrel raised his hand. "I'll put a herd together and get back to you."

"The sooner the better."

"Soon, then." Squirrel strode away, a man on a mission.

Ben had no doubt he'd come through. And watching him, Ben realized that was how he needed to be. Confident. Secure. A man who knew what he wanted and what he was doing—even if he didn't feel that way inside.

That was the Benjamin Warley he needed to show San Antonio.

CHAPTER 3

T HE LUNCH CROWD WAS gone, and Kenna was cleaning the dining room before the dinner crowd arrived when Mr. Brinkmann entered. He removed his hat and dipped his head toward her, as was his way.

"Miss McCrea, is your pa around?"

"I'll fetch him." She pushed through the swinging doors into the warm kitchen. "Pa, Mr. Brinkmann is here to see you."

Pa paused mid-reach to hang a skillet on the wall.

Kenna's stomach knotted. "What is it?"

Pa hung the skillet and untied his white canvas apron, hanging it on a peg. "I'll go see."

She followed him. Mr. Brinkmann had taken a seat at a table by the front window.

As Pa sat, she stepped forward. "Can I bring you coffee?"

"That would be good, lass." Mr. Brinkmann nodded.

Kenna whirled back to the kitchen and poured two cups from the pot on the stove, added a sugar bowl and small pitcher of cream to the tray, then whisked into the dining room. She served the men, then stepped to a nearby table and pulled a clean rag from the pocket of her apron. She rubbed at a non-existent spot as she listened.

"It's a good thing you're doing, helping the smaller ranchers," Pa said.

Mr. Brinkmann took a sip of his coffee. "I'll need good men to work for me, men who can ride and aren't afraid of hard work." He rubbed the drooping ends of his mustache. "And a cook."

Kenna smothered a gasp with her cleaning rag.

Pa nodded, his fingers laced around his cup. "Both are important for a successful operation."

"I want to work with the best, and that's you, Gus."

Pa shook his head.

Kenna's breath came back with a rush.

"You dinna want an old man, Squirrel. Go find a younger one."

"One of your sons?"

So much for breathing. Kenna stopped pretending to clean and stared at Pa, willing him to say no.

"My sons are good lads, but neither is a cook." Pa braced his elbows on the table. "They are good with horses, hard workers, and have already told me they want to go. I canna think of anyone I would trust them to better than you, my friend."

Kenna pressed the rag to her mouth again to stop the words of denial forming there.

"You'll find them at the livery," Pa continued. "You can tell them they have my blessing to go with you."

Kenna escaped to the kitchen, where she opened the back door and took a deep breath of the hot afternoon air. Vanora and Elva would return from their errand soon. She needed to pull herself together.

The bells jingled over the dining room door before the swinging doors swished behind her. Pa gripped her shoulders, his fingers pressing hard. She leaned back against him, teeth gritted against a rising sob. It wouldn't do for her to give in to her despair over the lads leaving.

Vanora and Elva still needed her.

So did Pa.

At least Pa had said no to becoming Mr. Brinkmann's chuckwagon cook. As bad as things were with Lloyd and Tyree leaving, it could have been much worse.

She closed her eyes briefly and breathed out a silent prayer of thanks.

Saddled and ready, Ben swung aboard his mustang for the first time. There was more than just the size of the horse to get used to. The Texas saddle boasted a wide, flat horn on the front. Ben had seen the same type of saddle on horses tied along the street, lariats coiled and hung from the horn. It made sense when working cattle. The saddle also had a full seat instead of the divided seat of the army's McClellan saddles. He could get used to that level of comfort for his backside.

He clicked to the roan and started down the street, passing freight wagons, buggies, horses, and mules, even a few donkeys. San Antonio was larger and busier than he'd imagined. Businesses of all kinds, from bakeries to cobblers, saloons to haberdasheries, flourished up and down multiple streets. Different languages peppered the air, as well as heavily accented English. It took Ben close to half an hour to work his way across town and onto the open prairie.

When he did, the smell hit him first—the burned hide of freshly branded cattle.

Before him spread a vast herd of cattle in every shade and pattern of red, white, black, brindle, and brown. Horns that spanned nearly as wide as his arms gleamed in the afternoon sun.

Ben took off his hat and mopped his brow before resettling it.

He had no idea how many cattle occupied the stretch of prairie in front of him, but it was more than he'd ever seen in one place.

Squirrel Brinkmann rode toward him on a bay mustang. The tall man's legs hung well below the horse's belly, but both appeared comfortable with the odd pairing. At least, it was odd to Ben. His mustang was no bigger than Squirrel's, but Ben was considerably smaller, so they were a better fit. A better fit by South Carolina thoroughbred standards.

Squirrel touched his hat brim. "Here's your first mixed herd, boss."

"Ben, not boss. That's McCoy."

Squirrel chuckled and pointed to the cowboys working among the herd. "Those boys won't never see Mr. McCoy down here, so you're the boss."

Boss. The name rested uneasily on his shoulders, but what Squirrel said made sense. "I didn't expect you to pull this together in just two days."

"News like yours spreads faster than a wildfire. Ranchers had already gathered their cattle, hoping to sell." Squirrel pointed to where two cowboys waited while two on horses roped an animal by horns and back legs. When the steer was stretched between the two horses, the men on the ground—one looking like the dark-haired stable boy who'd sold Ben the roan—pressed a glowing hot brand to its hide.

"They'll wear the road brand along with their original brand. It'll help us cut out the range cattle that'll drift in from time to time."

There was so much Ben didn't know about this work, but he was learning.

"Yours'll be the first herd to head north." Ben poked his thumb back toward town. "There are two other herds gathering to the east, but they don't expect to be ready to move for a few more days. I'd like you to go first since you've been through that country before."

"You said Hersey marked the trail." Squirrel shot him an unreadable look from under his wide-brimmed hat. "Does that mean I have to stay on it?"

Ben and Timothy had spoken at length about the trail as they'd erected mounds on their journey south. Timothy knew what he was doing, but he also acknowledged that things changed, things like river depths and bogs and the like.

"The mounds will guide you to the trail we found, but if there is a better way, use your own judgment."

Squirrel gave a satisfied nod. "We'll start this bunch north early morning after next. The beeves will all be branded and the cook outfitted by then."

"You found a cook?"

Squirrel nodded. "Not the one I wanted, but he'll be good enough."

"Who did you want?"

"Gus at the diner."

"A diner man?" The food had been something special. Ben fully intended to return for another meal, but he'd barely had time to turn around for the past week, so meals at the hotel had been more convenient. "For a chuckwagon?"

"Gus used to work for one of the ranchers as a sheepherder." Squirrel pointed to the northwest. "I first met him out there. Never ate so good before or since. Him and his wife... such a tragedy when she died."

Wasn't it always? His mother had died after childbirth many years before. Ben cleared his throat. "I'll be here at daybreak for the start."

"Be here an hour before." Squirrel reined his bay around and cantered back to the herd.

An hour before. Maybe trail life wasn't so different from army life—just littered with cattle.

Ben pointed the roan back toward town. He patted the animal's neck. "What do I call you?" His personal mount needed a proper name. "Hmm... how about Rusty? You're the right color for it."

The horse ignored him but picked up into a canter at the slightest touch of Ben's heels. The boy at the livery had been right, well-trained and willing.

Instead of heading to the hotel, Ben dismounted and tied Rusty in front of the diner. The scents of seared meat and something spicy greeted him at the door. The younger girl was washing tables—all of them empty.

"Am I too late for lunch?"

In the kitchen, Kenna caught the rumbling voice and dried her hands. The new man in town was back. She'd not heard another voice like it, so it must be him. It was a little past lunch, and Pa had stepped out, but she could cook a steak, and there were still several pieces of dried-apple pie.

Vanora scooted in the door. "Got a customer, the new fellow from a few days ago." She put a coffee tray together with the ease of long practice.

"You'll need to wait on him. Pa stepped out and Elva went with him."

Her sister straightened, holding the tray, so grown-up for a twelve-year-old.

How long before this one didn't need Kenna anymore? The twist to her heart was bittersweet. They were her siblings, not her children, but still...

Vanora disappeared through the doors, her voice carrying questions as well as the man's deep answers. Such a nice voice.

"Steak rare, wedge of pie," Vanora called out.

Kenna slapped a steak on the griddle she'd already scraped clean, its sizzling steam adding to the grumble in her middle. She pulled another from the pile and added it beside the first. She and Vanora needed to eat too.

Vanora bustled back into the kitchen, a flush on her cheeks. She leaned close to Kenna. "He's got such nice manners. And that voice? I'd love to hear him sing."

Trust Vanora to think of that. She loved music of all kinds.

"Set us a table in the back, and we'll eat where we can keep an eye on him should he need anything."

Her sister gathered the plates and silverware and whisked back through the swinging doors. Kenna had the man's plate ready with steak, grilled peppers and onions, plus a large wedge of pie on a smaller plate when Vanora returned. She cut the other steak in half and fixed plates for herself and her sister, carrying them into the dining room.

Vanora's laugh filled the room, responding to whatever the stranger's rumbling comment had been, then she joined Kenna at the back table.

"What was that all about?"

"He told me how poorly he'd eaten on the way here from Kansas. Can you imagine? Riding all that way for a bunch of cattle?" Vanora shook her head.

"Kansas?" Kenna's hunger fled. "Then he's involved in the cattle drives?"

Vanora lifted one shoulder and let it drop. "Sounds like it."

Was he the man who was taking her brothers away? Sitting in their dining room, stuffing a steak she'd cooked into his mouth. She wished she'd spit on it.

Shame heated her face. Where had that thought come from? She'd never do such a thing. She'd been raised much better than that. Squirming on her chair, she stabbed her half of the steak and cut it with more vigor than required.

The bells jingled as Pa and Elva came in the front door. Elva scampered to Kenna's side and snitched a bite of steak off her plate. Not that it mattered. Kenna's appetite was gone. She pushed the plate in front of an empty chair and motioned for Elva to sit and eat.

"Ah, a late customer." Pa slipped off his hat. "I trust my daughters have seen to your meal."

The man nodded, swallowing his mouthful before saying, "I wouldn't have known it wasn't you who cooked it. It's just as tasty as the first time I was here."

How could a man no larger than he have such a voice? And he used it to praise her cooking. Her shameful thought of moments before poked deeper into her conscience.

"My Kenna is a fine cook." Pa beamed her way before turning back to the stranger. "I am Gus McCrea."

The man set his silverware down. "I heard your name this morning. Squirrel Brinkmann said you were the best trail cook in the area."

Pa waved in dismissal.

The other man stood and offered his hand, which Pa grasped in greeting. "Ben Warley. I'm here as stockman for Joseph McCoy."

"Squirrel mentioned your name." Pa rubbed his beard. "My two sons, they've signed on with him for the drive."

"I hear he's one of the best." Mr. Warley gave a wry smile. "He's a good negotiator, I can tell you that."

"He dinna come by his name dishonestly, that one." Pa laughed. "He could talk a squirrel out of a nut tree. But excuse me, I dinna mean to disrupt your meal. Please, sit and eat."

Pa turned and approached their table.

"How would you like to see the herd where your brothers are working?" he asked. Vanora and Elva both agreed with excited chatter, but Pa's eyes stayed on her. "Kenna?"

She wiped her mouth on a napkin, then nodded. "Yes, we should."

"Good." I'll rent a buggy from the livery. He headed for the back door, but stopped and turned. "Just put the last dishes in to soak. You can wash them when we return."

Mr. Warley stood and dropped coins on the table. He settled his hat, then touched the brim when he noticed she was watching him. "Good day to you, Miss McCrea."

Kenna nodded, her mouth too dry to answer. He was the man who was taking her brothers away. The man responsible for splitting up her family. He should be ugly and nasty, someone she could loathe.

Not a neat, polite man with a subtle accent she couldn't place. An accent that added mystery to the rumble of his voice.

The bells jingled over the door as he closed it, pulling her out of her musings.

"Hurry, girls," Pa called from the kitchen. "This might be our last chance to see Lloyd and Tyree."

"You mean... ever?" Elva's squeaked out the last word.

She hugged her youngest sister. "Of course not forever, but Kansas is a long way away. It'll take them months to drive the herd that far, and then weeks to return to us."

If they ever did.

Kenna's heart twisted at the thought.

CHAPTER 4

T HE TELEGRAPH OFFICE WAS cramped and stuffy, the rhythmic click-
ing of the telegraph machine mingling with the *scritch* of pencil against paper as the clerk transcribed the nonsense into words.
Ben waited for the machine and man to stop before stepping to the
counter.

"Any telegraphs for me?"

"No, sir, Mr. Warley." The clerk raised a hand without looking up,
pointing in the direction of the hotel. "I'd have sent it right over if there
was."

"I have one to send." Ben pulled the carefully worded note from his
shirt pocket. He wasn't too sure how McCoy would react to the change
in plans Ben had made by hiring Squirrel directly, but with what the
man had accomplished so far, he was sure McCoy would be satisfied
with the results.

At least, he fervently hoped so. His entire future might hang in the
balance.

If he failed—and caused McCoy's grand scheme to fail—his name
wouldn't be worth Confederate scrip. If he failed, he'd never outrun
the stigma of it. Even he, a younger son of Southern privilege who
had rarely concerned himself with business before, could see the
large-scale implications of McCoy's plans. Implications for those in
Texas and those in the east, and pretty much every place in between
that would thrive on the business pushed their way.

At a time when the country desperately needed something to thrive,
Ben couldn't afford to mess anything up. He was back in the South,
even if it was as far from South Carolina as he could get. He was among
his own people. There was hope for a future for him here.

After he paid the bill for the telegraph, Ben mounted Rusty and rode out to view the two other herds being gathered. Both looked pretty much the same, although with fewer cattle. He spoke to the trail bosses, who assured him they'd have full herds and be on the trail within the week.

Then, maybe because he had so much riding on it, Ben returned to Squirrel's herd. The lanky trail boss saw him coming and rode to meet him.

"Everything okay?"

"Just taking a last look before I return to town." Ben tipped his head toward where the other herds waited. "Looks like you'll be out a few days before the others."

"That'll give us the first grass." Satisfaction flowed through Squirrel's reply.

A herd of horses moved into view. There must have been a hundred of them. Maybe more. Ben pointed toward them. "Are you moving horses as well as cattle?"

Squirrel leaned on his saddle horn. "You've never moved cattle, have you." It wasn't a question.

Ben prickled a bit under the scrutiny. "Not this many, and not so far." After all, he'd helped gather cattle more than once when Father decided the slaves were more valuable working other areas of their small plantation.

"I'll need every one of those horses"—Squirrel pointed—"to keep the men mounted and moving. We start before sunup and ride night watch until we start out again. Ten mounts per man, and pray we don't lose any along the way."

Ten mounts per man? Ben's mind whirled over the cost of all those cow ponies. McCoy wasn't going to be happy if...

One of the cowboys broke off from the herd of horses and galloped toward a buggy.

Gus and the McCrea girls had dismounted and stood around it, the youngest waving at the cowboy.

"Gus and his girls came to say their so-longs to Lloyd and Tyree." Squirrel supplied the names. "Both good young men. Hard workers. I'm glad to have them along for the drive."

Another cowboy joined the group, and even from a distance, Ben could see the resemblance to the red-haired oldest daughter.

The oldest daughter who had caught Ben staring and was glaring in his direction. What had he done to offend her since lunch?

Squirrel chuckled. "Miss McCrea raised her siblings since their mother's death, back about the time the war started." He tipped his hat to the young lady in question, and she turned her back on them and tightened the lacy shawl draped around her shoulders. "She's none too happy that we're taking her brothers away."

There was nothing Ben could do about that, but he had a pang of regret all the same. Some of it may have been from missing his own sisters. Most of it was likely from feeling the scorn of such a pretty woman.

He wouldn't mind getting to know her better once the herds were on the trail and things slowed down. Nobody in San Antonio knew his background. He was building a new life for himself. It should include a wife and children.

Miss McCrea was easily the prettiest woman he'd seen since he'd arrived. She'd been pleasant to speak with until she'd learned his connection to the cattle drives. But she should get over that with time. And if she could cook half as good as her father...

Plates clattered into the basin as Kenna washed their lunch dishes before the supper crowd arrived.

"If you canna wash the plates without breaking them, let your sister do it." Pa crossed his arms, head cocked to the side. "What has your temper up?"

Vanora nudged her out of the way and grabbed the dish cloth. Not that she wanted to wash, no doubt, but so she'd be close enough to listen.

Kenna wiped her hands dry and faced Pa. "I wish the lads weren't leaving us."

"Kenna." Pa opened his arms, and she slid into them. "You canna stop the passage of time. Lloyd and Tyree must go and make their own way in the world. You canna keep them tied to your apron strings."

"I know." Her voice was muffled against his shoulder. "But I don't have to like it."

"I dinna like it much myself, but I have no room to complain. After all, I left my family to cross an ocean, knowing I would *never* see them again." He pushed her away and cupped her chin in his fingers. "They aren't nearly as far away as Scotland."

How could Pa have done it? How could anyone turn their back on their family and ride—or sail—away? Kenna wanted them to stay together for always. Oh, not in the same house, but was it too much to ask that they live in the same county?

Her bottom lip trembled, and she blinked back dampness.

"Take a short walk." Pa's voice was low, understanding written in the creases of his forehead. "We have a half hour or so before customers arrive."

"Thank you, Pa." She gave him a quick squeeze, shucked out of her apron, and fled through the back door into the alley. Had it been just days ago that Tyree had chased Elva with the snake, and Kenna had feared he'd never grow up? What she wouldn't give to see him—even with a snake—coming toward her now.

She turned in the other direction and meandered around the building. The street out front was busy, as busy as she'd ever seen it. Cowboys in their dusty clothing, Mexicans, ex-slaves, and even one young cowboy with hair as red as Tyree's. They rode by or leaned against the walls of businesses up and down the street. Some on errands for the ranchers they worked for, and others hoping to get hired by trail bosses.

More men eager to ride off and leave loved ones behind.

Kenna caught a glimpse of a familiar hat and a red roan horse she'd seen before. She stepped back into the space between the diner and the barbershop next door.

Mr. Warley didn't glance her way. Either he hadn't seen her among all the other people along the street, or the way she'd pointedly turned her back on him earlier had warned him off.

Which was fine.

She wanted nothing to do with the man who had lured her brothers away, even if he did have pleasant manners and the most intriguing voice.

If McCoy had ordered Ben to get a herd together and start it up the trail within ten days of arriving in San Antonio, Ben would have called the man a fool to his face and walked out of Red's bar. He couldn't have known the depths of the ranchers' desperation to move their animals. Sprawled before Ben was McCoy's dream—but it was the ranchers who were taking the real risks.

He shifted in his saddle, stifling a yawn. He hadn't been up this early since leaving the cavalry. Dawn was barely flirting with the eastern horizon, lighting the landscape but not coloring it yet. Already, the cowboys before him were fed, saddled, and starting the cattle moving.

Like a wave of horns and hide, the cattle milled around where they'd been bedded down for the night. The circling cowboys kept them together, waiting for what, Ben had no idea. The chuckwagon, pulled by six strong-looking mules, had rolled out a good quarter of an hour past. The remuda—what they called the herd of horses—had followed with two cowboys keeping them bunched together.

A shout came from the north side of the herd. Even in the low light, Squirrel stood out with his height. Standing in the stirrups, he whooped again, hat in his hand and circling above his head. Answering shouts followed, more hats were waved, and horses were pressed up against the milling cattle. Amazingly—or so it seemed to Ben—the cattle moved off into a line several animals wide. They walked calmly, raising dust with each step.

Rusty snorted and shook his head.

"We're on the wrong side of the herd, that's for sure." Ben guided the horse out of the way of the dust and watched for several more minutes as the cattle unwound into a long line. The first steps toward Kansas were nothing remarkable. Few onlookers had risen early enough to witness it. With a little luck, and owing a lot to the savvy leadership of Squirrel Brinkmann, they were seeing history in the making.

And not the start of a colossal failure.

How she didn't spill the coffee, Kenna had no idea. Her hands weren't steady, and neither was her heart. She'd longed to see Lloyd and Tyree off that morning, but Pa had been against it. It wasn't right to bother men while they were working, he'd said. Their visit the evening before, when both lads had walked into the kitchen just before dark, had been their parting.

Kenna finished filling customers' cups and returned to the kitchen.

Pa nodded toward three plates heaped with steaks, eggs, and biscuits.

With a sigh, she gathered them and slipped back through the swinging doors, barely avoiding a collision with Vanora, who'd cleared off a table and carried a tray stacked with dirty dishes. The diner was busier than it'd ever been, the result of all the people drawn to San Antonio by the lure of work and cattle sales.

Keeping busy would help stop her from brooding over her loss.

She delivered the plates to a trio of cowboys who must not have hired with an outfit yet. Once they did, the chuckwagon cook would feed them. As she turned, the bell jingled over the door.

Mr. Warley entered, removing his hat as he did.

Anger churned low in Kenna's middle. If he hadn't come to San Antonio, her brothers would be right down the street at the livery stable mucking stalls or grooming horses or running errands. But no, he had to show up and ruin everything.

Part of her knew her anger was a result of the fear she carried for her brothers' safety, but that part wasn't strong enough to redirect her.

He chose a seat at a small table in the corner, and she marched to his side.

"Breakfast is steak, eggs, and biscuits." Her words came out crisp and sharp.

He blinked up at her, forehead creasing. "That sounds fine."

She whirled and stomped into the kitchen. "Another plate."

Pa paused with his spatula mid-air. "What is wrong?"

"*He's* here."

Pa's beard bristled, a sure sign he was gritting his teeth. Then he slammed down the spatula. "Who is he?"

"That man, Mr. Warley, who got the whole town stirred up." She kept her voice down but jabbed a finger toward the dining room. "The one who took Lloyd and Tyree away."

Picking up the spatula again, Pa shook his head. "Kenna, you doesna have the right of it. He dinna take the lads away. They chose to go." He flipped eggs, two at a time, then turned back to her. "You canna blame the man for offering them opportunity."

"I can."

"Lassie." Pa flipped the steaks, then set the spatula down. "Mr. Warley offered a good opportunity to not only our lads but many people in this town. Look at our dining room. We are benefiting from his presence as well. We can meet some needs. For instance, your sisters need new dresses and shoes."

"You mean it, Pa?" Elva stood on a stool to reach the wash basin where she scrubbed dishes. It wobbled when she practically danced in eagerness for his answer.

Kenna steadied her but didn't reprimand her. After all, a new dress was a heady thing for the little girl who'd always worn Vanora's hand-me-downs.

"I do." Pa turned his attention back to Kenna. "And you could use the same. Dinna bite the hand that feeds you." He loaded two plates and shoved them at her. "Life changes. You canna stop it. Smile and wait on the customers like you always have."

Kenna bared her teeth at him in more of a snarl than a smile.

Pa chuckled and shook his head before cracking more eggs onto the griddle.

And so life went on as if Lloyd and Tyree weren't taking a part of her heart with them. The anger drained almost as quickly as it'd flared. Pa was right. She was behaving unreasonably.

And she wasn't being a very good example for her sisters.

She composed her face into a proper—if not heartfelt—smile and reentered the dining room. After delivering the plates to the appropriate table, she returned with the coffeepot and approached Mr. Warley.

"You take it black, if I remember correctly." She poured the inky liquid into his cup.

He edged back in his chair, as if concerned she might dump the scalding coffee in his lap.

Kenna's cheeks warmed, but she held onto her smile. "I apologize for being short with you when you entered, Mr. Warley."

"I hope it wasn't something I said or did, Miss McCrea."

"Not intentionally." She kept her voice low, although conversation buzzed around the room loud enough to cover anything short of a bellow. "But my brothers left with the cattle herd this morning and..." She swallowed against the lump that tightened her throat.

"I'm sorry if that distresses you, but I'm assured they are in the best of hands with Squirrel Brinkmann."

Kenna nodded. "Pa thinks so. He's known Mr. Brinkmann for many years. We all have. But it's hard to have the lads gone."

"I know what it means to lose a brother." His brown eyes met hers, somber in their depths. "I lost my oldest brother in the war. There were three others who died as infants."

"Oh." Kenna was lamenting her brothers riding away while this man had lost so much more. He must find her worries ridiculous. "I'm sorry."

"So am I."

"Kenna! Plates up!" Pa shouted from the kitchen.

"Excuse me." Kenna scurried to the kitchen and grabbed three filled plates, one of them bound for Mr. Warley. She slid it in front of him, seeing him a little differently. She still couldn't place his accent, but it wasn't nasal enough to be Northern. A Confederate then.

One who had lost a brother to the cause.

CHAPTER 5

W HY HAD BEN TOLD Miss McCrea about his brothers? The twins
had died before he was born, and he'd only had a glimpse
of little Adam beside their mother in the casket. Peter, though... the
loss of Peter left an ache that would never be completely filled. Peter
should have married and had children to carry on the Warley name.
His children should have inherited the plantation their great-grandfather had molded from the wilderness.

Now the plantation was gone, and only Ben remained to carry on
the family name.

He shook off the gloomy thoughts and cut into the steak, chewing
a bite while he watched Miss McCrea serve others in the diner. She
was graceful and efficient, smiling at the men who nodded their thanks
before tucking into plates of savory goodness she set before them.

And savory it was.

The food at the hotel was good, but there was something special
about the diner. And it wasn't a secret. Ben had been lucky to arrive
when he had. A line formed outside the door, hungry men waiting for
a table.

He lifted a hand to catch Miss McCrea's attention.

She hurried to his side. "More coffee?"

"Not yet." He gestured to the door. "But if any of those men care to
join me, there are two empty seats at this table."

She cast him a truly beautiful smile then, not the polite one he'd
seen before, and it shot a jolt clear down to his heels. Wow. He hadn't
expected that. But before he could unravel what it meant, two men
dressed in town clothes took the empty seats at the round table and
introduced themselves. They were brothers who owned a mercantile

across the street, and both thanked him profusely for the business he'd stirred up in San Antonio.

Ben nodded and responded automatically, his attention on the flame-haired woman with a plate in each hand, aiming her polite smile at another pair of customers. Just the polite smile. The other one... that one she'd aimed at Ben alone.

He wasn't in a position to consider courting anyone—not yet. He had a job to do. But when he was suitably established in San Antonio as the prosperous business associate of Joseph McCoy, when he'd settled into his new life, Miss McCrea would be his first choice for a woman to court.

While she didn't want to admit it, even to herself, there was less work for her with her brothers on the cattle drive. Less clothing to wash and mend, which meant she had time to sew dresses for Vanora and Elva. She was even planning one for herself.

Pa'd been right about the money. Not only the increase in business—which was substantial—but it cost them less to feed the family with Lloyd and Tyree away. Those boys ate like a pair of starving coyotes. Pa liked to say they both had hollow legs to fill.

It'd been two weeks and more since they'd ridden north. Two weeks without a word. Pa had told her it'd be that way. Even though they'd pass near towns, the cowboys wouldn't be allowed to leave the cattle to mail letters and didn't have the money to send a telegram.

Still, she'd trade the new dresses and full larder for a letter at the post office or their grinning faces at the breakfast table.

It was just Pa, the girls, and Kenna this morning. As always, they breakfasted early, before Pa opened the doors for customers.

"Tomorrow after church"—Pa wiped his mouth with a napkin—"I thought we'd pack a picnic and take it to the river."

Elva squealed. "Can we fish, Pa?"

He ruffled her braided hair, loosening curls Kenna had labored to contain. The poor girl had inherited the unruly hair along with their mother's red hue.

"I dinna see why not."

"And can we eat fish for our supper?" The girl's eyes practically glowed.

Vanora leaned forward in her chair. "Fish would be so good."

Kenna wouldn't mind a change from beef either.

"We canna count on it. The fish have to cooperate first." Pa chuckled. "After the breakfast crowd, you girls can turn rocks for worms." He wagged a finger. "Watch for snakes."

Elva gave a solemn nod, glancing at Vanora. The older girl took her sister's hand. "We will, Pa. I'll make sure."

Kenna couldn't have made a noise past the lump in her throat. Vanora was only twelve but so grown-up. It wouldn't be long before young men came sniffing around. She looked like Lloyd, with her sleek dark hair and skin that tanned under the Texas sun. Her mane was braided in a single line, not a strand out of place. She was far too grown-up for Kenna's peace of mind.

A thump of boots on the boardwalk outside the diner broke the moment.

"Clear the dishes, lassies. We've customers to feed." Pa pushed away from the table and unlocked the door, greeting men by name as he did with the regulars every morning, warning them that they were early and it'd take a minute to prepare their plates. "Coffee, Kenna." He hollered for no reason other than habit.

Kenna was already halfway to the tables with the full coffeepot in her hands.

"I'll take some of that." A young man Kenna didn't recognize grabbed a cup off his table and thrust it at her. "Especially from a sweet-looking thing like you."

Kenna shot a glance at Vanora and Elva, who scurried into the kitchen. Pa took a step closer as Kenna filled the cup. Pa wasn't a tall man, but he was powerful. Burly in a way that wasn't fat. The younger man snickered, took a swallow of the scalding liquid, and winced, his eyes never leaving Kenna.

With any luck, it would sear his throat and shut him up.

Pa had told her to write two choices on the chalkboard for breakfast—steak and eggs, or beef hash over biscuits. She took orders, jotting them down on a tablet, and hurried back to the kitchen.

"Watch that one, lass." Pa pointed his egg-splattered spatula toward her. "I dinna like the looks of him."

"Me either." Kenna loaded plates with hash and biscuits. "You girls stay back here. I'll serve and bus the tables until that one is gone."

She delivered the first plates, then returned for a second round of coffee. As she poured a cup, someone touched her backside. Pa had added two more tables to accommodate the extra customers, and they were close together, but they weren't close enough for that touch to have been accidental, and she knew who was seated behind her.

Kenna whirled, letting the bottom edge of the enamelware coffeepot collide with the side of the cocky stranger's head, hot coffee splashing from the spout onto his chest.

He yelped and jumped up, knocking his chair over while slapping at his coffee-soaked shirt. "Why you—"

"I'm sorry." Kenna grabbed a glass of water from the table and doused the coffee staining his front. "That'll take care of the burn."

He reared his arm back.

Kenna flinched and ducked, but the blow never reached her. She glanced up in time to see Mr. Warley twisting the stranger's arm behind his back and holding it there. The mild man with nice manners transformed into someone with whipcord strength and steely determination.

"I believe you owe Miss McCrea an apology," Mr. Warley said.

"The bi—" The word was cut off as the stranger rose onto his toes, his face pulled into a grimace.

Several other customers came to their feet.

The cocky stranger sagged in Mr. Warley's hold. "Okay, let me down."

"The apology?"

"It doesna matter." Pa stood in the doorway of the kitchen, his largest skillet in one hand. "He's leaving. He isna welcome here again."

Mr. Warley gave Pa a firm nod, then walked the stranger out the door, giving him a none-too-gentle shove into the street.

Several harsh and vulgar words flew back their way, but Mr. Warley dusted off his hands and turned to Kenna, once more the well-mannered gentleman. "I see you have beef hash this morning. That sounds perfect." Then he joined two other men who were reseating themselves at a table near the window.

Pa nodded and returned to the kitchen.

Kenna followed Mr. Warley and poured his coffee. "Thank you." If her voice came out a bit shaky, who could fault her?

"I just happened to be closest when he pulled that stunt." Mr. Warley gestured to the men around him. "These gentlemen would have done the same."

There was a murmuring of agreement from around the room.

Mr. Warley leaned closer and dropped his voice. "Nice shot with the coffeepot. I hope you didn't dent it on his thick head."

The other men at his table hooted over the remark.

Kenna's face heated to the roots of her hair.

"I admire a woman who can take care of herself." Mr. Warley's sincere words took some of the embarrassment away.

But the blush remained—or maybe was intensified—at the honest regard in his eyes.

Ben let Rusty wade into the river outside of San Antonio and pull in a long drink. It was hot enough to fry eggs on the rocks lining the river. Ben removed his hat, mopped sweat from his brow, and resettled the hat on his head. It kept the sun from frying his brains.

He'd ridden out to visit two more herds forming outside of San Antonio for the long drive to Kansas. They had to gather farther from the city now, the near grass having been grazed off by the first herds. They needed rain, but he'd been told not to expect any for weeks. Other than the heat, nothing about San Antonio reminded him of South Carolina... which was just as well.

He didn't need reminders of his past.

Ben had inspected both herds. McCoy would be pleased. The ranchers organizing them had imported English and Scottish stock to improve their herds some years ago. They weren't all longhorns, either.

There were short-horned cattle in the mix. Some of the beasts were even polled—lacking any horns at all—or what the cowboys called muleys. Those crossbred animals were thicker and fleshier than the wild longhorns. Both herds were stocked with well-finished beasts. If they didn't walk all their weight off before they reached Abilene, they'd draw top dollar at the eastern markets.

A high-pitched squeal caught Ben's attention.

Rusty jerked his head up, water dribbling from his lips, ears pointed upstream.

"Let's see what that's all about, shall we?" Ben nudged the horse onto the bank and turned in the direction of the sound.

"I caught one!" The words cut through the thick scrubby brush that grew along the river's edge. A young female voice he'd heard many times before. The youngest McCrea, Miss Elva. He clicked his tongue, and Rusty broke into a canter.

They circled a patch of brush and trotted into a wide opening along the riverbank. Gus stood over his youngest, one hand on her fishing pole, the other around her waist as they worked the fish toward land. Miss Vanora bounced on her toes, her hands clasped under her chin.

But it was the other Miss McCrea, her wayward red curls ignoring their pins, who held Ben's interest. She had one hand on her hip and the other over her mouth, squinting in merriment as the fish flopped out of the water and back in with a splash.

Then she noticed him.

He had no right to feel the way he did when her blue-gray eyes met his. She dropped her hand to flash him one of her beautiful smiles. A man could get lost in those smiles—be content to be lost there. Perhaps once the cattle drives were—

"Mr. Warley!" Miss Vanora waved at him, pulling Ben's attention from her sister. "Come watch Elva catch a fish."

Ben dismounted and led Rusty to a sturdy branch and tied him there. The horse stripped away a mouthful of tasty willow leaves and munched.

"Come and see, Mr. Warley!" the youngest girl shouted, peering around her father until the fish gave another tug, which she answered with a squeal.

"Pay attention, lassie." Gus chuckled. "We canna eat a fish that gets away."

"Look what we have already." Miss Vanora pointed to a round basket holding several large fish.

"Think there'll be enough for lunch tomorrow?" He waggled his eyebrows at the dark-haired girl.

She laughed, one hand over her mouth in a pose very like her older sister from moments before. "I don't think so."

"Ah, here we are." Gus hauled the wiggling fish onto the bank while Miss Elva squealed again. "The grandest one yet."

"That makes six," Miss Elva said.

"I caught three of them." Miss Vanora twisted the ties of her bonnet around her fingers.

"Aye, that you did." Gus removed the fish from the hook and slipped it into the almost full basket, where it flopped a couple of times before giving up. He nodded a greeting to Ben. "She's the best fisherman of the lot—including the lads. Has the patience of Job, and that's a fact."

Ben turned to Miss McCrea. "And how many did you catch?"

Her face colored, almost hiding the smattering of light freckles that bridged her nose. "Not a one, I'm afraid."

"She never does." Miss Elva grinned wide enough to expose a fresh gap from a missing tooth on one side. "She falls asleep."

Gus roared with laughter, the younger girls giggled, and Miss McCrea rolled her eyes.

"I'm not much of a fisherman myself," Ben admitted.

Miss McCrea shot him a grateful glance.

"But my wee lassies are." Gus wrapped an arm around each of the younger girls. "And so we'll eat well for supper. You'll join us, Ben?"

"I'd be happy to, if you're sure you have enough."

"Wait until you have Pa's fried fish." Elva's eyes gleamed. "They're the best ever."

Gus hefted the basket while the younger girls gathered the poles. Ben offered Miss McCrea his arm and walked her to the buggy. He assisted Gus in hitching the horse, then mounted Rusty and rode alongside.

He allowed himself to enjoy the moment, to be a small part of the family outing. How long had it been since he'd had anything like a family outing?

Since before the war.

A lifetime ago.

Dark clouds pressed against the happiness of the occasion, and it took all Ben had to shove them aside. The war was over, but the healing had barely begun. He had to establish himself as someone other than a small plantation owner's younger son—one who'd switched allegiance and turned his back on his country. He had to completely rebuild his life.

He had to learn to be someone other than the Ben Warley of before the war.

CHAPTER 6

I T DIDN'T ESCAPE KENNA'S notice that Mr. Warley rode on her side of the buggy—not Pa's. It hadn't escaped Pa's either, if his sidelong glances meant anything. Or her sisters', who twittered like a pair of birds in the buggy's back seat. Kenna's stomach knotted in a not-unpleasant way. A way she hadn't felt before but instinctively knew was related to the man on the horse next to her.

Though she'd been just twelve years old when Ma died, her mother had prepared her for what it meant to be a woman. Had told her things—things she should be passing on to Vanora. She owed it to her sisters to share those things. She had to provide what their mother would have. What Ma would expect her to do.

She glanced at Mr. Warley and the knot increased, but she had no right to be thinking of him at all. Not while Vanora and Elva still needed her.

"How far do you expect Squirrel's herd to have gotten by now?" Pa's gruff voice cut through Kenna's wayward thoughts like a hot knife through butter.

"He was hoping to make fifteen miles a day in good weather over good ground, but said some days might be more like ten or twelve. And he assured me that they'd go slow enough not to walk all the weight off the cattle."

"Nobody wants a stringy piece of beef." Pa chuckled. "Not even those Yankees up north."

"Were you in the war, Mr. Warley?" Elva asked.

Kenna sucked in a breath of hot air to reprimand her sister, but Pa touched her sleeve. She snapped her mouth shut. Pa must want to know the answer... but why?

"I was, Miss Elva," was all the man said.

Elva seemed to think it was enough, or Vanora had a hold of her. Either way, she stayed blessedly silent for the rest of the short ride home.

Kenna couldn't help but wonder which side Mr. Warley had fought on. She still couldn't place his accent, but she'd bet her last silver button it wasn't Yankee.

Pa dropped them off in the alley behind the diner while he headed to the livery to return the horse and buggy. Mr. Warley rode on with him.

Kenna took the basket of fish into the kitchen and had them cleaned and ready to cook by the time the men returned. Vanora had peeled and sliced potatoes. Elva had the table set with their best Sunday dishes, the ones Ma had gotten from her mother. They were chipped and the finish cracked, the golden edges worn away in many places, but still precious to Kenna. Still a link to the mother Vanora and Elva could barely remember.

Mr. Warley stopped just inside the door while Pa fired up the stove, banging pans and getting ready for the fish fry. "What can I do to help, Miss McCrea?"

"Nothing. You're our guest."

"Please, I like to be useful."

"If you're sure." She grabbed a pair of buckets from near the door. "We could use fresh water. Elva can show you to the San Pedro canal." It was the local water source designated for drinking and cooking.

He took the buckets and turned to Elva. "Lead on, Miss Elva." Then he followed her out the door.

"He's a nice young man," Pa said.

Kenna's face burned. "He seems to be. But we know very little about him."

Pa scratched under his beard, then grinned at her. "But enough to catch my lassie's eye."

"Don't start matchmaking. We've too much else to do."

"I wouldn't mind being matched to someone like Mr. Warley," said Vanora, a dreaminess in her voice.

Kenna huffed and glared at Pa.

He shrugged before adding more grease to his largest skillet and dumping in Vanora's potatoes.

Kenna sat on a low stool and motioned Vanora to come closer. "You're just twelve, dear. Far too young—"

"I'll be thirteen in October." Her deep brown eyes held sincerity without a trace of rebelliousness—which Kenna was thankful for. "You took over for Ma when you were twelve."

"Only because I had to."

"I know, but I'll be old enough to take over from you soon, and then you'll be free to match up with someone... maybe even Mr. Warley. You two would make a lovely pair."

So that was where her sister's mind had gone. Relief flooded Kenna.

"I think I'll stay close a bit longer, if you don't mind." She gave her sister a quick squeeze. "But the day will come when you don't need me around anymore."

Vanora returned the brief hug. "I'll always need you, but maybe not always in the same way."

When had her introspective sister grown up? Kenna blinked away a sheen of dampness, then stood. "Let's help Pa with supper, shall we?"

Kenna enjoyed the supper, enjoyed the banter between her sisters, Pa's discussion of the cattle drives with Mr. Warley, and being allowed to relax at a table for a while. But when the evening wound down, she made sure it was Elva who escorted Mr. Warley to the door and bid him goodnight. It wouldn't do to encourage the man.

Wouldn't do for him? Or for her?

Ben dismounted, covered in dust and sweat that belied the calendar insisting autumn had arrived. But then, what did he know of autumn in Texas? He unsaddled and brushed Rusty, then turned the animal into the livery corral for a good roll. Ben and the mustang had grown close over the summer months. He leaned against the top rail of the corral and remembered his first impression of the mustang. He'd been wrong about a lot of things. Rusty might not have the body of a thoroughbred, but he certainly had the heart of one.

Ben dusted himself off as best he could. He'd stop by the telegraph office, then head to the diner for one of Gus's steaks and whatever he'd prepared to go with it.

Ben had never eaten so much steak in his life, maybe not in all his twenty-four years combined, but beef was cheap and plentiful in Texas. And it came with a smile from Miss McCrea or a giggle from one of her sisters, so it was worth it.

With summer whittling away, no more cattle to start north, and Mc-Coy's telegraphs ecstatic over the success of the drives, Ben had been working up the nerve to ask Gus if he could call on Miss McCrea. Since moving out of the hotel and into a boarding house, Ben had frequented the diner around noon almost daily. Miss McCrea's attitude toward him had thawed once he'd shared about losing his brothers. Her smile, while never crossing to flirtatious, was surely an encouragement. An evening walk along the river, perhaps, or even walking her to church on Sunday, would be a fair start to what might lead to the family he wanted.

His boots thumped on the worn floor of the telegraph office, bringing the clerk's head up in his direction.

"Mr. Warley, I was just on my way to the boarding house to deliver a message. You've saved me a walk."

"A happy coincidence, then." Ben took the folded and sealed paper. "Thanks."

"Hold your thanks until after you read it." The machine at the clerk's elbow started to jiggle. "Excuse me."

Ben stepped outside and squinted into the sun's glare. The calendar had just turned to September, but the sun was as hot as ever. Did San Antonio never cool down? He slapped the paper against his palm and debated waiting to open it until after he ate. From what the clerk said, it wasn't good news.

Bad news had a tendency to spoil a man's lunch.

The herds that had already arrived in Abilene had made it through in good order, a few head lost to injury, illness, and Indians—which was to be expected—but McCoy had sent his hearty congratulations along with orders to ride out to all the area ranches and start plans for more herds to drive north beginning in early May. Ben had been out to the Triple S all morning doing exactly that. Frederick Schmidt had been disappointed to miss the summer drives. He was raring to go in the spring and promised the largest herd yet.

Ben tucked the note into his pocket. Whatever it was, it could wait until his stomach was full. He strode to the diner and entered to the jingle of its bell. The place was nearly empty, it being more than an hour past noon.

"Hello, Mr. Warley." Miss Elva grinned at him, exposing the slight gap to one side where a new tooth had mostly grown in. "Sit wherever you like. I'll tell Kenna you're here."

He picked the small round table near the front window that he was coming to think of as *his* table. Kenna—Miss McCrea—arrived with a coffeepot, and his heartbeat kicked against his ribs.

"Have you heard?" She poured his coffee, a lovely smile curving her lips.

"Heard what?"

"Mr. Brinkmann is back. Lloyd and Tyree came home with him."

"I'm happy for you." He was, but there was a hollow thump inside him as well. What would it be like to rejoice over a brother returned? He'd never know.

"They arrived late last night. Oh, and Mr. Brinkmann was asking after you. I told him you're generally here for a late lunch." She started for the kitchen. "I'll fetch your plate."

Squirrel asking for him? Ben pulled the note from his pocket. Maybe he'd better read it.

September 3, 1867

Mr. Ben Warley, San Antonio, Texas

Squirrel to arrive shortly. Good man. Railroad confirmed cars to haul cattle second week of December for Christmas market. Need cattle here by then.

Joseph McCoy

What? Ben leaned back against his chair and stared out the window. He didn't know much about the day-to-day work of moving a huge herd for hundreds of miles, but even he knew it would be much more difficult as winter approached. Less nutritious grazing. Cold weather and freezing rivers. Harder on men and animals both. Dangerous, even.

Miss McCrea reappeared with his plate. He thanked her and cut into the meat without much enthusiasm. How could he eat when such news had been dumped on him? Schmidt at the Triple S was his best chance for amassing the numbers of cattle needed, but he'd missed the early drives due to a lack of capable and willing men to work them.

Where would Ben find those men now?

He paused mid-chew. The McCrea boys were back. Surely that meant others had returned as well. That put things in a better light. He cleaned his plate, anxious to find Squirrel and see what he knew. Ben didn't wait for Miss McCrea to return for his plate. He left the coins for his meal beside it on the table and left.

Kenna slipped the coins into her apron pocket and watched Mr. Warley stride away. How odd. He normally lingered over his meals. She brushed away the sting of disappointment.

While he came in almost every day and seemed to enjoy their brief chats, he'd never given her reason to think she should read more into his visits than the appreciation of Pa's cooking. For her part, she was diligent not to encourage him. She sighed and gathered his dishes and some from the table across the room. The lunch crowd was finished for the day.

She headed to the kitchen and dumped the dirty plates into the wash basin, then stretched her back. "That's the end of it, Pa."

"Good." He pulled several more steaks off the pile and slapped them onto the stove. "Elva, run and tell your brothers it's time to eat. They'll be hanging around the livery."

"Yes, Pa." Elva wiped her hands dry and scooted out the back door.

Kenna rolled up her sleeves and plunged her hands into the soapy water. "It's so good to have them home."

"Aye." He paused and leveled a glance her way. "But dinna get too attached to having them here."

"But—"

"They have tasted independence. They willna wish to live under my roof much longer."

She started to speak, to refute what he said even as her heart recognized its truth, but he stalled her with a raised hand.

"And that's as should be, lass."

It was, but she didn't want to hear it. Didn't want to think about it. Couldn't stand the thought of her family breaking up.

The back door burst open, and her brothers spilled into the room, Elva close behind.

Tyree pulled in a long breath, his broad chest swelling. "I'll never tire of that smell, Pa."

"Sure beats the slop we've been eating for the past few weeks," Lloyd said.

"Was the chuckwagon cook that bad?" Kenna asked. She'd heard Squirrel had hired the best in the area—aside from Pa.

"He was fine"—Tyree snitched a cold biscuit and shoved half of it in his mouth, then mumbled around the mass—"but we were on our own for the trip back. And Squirrel can't cook any better than the rest of us cowboys. Cookie stayed in Kansas."

"Why did he stay?" asked Pa.

"It's a brand-new town," Lloyd said. "They needed a cook at the bar, the only place serving any food until McCoy's new hotel is fully operational. Cookie already has a job lined up there when it is."

"Well, I'm just glad that you're both home." Kenna moved to the base of the stairs. "Vanora! Come down for lunch."

Her middle sister appeared, nose red but eyes bright. She'd been fighting a cold for several days, but Kenna wouldn't deprive her of the chance to eat lunch with their brothers.

As they'd done ever since Pa had opened the diner, they filled their plates and filed into the empty dining room to have their family meal. Kenna sat with a sigh, happiness spilling over inside as Pa offered a prayer for the meal.

"There's talk of one last drive pushing north." Lloyd reached for a biscuit from the bowl in the center of the table. "If it happens, reckon Tyree and I will sign on again."

Tyree nodded, mouth too full for anything else.

Kenna stifled her groan, catching Pa's warning glance from the corner of her eye. After all, nothing was sure yet. It was just talk. Men may say women were gossips, but they had as much tittle-tattle to wade through as any circle of women ever did. Talk had as much chance of being wrong as being right.

And even if it didn't last, their domestic bliss, Kenna was going to enjoy every minute she could while it did. She cut a piece of savory steak and popped it in her mouth.

"So you knew about this already?" Ben spat the words out as he waved the note from McCoy at Squirrel.

"He wasn't sure he could get the railroad to cooperate." Squirrel shrugged, one relaxed hip propped against the doorframe. "He doesn't have the feed to overwinter cattle in Abilene, so it was just an idea when I left."

"Did you return with enough cowboys to manage another herd?" Ben pulled back the curtain from the window of his upstairs room at the boarding house. There weren't many men in view, and those were busy doing something, not lounging around in front of buildings.

"Over half returned with me, and a trio of other men who were traveling this way. They've indicated a willingness to work a drive. We'll have to scare up a few more."

"Frederick Schmidt has a herd he wants to move in the spring. It wouldn't take much to convince him to let them go now." Ben faced Squirrel. "But tell me the truth. Can a herd be moved this late in the season?"

Squirrel scratched his jaw. "I won't lie, there will be increased risks."

"What kind of risks?"

"Harder on the men than the cattle. Cattle can handle the cold. Swimming rivers will mean having to build fires and dry men off to prevent frostbite. That'll slow us down. I'll need to rotate the night riders more frequently for the same reason. Can't have men losing their toes or fingers out there." He eased his weight from one foot to the other. "There should be enough grass left to graze the herd and horses if we swing a little wide of the original trail. The hardest part will be finding a cook—I mean a really good cook—to keep the men well fed. Men need to eat more in cold weather. They need hot food."

"Isn't the cook you used before good enough?"

"Oh, he is, but he stayed in Abilene."

Nothing was ever easy. Ben had learned that early in the war. Until then, he'd had little to worry about. His father had run the plantation. The slaves had done the bulk of the labor. Peter had learned at their father's elbow. Ben had done little other than amuse himself and hone his skill with horses. What he wouldn't give to go back to those idyllic days.

He slumped onto the bed. "I was at Schmidt's place this morning. Let's head back out tomorrow and talk to him. He doesn't have the men to work it, so we'll need to scare up a crew."

He'd been so close to speaking with Gus about Miss McCrea, but he'd need to put that on hold. He wouldn't ask until he knew he had time to do a proper job of courting. And that meant waiting until after this last herd was on its way north.

CHAPTER 7

"**T**HREE STRANGERS IN THE dining room," Kenna said as she swept through the swinging doors, both arms loaded with dirty dishes. She slipped them into the wash basin for Tyree to scrub. The lads were making themselves useful. Vanora was still sniffling, and Elva had started coughing after lunch, so Kenna had sent them both upstairs to lie down.

Lloyd stacked the plate he was drying and glanced into the other room. "I know them." He picked up another plate. "They rode from Abilene with us. All three are Yankees fresh out of the cavalry, but they seem nice enough."

"Yankees?" Kenna put her hands on her hips.

Pa pushed two loaded plates her way. "We've fed Yankees before, and we will again. The war is over."

"Besides," Tyree said, "we met a lot of Yankees on the trail. They ain't much different from you and me." He gave her a cheeky grin.

"Yankees." She gathered the plates and her resolve before entering the dining room. After delivering the plates to a couple of regulars, she grabbed the coffeepot and approached the strangers' table.

"What can I get you men?" She couldn't bring herself to say *gentlemen* to a bunch of Yankees.

One man pointed to the plates she'd just delivered. "Steak and potatoes look fine to me."

The other two asked for the same.

Kenna poured their coffee and was almost to the kitchen door when the bell jingled.

Mr. Warley walked in, removed his hat, and then froze when he spied the trio of Yankees.

One of them rose. "Ben? Benjamin Warley?"

The other two came to their feet as well. Was there going to be a fight in the dining room? She thrust her hand to open the swinging door, but Lloyd was already there, Tyree a step behind.

"It's good to see you." The first one who'd stood grabbed Mr. Warley's hand and pumped it. "Had no idea you'd come to San Antonio. Last I heard, you was heading to Abilene to see Red."

"I did." Mr. Warley retrieved his hand and shifted his feet. "I took a job for Joseph McCoy. He sent me here."

"I'd say you landed on your feet right enough." One of them guffawed. "You look like a big-city dandy in them duds."

"Join us." The third man grabbed an empty chair from a nearby table. "We can catch up on what's happened since you left the cavalry."

Kenna stepped forward to fill Mr. Warley's coffee cup as those last words sunk in. *Since you left the cavalry.*

Mr. Ben Warley was a *Yankee?*

Ben dropped onto the chair someone had pulled over for him. His brain refused to work past the shock of seeing the three men seated around him. Jake, Vernon, and Charlie had been the closest friends he'd had in the U.S. Cavalry. Vernon was another Galvanized Yankee. Jake and Charlie had been raised in the western territories, had no experience with the War between the States, and had never treated Ben as anything other than a fellow cavalryman.

Miss McCrea poured his coffee, but her lips were pressed in a firm line. An unsmiling line. When her blue-gray eyes met his, there was no warmth in them. None of the men around him wore any indication of having been in the U.S. Cavalry, but she'd overheard. Disapproval rolled off her like a dust cloud before a storm.

"How long you been here?" Vernon asked.

Ben pulled his attention back to his fellow cavalrymen. "Since the first of June."

Miss McCrea's dark-haired brother, the one who had sold Rusty to Ben, came to the table. "You fellows know each other?"

"Know each other?" Charlie slapped his palm on the table. "We rode together out of Fort Dodge."

Ben winced at the bold declaration and wished Charlie had kept his voice down.

Heads around the diner swiveled their direction. Most of the looks were no friendlier than Miss McCrea's. They were deep in the South. Charlie would do well to remember that.

Jake poked a thumb toward Ben. "This son-of-a-gun saved my bacon when a horse took an arrow and dropped from under me during a skirmish. You should have seen him, riding at a flat-out gallop straight toward me. I stuck my arm in the air, he grabbed it, and the next thing I knew, I was behind his saddle and hanging on for dear life, arrows and bullets whizzing on either side."

"Not just on either side." Ben remembered that moment all too well. "We had to dig two slugs out of my horse's rump back at the fort. He was a good mount. He healed up and was back in action within a month."

Vernon pointed at Ben. "Only because you knew what to do. I never saw a man any better with horses. Not ever."

"That's a fact," Charlie said. "The way you ride, doctor, and can even shoe a horse in a pinch."

Miss McCrea's brother stuck out his hand. "We never properly met when you bought the roan mustang from the livery. I'm Lloyd McCrea."

He stood and shook the young man's hand. "Ben Warley."

Lloyd held onto his hand for a moment, recognition flickering in his dark eyes. "You the one who hired Squirrel?"

Ben nodded.

The young man grinned and waved the other brother over. "This is my brother, Tyree. We were both on the drive." He announced that loudly enough to be heard outside the diner.

The mood in the dining room relaxed as if Ben's connection to Squirrel meant he wouldn't be condemned for being a Yankee. But if they knew the whole truth, condemnation would fall on him like an ax. A Yankee was bad enough, but a Galvanized Yankee? Someone from the South who'd deliberately turned his back on his country? He'd be run out of San Antonio for sure, if not worse.

Worse like the neighbors in South Carolina, who'd torched his boyhood home and every single outbuilding when they'd learned what he'd done.

"Pa, he's a *Yankee*." Kenna forced the words out in a hoarse whisper, ignoring the noise her brothers were making in the dining room.

Pa flipped a pair of steaks on the griddle. "Who's a Yankee?"

"Mr. Warley." She pointed toward the swinging doors. "And he's out there at a table full of other Yankees. In our diner."

Pa wiped his hands on his apron and strode to the swinging doors. He didn't enter the dining room, just watched over the top and listened for a moment, then he turned back to Kenna.

"We canna live in the past." He shrugged. "The South dinna win the war, so we are citizens of the United States of America again."

"Pa." Kenna tried not to gape, but she could barely believe her ears. "What about the fight for independence? Were not your own people Jacobites who fought long and hard for the same?"

"Aye, and where did it get them?" Pa returned to his griddle, slapping perfectly-cooked steaks onto plates and heaping the sides with potatoes and greens. "The war is over, Kenna. Dinna hold on to the past."

"But you know Southerners have joined with Maximilian and—"

"Maximilian is dead." Pa raised a hand to stop her next words. "And there is no power to replace him that will assist the South. It's over, Kenna. Let it be." He shoved the plates toward her. "Feed the men. We have a good life here. There is no need to stir up battles of any kind."

Kenna took the plates and delivered them to the Yankees and Mr. Warley—also a Yankee.

Lloyd shifted to the side to give her access.

"Can I get you anything else?" Her words were clipped and drew a raised brow from Tyree. She could have offered him the same for cavorting with Yankees.

"I'll take a slab of pie when my plate's clean," the tallest said. Heads bobbed around the table, including Mr. Warley's.

"Four plates of pie." Kenna whirled, but not before catching the regret in Mr. Warley's expression. Well, it served him right for leading her to think he wasn't a Yankee with that funny accent of his.

Never had it taken men so long to eat a meal, not that her brothers helped as they gathered other chairs and joined the Yankees while dishes piled high in the kitchen and Kenna was left to herself to serve, clear, and clean. She had built a powerful head of steam by the time the last man exited the front door.

"Tyree." She all but snapped his name when her brother moved to follow the other men outside. "I could use your help." She jerked her head toward the kitchen.

He frowned, obviously on the verge of ignoring her, but Lloyd stepped between him and the door, pointing toward the kitchen.

"Kenna can't do it all, and the wee lassies are ill. Come, brother. Pa needs our help."

"We're cowboys. We shouldn't be wearing aprons and scrubbing pans."

"We're unemployed." Lloyd gave Tyree a gentle shove. "And Pa is feeding us, so we pull our weight as we always have."

Kenna fumed between being angry with Tyree for his near disobedience to her and being sore that Lloyd had stepped in and handled Tyree like a... like a man. Her older brother winked at her as he followed Tyree to the back, rolling up his sleeves.

Not only didn't they need her anymore, but now Lloyd was stepping into the leadership role she'd assumed so many years ago.

Kenna sank onto a chair, cleaning rag hanging uselessly from her hand. Her whole world was changing. Her brothers left as boys, then returned as men, and a man she'd come to view as a friend turned out to be nothing but a Yankee. She wasn't sure she could handle it all. She pressed the palm of her hand against her forehead.

What choice did she have?

Cattle spread before Ben across land west of San Antonio that had already been grazed off once that year, but with enough fall growth to keep the animals for a few days until they started north.

Frederick Schmidt agreed to send his cattle north even though they couldn't leave until mid-September. Ben introduced him to Squirrel, and the two Germans linked up like long-lost brothers. The problem—same as before—was finding enough men to handle the cattle. Of those who'd returned with Squirrel, only a handful had agreed to another drive.

Lloyd and Tyree McCrea had been the first.

Ben flinched at the memory of Miss McCrea's face when they'd accepted Squirrel's offer at the diner over lunch the week before. She'd barely spoken to Ben since learning that he'd ridden for the U.S. Cavalry, but that day... that day, he fancied he'd seen more than just anger in her eyes.

He'd seen loss, despair, and hurt.

He'd almost pulled the plug on the drive. He probably had the power to do it, although it wasn't exactly settled by his agreement with McCoy, but in his mind, it would equate to a failure.

And failure wasn't an option. Too many others depended on his doing his job well.

Yet, as he sat on Rusty looking over the milling herd, failure once again raised its ugly head and stared straight at Ben. Even with Schmidt's extra hands signed on, they were short at least three riders and a cook. Where were they going to find them?

Beside him, Squirrel shifted on his saddle, the leather creaking in the early morning stillness. "There's a settlement just south of town a ways where I could probably scare up a few more cowboys, men who can ride and work the cattle."

"Then why haven't you been there?"

Squirrel removed his hat and scratched over one ear before jamming the hat back on. "Thing is, they're all black men down there."

Ben swiveled to get a better look at Squirrel. "Slaves?"

"Not anymore, no. Just men. Men who can ride and keep the cattle moving."

"But who would be willing to work side by side with freed slaves?" Ben asked. "You'll lose the rest of the cowboys you've signed on."

"Well." Squirrel shifted again, his horse taking a step in protest. "I don't think so." He leveled a glance at Ben. "I think they'll be fine with it. After all, they'll still earn themselves a paycheck."

"So what's stopping you?"

"You."

"What?"

"You can fool a lot of folks with how you talk, but if they listened better, they'd know you're not a true Yankee." Squirrel gazed across the herd. "Vernon let slip that he was a Galvanized Yankee, and I figure you for the same."

Ben's stomach dropped. "I suppose you resent working for the likes of me, then."

Squirrel leaned to the side and spit a stream of tobacco juice into the dirt. "No, sir. I figure the war made a lot of men do things they'd rather not have. But it's over, and we have beeves to move." He squinted at Ben. "If you're good with moving them using black cowboys, that is."

"Of course. Why not? If they can do the work."

"At equal pay with all the other cowboys." Squirrel's jaw firmed beneath his drooping mustache. "A man works for me—any man—he deserves to be paid an honest wage. I won't back down on that."

Paying slaves. Ben gritted his teeth. What would his father think of that? Would he see the need to move all those animals north at any price? Or would he stand on his principles that an inferior race should be treated as such? Would he see Ben as a failure if he agreed to Squirrel's terms?

Failure. The word rode him like a hair shirt.

McCoy was waiting in Abilene for the cattle spread out before him. If hiring former slaves was the only way to move them, then that's what they'd do.

He gave Squirrel a tight nod. "Do it."

The man beside him relaxed in his saddle. "That'll get us one step closer, but we still need two more things."

"A cook and a wrangler for the remuda to handle the horses."

Squirrel nodded.

"The older McCrea son, Lloyd, he seems to know what he's doing with horses."

"I agree, and in a couple of years, I'd put in him charge of the remuda. But he's young. Care of the horses is too important."

"Maybe you'll find a slave—ex-slave—who knows horses. Some of them must."

"You're likely right about that. But a cook?"

"Who else is there, other than those people?"

Squirrel twisted on his saddle and looked back toward town. "McCrea turned me down flat in the spring, but with both of his sons going, maybe I can change his mind this time."

That would leave Miss McCrea and the girls all alone at the diner. Ben didn't believe Gus would do it, but Squirrel had known him longer. "Worth a try."

Squirrel gave him a narrow-eyed look that Ben couldn't read.

"I've had the chuckwagon stocked and loaded with extra blankets. I think we'll get this pulled together in time to roll out in three days."

Three days.

Leaving in mid-September for a drive that would take longer than normal due to the weather and grazing needs. They'd be lucky to reach Abilene in time for the Christmas shipment east.

But failure still wasn't an option, so they'd do what it took.

Even hiring ex-slaves.

Kenna had a bad feeling. It worked its way into the tension of her shoulders, her inability to sleep, and the sharpness of her words. Pa had called her out for her snappishness too many times over the past week.

He was right, but she couldn't seem to control it.

At night, her dreams were unsettling. The most persistent was the storm that approached from the southeast, huge clouds rolling toward them with fierce winds. As hard as she tried, Kenna couldn't get her sisters and brothers all together under shelter. She'd turn her back and one would go missing. She'd rush into the wind to find them, only to return with that one and find another gone.

She'd smothered a yawn and put the last cleaned pan back on the stove for the supper crowd when the bell jingled over the front door.

Who would be coming in at this hour? She snapped her towel and hung it on the line they kept strung for that purpose.

"I'll see who it is." Vanora scooted through the swinging doors, likely as much to avoid Kenna's ill humor as to see the visitor.

"Miss Vanora, is your pa about?"

Kenna snorted at the familiar voice. What did Mr. Brinkmann want now? Wasn't it enough that he was taking her brothers away again?

"Wait right here and I'll fetch him." Vanora sprinted through the kitchen and out the back door. Pa had gone for water moments before. She'd catch up to him at the canal.

Kenna was tempted to stay in the kitchen and pretend to be busy, but her work was done, and good manners required her to greet their guest. She gritted her teeth and pasted on a smile before entering the dining room.

"Mr. Brinkmann, it's good to see you."

"Is it, Miss McCrea?" Understanding softened the sun wrinkles around his eyes.

"It's not you, personally, you know. It's just..." She turned her face away and blinked back the threatening dampness.

"They're good men, your brothers, hard workers but not reckless. They watch out for each other too. You'd be proud of them if you saw them out there."

"I'm sure I would, but I'd much rather have them home."

Mr. Brinkmann nodded, then glanced behind her as Pa entered the room with Vanora behind him.

"McCrea, I need a chuckwagon cook."

Kenna whirled to face her father, willing him to refuse again with every fiber of her being.

"Aye. The lads told me." He glanced at Kenna, then addressed Squirrel. "I've been expecting you."

CHAPTER 8

"PA YOU CANNA BE serious." That his Scottish burr had slipped into *her* speech signaled Kenna was past upset. She was furious, or frightened, or both. Her palms stung as her nails bit into them.

Vanora left the room, likely to wait out the storm upstairs with Elva.

Pa moved away from the door after seeing Mr. Brinkmann on his way. His shoulders were back, barrel chest forward, head lifted. A light in his eyes made Kenna's heart twist like a wrung-out dishrag.

Nothing she said or did would change his mind.

He was a man on a mission, a man in charge, and a man about to do what he'd wanted to do all along.

Kenna had always known that the diner had been Pa's fulfillment of his promise to Ma all those years ago. Kenna didn't have to close her eyes to dredge up the scene, Ma on the bed in the back of the wagon, Pa by her side. Ma had begged him to take her children to town and raise them there, away from the hardships, the weather, and the snakes. She'd begged him to be sure they got a proper education. It'd been the only time she'd ever seen tears in Pa's eyes. He hadn't even cried as they'd buried Ma, but he had in the wagon beside her bed. The bed she'd died in hours later.

"Lass." He gripped her shoulder. "We'll keep the family together."

"You mean...?" Words escaped her, and she stared at him open-mouthed, like a fish on the riverbank.

"Aye. We'll go together, all of us, like we used to do."

"But Pa—"

He raised his hand, stopping her mid-speech. "The wee girls are old enough to be a grand help, as they are here. We'll see the lads at mealtimes every day. It'll be good, lass, you'll see." His voice was kind, but there was no give in it. "And we've just three days to teach you to drive a team."

"What do you mean?" Kenna's head spun. It was as if she couldn't understand Pa's words, as if he were suddenly speaking Gaelic—a language he'd never taught his children.

"I canna drive both the chuckwagon and the McCrea wagon, which we'll need for you, the wee lassies, and our household belongings. I'll be counting on you to drive it. You'll have a place to sleep off the ground, and a dry place to ride when it rains or snows."

"Snows?" She couldn't seem to put a whole sentence together.

"Aye. We'll see snow before we reach Abilene. You'll need to buy warm fabric for clothing to outfit you and your sisters. There will be time to sew in the evenings around the fire." A soft expression crossed his rugged features. "Just as your Ma used to."

For a moment, Kenna could picture it, Ma sitting by the fire with needle and thread in her hands, usually mending clothing for Lloyd or Tyree, contentment on her face.

Pa cleared his throat. "There is much to do. Lock the front door and post a closed sign."

"We'll not feed the supper crowd?"

"Nay, lass, so you'll need to salt the meat and pack it in a barrel. Crate everything else and I'll add it to the chuckwagon. We'll need every minute to sort and pack and ready ourselves. But first"—he plucked his hat from the table—"I must see the banker about purchasing the diner."

Kenna's shoes might as well have been mired in a bog. She couldn't have moved if she'd tried. "You mean"—her voice came out in a squeak—"we won't return to San Antonio?"

Pa fiddled with his hat and then slapped it on his head and faced her. "Nay, we willna return. The lads and Squirrel have told me much of Abilene, a new town with new possibilities since the railroad came. Jobs offered by the railroad where the lads might move up in the world. We will make a new start there, all of us. Together."

Together.

Kenna clung to that word. As much as she hated the idea of leaving, of going out in a wagon again, of learning to *drive* a wagon, she'd give up almost anything to keep the family together.

Including San Antonio, their diner, and everything that made her feel safe.

"We have enough men for the drive, then?" Ben asked Squirrel, both men once again looking over the herd as the last batch of cattle was trailed in. They didn't need to road-brand the animals, since all of them belonged to Frederick Schmidt's Triple S ranch and wore the 3S brand.

"Yup, hired two black men. One—George is his name—handy enough with horses to be the wrangler's assistant."

"Still no wrangler or cook?" Plans were to leave on Saturday at daybreak—in less than forty-eight hours.

"Oh, we got a cook." Squirrel's grin lifted his drooping mustache. "The best."

"You mean to tell me McCrea agreed?" That explained the diner being closed the evening before when he'd walked past.

Squirrel nodded. "Without a fuss. Seems his boys had him all softened up toward the idea." Squirrel squinted at the herd. "But there was a stipulation."

Did nothing ever happen smoothly? "Which is?"

"He'll bring his daughters along in a separate wagon."

"On the cattle drive?" Rusty shifted under Ben, reacting to his agitation. "That's ridiculous—too dangerous. You can't allow it."

"I can and I have."

"Well, I won't." Ben jabbed his finger at the chuckwagon parked to the side of the grazing herd. "I've heard enough to know crossing rivers with a wagon is too dangerous, much less *two* wagons and one of them filled with *women*."

"It's also too dangerous to trail cattle with wet, cold, hungry men." Squirrel's expression didn't budge. He was deadly serious.

About taking women—two of them mere girls—on a cattle drive. It was preposterous. Ben wouldn't condone it. He couldn't.

"Of course, were you to come along as wrangler, you'd be nearby to see to the safety of the misses McCrea. We keep the remuda near the chuckwagon most of the time."

Squirrel's voice was expressionless, but Ben knew he'd been manipulated. If he refused to work as the wrangler, he'd leave Miss McCrea and her sisters under the protection of their father alone. He had no doubt about Gus's abilities, but one man with two wagons and three daughters? The odds weren't in his favor.

Ben glared at Squirrel. "I can still cancel this drive."

"You could, but you won't." Squirrel twisted to face Ben. "You've already sent a wire to McCoy telling him we're leaving on Saturday. All those men out there, they've been working for almost two weeks without pay. You'd owe them. And if you back out, you'll lose the trust of the other ranchers in this area. Maybe in all of Texas."

He was right, but that didn't make it sit any better with Ben. He wheeled Rusty around, allowing him to bump into Squirrel's mount. "All right, you win, but listen to me and listen good. If anything happens to those girls, I'll hold you personally responsible."

The older man nodded, his face devoid of any triumph that his ploy had worked. "You can't hold me any more accountable than I'll be holding myself."

Ben dug his heels into Rusty's sides and hung on as the agile mustang sprinted toward town. Maybe there was still time to talk sense into Gus.

Kenna fumbled with the stiff leather reins. Why couldn't she get the hang of them? She swallowed her fear and despair, then gathered them back between her fingers as Pa had shown her several times. The lead team's reins over her first fingers, the swing team's reins between her first and second fingers, and the wheel team's reins between her third and little fingers.

"You're doing grand, lass." Pa sat beside her on the wagon's high seat.

"I'm not." She did her best to keep the fear out of her voice. "I was never meant to drive a wagon, Pa."

"You're a McCrea, through and through. You can do whatever you set your mind to, or I'd not ask it of you. I'd not entrust your sisters to you. I dinna have any doubt."

Kenna had enough doubts for both of them. Cooking she could do. Sewing, washing, tending her sisters, keeping the diner and their home clean and neat. But driving six strange mules hitched to their new canvas-covered wagon?

"Give the reins a flick and call to the lead mules. They'll respond." Pa slipped his arm behind her back as if to fortify her. "I bought the best-trained mules to be had."

She closed her eyes and fumbled to remember the names of the leaders. The rest were a blur from Pa's introductions and instructions on harnessing. Not only must she learn to drive, but to harness, un-harness, and care for the beasts as well. Pa would be busy with the chuckwagon's team.

Kenna opened her eyes, adjusted the reins one last time, and then flicked them. "Get up, Jack. Get up, Hobbs."

She almost dropped the reins and grabbed onto the seat when the large wagon jerked into motion.

"That's right, lass, you're doing grand."

"I'm not doing anything." The mules were heading down the street on their own.

"I told you they were well trained. They know their job." Pa's arm tightened around her for a brief moment. "Once we're out of town, I'll teach you how to do more."

They reached the edge of town as a lone rider raced in from where the herd waited. Kenna didn't take her eyes off the mules for more than a glance, but Pa waved at the man approaching.

"Pull up the mules, daughter."

Any fool knew how to do that much. Kenna hauled back on the reins and the mules stopped abruptly, banging together in their harnesses. The wagon jolted to a halt.

"Easy, lass. Go gently on the reins."

"Sorry, Pa."

He chuckled. "Takes practice is all."

The approaching rider slowed and lifted his face to them. Mr. Warley.

Kenna ground her teeth together to stop the words that wanted to spew forth. It was all his fault. If he hadn't ridden into San Antonio and stirred the whole hornets' nest of cattle drives—

"How does the herd look, Ben?" Pa asked.

"Are you really intending to take the girls on this drive?" Disapproval colored Mr. Warley's tone as he ignored Pa's question.

Kenna bristled. It wasn't that she disagreed with him. It was that he was bold-faced challenging Pa. She may share the same sentiments, but Pa was family, and Mr. Warley was a Yankee.

"My lassies can handle the trail." Pa straightened on the seat. "They were born to it."

Mr. Warley removed his hat and wiped his brow before resetting it. "There are dangers—"

"Aye." Pa glanced at Kenna. "We canna forget the dangers, but we canna live in fear of them either."

That was meant for her, not Mr. Warley. Had she been living in fear? Of course she had. Fear of losing her brothers. Fear of once again living out of a wagon. Fear of driving the mules.

Fear of change.

She squared her shoulders and firmed her grip on the reins. "Mr. Warley, my sisters and I are McCreas. We can do whatever we set our minds to."

Even when it frightened her half to death.

She was as crazy as her old man.

There was nothing Ben could do to keep them from going on the drive, but he couldn't bear the thought of something happening to her or the younger girls. He'd grown fond of her—of all of them—while eating at the diner for the past three and a half months. At least working as the wrangler, he'd be nearby to keep an eye on them.

"I'll be joining you on the drive."

"You?" Gus's eyebrows rose.

"As wrangler." Ben shrugged. "Squirrel couldn't find anyone else."

"Being ex-cavalry, you must know horses." Was that approval in Gus's voice? He'd have given anything to hear that a few weeks ago when he'd been contemplating approaching Gus about courting his daughter. But it was useless now. Ben had gotten no more smiles from Miss McCrea since Jake, Vernon, and Charlie had arrived and spilled the beans about Ben's past. *She* didn't approve of him being ex-cavalry. While not exactly hostile, the friendly camaraderie they'd developed had shriveled and died.

He missed it. He'd give just about anything for a thawing of her attitude toward him.

Gus studied him for a moment, glanced at the chuckwagon, then back at Ben. "Can you drive a six-hitch of mules?"

Ben nodded. He'd learned to handle mules in the army.

"I have the chuckwagon to prepare and dinna have much time. If you could school Kenna in the art of handling the team, I would appreciate it."

"Pa—"

"Take me to the chuckwagon, lass. We've no time to waste. Call to the leaders and flick the reins."

Miss McCrea did what he said. By her slight gasp, she was anything but confident at the reins. And Gus expected him to teach her enough to drive the wagon by Saturday daybreak?

On the other hand, it would mean time spent with her. Perhaps without anyone interrupting them or food to serve or tables to clean, they could get back to a friendly footing. He'd give it his best shot.

Gus climbed down at the chuckwagon.

Ben dismounted and tied Rusty to the back of the wagon before taking the seat beside Miss McCrea. The lady slid as far over as the high seat would allow and brushed her skirt out of his way, as if he might contaminate it.

A less than promising start.

"She dinna need to learn it all in one day," Gus called over his shoulder. "You can get her started and tomorrow teach her the finer points." He waved his hand, never looking back, as he opened the rear of the chuckwagon and stuck his head inside.

"Well." Ben settled next to Miss McCrea, keeping to his side of the seat with a few inches of space between them. "What have you learned so far?"

"That the mules must always be hitched in the same order as three pairs, and the pairs always on the same side of each other. The lead mules are the smartest, and the wheel mules are the strongest." She blew out a breath, then looked at him for the first time. "I can get them started and stopped."

"That's a fine start, I'd say."

"It won't get my sisters and me safely to Abilene." The words were flat, but with a budding determination he sensed more than heard.

"Don't worry, Miss McCrea. As wrangler, I won't be far from the wagons. If you get in trouble, just call out."

"You'll be needed with the horses."

"Squirrel hired an assistant wrangler. If he's worth his salt, he can handle the remuda long enough for me to assist you."

A tentative smile was his answer, and it caused something warm to stir deep in his chest. Something he ought not to dwell on with the drive ahead of them. He might not know much, but he knew the drive would take everything they had... and maybe then some. There'd be no time to think of pursuing the lovely Miss McCrea, even if her father allowed it.

But maybe they could be friends.

Shoving those thoughts aside, he showed her how to turn the mules and back them up, then had her drive the rig in figure eights, changing direction twice. They finished with a wide circle of the herd while weaving around stunted trees and large rocks in their path.

At some point, the inches between them on the narrow seat had disappeared. The mantle of disapproval she'd worn for days had fallen away. Her hair had escaped its pins and defied her bonnet. By the time Ben was satisfied she could handle the team, it waved in the breeze.

He almost hated to admit it—because it took away an excuse for her to stay in San Antonio—but once she'd gotten over her fear, she'd shown she could handle the mules. Gus had said Ben could show her the finer points the next day. And on the day after that, they'd be heading north to Abilene.

But Ben would enjoy one more day of instruction before the real work started.

CHAPTER 9

I T WASN'T YET DAYLIGHT, but Ben had been in place for close to an hour. Including Rusty—he hadn't wanted to leave his personal mount behind—there were one hundred and forty-eight horses in the remuda. They were mustangs, quick and agile and able to outrun the fastest cow or steer in the herd. Ben's opinion of the small western horses had risen considerably after seeing them in action.

The evening before, each cowboy had been allowed to choose one horse. Then they'd started over and each chose a second horse. It continued until the cowboys had ten horses that were theirs for the drive. Each man was expected to care for his own animals, but Ben would oversee the general welfare of the remuda and get them from one stopping place to the next.

Along with George.

Meeting the huge man that morning had made an already tense morning worse. Ben was working side-by-side with an ex-slave. An ex-slave hired on at regular wages. What would his father have said about that?

Father was dead. Peter was dead. Amelia and Pauleen were married and raising their families in South Carolina. Ben was on his own, forging a new life on a new frontier with people he'd never have spoken to in the past.

He fought the memories of lazy days beside the river, picnicking along the grassy banks, slaves doing all the heavy labor, top-quality horses to ride or drive, and pretty girls in wide hoop skirts to grace his arm when he wished.

Nothing about his life was easy anymore.

But Ben couldn't change it. He'd agreed to be the wrangler. The success of the drive hinged on the health and well-being of the mounts in his charge. Added to that, he'd assured Gus he'd stay as close to the McCrea's wagon as he could. That he'd help watch over the girls.

A Southern gentleman didn't go back on his word.

He shifted on his saddle, the creaking of leather breaking the morning stillness, and pushed away the memory of his loyalty oath to the Union.

George approached from the direction of the remuda, looking ridiculously large on the mustang under him. Seeing any dark man on a horse would take getting used to. Father would never have allowed—

"Mr. Warley, suh." George made a brief eye contact and then looked away. "Them horses is restive, suh. We best be moving them soon."

Ben bristled at being told what he needed to do. The milling remuda hadn't escaped his notice, but he'd decide when they moved. While he wasn't in charge of the drive—that was Squirrel's position—he wasn't leaving without the wagons. He'd made that plain to Squirrel already, and the lanky man had agreed.

Before he could voice a reprimand, Squirrel wheeled his horse away from the chuckwagon and galloped in their direction. It was no wonder Squirrel, as the trail boss, was allowed two more horses in his string than the rest of the cowboys if he rode this hard from the very start. The mustang skidded to a halt in front of Rusty, who shied and danced, forcing Ben to calm the mount.

"Gus is ready." Squirrel didn't bother with the niceties of a greeting. "I want you and George to lead the way with the remuda. We'll stay on the trail you and Hersey marked until I say otherwise." He glanced from Ben to George and back again. "Ready?"

"Ready as we'll ever be," Ben said.

Squirrel nodded, then glanced at George.

"Yes, suh."

"Move 'em out." With those parting words, Squirrel spurred his mustang and shot toward the southern edge of the mass of cattle.

Ben lifted his reins and urged Rusty forward, tipping his hat to Miss McCrea on the second wagon's seat as they passed.

Behind her, standing in the wagon's bed, were Miss Vanora and Miss Elva, the older girl's dark eyes shining as he rode by. Miss Elva, however, looked pale and a little lost.

Miss McCrea spared him barely a glance, her hands firm on the reins as he'd schooled her, feet encased in new boots and braced against the wagon's kickboard, bonnet covering her red curls to keep the sun from her face and the dust from her hair. She was as ready to drive as Ben could prepare her in two short days. She'd learned fast and well.

He was proud of her.

Perhaps the thawing between them would continue as the drive went on.

He pulled up alongside the chuckwagon.

"You ready, Gus?" he asked.

A grin split the older man's beard. "I dinna think I'd be behind the reins of a fine team again. I'm more than ready, I'm home."

"Then let's start this drive." Ben pointed George to the rear of the remuda. "You take the drag"—the term he'd learned from Squirrel that meant riding in the back of the herd and eating all the dust—"and I'll take the point."

Ben headed toward a black-legged bay with a large white star on her forehead. An older mare, she was the most dominant horse of the bunch. She laid her ears back at Rusty as they approached, but Ben twirled the long ends of his split reins and directed her to move along. A well-muscled buckskin mare joined her on one side, and a slab-sided black on the other. Ben moved Rusty to the side, and the rest of the horses followed after the leaders at a brisk walk. Since most of the horses had returned to San Antonio from Kansas with Squirrel, they were trail-broke and moved out easily.

The jingle of harness and the rattle of wheels announced the wagons following. Already, the dust had risen enough that Ben could see only the outlines of the vehicles. Gus would drop back far enough to avoid the worst of the dust but remain within shouting distance of George at the back.

Ben took up his position to the left of the leaders, keeping far enough away that the following horses wouldn't shy from him.

It was a rather anticlimactic start to a new adventure—one Ben wished he weren't along on—but anticlimactic was far preferable to chaos.

The wagon lurched beneath Kenna, and she steadied her feet against the kickboard as Mr. Warley had instructed her, hands on the reins and shoulders squared. Vanora laughed while Elva squealed and grabbed Kenna from behind, practically strangling her.

"Vanora, control your sister while I handle the mules." The vice around her neck released, and Kenna drew in a deep breath. "I must pay attention to what's ahead of us, so you two will have to take care of each other."

"I'm fine." Vanora's high spirits were clear in her voice. "It's Elva who's the 'fraidy cat."

"Vanora!" Kenna turned her head just far enough to frown at her sister. "Wherever did you hear that term?"

"From Carl, one of the cowboys."

Was that a blush on her sister's face? Kenna didn't dare take a second look as the wagon's front wheel dropped into a depression, tilting them all off-balance.

Elva squealed again.

"Sit down, both of you," Kenna snapped. The rustling behind satisfied her that they obeyed.

As if she didn't have enough to worry over, she didn't need some cowboy sniffing around Vanora. The girl wasn't yet thirteen. Oh, what had Pa been thinking to drag them along on this drive? She braced her feet as the back wheel dropped and rose out of the same depression, then guided the mules until they were directly behind the chuckwagon. Mr. Warley had advised her to do that, knowing Pa would find the easiest path for the wagons.

The ex-slave who had ridden up with Mr. Warley appeared at her side. He ducked his head. "Everything all right, miss?"

"My youngest sister is a little scared." Which was an understatement.

"Ain't no call to be worried, little missy." He raised his voice enough for Elva to hear. "Anything go wrong, George be nearby to help."

Kenna gave him a smile, but he barely raised his eyes to her before he pulled a neckerchief over his nose to block the dust and rejoined the remuda. She'd never had much to do with the dark-skinned people who populated the area south of San Antonio. They came into town sometimes, always in a group, but never to the diner.

"See, Elva?" Vanora's voice took on a patient tone. "That man is nearby if we need help, and Mr. Warley and Pa are just ahead of us. They'll keep us safe. Isn't that right, Kenna?"

"Of course. Nothing to worry about." Kenna lied through her teeth. She'd heard enough stories of what could go wrong on cattle drives, but Elva needed encouragement. "We have all the help we need."

"And Kenna is doing a fine job driving the wagon." Vanora giggled. "Did you ever imagine our sister would become a mule skinner?"

Elva's answering giggle made the corners of Kenna's lips twitch.

She may be a mule skinner, but she was the most reluctant mule skinner ever.

When Gus called the wagons to a stop around noon, both to give the mules a rest and to feed the cowboys, Ben circled the lead mares and eased them to a halt near a thick patch of brownish grass.

George brought up the rest of the remuda and rode on the opposite side of the horses until they settled down to graze.

Gus had dropped the tailgate on the chuckwagon and hoisted a white flag to let the cowboys know lunch was ready. A bucket of water with a dipper rested next to the pile of biscuits baked that morning and filled with slabs of cold bacon.

Ben drained two dippers of water first, then grabbed a biscuit.

"Oh, no!"

The shout stopped his hand halfway to his mouth.

Hooves thundered toward him. He twisted and half-jumped, half-fell out of the way of a running mule. Before he could get his feet firmly planted on the ground, George—still mounted—had cut off the mule and was hazing it back toward the family wagon where Miss McCrea stood still, both hands over her mouth.

"Lass?" Gus was drawing water from a barrel on the side of the chuckwagon.

"I'll check on her." Ben hurried to Miss McCrea's side. "Are you hurt?"

She shook her head but didn't lower her hands.

"He didn't harm you?"

Another head shake, but her freckles stood out in bold relief against the paleness of her face.

George had caught hold of the mule's halter and led the beast to them. He dismounted, dropping the reins of his horse and bringing the mule closer. "He ain't a bad sort, miss. Reckon he just got hisself a little spooked."

"Picket him and unhitch the others," Ben ordered George, then returned his attention to the frightened woman in front of him. "I promised you we'd be nearby if you needed help."

A weak chuckle brought a little more color to her face. "I didn't think it would happen so soon. We've hardly left San Antonio."

"It'll get easier once you've done things a few times and the mules are used to you."

"Will it?" The near-panic was gone from her eyes, replaced by a weary sadness that twisted something inside Ben.

"Of course it will. May I assist you with anything else?" Because he'd love a reason to stay close to her for a little longer.

But his question seemed to snap her out of her melancholy. "I believe I can handle the rest. But thank you." She strode to the next mule to be unhitched, determined puffs of dust defining each step.

George approached and helped with the rest of the mules.

So much for handling it by herself.

Ben snorted and returned to the chuckwagon. He had no reason to feel rejected, but he did.

He retrieved his biscuit and bit into it. Nothing like Gus's meals in the diner, but for the cowboys riding up to grab something to fill their bellies, they were manna from heaven.

The men rode in, generally in pairs, to rope fresh horses, swap their saddles off the tired mounts, drink their fill, grab a biscuit, and hightail it back to the cattle. The sweaty horses would drop to the dirt and enjoy a good roll before George moved them into the remuda. Tired as they were, they gave him no trouble.

Ben roped one of his spare mounts, a black-and-white pinto mare with blue eyes. None of the cowboys had wanted her, quoting some superstition about blue-eyed horses. Many of the cowboys had also voiced the opinion that spotted animals were inferior. Ben stripped

Rusty and turned him loose, then transferred the saddle to the pinto and tightened the girth. She gave a grunt and a halfhearted kick, but once Ben swung into the saddle, she relaxed.

The McCrea women were sitting in the shade of their wagon. Miss McCrea had pulled off her bonnet and was fanning her face with it. The younger two were eating.

Ben approached and removed his hat. "Would you like a break, Miss McCrea? George can handle the remuda for a while, and I can drive the wagon."

"I don't think so, Mr. Warley." She tidied her hair and replaced her bonnet. "We should start as we intend to go on." She snapped the ties into place. "The wagon is my responsibility."

If there was one word that summed Miss McCrea up in a nutshell, it was responsible. He'd heard enough of her story to know she'd raised her brothers and sisters since their mother's death, and she couldn't have been much more than Miss Vanora's age when she'd taken on the task. Not only raising her siblings but helping her father run the diner and doubtless the house above it.

How different from his upbringing of plenty and privilege.

If he'd grown up with more responsibilities, would he have been a better soldier? Would he have stayed true to the South? Would he, even now, be sitting on the front porch of his childhood home overlooking everything green and familiar?

He'd never know the answer to those questions.

Signing up for the Confederacy had been assumed, as it had been for every son of a South Carolina landowner. Pledging loyalty to the Union at Rock Island prison camp in Illinois with Emmet—his cousin—had been a practical decision. Conditions had been horrible in the camp. There hadn't been enough food, shelter, or clothing for all the men penned inside. Emmet had signed the loyalty oath as well, but he'd returned to South Carolina, sneaking off in the night after he'd failed to get Ben to agree to join him.

Emmet had returned to South Carolina a hero. Pauleen had written of the fuss he'd created. The same fuss that had declared Ben a traitor and ended with his family's plantation burned to the ground. Not by the Yankees, who hadn't arrived there yet, but by his neighbors. His former friends.

But that was all behind him. Before him stretched the prairie and another chance to succeed in starting his life over.

He glanced back at Miss McCrea. To fully start over, he'd need a wife. With her thawed attitude toward him the past couple of days... dare he hope?

CHAPTER 10

EVERYTHING HURT. KENNA RUBBED her shoulder, but that added to the ache in her back. Her knees were stiff from bracing against the wagon's kickboard. Sore spots between her fingers hinted at blisters even though she'd worn the heavy leather gloves Mr. Warley had insisted she purchase. Her eyes burned from the dust raised by the chuckwagon.

Kenna was a mess.

She sneezed hard enough to startle the mule she was brushing. What was its name? The animal turned its face to her, a smallish white mark in the center of its dark forehead—Cigar. Pa had told her to memorize their names because mules were smart and knew their own names.

"Sorry, Cigar, it was the dust from your coat." Like the dust everywhere. She'd worked harder than ever to keep her wayward hair covered, but the ends that had escaped were stiff with the stuff.

Two more mules to brush, the wheel mules, Soulful and Manny. Manny was easy to remember, since he was the only red mule on the team. Soulful's back legs were white almost to the hocks. Kenna led Cigar to where three others were already grazing and turned him loose. Pa said there was no need to picket them this far from San Antonio. The mules were tired after a full day pulling the wagon, and they wouldn't try to make their way back such a great distance.

Hopefully, he was right.

She returned to the wagon, where the assistant wrangler had already unhitched both wheel mules. He touched the brim of his hat and ducked his head. "I thought to lend you a hand, miss."

"Thank you, Mr..."

"George, miss. Just George."

She passed over the brush she'd been using. "Thank you, George."

The assistant wrangler was a large man, both tall and broad, not fat but powerfully built. Everything about him said he could snap her in half if he wanted to. Kenna had little experience around men like him, but he'd been courteous from the start, and his willingness to assist her took a load from her aching muscles.

She'd sent Vanora and Elva to help Pa make dinner, so Kenna climbed into the wagon and shook their blankets out the back opening to remove as much dust as possible. She drew a scant half bucket of water from one of the barrels mounted on the wagon's side. Breath hissed between her teeth when her bare hands hit the water. Blisters for sure. She bathed her face and neck, both stinging from a day in the sun despite her bonnet, then set the bucket aside. They would wash in it before bed. Maybe even again in the morning. One of the things Pa had stressed—numerous times—was never to waste a drop of water on the trail. She tidied her hair and resettled her bonnet before joining Pa and her sisters.

"Kenna?" Pa asked. "Your mules are tended?"

"George is seeing to the last pair."

Pa nodded, then pointed to a bowl of potatoes near Elva. "Cut those for frying."

"What should I do with the peels?"

"Leave them on. We waste nothing from here on out." Pa mopped his brow.

Elva looked up from scrubbing the potatoes in a small bucket beside Pa's workbench. She wrinkled her nose. "I don't like the peels."

Kenna didn't either, but saying so wouldn't help anything. "I expect we'll get used to the changes soon enough. And peels are better than hunger."

Her youngest sister didn't seem satisfied, but she kept scrubbing.

Vanora coaxed the fire under a pair of huge coffeepots. She fetched pieces of wood taken from the sling under the chuckwagon. Mr. Warley and George had tossed wood into the sling throughout the day, picking up whatever they saw that would burn. Kenna subdued a shudder at the thought of what they'd be burning once they reached the long stretches of treeless prairie.

Cattle droppings.

Herds that had gone before would have left plenty in their wake, baked by the sun and dry enough to burn. It would be up to Vanora and Elva to collect them and stow them in the sling. In the evenings, they'd cook over the burning droppings. Kenna didn't want to think about the smell.

Potato peels were nothing compared to what was coming.

"Miss McCrea?" Mr. Warley approached. "Do you need help with the mules?"

"Thank you, no. George is seeing to the wheel team while I help Pa."

"Oh." Mr. Warley's expression changed into something Kenna couldn't read. Was he unhappy that George was assisting with the mules? Should she have refused his offer? And yet, Mr. Warley was offering his assistance.

"Then I'll return to the remuda and check the horses coming in." He touched his hat and strode away.

"Odd," Kenna said.

Elva grinned at her. "He likes you."

"What?"

"He likes you." Her sister shrugged and then plunged another potato under the water. "That's why he wanted to help you, but you let George do it."

"I'm sure you're mistaken—"

"She's not." Vanora shook a broken branch from the sling at her. "You should encourage him. I like Mr. Warley. If he were to look at me like that—"

"Stop it." Kenna smacked the flat blade of the knife against the cutting board. "You're far too young to be looking at any man, Vanora. There'll be no more such talk, do you hear?"

"But you're not too young." Elva's pixie grin was gone, replaced by a wide-eyed earnestness. "And I like Mr. Warley too, but not for me. For you, Kenna."

Face burning from more than the sun, Kenna savagely attacked the potatoes. "We have a crew of cowboys to feed and look after. There will be no more talk of men on this drive other than the feeding of them." She gave a final chop and glared at her sisters. "Am I understood?"

They both muttered agreement, but Vanora harbored a lingering smirk that worried Kenna. The girl would warrant a close eye on her. She'd speak to Pa and make sure Vanora was busy behind—or preferably inside—the chuckwagon whenever the men were gathered nearby.

If ever Kenna had missed Ma, it was now. How had she managed five children in a wagon following a flock of sheep for all those years? Pa had been with her, of course, and they'd worked as a team. Kenna remembered that. There had been good times—as well as hard times—then too.

What would it be like to have a man working beside her in such a fashion? Mr. Warley's face flickered across her mind's eye, and she mentally batted it away. Even if her sisters were correct, and she wasn't about to admit they were, he was a Yankee.

A Yankee who'd taught her to drive the wagon when surely he'd had many other tasks to complete before the drive. She'd taken up far too much of his time already, and that was the end of it.

She gave the potatoes one more whack.

By the time the herd caught up with the remuda and wagons, Ben's humor was testy at best. It shouldn't be, but it was. And why? Because George had been the one to capture the runaway mule at the noon stop. And George had been the one to assist Miss McCrea at the evening stop. And George had received the first plate of supper dished out by Miss McCrea.

Ben should have eaten then, too, but he wasn't going to sit next to an ex-slave, and it would have been seen as nothing short of surly to do otherwise. Or maybe it wouldn't have. After all, Miss McCrea was a Southerner. Maybe she understood the need to keep the races separate.

Clawing at Ben wasn't the ex-slave part, however. He knew how he looked next to the hulking black man. Ben had no illusions about his physical appearance. At best, he was ordinary. Without the trappings of his father's name and wealth to prop him up, Ben was a nondescript nobody.

That was what galled him as he waited to check over the next round of horses.

A group of five cowboys raced toward the remuda, raising enough dust to cover a small town. Before Ben could yell a warning, Gus stormed away from the chuckwagon, arms waving wildly, and covered the men with choice words. As well he should. As bad as scattering the remuda would have been, ruining everyone's dinner would have been worse.

The chastised bunch of cowboys walked their horses the rest of the way.

The first one to dismount was an ex-slave with a deep scowl. He dropped his reins and lifted one of his mount's hooves.

Ben hurried to his side. "What's the problem?"

"The shoe." The man leaned back so Ben could see.

A nail was missing, the shoe loose but still in place. "Strip your gear, and I'll set another nail."

The older man shook his head. "I'll do it."

Ben straightened and crossed his arms. "I'm the wrangler. It's my job."

The dark man let go of the horse's hoof. He didn't have the decency to look away, as a slave would have, but met Ben with a deliberate stare. "For the drive, he be my horse. Squirrel say so. I take care of him."

"What makes you think you can—"

"I done been head groom for my *massah*." The man stressed the title as if it were a curse. "There be nothing I can't do around a horse."

"If that were true, Squirrel would have assigned you to work with me." George could handle the animals—he'd proved that when he'd caught the runaway mule—but he hadn't given any indication that he could shoe a horse.

"But he didn't."

Of all the insolent... "What's your name?"

"Leppo. And I may 'a been a slave once, but I ain't no more."

The man was trouble, pure and simple. If it were up to Ben, he'd fire him for his insolence. But it wasn't. Ben was in charge of the horses. Squirrel was in charge of the men and cattle. And Ben had told him to hire the ex-slaves.

"Fine. Fix the shoe. The tools are in the chuckwagon."

Ben left him to check on the other animals, but he kept an eye on Leppo's movements. Sure enough, the man knew what he was doing. In a few minutes, the mustang's shoe was secured, and the horse grazed with the rest of the remuda.

Squirrel rode in half an hour later and dismounted a weary chestnut, his sixth horse of the day. Ben stalked toward him, anger rising with each step.

"What's stuck in your craw?" Squirrel barely glancing at him.

"You didn't need me for this drive." Ben pointed toward Leppo, finishing his dinner near the chuckwagon. "Leppo is qualified to work as a wrangler, and yet you didn't even make him assistant wrangler. Why?"

Squirrel stripped the sweaty horse of its tack, dropped the saddle to the ground, and faced Ben. "Because according to men who know you, you're the best with horses to be had—and I like to work with the best. As for not making him your assistant, it appears you've already butted heads. I don't need my wranglers at each other's throats for the duration of this drive."

Ben wanted to argue, but before he could form a logical rebuttal, Squirrel clamped a hand on his shoulder. "And I knew you'd watch over Gus's girls." He gave Ben's shoulder a companionable shake, then headed for the chuckwagon.

That brought Ben back to the root of his discontent. How was he to assist and watch over the Misses McCrea—

Oh.

Tomorrow, he'd send George to ride point, and Ben would eat the trail dust in the drag position. The position closest to the wagons—the position typically given to those of lower rank. And the position that would allow him easy access to Miss McCrea.

For that, Ben could swallow his pride.

Morning had always come early with a diner to run, but the inky blackness of the prairie made waking up more difficult. Kenna groaned as she rolled over on the narrow bunk in the wagon. Or maybe it was more difficult because she was stiff and sore. When she stretched, her spine snapped like popping corn over a roaring fire.

She rose and dressed as quietly as she could. She'd let her sisters sleep for another half hour. Twisting her hair into a quick bun, she pinned it in place and tied on her bonnet. After pulling on the sensible boots without buttons she'd bought for the trip—another purchase Mr. Warley had insisted on for all the girls—she climbed out the wagon's back.

Stars peppered the sky, and not the slightest hint of light marked the eastern horizon. The central fire near the chuckwagon had burned down to a bed of glowing coals. Loosely ranged around three sides of it were the dark lumps of cowboys sleeping while they could.

Kenna cocked her head and listened. The wind swept over the landscape, but there was something else. Something... musical.

"Carl, one of the young men, he play a mouth-organ."

Kenna gasped as George emerged from the darkness.

"A mouth-organ?"

"Calms the cattle. Keeps 'em happy and settled."

"Yes, of course it does." Whatever it was. "I best be helping Pa."

"I came to check the mules for you, miss. Then I be about my business."

"Thank you." She hurried to the chuckwagon, more than a little unnerved to have been speaking to a man by herself in the dark. But then, this wasn't San Antonio. There were no societal rules out here. At least, none she knew of.

"You're up early, lass." Pa kept his voice low as he prepared the two massive coffeepots. "How are you feeling?"

"Older than my years."

Pa chuckled. "You'll toughen up soon."

"Pa?"

"Yes?"

"What's a mouth-organ?"

Pa's rusty chuckle warmed the air between them. "A harmonica. I heard it earlier." He paused. "Where did you hear that name for it?"

"George called it that. He's checking the mules for me."

Pa straightened and stared into the darkness toward the family wagon. "Is he now?"

"He's been very helpful and polite." Pa had come to Texas as a young man and settled in an area where slaves were common. Kenna couldn't remember him ever giving an opinion on slavery one way to the other. They'd never owned a slave—of course. McCreas did their own work, did it well, and took pride in it.

"Pa, what do you think about the freed slaves on this drive?"

He rubbed his beard for a moment, and then turned back to his coffeepots, answering over his shoulder. "I think Squirrel is right. If a man does a day's work, he deserves a day's pay."

That seemed fair to Kenna. The war had been for independence as far as she was concerned. The Yankees had refused to let the South go its own way and become its own country because they were like the English against the Scottish. They wanted to dominate.

And yet, since the end of the war, very little had changed for Kenna and her family. Pa had kept Lloyd and Tyree out of the fighting because of their ages. Even though boys they knew had gone to fight, neither had defied Pa and run off to join the Confederacy. She'd not thought to question it before. There was always too much work to be done to worry about such things.

It wasn't the time to dwell on the past. She busied herself making biscuits. Pa had told her how much to make the night before when she'd prepared the starter. She was stacking the loaded cast iron ovens with coals between them when the coffee's rich aroma roused the cowboys sleeping nearby.

Mr. Warley was the first to the fire. "Good morning, Miss McCrea."

"Good morning." Kenna glanced to the east, where a thin film of gray outlined the horizon. "Or at least, it will be."

He gave her a slow grin. "I was warned that mornings started early on the trail. Squirrel came in for a fresh horse at least an hour ago. I've no idea if the man slept at all last night."

Another man joined them, one of the trio of ex-cavalrymen who'd been to the diner the day she'd learned Mr. Warley was a Yankee.

"You get used to it." The man's jaw cracked with a yawn. "Eventually." He held out a cup, and Kenna filled it with coffee. No cream or sugar. The men drank it strong, black, and hot enough to scald their throats.

"I'll see to your mules," Mr. Warley said.

"George already has." Kenna said the words over her shoulder, pouring cup after cup of the strong brew as the cowboys filed past.

Mr. Warley strode away, probably to see to his many other duties as wrangler. If there was one thing Kenna had learned, it was that every person on the drive was essential. Everyone had a job to do and every job contributed to the success—or possible failure—of the whole drive.

Pa flipped steaks on a grill over the fire, Vanora took over the coffee duty, Elva stacked plates nearby for when they were needed, and Kenna opened the ovens, scooping out golden-brown biscuits. They might be out on the prairie instead of in their safe diner but—aside from the wagon and mules, dust and wind—the work wasn't much different.

For some unknown reason, that brought a wave of satisfaction to Kenna.

CHAPTER 11

T HE FOURTH DAY ON the trail, and Ben couldn't remember what it felt like to be clean. Everything was dusty. Even more so since he'd taken to riding drag on the remuda. They worked in dust and slept in dust. Even Gus's food—tasty as it was—had a hint of dust to it.

They'd eat well tonight, dust or not. One of the steers had broken its leg. Nobody seemed to know how it happened, but in the crush of bovine bodies and long, curved horns, it wasn't surprising. After they'd crossed a creek and stopped for a noon rest to let the cattle graze, the McCrea boys had hazed the wounded animal from the herd. Lloyd helped Gus butcher it on the spot and pack the meat in salt. Better than leaving it for the coyotes.

Squirrel came racing in at his usual speed, slowing his lathered horse to match pace with Rusty. "Everything quiet?"

Ben removed his hat and wiped a layer of dust and sweat from his face. "Quiet as a church mouse."

"Good. Enjoy it while we can."

"Quiet I don't mind, but this dust—"

"Enjoy that while you can too." Squirrel pointed to the west. Something smudged the distant horizon. "I don't like the look of that."

Ben squinted, wishing—not for the first time—that he had better distance vision. "Storm brewing?"

Squirrel leaned over and spit. "'Fraid so. And these cattle are barely trail broke. Keep your eyes open and keep the horses out of the way if that herd breaks loose."

Stampede.

Ben knew about them, of course. Everyone had heard the stories, but the thought of seeing one firsthand was... unsettling. Stampedes and river crossings were the two most dangerous situations on a drive. The most costly in animals and men either wounded or killed.

"Keep the remuda bunched and the lead mares close to George." Squirrel cast Ben a quick glance. "Or take the point if you think it better."

"George is good with the horses." Ben had to force the words past his teeth. "He can handle them." It rankled that even with George on point, the large man still offered a hand to Miss McCrea once the remuda was settled for the evening.

And she accepted his help.

Help she didn't accept from Ben.

Four days, and he hadn't been able to get past the polite exchanges she offered to everyone other than her brothers.

Squirrel shook out his lariat. "I appreciate you eating dust to keep watch over the girls, especially with a storm brewing." He rested the loop on his shoulder and grinned at Ben. "But it wouldn't hurt to let George ride drag sometimes too."

"I'm fine." Ben did his best to keep the surliness out of his tone.

"Uh-huh." Squirrel rode off, tossing his lariat over the neck of his next mount. He had his tack off the weary horse and onto the fresh one before Rusty caught up with them. "Mind those clouds."

Ben touched his hat brim as Squirrel sprinted away.

At least rain would lay the dust for a while. That would be a welcome change.

The wind hit before Pa had called a halt to make supper. The canvas of the McCrea wagon snapped behind Kenna, the tug of the wind swaying her on the high seat. Elva squealed from the back, she and Vanora having climbed aboard as the dark clouds had borne down on them. Vanora hushed her.

Tanny, one of the swing mules—the middle team—shied at the popping canvas, but his steady teammates ignored him. Long ears swiveled, but they kept their plodding pace.

Pa shouted something, and Mr. Warley rode to him.

Kenna was too far away to hear their words, even without the wind, but something was amiss. She flicked the reins and the mules picked up speed. They closed the distance between the wagons as Mr. Warley rode toward her.

"Gus says he'll hunt for a likely place to weather the storm." His voice was loud, nearly carried away on the storm. "Park your wagon alongside his." He glanced at the remuda, then back. "Unhitch the mules as soon as you stop, don't worry about grooming them, and get into the wagon. Stay there with your sisters until Gus tells you otherwise."

Fear pebbled the skin on her exposed forearms. "We will," she shouted over the growing moan of the wind.

Mr. Warley rode off, and Kenna firmed her grip on the reins. The lead mules had their heads up more than normal, but neither fidgeted or balked. Manny—the red wheel mule—began to prance behind Tanny.

"Tanny, Manny. Easy, boys," Kenna called, the words whipped from her lips. But the animals heard, their long ears swiveling back toward her. Manny settled, but Tanny continued to jig in the harness. His partner, Cigar, nipped at him, then they all settled down and leaned into their harnesses as the rain reached them.

The drops stung, driven by the wind, and within moments, Kenna was soaked to the skin. In the deluge that followed, she could barely see Pa's wagon in front of them. The mules, however, seemed to know what to do and pulled in closer behind the chuckwagon.

"Kenna! We're getting wet," Vanora yelled above the pounding of rain against the canvas.

Kenna didn't dare turn her attention away from the mules, but she called over her shoulder, "Close the back canvas. Then unfold the tarps. Cover the bunks and crawl under one of the tarps to keep dry." How she wished she could do the same. Her soaked bonnet did little to keep the rain off her face, and it let a stream of water run down between her shoulder blades.

Then the chuckwagon stopped.

Pa came around and took Jack by the bridle, leading him until their wagon was tight beside the chuckwagon. "Get them unhitched!"

She set the brake, wrapped the lines, and scurried off the high seat, landing with a squishy splash in the mud, thankful once again for the sturdy boots she'd purchased. Pa stepped back to tend his team while she unhitched hers. There'd be no brushing or cosseting the animals this evening. Instead of the vigorous roll they usually indulged in, the animals stood tails to the wind, heads down, gathered in a bunch. They didn't care for the rain any more than Kenna did.

"Come." Pa gripped her elbow. "We'll wait out the worst of it in the wagon." Instead of going to the chuckwagon, he entered the family wagon with Kenna. "My smart girls." He beamed at Vanora and Elva. "You kept your beds dry."

Vanora looked at Kenna and opened her mouth, but Kenna shook her head. Pa didn't need to know she'd directed them. Let them enjoy his approval.

"We can sit on the other bunk, Pa. The tarp will keep our soggy clothing from the bedding."

"Pa, how will we feed the cowboys?" Elva asked, peeking around Vanora but staying under the tarp.

"Nobody will eat until the storm passes."

"Those poor cowboys." Vanora glanced out the front of the wagon where they couldn't fully close the canvas, but the overhang kept out the rain. There was nothing to see but billowing gray sky.

"Those poor horses," Elva said. "At least the cowboys have hats."

Kenna chuckled. How like her tenderhearted sister to worry about the animals.

A great gust of wind struck, the wagon swayed, and the chuckwagon creaked and clanked beside them.

Elva squealed.

"It's all right, lassie." Pa gripped her little hand but stopped her when she would have crawled across the space and into his lap. "Stay where you are. I'm too wet to hold you."

A streak of lightning cut through the gray sky, and Kenna held her breath. She counted slowly to seven before the long, low rumble of thunder followed. It wasn't too close. Yet. The pressure against the canvas eased as the wind diminished.

"The worst has passed," Pa said after several minutes without the wind picking up again and the thunder keeping its distance. "I'll go see to the chuckwagon. You lassies stay in here for a wee bit longer."

"I can help—"

"Stay, lass." He patted Kenna's knee. "It will be over soon. These kinds of storms pass as fast as they strike. We'll all have to work to feed some very hungry, very wet men soon."

The wagon swayed as he jumped from the back, closed the flap again, and sealed them in.

"Gus!" A shout followed along with sloppy hoofbeats. "One of the men is hurt. They're bringing him in. He'll need space in your wagon."

Kenna's heart dropped.

Lloyd? Tyree?

"Stay in the wagon." Kenna ordered her sisters, then rushed into the rain. The wind had subsided, but the deluge still made it hard to see very far. She slipped in the mud but kept her feet under her as she rushed to the other side of the chuckwagon. "Who is it, Pa?" She could barely get enough breath to ask, her throat clogged with fear.

"I dinna know. Spread a tarp over my bed."

"But where will you sleep, Pa?"

"I'll sleep on the ground like the rest of the men. As cook, it's my job to see to the sick and injured."

He hadn't told her that before, but it made sense. Who else was there? She entered the cramped chuckwagon and did as he'd said.

The splash of hooves in mud announced the arrival. Kenna sucked in a deep breath and braced herself at the opening in the side of the chuckwagon. Two cowboys lifted a man off the back of a horse and carried him toward her. They hoisted him inside, and he cried out in pain. It was one of the ex-cavalrymen, the one they called Vernon.

Kenna released her breath in a rush. Not that she was happy anyone was injured, but she couldn't help the relief at seeing it wasn't one of her brothers.

Or Mr. Warley.

With the horses bunched and settled to wait out the storm, Ben approached the chuckwagon. He'd seen the man brought in and the cowboys' hasty return to the herd. They'd need all hands to keep the animals quiet and contained. But Gus might need help too.

"Anything I can do?" he called into the chuckwagon. The rain had reduced to a steady drizzle, so he could see clearly to the bunk.

It was Vernon. The easygoing man's face was tight and pale, his knuckles white from gripping the edge of the tarp-covered bed.

Miss McCrea crouched beside him next to her father.

"Leg's busted. I'll need someone to hold him." Gus looked up, his brow wrinkled and plastered with strands of wet hair. "Call George. I'll need you both."

Ben nodded and turned, almost walking into George.

"I heard," the big man said.

Gus came out of the wagon and motioned Miss McCrea to follow. "George, you climb in there and hold firm on Vernon's shoulders. Dinna let him move when I pull. Ben, you climb in after and keep pressure on his hips. Pin him down on the bunk. Dinna let him rise up."

Once George was in position, crouched into a space that barely held him, Ben entered and did as he'd been told. "I'm sorry, Vernon."

"Not as sorry as me." His friend managed a shaky grin that ended in a grimace.

"Stand back, lass." Gus wedged himself into the small space left, looked both George and Ben in the eye. "Ready?"

"Yes, suh." George's voice sounded too loud for the crowded wagon.

Ben nodded, pressing his palms against Vernon's hipbones.

"Relax as best you can, Vernon." Gus removed the man's boot, drawing a ragged breath followed by a groan. Gus cut away the pant leg covering the broken limb, the break a hand-span beneath the knee. "Dinna fight me. It must be done."

"Just do it," Vernon said between gritted teeth.

With no more warning, Gus jerked on the broken leg.

Vernon screamed.

It took everything Ben had to hold him on the bunk.

George grunted, one of Vernon's arms connecting with the man's chin, but he didn't loosen his hold.

The grating of bone moving against bone accompanied Vernon's collapse into blissful unconsciousness.

"Done." Gus mopped his brow, then bent over the leg again. "His foot is straight. The lump on the side of his leg gone. The bone snapped into place." He turned to the opening of the wagon. "Find me the straightest pieces of wood you can, lass. Three of them. He'll need a splint."

"Yes, Pa."

"What else can we do?" Ben asked, his insides a touch wobbly.

"I can tend him from here. You did well, both of you." Gus moved out of the way so Ben and George could climb out into the drizzle.

Miss McCrea was sorting through the wood in the sling.

"Stay with the horses and keep an eye on them," Ben ordered George.

"Yes, suh."

Ben went to Miss McCrea's side. "Let me help."

She pointed into the sling. "There's a long straight piece in the middle, just out of my reach."

Ben grabbed it and a second piece of similar size. "Will these do?"

Miss McCrea shrugged. "I hope so. I've never done anything like this before."

"Me either."

She wiped the rain from her face, her lips trembling. "That could have been Lloyd or Tyree—"

"But it wasn't." He resisted the urge to pull her into his arms for comfort. "Your brothers are safe, and the herd didn't stampede."

"Stampede?" Her eyes rounded, color fading from her cheeks.

He was an idiot. He gentled his voice as much as he could. "It sometimes happens in a storm, but these cattle handled it well."

"Yes." She glanced toward the herd, a dark mass a hundred yards or so away. "They did."

"Kenna?" her father called.

"Coming, Pa." She patted Ben's arm. "Thank you. I couldn't have done what you did."

He touched the brim of his dripping hat. "Glad to help."

She hurried to the chuckwagon with the pieces of wood in her hand.

Ben covered the spot on his arm where she'd touched him. Even through his soddened sleeve and leather glove, he imagined a warmth there.

CHAPTER 12

B EHIND THE RAIN HAD come a cold spell, although early in the year for it. Kenna wrapped her woolen shawl around her shoulders before stepping out of the family wagon. Dawn was still an hour off, but Mr. Brinkmann had said they'd push on through the mud as if it were any other day. As if one of the cowboys hadn't been grievously wounded. His words had seemed cold-hearted at first, but Pa had agreed that they couldn't stay where they were. Vernon needed a doctor.

Her boots didn't splash in the mud, but the gooey mess sucked at her heels as she made her way around the chuckwagon. Pa was already setting the coffeepots over a blazing fire. She joined him and held her bare fingers out to catch some heat.

"'Morning, lass." Pa's eyes were haggard. Had he slept at all last night? "Get the biscuits started while I see to Vernon."

"How's he doing?"

"Fair enough, but I canna do what a real doctor can." Pa brushed his hands down the front of his apron. "Squirrel says there's a town northeast of here. I dinna like the idea, but we'll have to split up."

"You'd drive him to the town?"

"I can pick up a few supplies while I'm there."

"But... feeding the men?"

"Aye, will fall to you. I have beans soaking for tonight. I should meet back up with you tomorrow morning."

"Pa, I don't even know how to make the coffee in those pots."

"You dinna know how to drive a team of mules last week either." He gave her a pleased grin. "And look at you now."

"But if we run into trouble—"

"Dinna worry, lass. Ben will be close by. And George. I think either would take a bullet for you and your sisters."

They'd both been helpful and attentive, although Kenna was careful not to encourage Mr. Warley's attention. He was, after all, a Yankee. Pa didn't think it mattered anymore, but Kenna wasn't so sure.

"I'll help Vernon see to his needs, and then move him into your wagon. You'll need the chuckwagon to feed the men."

"I'll set the biscuits to baking. Shoo the girls out to help me."

Pa strode off, and Kenna got busy.

The last of the cowboys had finished eating and were saddling their mounts, ready to join those holding the herd, when Pa handed Kenna a plate of biscuits and a cup of coffee.

"Vernon may need help sitting up to eat, but I'm sure you can manage. The lassies and I will finish cleaning and packing the chuckwagon. I'll hitch your team to it since you're used to them."

She took the plate and cup and entered her wagon. Vernon was laid out with his leg propped up on a narrow box Kenna used to hold her sewing notions.

"Ready for your breakfast?"

He opened his eyes, the lines around them marking his pain. "Thank you, miss."

She steadied his splinted leg while he pushed himself upright enough to eat.

"Gus says he's taking me to a town to find a doctor." He grimaced. "It's sure I won't be more than a hindrance here."

"I'm so sorry you were injured."

He shrugged. "Part of life is being knocked down and getting back up again. Learned that in the war."

"I guess even Yankees got knocked down sometimes." Kenna kept her voice level.

Vernon snorted. "I wasn't a Yankee when I got knocked down."

"I don't understand."

"I turned Yankee to get my freedom back."

"You mean"—she floundered for the right words—" you mean you're a Galvanized Yankee? You changed loyalties during the war?"

"I was in a prison camp. The war was over for me. My home had been demolished by the Yankees. It wasn't much, just a cabin on the side of a mountain, but it'd been in my family for generations." Another shrug. "I didn't lose as much as Ben did, mind you, but I didn't have nothing to return to either."

Kenna snapped her sagging mouth shut. "Mr. Warley? He's a Galvanized Yankee too?"

A Galvanized Yankee. A man who'd turned his back on his country. A traitor.

Kenna kept the mules at a steady pace, following to the right of the remuda, trying not to watch for Mr. Warley as he trailed after the horses, urging the slower animals to keep up when they lagged behind.

If she hadn't known what to think of him before, she certainly didn't now. Things started to settle into place, however. The way he ordered George around as if the man were still a slave, for one thing. Vernon said that Mr. Warley had lost more than he had. More meaning... slaves?

"Will we stop for the noon rest soon?" Elva asked, walking beside the chuckwagon. She and Vanora were helping by picking up sticks and tossing them into the sling.

"Mr. Warley said he'd let me know when and where. We'll wait for him to tell us." Imagine, her taking orders from a Galvanized Yankee. But he knew better what the horses and cattle needed than she did. She'd have to trust him.

Trust a Galvanized Yankee.

She couldn't keep the title from circulating through her thoughts.

What made a man turn his back on his country?

And what kind of man would do it?

The same kind who'd taught her to handle the lines of a six-mule hitch.

Nothing made sense anymore. Why couldn't they be back in San Antonio in their safe diner, waiting on paying customers, instead of living out of a wagon battling first dust and heat, and now mud and cold? If she hadn't needed to keep her hands on the reins, she'd have rubbed the gooseflesh from her arms.

A trio of cowboys approached, including the other black man besides George, heading for the remuda. It happened often during the day, the cowboys changing mounts. They usually nodded in greeting as they passed, but nothing more. The dark man, however, met her glance with a bold stare. He was older than most of the cowboys, and there was something about him that made Kenna uneasy.

As if he sensed it, he flashed her a grin with no humor behind it. Like a cat staring down a mouse.

Kenna looked away and pretended not to hear his laughter.

"Was he bothering you?"

She jerked at Mr. Warley's voice. Where had he come from? "No, not bothering. Not exactly."

"I'll keep an eye on him."

"Thank you, Mr. Warley." She straightened on the bench seat. "I don't think it'll be necessary." What was worse, to be mocked by the cowboy or guarded by a Galvanized Yankee?

"Let me worry about that." He touched his hat and rode to the back of the remuda.

Kenna relaxed, but was it due to his leaving? Or his willingness to watch over her?

Miss McCrea's cool response to Ben was as drastic as the temperature drop. What had sparked it? They'd seemed to be getting back to a friendly footing until that morning. He'd assumed she'd been extra busy, what with Gus pulling out and taking Vernon to the nearest town to find a—

Vernon.

Ben ground his teeth together. That must be it. The man couldn't keep his mouth shut. He'd told Squirrel, after all, so he'd probably told Miss McCrea as well. She might have gotten over Ben being a Yankee—in time—but she'd just tossed his offer of protection back in his face.

She'd rather be harassed by an ex-slave than protected by a Galvanized Yankee.

So much for Ben starting over. He'd been manipulated out of San Antonio by Squirrel, and now he'd been found out by the one person he most wanted to impress.

In the back of his mind niggled the truth—he'd have had to confess his circumstances to her sooner or later anyway, if he'd won Gus's permission to court her.

He gave a dry laugh that had the pinto mare he rode swiveling her ears at him. He patted the black-and-white neck. "Never mind. No reason you should understand me. I hardly understand myself."

Everything had been perfect before the war. His life carefree and easy.

The Confederate cavalry hadn't been either. Seeing boyhood friends shot from their saddles, never enough to eat, rarely enough sleep, and always the fear of Yankees over the next hill or through the next grove of trees.

The prison camp had been even worse. Crammed in railroad cars so tightly they couldn't lie down, he and his fellow prisoners had arrived hungry, thirsty, filthy, and exhausted. Sleep could be had within the prison walls, but food and water were scarce, bathing out of the question. They were given just enough to stay alive, but barely. Most of the men grew sick and weak. Many died.

Emmet had heard the rumblings of a loyalty oath first. Pledge to the Union and be shipped west to man the frontier forts. They could fight Indians instead of hunger, illness, or each other. They'd not be expected to aim a rifle at their fellow Southerners. They wouldn't fight against their own people.

Whether the prison had run out of food entirely, or whether they'd withheld it to gather more signatures, Ben didn't know. But when the soldiers arrived and set up a table to swear men into the U.S. Cavalry, Ben had gotten in line. Emmet followed, but reluctantly, muttering about being a turncoat.

They'd signed the oath, been given uniforms, and then loaded on another railroad car, one bound for Kansas City. At least in that one, they'd had enough room to lie down and enough food and water to sustain them.

In Kansas City, Emmet decided to desert. After all, he hadn't really changed his loyalty. He'd lied to get his freedom. He urged Ben to run with him, and then called him every sort of a coward when he refused.

Ben wasn't sure himself why he hadn't run with his cousin. He hadn't felt any more a Union soldier than Emmet had, but something inside of him had balked at running away. Even now, sitting on a horse in the middle of the Texas prairie, he couldn't say for sure why he'd stayed. But he had. And Southern folks would never forgive him.

Like Miss McCrea.

It was time to stop looking in her direction. If Ben was going to build a new life for himself, it would be without the fiery-haired woman driving the chuckwagon. Sadness gathered in a lump at the base of Ben's throat. But he straightened in his saddle and set his face to the north.

He still had a job to do. He'd see the cattle to Abilene. Failure wasn't an option.

And he'd watch over Miss McCrea as he'd promised, whether she liked it or not.

The weather had returned to normal, and Kenna sweated under the blazing sun. She sat back on the high seat of the family wagon, her mules plodded along behind Pa on the chuckwagon. Dust billowed around her, but she'd grown almost numb to it.

At least she didn't have to pick up dried cow dung.

They'd run completely out of trees the day after Pa had rejoined them once he'd delivered Vernon to the doctor. That had been... Kenna squinted into the distance and counted out five. Five days. Each one a repeat of the day before. Rise early, feed the men, drive the wagon, feed the men, drive the wagon again, feed the men again, wash or mend clothing, followed by sleep. Then do it all over again the next day. And the next.

The diner had a routine as well, but there'd been occasional breaks for fishing at the river or shopping or attending church. There was nothing out on the prairie. Nothing but the wind and the dust and the heat.

Vanora stumbled, then stopped and rubbed her ankle.

"Are you all right?" Kenna called.

"Can I ride for a while?"

They needed the cow dung to cook with, but surely they had enough for tonight. "Climb in."

"Me too?" Elva asked.

"You too. Come on." Kenna didn't slow the wagon. Her sisters had become adept at grabbing hold and climbing over the tailgate while the mules shuffled along.

"Thank you." Elva wrapped her arms around Kenna from behind. "I'm so tired."

"Why don't you lie down? Take a nap if you can. Vanora too."

Both sisters thanked her, and the bunk creaked under their slight weight. In a matter of moments, their deep breathing could be heard between the gusts of wind. They were so young. Kenna rubbed her eyes with the back of her wrist, keeping the reins woven between her fingers. They were all tired.

"Are you well, Miss McCrea?" Mr. Warley asked.

She coughed and nodded. "Just clearing out the dust."

"Much as I don't like it, the mud wasn't any better."

Kenna pressed her lips together, refusing to be drawn into small talk. Mr. Warley got the hint—as he always did—and eased his horse away from the wagon. Would he ever just leave her alone? She might be miserable, but she didn't need the attention of someone like him.

Hoofbeats came from behind, cowboys looking for fresh horses. Kenna was getting used to the ebb and flow of them now. She even amused herself sometimes by guessing which ones were due for re-mounts.

This time would be Leppo.

She'd learned his name when she'd asked George. He'd seemed concerned about her questioning, and ever since, either George or Mr. Warley happened to be nearby when the older black man changed horses.

It wasn't Leppo's color that bothered Kenna. George was much darker, and she was very comfortable around him. It was Leppo's demeanor—the way he looked at her—that made her skin crawl.

So when Mr. Warley once again drew his horse close to the wagon, she not only nodded to him, she gave him a wan smile. After all, she had her sisters' safety to think about too, didn't she? He'd been content to ride along without small talk for the past few days, so it wasn't like they were becoming friends.

And Galvanized Yankee or not, Mr. Warley never made her skin crawl.

CHAPTER 13

T HEY WERE APPROACHING THE first major river to ford. Ben leaned forward and rubbed Rusty's neck. "I sure hope you're a swimmer." They'd crossed a number of creeks and one boggy stretch without incident, but the cowboys assured him they'd have to swim the river winding in front of them.

But not yet.

Squirrel's orders were to wait for the cattle. The cowboys would cross first. They'd pushed the animals hard since the last watering, so they were thirsty. That should make them easier to drive into the river and force across.

Then they'd need to float the wagons over. The undersides of both wagons were sealed with pitch. They were, in essence, wheeled boats. But mules weren't the best swimmers, so they'd have to unhitch them and swim them over, then rig ropes and use horses to ferry the boats. It wasn't a major operation if everything went according to plan.

But when did that ever happen?

Gus thought the girls should stay in the wagon and float across on it. Squirrel was in favor of the girls going over behind cowboys on the best swimming horses the outfit had.

Ben wished they had a bridge.

But if wishes were horses, beggars would ride.

He blew out a sigh and aimed for the chuckwagon. "What can I do to help, Gus?"

The cook poked his head from the wagon's side entrance. "We canna move until Squirrel gives the go-ahead. I'm tying anything that canna get wet to the top hoops."

"Won't that make the wagon top-heavy?"

Gus shook his head. "The heavy stuff is packed in water-tight bar-rels." He moved back into the vehicle.

Ben caught sight of the large calendar Gus had nailed to the back of the chuckwagon. Every morning, the cook scratched an X through one box. It was September twenty-seventh, just two weeks into the drive. In all likelihood, they had more than two months left to go. Ben couldn't remember how many rivers he and Timothy had crossed on the way down. Too many. And each one getting colder this time of year.

He reined Rusty around to the back of the McCrea wagon. "Need any help, Miss McCrea?"

Miss Vanora stood at the tailgate, her eyes shining. "Pa told us to tie our clothing and other important things to the top of the wagon." She moved aside to show him the odd assortment of bundles dangling from the high hoops. "Isn't it exciting?"

The elder Miss McCrea was tying another bundle, keeping her back to Ben.

Exciting? That wasn't the word Ben would have chosen, but better if the girls saw it as an adventure. "It'll be a new experience, that's for sure."

"I'm scared, Mr. Warley." Elva inched toward the back of the crowd-ed wagon.

So was he, but he couldn't admit it. Scared that something would go wrong with the wagons. But before he could say anything, a distant shout reached them.

The herd was coming. By the cloud of dust and rumble of hooves, it was coming fast. Squirrel meant to plunge the thirsty beasts right into the river and force them across by the pressure of the cattle behind them. Cowboys—still unseen through the dust—yipped and whistled and shouted. Some of the cattle bawled in protest, but the mass surged forward. They passed where the wagons were stopped and picked up speed down the gentle incline to the river. Cowboys—finally visi-ble—swung lariats and continued to make noise.

It was a spectacle to behold. The animals flowed like a river them-selves, packed so tightly that, if one of them went down, it'd be tram-pled to death by the rest.

The cowboys kept their horses well outside of the crush.

Squirrel raced along the side, passing between the herd and the wagons. Two others flanked him, and three more rode on the opposite side of the herd. In a movement not unlike an orchestrated dance, the six riders pressured the lead cattle into the rushing water. The horses snorted but stood their ground in the shallow edge. One pawed at the water, sending it spraying in all directions. More cowboys were spaced like the sides of a funnel while the drag riders whooped and hollered and kept the back of the herd pressing forward.

"Bring the remuda and mules over right behind the cattle!" Squirrel yelled from the river.

Ben reined Rusty around. "Time to find out if you're a swimmer or not." He touched his heels to the mustang's flanks and joined George, who'd been holding the horses in place. They were no longer grazing, the cattle having drawn their attention. Several had their heads up, ears pricked, nostrils wide, ready for what came next. Most had been through these rivers before, so Ben wasn't worried about them.

"Let's go," he said to George, and they moved the remuda to the back of the herd. Ben pulled his neckerchief over his nose against the dust and swung the long ends of his split reins. "Move out. Git up there."

The first horses hit the water, some practically jumping in. The cattle were already climbing the bank on the far side a short distance downstream. The current was strong enough to make swimming straight across impossible. Ben had to chase after two horses who broke away to avoid the water, but Rusty was fast and circled them, turning them back to the rest. And horses being horses, they decided they'd rather stay with the herd than strike out again. The mules followed, several of them braying in protest. Miss McCrea's red mule set to bucking when its feet got wet but finally swam after the others.

George spurred his horse into the water after the red mule, and Ben did the same. Rusty went in willingly enough, but when his hooves didn't strike bottom, the mustang fought to turn back to shore. "Easy, boy, just follow the rest of them. You can do it."

Rusty fought him instead, the mustang's head going underwater and bobbing back to the surface.

"Toss me a rein." George stretched out his hand.

"We're fine," Ben yelled back. But they weren't. Rusty was tiring himself out fighting both Ben and the current.

Then George was beside him, his mustang swimming beside Rusty on the downriver side, pushing the roan along. When Rusty's feet gripped the riverbed, he lunged to the bank where he stood with sides heaving.

Ben dismounted and loosened the horse's girth.

"Be his first time in a river with a rider on his back, I allow," George said. "He'll do better next time."

Ben glanced back at the rippling water, and then at the large man who'd rescued him. "Thank you for the help."

George grinned, an ear-to-ear grin without an ounce of I-told-you-so in it. "Anytime."

What would Ben's father have said about that? But there wasn't time to wonder. They still needed to ferry the wagons across.

Lloyd rode to Ben leading the pinto mare. "She's a strong swimmer. I remember her from the last drive."

"Thanks." He transferred his saddle from Rusty to the mare. "Sorry to hold everyone up."

"You aren't." Lloyd pointed to where several others were transferring tack to fresh horses. "It'll take most of us to get the wagons across. Everyone is saddling their best horse. Tyree and I are returning to bring the wee lassies over."

"And Miss McCrea?"

Lloyd frowned and shook his head. "She and Pa will stay in the wagons."

He obviously didn't like that idea. Neither did Ben. If the wagons went down, they could be trapped underwater. But on the other hand, aboard the wagons they could tie off lariats that slipped or even help shift weight inside the wagon if necessary.

Tyree rode toward them, and Lloyd moved away, the brothers hitting the river together, their horses swimming for the other side.

Squirrel whistled and waved the rest of the men to join him. He laid out the plan. They'd attach lariats to the wagons and keep their horses on the upstream side, swimming and pulling one wagon at a time across the river.

They waited until the McCrea boys reached the far side. Each deposited a wet and bedraggled sister on the riverbank before heading back across the river and tying their lariats to the wagon.

"We'll take the chuckwagon first," Squirrel said. The men too up the slack in their ropes.

"Just don't dump me, laddies," Gus called from his perch on the seat.

"Ain't nobody we take better care of than the cook!" Jake shouted. Several laughed and agreed.

Ben dallied his lariat to the horn of his saddle and waited. Three men dismounted and pushed the chuckwagon into the river while the rest pulled. The pinto struck out into the current, only to be towed sideways when the weight of the wagon left the river bottom.

"Turn the horses!" Squirrel yelled. "Aim them upstream."

It seemed to take forever, but finally the wagon's wheels struck bottom. They waited, holding the ropes tight, while Gus and his boys unloaded the harnesses and hitched the mules to pull the heavy wagon onto the bank.

The pinto rested beneath Ben, and when it was time to return for the second wagon, she wasn't even breathing hard.

But Ben was. Miss McCrea's wagon was next.

Kenna's heart had stopped when Mr. Warley's horse had floundered in the water. If not for George, what might have happened? But the large man had been there, and they made the other side safely.

Kenna's heart had beat in her throat until Lloyd, Tyree, Vanora, and Elva emerged from the water on the other side of the river. Elva had squealed when they entered the water, but she'd minded Tyree's instructions and clung to him like a cocklebur. Vanora had probably enjoyed it. That girl.

Kenna's heart had eased when Pa had crossed with the chuckwagon in perfect order.

Now the cowboys swam the river one more time for her. She sat on the high bench seat and tried not to think of everything that could go wrong.

The first one to reach her was Mr. Brinkmann, riding a different horse. Several of the men had saddled fresh mounts. Mr. Warley still rode the pinto. Lloyd and Tyree had stayed on the far bank and were harnessing the mules to pull her wagon the rest of the way from the river. Pa watched from the bank next to Vanora and Elva, twisting his hat between his hands.

"All set, Miss McCrea?" Mr. Brinkmann asked.

She nodded, not trusting her voice.

"Just like before," he called to the cowboys. "Last crossing and then we can dry out."

The wagon jostled under her as the men tied and snugged the lines. Three men dismounted and pushed it toward the water, the others riding alongside.

Kenna sucked in a deep breath and tried to form a prayer, but her mind went blank and all she could do was grip the seat.

The moment the wagon floated, it swung into the current. Seeing it happen to Pa's wagon hadn't prepared her for the feeling of utter helplessness. The strong legs of the horses, the lariats, and the sturdy wood of the wagon's bottom were all that kept her from being washed downstream. She wanted to squeal like Elva, but of course, that wouldn't do. Not for a woman her age. Instead, she focused on Pa watching from the opposite shore. He walked along as the wagon drifted, keeping in her sight. They were almost across—

The wagon lurched to the side, and Kenna lost her grip. She slid toward the downriver side, grasping for anything to stop her fall. Her legs hit the water, but she held on.

"Miss McCrea!" One deep shout stood out from the rest—Mr. Warley.

"Ben! Stop!" Mr. Brinkmann's yell came with another lurch of the wagon.

Kenna slipped more, the water coming to her waist.

Mr. Warley and the pinto came beside her. He thrust out his hand. "Take it!"

Kenna grabbed it, the current pushing her into the pinto's side.

"Hold on to my saddle, but let the mare pull you through the water. She can't carry us both." Mr. Warley slid off the other side of the horse while keeping his grip on the saddle.

The mare struggled toward the bank, thankfully not far away, until her feet hit bottom. She pulled Kenna from the water with her, and Mr. Warley too. What a brave little mare.

Kenna made it to the bank about the same time her wagon did, but it listed badly to one side, its front wheel smashed by whatever it had struck on the river's bottom.

The saturated fabric of her skirts made walking difficult, but Pa had his arms around her before she took her third step out of the water.

"Are ye all right, lassie?" His Scottish burr thickened with his distress. "If anything had happened to ye—"

She squeezed his arm. "Nothing did. It was just as you'd said. Mr. Warley was looking out for me."

But someone not pleased was Mr. Brinkmann, who approached them looking like the he was about to explode. "Ben! You disobeyed my direct order back there. You left us a man short to move the wagon and put us all in danger."

"But I protected Miss McCrea, and that was my top priority."

"I don't care—"

Mr. Warley stood toe-to-toe with the trail boss, albeit a half a head shorter. "You and the others can swim, and your horses can swim"—he jabbed a finger at Kenna—"but her dress would have dragged her to the bottom."

Mr. Brinkmann seemed to chew on those words for a moment.

Kenna glanced at Pa, who still had his arm around her but managed to look menacing all the same. And behind him stood George, twisting his horse's reins in his hands.

Kenna had her protectors.

Mr. Brinkmann dropped his head, then looked up. "You're right. I should have seen that myself." Then he directed his attention to her. "I'm sorry, Miss McCrea."

She summoned a smile. "I understand."

"We'll get the spare wheel on the wagon and haul it out. Gus, build a roaring fire and dry your girls out." Mr. Brinkmann stalked away, barking orders with every step.

Pa let her go and stuck out a hand to Mr. Warley, which he grasped. "I canna thank you enough for what you did out there. That took guts. If the wagon had toppled, it would have pinned you both beneath it."

Mr. Warley nodded toward George. "If he hadn't seen me across on the first pass, I wouldn't have been there. I guess he deserves the thanks."

"No, suh." George looked toward the puffy clouds overhead and then back at them. "Wasn't me. They was someone else watching down on us. Glory be."

Kenna remembered her attempt at a prayer, and in her heart, she agreed with George. There were still hundreds of miles and more rivers to cross before Abilene. It was good to know they weren't on their own.

CHAPTER 14

I T'D BEEN TEN DAYS since they'd almost lost the McCrea wagon, ten incredibly busy days, covering a long stretch with little water. Ben and George had needed to ride night watch on the horses to keep them from straying in their thirst. They split the shifts, so both of them were short on sleep.

Rusty was restive as they waited along the banks of another river. Ben patted the roan's neck. "I think you deserve another chance, and this river isn't nearly as wide as the last."

"I think you's right, suh." George had dismounted and was snugging the girth of his fresh mount. He wiped the cold drizzle from his face and looked up at Ben. "Everyone deserve a second chance."

Ben shifted on his saddle. Ten days ago, he wouldn't have been sitting next to George, he'd have kept his distance, ordered George to be elsewhere, or would have ignored him altogether. But since that day in the river, when George had circled his horse back and helped Ben cross, their relationship had altered.

What would his father think of that?

Maybe, if his father had been in that river with a panicked horse, he'd be thinking the same as Ben.

George was a good man. Not a good *slave*, not a good *ex-slave*, but a good *man*. Ben still wrestled with shame that he hadn't been able to see it before.

"Good men aren't afraid to give those second chances, are they?" Ben asked.

"No, suh. I reckon they ain't."

The first shouts from the herd reached them. There was no dust to give warning since the drizzle had started the night before and plagued them the whole day. No need to worry about getting wet in the river. Anything not covered by their oiled slickers—and half that was—had already been soaked through. The sun glinted above the western horizon. Hopefully, Squirrel would let them strike camp once they crossed. Those not guarding the herd could huddle under Gus's tarps and dry out for a while.

"We best get the remuda and mules ready." George mounted and rode toward the animals.

Ben kept Rusty back for another few moments, debating his decision to give the roan another chance at a river. But catching sight of Miss McCrea sitting tall on her wagon, awaiting her turn, clinched it. If she could brave another crossing on the same wagon, he could do as much with the same horse.

And he'd grown uncommonly fond of the roan mustang since they'd left San Antonio.

"Come on, Rusty. You've done it once with a little help. You can do it solo this time." He followed George, and they gathered the horses and mules into a bunch.

As before, the cattle were thirsty and moving fast. The lead and swing cowboys created a funnel with their horses, and the drag cowboys pushed the animals through. One advantage of trailing the herd in the fall was not having to worry about swimming any calves across. The animals were all large and strong enough to make it over.

The horses and mules went next, with Ben and George flanking them. Rusty snorted and pranced on the riverbank, but when Ben applied his spurs, the roan splashed into the water. This time, there was no fighting, no panic. The river was shallower than the first one, and Rusty didn't start swimming until near the middle. Within a few yards, his hooves had gained purchase in the riverbed again, and they climbed to the other side.

Rusty was still shaking the water from his hide when Lloyd and Tyree swam their animals back across for the girls. But Lloyd had a third horse on the lead behind them. What was that for?

Then Ben caught sight of Miss McCrea, no longer sitting on the wagon but standing next to it and wearing a pair of britches. Britches!

Ben almost fell off his horse.

"If that ain't the dad-gummest thing I ever did see," George said beside him.

Ben's Southern-gentleman sensibilities might have been unseated a few years ago by the sight of a woman in britches, but he'd seen too much since then. And it was the logical solution to the heavy dress that could have killed her on the last crossing.

She approached a sturdy bay Lloyd had taken across for her, one from Lloyd's own string, a reliable horse. Her brother helped her mount, then the younger girls scrambled behind their brothers and they all came across.

The wagons were easy to float the shorter distance, and by the time everything was on the north side of the river, the drizzle had stopped. Squirrel called a halt for the night. They'd made the crossing without a single incident.

Ben finished his duties as wrangler and approached the chuckwagon. Miss Vanora filled his cup, and Miss McCrea—properly attired in her apron-covered dress—handed him a plate loaded with beef and potatoes. She served them with a smile.

Not quite the beautiful smile he'd seen back in San Antonio. They hadn't spoken of the war, and he sensed it hung between them like a sheer curtain over a sunny window, but she wasn't frosty toward him anymore.

That was worth something.

"Enjoy the potatoes," she said. "It's the last of them."

"What comes after potatoes?"

"Lots of cornbread and beans."

He grinned. "I like both of those just fine."

"You'll get sick of them soon enough." Tyree reached for the plate his sister was filling. "Even Pa can only do so much with cornmeal and beans. Of course"—he leaned to the side, peering behind his sister—"Pa could always cook a rattlesnake or two for more variety."

Miss Elva squealed and clung to the back of Miss McCrea, who waved a dripping ladle at her brother. "If you don't stop that nonsense, you'll be lucky to get corn mush to eat for the next week."

Tyree danced out of the ladle's reach and laughed before returning to the men seated around the fire.

"It's all right." The eldest Miss McCrea gave her youngest sister a quick hug. "You know he just says those things to tease you."

"I don't like it."

Ben leaned down to the girl's level. "You know why brothers do those things to their sisters?"

Miss Elva shook her head.

"Because they're too timid to say 'I love you.' And they think teasing shows it."

"Really?"

"Yes, miss. That's a fact. You can take it from someone who has two younger sisters of his own."

"You do?" Her face lit up. She was going to be a heartbreaker in a few years—just like her sister.

"Their names are Amelia and Pauleen," Ben said. "They're both married and have children of their own." He winked at her. "I can't bother them anymore."

"Back to washing now." Miss McCrea shooed Miss Elva toward the pile of dirty plates then turned back to him. "That was nice of you."

"All true." It was the first time they'd made small talk since Vernon had been injured. A step in the right direction.

"Well, it was nice just the same."

Another cowboy came for his meal, so Ben stepped away. It was going to be a damp, cold night, but the warmth was flowing between him and Miss McCrea again, so what was a little thing like the weather?

The nights were getting colder. Kenna pulled another blanket from the storage box under her bunk and spread it over her sleeping sisters. Vanora had been miffed to be sent to bed early with Elva—she thought herself too old to be ordered to bed—but the girls were exhausted from walking all day beside the wagons, picking up fuel for the evening fires.

They needed more than one fire now. One to cook, but two others for the men to warm themselves, especially when they came in off night herd duties. Mr. Brinkmann was adamant that the men take off their gloves and boots and thoroughly warm their feet and hands. She'd always liked him, but her respect for the trail boss had grown, seeing how much he cared about not only the beasts in his care but the men he led.

A cattle drive without such a man in the lead would be a disaster. She could see that. They'd been on the trail for four weeks. Pa estimated they were covering ten to twelve miles most days. That put them somewhere around three hundred miles from San Antonio.

Not even halfway to Abilene—and the hardest part of the journey was still ahead.

Kenna tucked the blanket around her sisters, gathered her mending basket, and slipped out of the wagon to join Pa by the fire.

"You should find your bunk like your sisters, lass."

"But the mending won't do itself." Kenna pulled a crate closer to the flames so the light would show on her work. Vanora had tripped on her skirt again and pulled out the hem. Kenna should have hemmed it shorter as she had Elva's, but she wasn't comfortable with her older sister's legs being exposed to the cowboys. The one called Carl was already making cow's eyes at Vanora, who wasn't doing anything to discourage him.

Kenna threaded her needle.

"Once we reach Abilene, Vanora will need new clothes. I suppose it'll be time for her to wear full skirts."

Pa slipped the pipe from his mouth and faced her, the firelight casting shadows across his bearded face. "She canna be old enough for such."

Kenna sighed. She wanted to agree with him, but what was the point? The truth was, her sister was growing up. "She'll be thirteen next week. I was wearing full skirts at twelve."

"You had to, lassie." He replaced the pipe and spoke around it. "There isna need for Vanora to grow up as fast as you did."

"Not by need, by want." Kenna sewed a few stitches in silence. "She's growing up faster than Lloyd or Tyree did."

"That's what the lassies do, I suppose. I first met your ma when she was Vanora's age."

"Pa." Kenna let the mending settle into her lap. "Vanora bears watching, especially around Carl."

Pa straightened on his camp chair. "What's this?"

"Hush. No need to raise your voice." Kenna scanned the other fires, but no one was looking their way. "I'm sure it's innocent enough, but he's interested in her, and she's not disabusing him of the notion."

"I'll speak to her."

"I'd appreciate it."

He tilted his head and studied her. "I dinna have to do that with you, lass. Why not?"

"You know why. You and the children needed me."

"Needed, aye." He stroked his beard. "But you have more than done your duty to our family. You should keep your mind open to the possibilities, Kenna. I wouldna see you become an old maid."

An old maid? Kenna had turned twenty last spring. Hardly old. But Ma had married Pa when she was just seventeen. She'd had Kenna holding onto her skirts and Lloyd rounding her belly at Kenna's age.

Kenna wanted a family of her own someday. There was plenty of time to find someone to spend her life with. After all, the prairie was ripe with men and wanting in women. She glanced at those gathered around the other fires, light from the flames creating silhouettes of some and highlighting tired, creased faces of others. George's hulking frame was easy to pick out, which meant Mr. Warley was with the remuda.

If he hadn't come for her in the middle of that river...

But there was no use thinking of him or any of the other men on the drive. She'd never marry a man who trailed cattle for a living. Kenna wanted security above all else. A house to call her own. A husband who returned to her each evening. Was it too much to wish for?

She hunched over her mending, turning it to catch more of the fire's light. Better to concentrate on what needed doing than consider her future. She couldn't do anything about that until they reached Abilene—if then. She and Mr. Warley were on friendly terms again, but that was all there was to it. He was still a Galvanized Yankee, a traitor to his country, and so proved he couldn't be trusted.

But Kenna wasn't sure she could hold onto that belief anymore.

According to Gus's calendar, they were smack in the middle of October. Ben waded into the river they'd just crossed, clothes and all. It was warm enough for a bath, and likely the last they'd have until they reached Abilene. The nights were getting colder, a combination of moving steadily north and the season turning.

The river was a small one, barely over Ben's head at its deepest. He plunged into the chilly water and surfaced, shaking his too-long hair. He should have visited a barber before leaving San Antonio, but there hadn't been time.

He'd had a pupil to school in driving mules.

"What are you grinning at?" Charlie splashed water at Ben. "The water's cold enough to turn my blood to mush. Southern boy like you ought to be frozen through."

Three others had joined them for the impromptu bath and laughed at Charlie's remark.

"Guess I've lived in the North long enough to get used to it."

"Well, I sure ain't." Carl, the youngest cowboy on the drive, splashed his way to the riverbank where they'd left their clean—or at least cleaner—clothing.

That's when Ben felt the rumbling of ground.

Before he could blink, two of the men who'd been on Squirrel's previous drive took off for the riverbank. One yelled "Stampede!" over his shoulder.

Ben's blood ran cold.

It took him forever to reach the bank, the water pulling at his wet clothing, slowing his legs. He climbed out as the first two men halted on the rise above the bank. One of them exhausted a large vocabulary of profanity followed by the shout, "Buffalo!"

Then they were all stuffing wet feet into boots before running to their mounts.

Ben had shifted his saddle from the pinto mare to Rusty before he'd jumped in the river. He hit the leather with a squish, his wet britches slopping into the seat. But there was nothing to be done other than ride and ride hard.

Squirrel was on top of the rise near the river, shouting orders. Those with the cattle stayed put, tightening the animals into a group they could hopefully control. The rest of them raced toward the oncoming buffalo to turn them away.

Ben's mouth dropped at the sight.

He'd thought their herd of cattle was huge. It was nothing compared to the herd of charging beasts heading their way and closing in fast. Each buffalo was fully twice as large as a single steer, and the mass of moving creatures was intimidating.

Several of the horses thought so too.

Jake's horse started to pitch. The man had all he could do to stay in the saddle. Several other horses were white-eyed and snorting, even at a gallop.

Ben leaned low over Rusty's neck. "Steady, boy. If that bunch hits our cattle, they'll scatter them like leaves in the wind."

The roan's ears swiveled back toward Ben, and the game mustang charged on.

Squirrel raced at Ben's right, Lloyd and Tyree close behind.

"Turn them north, away from the river!" the trail boss yelled.

With half of the men guarding the herd, even with Ben and George both riding with the cowboys approaching the herd, they were only ten men on mustangs against that shaggy, thundering horde.

Then Squirrel drew his pistol and fired repeatedly into the air.

Ben froze in his saddle.

The rushing mass turned into blue-coated men. The acrid scent of gunpowder stung the air. The thundering turned into the compression of air caused by cannonfire.

He was back in the war.

Ben let loose the rebel yell that had motivated his fellow soldiers in every battle since First Manassas.

When he drew his pistol, he didn't point it in the air, he fired into the menace bearing down on them. Two of the enemy dropped as he emptied his pistol. Then someone was beside him, grabbing the bridle of his horse, someone who pulled him away from the charge. Why? He blinked to clear his vision, then recognized the large black man wrestling his horse to a stop and halting Ben's along with it.

"What are you doing?" Ben tried to gain control of his horse. "They're getting away!"

"They is, suh. But you turned 'em. You sure enough turned 'em good."

"But they're—" Ben glanced at the flow of buffalo turning to the south.

Buffalo?

He'd been right in the path of their stampede until George hauled him to safety.

Where were the blue-bellies they'd been facing?

"I reckon you got a little confused, suh." George. It was George sitting next to him on a lathered, blowing horse.

"Buffalo?"

"Yes, suh."

Ben rubbed his eyes and shook his head. "I could have sworn..."

"Best we go back and check them horses, suh." George released the roan's bridle.

Rusty, that was the horse's name. Rusty, a mustang. Ben was on a cattle drive.

What had just happened?

He shivered in his wet clothing, even though the sun still hung above the horizon.

"Come on, Mr. Warley." George reined his horse around, and Ben let Rusty follow. "It might be best to keep clear of the trail boss for a little while. He shore looked fit to shoot you when you cut across in front of him and started firing into them buffalo. I thought you was going to charge right into them." George glanced at him. "But you done turned the herd, even if not in the direction the boss wanted. That'll count for something."

Ben tried to piece things back together. He wasn't in the war. Those buffalo weren't Yankee soldiers. And the large man beside him wasn't a slave. Not anymore.

He was the man who'd probably saved Ben's life for the second time since they'd left San Antonio.

CHAPTER 15

I T HAD TAKEN JUST moments to hitch the mules, even without George or Mr. Warley to help. Kenna had the task down to the fewest movements possible from so much repetition. She'd sent Vanora and Elva to pack the chuckwagon while Pa hitched his team. They wouldn't know what direction to take until they saw the buffalo, but they needed to be ready to run.

The ground rumbled under her feet, and even stoic old Cigar had grown restive as she'd hitched Jack and Hobbs ahead of him.

The cowboys holding the herd had their hands full. They were all but racing their horses around the bunched mob, slapping ropes and reins at any animals that appeared ready to break from the herd. The cattle bawled and pawed the ground and milled against each other. The rattle of horns against horns, the whinny of frightened horses, all added to the thundering of buffalo hooves until the tension was thick enough to fog the air.

Then came the gunshots.

As much as she wanted to know what was happening, as much as she wanted to run for the small rise so she could see over it, she held her mules in line and waited. And prayed. Lloyd and Tyree were out there. And Mr. Warley.

Then came a blood-curdling yell—like nothing she'd ever heard before—followed by more gunfire and shouting. Kenna was on the verge of calling for her sisters when the shouting turned to triumph. A few more gunshots peppered the air, but the shouts were moving away from the encampment.

They'd turned the buffalo.

Relief stole the strength from her legs as Kenna grasped Jack's harness to stay upright.

"They did it!" shouted Pa. Vanora and Elva both cheered.

The cowboys, however, still worked the cattle, slowing their horses and starting to sing to the beasts. Several more cowboys topped the rise and joined them.

Then George and Mr. Warley came into view and veered off toward the remuda, which had stayed in the small depression where they'd been settled down to graze before the ground had started shaking.

Another cowboy came racing toward the chuckwagon, and Kenna's heart lifted. It was Tyree. He brought his black horse to a sliding stop and jumped from its back.

"Pa! We got buffalo to cut up."

"They shot one?" Pa asked.

"Ben did. He shot two of them." Tyree pointed behind him. "You should have seen him take off at that herd. He pulled his pistol, shouted like the devil himself was on his tail, and started shooting. I thought Squirrel was going to have a fit, but it worked. The herd turned and they're heading south, swimming across the river." The words poured from her brother's lips, excitement sparking in his eyes.

He loved this.

She hated it.

He could have been killed out there. Lloyd could have been killed. If the buffalo had reached the wagons, they all might have been killed.

But Mr. Warley had turned them.

"What happened out there, Ben?" Squirrel's words were paced, even, not angry. "I gave orders to turn the buffalo north. That would have been the easiest route to move them. Then the next thing I see is you racing right into that charging herd and shooting the lead animals." Squirrel scratched the back of his neck. "I never saw the like. It was more than risky, it was pure foolishness."

His words remained mild and for that, Ben was thankful. But how could he explain what had happened when he didn't understand it himself?

"I don't know."

"Why did you disobey my orders? We'll start there."

"I remember what you said, but then the gunshots started and it was…" He took a deep breath, looked over the remuda toward George on the other side, then back at Squirrel. "It was like I was in the war."

"How was it like that?"

"They weren't buffalo anymore. They were Yankees. The pounding wasn't hooves, it was cannons." Even to Ben, the words sounded stupid. "I didn't think, I just reacted."

Squirrel sat for a long moment, squinting into the distance. Then he spit and wiped his chin with the back of his glove. "I've heard of something like that before."

"You have?" That oddly made Ben feel a little better. Maybe he wasn't pure crazy.

"Yup. Heard tell of a man south of San Antonio who they say brought the war home with him. Drove his wife and children out of their house with his fits."

Fits? Maybe he *was* pure crazy.

"They said all sorts of things would set him off, and he'd slip back into the war." Squirrel turned his squint toward Ben. "This ever happen to you before?"

"Never." And he hoped it never would again. His heartbeat was finally back to normal, but it had taken a long time to settle.

Squirrel relaxed and nodded. "Probably nothing to worry about then. They say that gent carried on from the time he arrived home."

"I never went home," Ben said. "I came out here and rode for the U.S. Cavalry for a couple of years."

"If you rode for the cavalry and nothing like this happened then, I'm guessing it was a one-time thing. A combination of the circumstances that reminded you too much of the war." Squirrel jerked his head toward the wagons. "You'd best get near the fire and dry out before you sicken with something. George can keep the horses calm, and the cattle have already begun to settle."

Ben reined Rusty around.

"And Ben."

He glanced back at Squirrel.

"Thanks. It might have been foolish and dangerous, but you turned those buffalo."

Ben's throat tightened as he rode off. He wasn't hero material, never had been, but it felt good to have done something to protect the herd, the remuda... and Miss McCrea.

Kenna handed plates of cornbread and freshly grilled buffalo to Charlie and Carl.

The cowboys were coming to the chuckwagon to eat in pairs, since all the other hands were needed with the cattle. Most of the animals had settled down to graze, some even lay down to chew their cuds, but there were still a few who bawled and pawed and snorted in their midst. They'd never seen the buffalo thanks to the small rise west of where they'd stopped, but they'd heard and probably smelled them. Pa said all it took sometimes was for one of those jittery animals to cut loose on a run and the rest would jump up and follow in a full stampede.

Charlie and Carl had changed into dry clothes. They were the last two to feed other than George and Mr. Warley, who were still with the remuda. And Squirrel. That man barely took time for meals on a calm evening, often taking biscuits or cornbread or even jerked meat to eat in the saddle.

Lloyd and the girls were helping Pa cut and salt as much buffalo meat as they had room to pack. If Squirrel would give them a day of rest, Pa could get more meat cured and packed away, but the trail boss said they couldn't spare the time. Everything hinged on them meeting the train in Abilene to ship the cattle east.

Making it safely and all together was what mattered to Kenna.

"Miss McCrea?"

Kenna jumped, so lost in her thoughts that she hadn't heard Mr. Warley approach.

"You're still soaking wet." Her words slipped out before she could check them, as if he were one of her brothers.

"Yes, miss. But I'm even more hungry than wet."

"Of course you are." She scrambled to fill another plate, choosing the largest piece of steak left for him. She handed it over but held on even when he gripped the plate's other side. "And thank you, for what you did."

He hadn't shaved in several days, but the growing whiskers didn't hide the flush that coursed over his cheeks. "It was nothing."

"That's not what Tyree said. He said you charged the buffalo all by yourself and turned the herd with your shooting."

Mr. Warley shrugged. "He might have embellished that a little."

She chuckled and released the plate. "You may be right. He has been known to color a tale from time to time."

He gestured toward one of the warming fires. "I'll just—"

"Those have burned down. Why don't you eat here by the cooking fire? I'm sure it's warmer and will help you dry out."

"Thank you." He stepped over to the fire and sat on a crate, plate balanced on his knees. They all ate like that, of course, but Mr. Warley looked more out-of-place doing it than the others. With his manners and bearing, he was meant to be in a dining room with a linen cloth on the table. He was too... refined for the prairie that surrounded them.

Kenna examined her callused hands. Even before the drive they had been rough and work-hardened. The leather gloves helped, but not enough. She'd grown new calluses between her fingers from handling the reins. As much as she hated to admit it, she was more suited to the prairie than the elegant dining room where she envisioned Mr. Warley.

"Do I smell buffalo steaks?"

Kenna whirled back to the workbench that extended from the back of the chuckwagon. "I'm sorry, Mr. Brinkmann. You caught me woolgathering."

He grinned at her, then glanced past her to Mr. Warley. "You're still sopping wet, Ben."

Mr. Warley lifted his plate from his lap and then set it down again. "I'll change after I eat."

"And in good company, I suppose." Mr. Brinkmann winked at her.

Kenna dished up his supper and handed it over. "I hope you enjoy it."

"I'm sure I will. Not much better than a buffalo steak." He raised the plate in a gesture toward Mr. Warley. "Thanks to Ben here, we'll eat well for a couple of weeks."

"Why don't you join him at the cookfire?" Kenna said. "It's built up."

"I'll keep an eye on things over here," he said over his shoulder, heading to the fire closest to the herd.

Now, Kenna had fed all but George. Pa, Lloyd, and the girls would eat when they finished the butchering. So she made herself a plate and pulled another crate near the fire.

"This is very good," Mr. Warley said.

He ate with those fine manners, cutting one piece at a time, and a small one at that. The other cowboys would shovel in huge bites, or even stab the meat and bite off chunks, not bothering to cut it at all.

"It'll be even better tomorrow after it's cured for a bit."

"Really?"

"Yes. Fresh meat is tougher than meat that's had time to cure."

"If you've learned that from your father, I'm sure you're right. He's the second-best cook I've ever known."

"Was your mother the first?" she asked.

"No." He chewed a last bite of his steak, then put his fork on his plate. "It was Lucy, our... cook."

Their cook? Then she'd been correct. He'd come from a family with money. Not a family that labored together daily in a diner to make ends meet.

Pa, Lloyd, and the girls approached, salted meat bundled in the buffalo hides slung across and lashed to the backs of two of Pa's mules.

"Excuse me." She carried her mostly untouched plate back to the chuckwagon's workbench. She'd feed her family and forget any ideas about Mr. Warley. Once they were off the trail, he'd return to his own kind, and she'd be serving customers in some eatery or another. But the thought left a hollow spot in her middle.

Ben sneezed, the force startling the pinto mare beneath him. He rubbed her neck. "Sorry, girl." He'd caught a cold.

They'd traveled far the past two days, pushing man and beast alike, covering a long stretch between reliable water sources. Squirrel had led them to a lake off the original trail Ben and Timothy had blazed. The cattle were drinking their fill. Ben and George had already let the remuda and mules drink. They'd get another long drink before full dark, and then again in the morning. There was a spring that fed the lake where the wagons could refill their barrels and the cowboys their canteens.

Ben wouldn't mind staying an extra day and resting up. He sneezed again, then fumbled for his handkerchief. The wind grabbed the large square of cotton fabric and whisked it away. Grumbling to himself, Ben dismounted and rescued it from a pricker bush nearby.

"Still feeling poorly, suh?" George asked.

"I've been better." He blew his nose and shoved the cloth into his pocket.

"Nights so cold, a body can't hardly get warm no more."

George had probably never been this far north. Ben's first experience with winter in the north had been at the prison camp in Illinois in October of 'sixty-four. Just three years ago.

It seemed like a decade.

Then he'd ridden guard on the supply wagons from Fort Dodge to Fort Garland, crossing a stretch of land as barren as one could imagine from western Kansas into Colorado. Riding through howling winter winds or broiling summer sun with no place to take shelter, constantly on the alert for hostile Indians, had changed Ben as even the war hadn't. It had hardened him, burying the remaining layers of the soft Southern boy he'd been.

But when Miss McCrea smiled at him, it touched that remembered softness.

Her gratitude over the buffalo incident had been sincere, he was sure of that, but her genuine smiles, the ones he'd so admired in San Antonio, still didn't shine his way. He couldn't read her like the girls back home. There were no fluttering eyelashes, no coy bowing of her head, no glances meant to be intercepted. She was a puzzle to Ben, but one he'd very much like to solve.

He sneezed again, then shivered despite the warm sunshine.

"I can handle the remuda, suh, if you needs rest and get to feeling better."

Ben was on the verge of refusing when another sneeze threatened to blow him out of his saddle. "That's not a bad idea. Thank you, George."

The big man's eyebrows rose to his hairline, eyes round and wide. "Yes, suh."

After the way Ben had treated him in the beginning, George had a right to be surprised at Ben's thanks. He was a little surprised himself. But working beside each other these last few weeks—as much as George rescuing him twice—had made him see George as a fellow human being, not someone who could be owned by another.

It wasn't quite an epiphany, but it was close. Ben ignored the imagined disappointment of his father and roped Rusty, transferred his saddle, and released the mare before he rode to where the fires were lit. He tied Rusty to the picket line.

Each rider kept a fresh horse saddled and ready for their night shift, or in case something unexpected happened. Those horses were picketed close to the fires, within easy reach. Several were already there, the cowboys on the first night watch rolled into their blankets and catching some sleep before they'd be called out to the herd.

Nobody wasted an opportunity to sleep on the cattle drive because such opportunities could be few and far between.

Ben followed their example, untied his bedroll from behind his saddle, and shook it out near the closest fire. He pulled the blanket over his shoulders and watched Miss McCrea working around the chuckwagon until the rest of the world faded away.

CHAPTER 16

"**W**E COULD MAKE ROOM in the wagon for you. It'd be no bother." Kenna passed a plate to Mr. Warley, whose eyes were as red as an angry bull's and nose almost the same shade. "A day of rest would go far to see you feeling better."

"I'll be fine." He clutched a blanket around his shoulders with one hand and took the plate with the other. "But thank you." He turned his head and rasped a cough. He left to huddle by the fire and eat.

Men could be so stubborn.

"What was that all about?" Pa wiped his hands on his dirty apron that covered his equally dirty clothing.

What Kenna wouldn't give for a day to do their washing.

"Mr. Warley is feeling poorly, but he refused the offer of riding in the wagon."

Pa studied the man from a distance. "He's a good hand with horses, but I dinna know how he'd shake out on the trail." Pa gave a firm nod. "He's done well." Then Pa went back to scraping the portable grill.

Leave it to another man to admire such stubbornness.

Kenna stirred the pot over the fire, the porridge releasing its cinnamon goodness into the air. She'd chopped dried apples into it for a special treat that morning. It was thick enough to stand on a plate next to the buffalo steaks Pa was grilling. A nice change from cornbread. She was dishing up plates for the two cowboys approaching when a scream came from the direction of the lake.

Elva.

Kenna dropped the plates on the bench and raced around the wagon toward the sound when another shriek split the air. It was followed by more shouts and an ominous rumbling, but Kenna lifted her skirts higher and ran faster.

Elva stood on a rock, hands clasped in front, mouth open with the next earsplitting cry. Vanora was running as well, coming from the far side of the rock, where she'd been filling buckets at the spring.

"What it is?" Kenna called.

"Snakes!" Elva screamed.

The rumbling grew louder, and Kenna could feel it in her chest. More buffalo? She couldn't waste time wondering.

"Stay back, Vanora!" Kenna thrust out the hand not holding her skirts. "Stand still, Elva, and be quiet. Don't arouse them."

She had no idea if the sound would inflame the snakes or not, but better to try and calm her sister.

"Stand still," she repeated. "I have to slow down and watch where I put my feet." Kenna put action to her words. "You're okay, sweetie. I'm almost there." By herself. Why hadn't Pa followed? Kenna didn't take her eyes off the dried prairie grass around her.

Then she spotted it—or them. The knotted snarl of slithery skin was too much for a single snake. They curved around the base of the rock Elva stood upon. The night had been cold, and the morning air frosted her breath. The cold-blooded things were probably half-frozen and clinging to the rock for its lingering warmth. Nothing moved as she approached. Not even a rattled tail twitched.

"Kenna!" Vanora was pointing toward the wagons.

Whatever it was, it would have to wait. Kenna held out her arms, drew in a deep breath, and moved as close to the rock as she dared. She could make out three heads and four tails in the tangle of snakes. "Elva, you'll need to jump to me. I'll catch you."

"I can't," Elva wailed.

"You'll have to. I don't dare step any closer." Kenna extended both arms and wiggled her fingers. "It's safe. Snakes can't jump." At least, she didn't think they could. But the ground was rumbling under her feet.

"Kenna!" Vanora yelled again, now racing toward her—and the snakes.

"Be careful. There are snakes."

"The cattle!" Vanora swerved around the rock near the water's edge, her buckets abandoned. Only then did the rumbling and shouting register.

Stampede.

Kenna whirled and watched, horrified, as the cattle swept around the wagons like a wave. Pa was on the seat of the chuckwagon, cracking his long whip and shouting.

"Kenna!" Elva wailed again.

Her sister's screaming had spooked the cattle. Kenna's stomach dropped as their family wagon disappeared behind the chuckwagon. But she and the girls were out of harm's way, Pa had the chuckwagon protected, and she needed to get Elva off the rock and away from the snakes.

"Move to the very edge of the rock. I need room to jump."

Elva did as ordered, her hands now firmly clasped over her mouth—even if it was too late.

Far too late.

Kenna gathered her skirts and jumped, her boots sliding on the rock until they found purchase. She waved her arms and caught her balance a split second before Elva clung to her and buried her face in Kenna's apron.

"Is it my fault?" Her little sister's words were muffled by the apron.

Kenna wrapped her sister in a hug and lifted her onto her hip, although she was too large to hold that way for long. "I don't know."

Vanora had stopped a safe distance away, her eyes wide and mouth open, watching the last of the cattle part in front of the chuckwagon and thunder off to the west, every cowboy on a horse in hot pursuit.

"Onto my back." Kenna swung her sister around. "Hold tight." She jumped as far as she could with the added weight behind her, clearing the snakes by a good two feet. She hiked Elva to a more comfortable position and kept walking.

Vanora hurried to her side. "Are we going to be in trouble?"

Were they? Pa was still on the wagon seat but no longer standing. He was sitting and watching them approach.

"Pa?" Kenna jogged closer, sensing more than knowing something was wrong. Terribly wrong. She let Elva down and shoved her toward Vanora. "You two keep back. Stay here." Then she broke into a run, the dry grass crisp beneath her boots. "Pa?"

"It's all right, lass. Dinna fret."

But it wasn't all right. One leg of Pa's britches was dark. Very dark. And wet.

"You're hurt." She started to climb onto the wagon.

"Find a strip of cloth," he said. "Anything to slow the bleeding."

Kenna pulled off the cloth she'd bound her hair with that morning as she reached the high seat.

"That'll do. Tie it here, lass, above the wound."

"What happened, Pa?"

"One of the beasts hooked me with a horn while I was climbing onto the wagon. It isna as bad as it looks."

But Pa's grimace told a different story.

Kenna had worried herself to a nub over Lloyd and Tyree. Never in her worst moment had she thought the one to get hurt would be Pa.

Ben gave Rusty his head and let the tired horse pick his way up and over the rim of the shallow canyon a dozen cattle had been hiding in. It was nearly dark, and Ben's empty stomach cramped. His breakfast had been trampled underfoot even before he'd swung onto Rusty, and there'd been nothing but riding since. Ben wiped his nose on the back of his forearm—not for the first time—and grimaced at the stiff fabric against his tender flesh.

Rusty dug his hooves into the soil and heaved them over the edge behind the docile knot of cattle. The beasts were as tired and hungry as Ben. It wouldn't take much coaxing to get them back to camp.

Or what was left of the camp.

He'd seen the McCrea wagon go down, but there was nothing for it. Nobody could have gotten in front of the mob fast enough to turn them away from the wagons. He'd also glimpsed the girls near the lake, well out of harm's way.

Thank God for that.

Gus had been on the chuckwagon wielding a long whip as if he'd been doing it all his life. Ben hoped he'd saved the chuckwagon. His belly groaned in agreement. He clicked to Rusty and swung behind the cattle, pushing them east. He'd lost track of his direction a time or two, but he knew he was west of the camp. With any luck, someone would be watching for him.

Or maybe the thirsty cattle would lead him back to the lake. Squirrel said they could smell water from a mile away. All Ben had to do was get them close.

Half an hour later, the last rays having dipped below the horizon behind him, he caught a faint shout. "Whoa, Rusty." Ben held still, searching the darkness around him. There, to his left, someone was waving a hat in the air. With a sigh of relief, Ben hazed the cattle in that direction. The man and horse trotted toward him, and when they got close enough, he recognized Lloyd.

"We'd about given up on you." The young man looked concerned even in the darkness. "Everyone else is back already. Squirrel sent a few of us out to look for you."

"Had a time finding these." Ben gestured to the cattle. "I saw them break off, and then they disappeared." He patted the roan's neck. "Truth to tell, it was Rusty here who found them in a depression I couldn't even see."

"I told you he was the best horse of that bunch."

"And you were right." Ben wiped his nose again. "Is your family's wagon a total loss?"

"The cattle pushed it over, but the wheels and axles are fine. Tyree and Leppo are working on some minor repairs, but it's drivable." Yet his voice lacked something.

"Anything else harmed?"

"Pa was gored."

"Gus?" Ben stomach dropped. "How bad?"

"Bad enough. He won't be doing much for a while. It's going to be hard on Kenna and the girls. I told him I would drive the other wagon, but Squirrel says he can't spare another man away from the cattle once we get on the trail again. Says they are too likely to spook again now that they've done it once."

George could handle the horses, leaving Ben to drive the chuck-wagon. And if Squirrel didn't like that, he could—

"But it's Elva who is taking it the hardest."

"Why?"

Lloyd rubbed a hand down his face. "She got scared by a snake—a whole nest of snakes—and screamed. Everyone thinks that's what spooked the cattle."

"And caused your pa to get hurt."

"Yup."

The poor girl. As if life on the trail wasn't hard enough already.

"But at least we'll have a couple of days to rest and recuperate," Lloyd said. "According to Squirrel, the beeves ran off at least twenty pounds each. He wants them to rest, eat, and drink before we move on.

Ben sneezed and wiped his nose again. Maybe he could wash out his shirt. And two days of rest sounded good to him, too.

Pa was stretched out on his bunk in the chuckwagon, having succumbed to the combination of blood loss and whiskey. Pa didn't hold with drinking due to his strict Presbyterian upbringing, but Kenna had convinced him that his wound had to be stitched closed, and he needed the alcohol to dull the pain.

She'd been terrified of having to do the stitching herself, but George had offered. Since he claimed to have done it many times in the past—and she never had—she'd willingly accepted. She'd sterilized the needle and thread in more whiskey, then handed them to George.

For such a large man, he had a gentle way about him. Pa had groaned a few times, but they'd made it through. George had left to check on the remuda. Although they hadn't galloped far and had returned with him easily enough, some of the horses were still restless.

Kenna had cleaned up the mess and removed her bloodstained apron. She needed to see to her sisters.

Vanora sat near the scattered remains of the cooking fire, Elva in her arms. The sight pinched something inside Kenna. She'd been the same age and had done the same thing, holding and comforting her brothers and sisters, after Ma's passing. Seeing Vanora in that pose was like looking back in time.

Vanora whispered something against the top of Elva's head, and the younger girl glanced up. Spotting Kenna, she scrambled to her feet and ran to her, burying her blotchy face against the front of Kenna's dress. "I'm sorry. I'm so sorry." Sobs wracked the girl's slight form.

"Shh... it's all right, sweetie." Kenna rocked her sister gently from side to side.

Vanora's face was almost as blotchy. Kenna extended one arm, and Vanora stepped into the hug and sniffled against the side of her neck. "It wasn't anyone's fault."

"But I"—Elva hiccupped—"I screamed and scared the cows."

Vanora sniffled again. "And I didn't keep her with me."

"Well." Kenna gave their shoulders a little shake. "I'm the one who sent you for more water."

"But"—Vanora raised her eyes—"it's our job to fetch the water."

"It's not my job to scream at snakes," Elva wailed.

"You can't help being afraid." Kenna released Vanora and stooped to Elva's level. "And you wouldn't have screamed if Tyree hadn't chased you with them so many times. But it's not really Tyree's fault either. Sometimes things just... happen."

"Then you're not angry with me?"

Kenna's heart twisted. "No. I can't be angry with you. You never meant for the cattle to run. They just did."

"Is Pa angry with me?"

"Of course he's not. In fact"—she pulled Vanora closer again—"he told me how relieved he was that we three were near the water when the cattle stampeded. It eased his mind to know we were all out of harm's way."

"You're not just saying that, are you?" Vanora asked.

Kenna smiled, trying her best to bring some normalcy back to the day. "I'm not. He said exactly that."

"Can we see Pa now?" Elva asked.

"Not yet. He's sleeping, and that's what he needs."

Vanora looked at the scattered fire, then back to Kenna. "Who is going to cook for the men?"

Who indeed? Once again Kenna was transported back through the years when she'd taken on the responsibilities of her mother. When she'd promised the dying woman that she'd see to the care of her brothers and sisters. This time, however, she'd have to step into Pa's place.

"I will." She straightened. "And I best get started. Vanora, I'm going to need those buckets of water. Elva, see if you can find the scattered plates and forks. Then wash whatever you recover." The men provided their own cups and knives, but they'd need to gather enough of the other things to at least feed a few men at a time.

The largest pot was on its side under the chuckwagon's sling. Kenna fished it out. One side was dented, but it wasn't broken. The grill, on the other hand, was bent beyond recognition. They'd be eating stewed or pan-fried meat for the time being.

Kenna scrubbed the pot and added water, then swung it over the fire she'd started with the dried cow dung. She didn't even notice the smell anymore. It was simply how things were. She was cutting salted buffalo meat into chunks and sliding them into the pot when a group of cattle appeared out of the darkness.

She spied Lloyd first and then Mr. Warley. Odd that she could pick out his silhouette almost as quickly as those of her brothers. He had a more formal way of sitting in the saddle that looked at odds with the mustang beneath him. But of course he did. He probably grew up riding expensive thoroughbreds with those fancy small saddles, not a cowpony with a working rig.

Best she remembered he came from a different class of people. A privileged class. The kind who hired people like her to do the things they didn't want to do for themselves.

Like cook. She dropped another handful of meat into the simmering water.

Mr. Brinkmann approached the fire, his steps slow. When was the last time the man had slept? He pulled his hat off and fiddled with it between his hands.

"Miss McCrea, I'm sorry about your pa."

She wiped her hands on her only clean apron. "It was an accident. I know my sister is—"

He held out a hand to silence her. "It wasn't Miss Elva's fault. Charlie spotted a trio of coyotes stalking the back side of the herd just before he heard her scream. He said they'd dodged toward the steers and stirred them up." He shrugged. "The cattle were still spooky from the buffalo, so it didn't take much to set them off."

Kenna pressed the back of her wrist against her forehead for a moment and let out a long breath. "I'd appreciate it if you would explain that to Elva."

"I'd be happy to." He took a step back. "We'll stay here for three days to let the cattle graze, rest, and drink. That should give Gus enough time to be able to handle the wagon again, because I'm sorry, but I can't pull a man from the herd until I'm sure it will trail peacefully again."

"I understa—"

"I'll drive the wagon." Mr. Warley stepped out of the shadows. "George can handle the remuda. It's well trail-broke, and it didn't spook much."

Mr. Brinkmann's brow furrowed in the flickering light of the fire, but he nodded. "If you're sure. Those horses are your responsibility."

"I'm sure."

The trail boss replaced his hat and strode toward Kenna's sisters, who were returning from the lake with their second load of water.

Kenna turned to Mr. Warley. "Thank you."

"It's the least I can do."

"The stampede wasn't your fault."

"No, but you and your family being here is." The firelight cast his features in bold relief, highlighting the concern in his eyes.

"I expect we'd have been here no matter who Mr. McCoy had sent to San Antonio." She realized the truth of her words even as she spoke them. She'd blamed this man for doing what he'd been hired to do, and if it hadn't been him, it would have been someone else. Her brothers were happy working the drive. Pa had been happy to leave the diner behind and strike out again. All Mr. Warley had done was offer the opportunity.

It was the men in her family who'd chosen their course.

And as always, Kenna was left to pick up the pieces. She couldn't waste time thinking about how it happened. It had, and that's what she had to deal with.

"Let's pray Pa is well enough to drive when we leave."

"If he can't, I will." He looked around the half-restored camp. "Until then, what can I do to help?"

She'd just classified him as among the privileged, yet here he was, offering to help. She lifted her hands, then let them drop. "Can you cook?"

"Not a lick."

"Can you haul water and fill the barrels? We lost all the water on our wagon, and the chuckwagon's barrels need to be refilled too." She pointed to her sisters, once again heading her way after speaking with

Mr. Brinkmann. "My sisters can help me with the meal if you can do that."

"I'd be happy to, miss." He tipped his hat and met the girls, taking the buckets from them and shooing them toward Kenna.

Well, he might be willing to pitch in after a disaster on the trail, but that wouldn't put them on equal footing once they reached Abilene. She needed to remember that.

CHAPTER 17

ONE OF THE McCREA wagon's barrels was cracked. Ben had turned it so the crack was at the top, but it wouldn't hold a full load. And if its metal band came loose... They couldn't afford to lose a water barrel.

Ben scratched his head, then glanced at the cowboys riding their horses at a walk around the herd. The cattle had settled for the night, likely too exhausted to run again if the devil himself arose in their midst.

With everything quieted down, perhaps Squirrel would loan Leppo to Ben to patch the barrel. Ben didn't like the man, didn't trust him, but he'd shown his skill in shoeing the horse and repairing the wagon. Maybe he could turn his hand at patching the barrel. He and George seemed the handiest at things like that, but George was needed with the horses.

It was worth asking.

Ben mounted the liver chestnut colt he'd saddled after turning Rusty loose. The chestnut was young and more than a little green. Ben had chosen him because of his size, being one of the tallest horses in the remuda. And probably the flightiest. He crow-hopped a few steps after Ben hit the saddle, ears pinned and neck arched.

"Easy, fella. We don't need you stirring up the cattle again." Ben got the horse under control, then headed for the herd. Squirrel was easy to spot. Ben halted next to him.

"A little chilly this evening," Squirrel said.

"It is." Ben jerked his chin toward the wagons. "One of the water barrels is cracked. I wonder if I could borrow Leppo to look at it. He seems handy at fixing things."

"He is." Squirrel gave him a long look. "But not the easiest to work with."

"I don't need to be friends with him, I just need him to patch the barrel if it can be done."

Squirrel rubbed his jaw, then paused to yawn. "We'll need every drop we can haul. We're about to enter another dry length of trail." He nodded to the right. "He's over there on the gray."

Ben clicked to the chestnut and approached Leppo. "Water barrel on the McCrea wagon is cracked and needs mending. Squirrel says for you to take a look at it." They both knew Ben had no right to order the man around, but Squirrel did.

With a glance Ben couldn't interpret, Leppo headed for the wagon. He dismounted, lifted the lantern Ben had left, and examined the barrel.

"Does Gus have the buffalo hides?" Leppo asked, not looking at Ben.

"I assume so. The meat was salted in them."

"I need one."

Ben bristled at the curt tone and lack of explanation, but he headed for the other wagon. Miss McCrea was climbing from the back.

"How's Gus?"

"Awake enough to drink a little broth, at least."

"That's good." Ben pointed to where Leppo waited. "Leppo needs one of the buffalo hides."

"Whatever for?"

"To fix the broken water barrel."

"With a buffalo hide?" She was clearly as perplexed as Ben.

"That's what he said."

"We emptied one of its salted meat." She reached under the wagon and pulled a hide from the sling. "It's too smelly to keep it in the wagon, so we stored it under here."

"Thank you." He took the stinky hide to Leppo.

"Take it to the lake and get it soaking wet. If you do not get it wet enough, you'll have to take it back again."

Ben held out the hide. "Do it yourself if you're worried I can't do it right."

"Can you shape wood"—Leppo held up a pair of sticks he'd gotten somewhere—"to fill the cracks?"

Probably. But probably not as well as Leppo. Ben spun and stalked to the lake, ignoring Leppo's humorless chuckle. He didn't like the man. Not one bit.

It wasn't quite cold enough to see his breath, but it must have been close as Ben arrived at the lake. He plunged the half-stiffened hide under the water, soaking his sleeves in the process. Might as well clean them off too. He sniffed in the brisk air. At least his nose had stopped running.

The hide resisted Ben's efforts at submerging it. He searched out a few large rocks and finally got it anchored to the lake bottom as someone approached on a horse.

George. He was the only man on the drive large enough to create that silhouette in the moonlight.

"What you doing, suh?"

"Soaking a buffalo hide."

"Why you want to do that?"

Why indeed? "Leppo says he needs it to fix the cracked water barrel."

George nodded, his face fully shadowed under his hat brim. "I reckon that would work."

Ben spread his arms. "How?"

George chuckled, but unlike Leppo's, George's lifted Ben's mood. "You gets it wet and soft and strap it tight to the barrel. As it dries, it shrinks and hardens." George nodded. "It'll mend a cracked barrel for sure."

Ben ground his boot heels in the dirt in frustration. "Leppo could have said as much."

"He ain't much for talking to white folks." George's voice went soft as he dismounted.

"But you do."

"It be different for me. Always was."

"You offer to help. You help Miss McCrea with the mules, you all but pulled me out of the river, and talk is that you're the one who stitched Gus's leg closed."

"Uh-hum." George shrugged. "I likes to be useful."

"Maybe you could teach Leppo."

"Lord knows I been praying for that man. Been praying for him for years."

It obviously hadn't done any good, but Ben didn't voice his thoughts.

George cocked his head and looked at Ben, not just a quick look and down as he so often did, but studied him for a moment. "You know how I learned to stitch folks up like I done for Mr. Gus?"

"No."

"Leppo."

"He taught you?"

"In a manner of speaking. Leppo be one of the most valuable slaves Massuh owned because he knows how to do a little bit of everything. But he be the most stubborn too. And proud."

Ben could well imagine that.

"Massuh don't like no stubborn slaves, and he shore don't like a proud one. He thought to beat it out of him." George shook his head. "But not Leppo. So Massuh, he try harder. I learned to stitch sewing Leppo's back shut after them lashings. So many times I done lost count."

Ben's stomach lurched. Not that he hadn't heard about slaves getting whipped. He'd grown up around men who talked of such things, but his father had never...

Or had he?

Memories flashed through his mind almost too fast to follow. He'd been a little boy still in short pants when Crooked Jim died. He was called Crooked Jim because of a bad leg. Ben had overheard someone once say he'd had a tendon cut during a beating so he'd never be able to run away again.

Had Ben's father done that?

"Suh?"

The word jerked Ben back to the present. "Yes?"

"I say that hide ought to be wet enough to use now. You want me to take it to Leppo?"

That would be the easy way out of dealing with the man, but Ben intended to finish what he'd started. "I'll do it. You best return to the remuda. I'll spell you once the barrel is mended."

George mounted and rode away while Ben wrestled the soaked hide from the lake. It had doubled in weight—or more. Ben's shirt and the front of his britches were dripping wet by the time he made it to the wagon.

But he stayed and watched as Leppo stripped the extra fat and membranes from inside the hide and then did exactly as George had described. It was an ingenious fix. Made from a simple buffalo hide. And while Leppo might have done the mending...

It was Ben's bullet that had provided the hide.

"Are you certain, Pa?" Kenna squinted into the rising sun, looking up at Pa on the chuckwagon's seat. "Your leg—"

"It'll be grand, lass, you'll see."

She saw all right. She saw the tightness around his eyes, the lines marring his forehead, and the grayness of his skin. And she'd bet cash money his hands weren't steady under his gloves. But the pig-headed, stubborn man wouldn't listen to her.

Lloyd had tried to talk Pa into staying on his bunk in the wagon too.

A perverse part of Kenna was glad Lloyd hadn't succeeded where she'd failed, but at the same time, she wanted to smack herself for the thought. Sibling rivalry had no place on a cattle drive.

And besides, Kenna was getting the last word.

"Vanora?" she called.

Her sister came at a trot, and Kenna boosted her onto the chuckwagon.

"What do you think you're about, lassie?" Pa asked.

"She's riding with you." Kenna crossed her arms. "And that's final."

Pa stared down at her, his beard bristling from pursing his lips, but in the end, he nodded. "Aye, lass. It could be for the best."

"I can learn to drive, Pa." Vanora said as Kenna headed to her own wagon.

She'd love to have overheard Pa's response, but the remuda was already on the move, and the wagons needed to start rolling. She climbed onto the seat as if she'd been doing it all her life, unwound the reins from the handle, and disengaged the brake. When the chuckwagon lurched into motion in front of her, she clicked to the lead mules,

Jack and Hobbs. They leaned into their harnesses without her needing to flick the reins.

Every animal on the drive had learned its job over the past five and a half weeks, and they'd all enjoyed the break of the past three days, so hearts and feet were fresh for the next leg of the journey.

A dry leg.

Squirrel had been impressed with Leppo's repair of the water barrel. It was the oddest-looking thing, the long buffalo hair waving in the wind, and it didn't smell the best, but it held every drop of water they'd dumped into it last evening. And if the smell tainted the water any, they could still use it for washing.

For that, she could and did thank Leppo. Not that he'd responded with anything other than one of his disturbing stares. He'd stopped riding close to the wagons early on in the drive, and she supposed Squirrel had seen to that. Or maybe George. The two former slaves seemed to be friends. Whoever had done it, she was thankful. Even if Leppo was handy, she preferred he keep his distance.

Unlike George, who'd made sure Pa's mules—as well as hers—were watered, groomed, and hitched that morning while Kenna had been busy cooking, feeding the men, and packing the wagons. It seemed every time she turned around, he was doing something nice for her.

So was Mr. Warley. But thinking about him set off warnings Kenna couldn't ignore.

Elva walked beside the wagon. "Kenna, what if I can't gather enough chips for all three fires?"

"Just do your best. If the men have to use the cook fire for warmth, then that's what we'll do."

"I will. I won't let you and Pa down." Her littlest sister—just ten years old—sounded so grown up.

It brought a lump to Kenna's throat. She coughed as if the dust were bothering her. "I know you won't."

Then Kenna stifled a groan. In all the hubbub of the stampede and Pa's injury and having to feed the men by herself, she'd almost missed Vanora's birthday. Kenna tried to remember the date on Pa's calendar. The twenty-first? Or maybe the twenty-second? Vanora's birthday was the twenty-fifth. How was Kenna supposed to do anything special for her sister in the middle of a cattle drive?

At the very least, she could bake a cake of some sort. No. More than one cake. The men would enjoy it as well. There were plenty of supplies in her trunk to sew a new bonnet in the evenings. One that would reflect her sister's maturity.

It pleased her to have worked it out, but ahead of her was a long day of dust and wind and backbreaking work once they stopped. She'd never understand why her brothers or Pa thought this a grand life. It was hours and hours of staggering boredom broken by heart-thumping danger, all of it layered in hard work and dirt. Already the clothes she'd laundered so carefully at the lake were stiffening with a layer of dust.

She sneezed.

Ahead of her, Mr. Warley turned in his saddle and stared until she nodded. He was always watching out for her, just like he'd promised. But did he ever see her as more than someone he needed to protect?

Did he ever see her as a woman?

With an unladylike snort, she pulled her thoughts back to what mattered—getting her family to Abilene in one piece. She hoped the cattle and horses all made it too, but it was her family who mattered. Once they arrived...

She had no idea what would happen then and no time to worry over it. Each day had sufficient worries of its own. She didn't need to think ahead and fret about what might—or might not—happen next.

Drive the wagon, feed the men, prepare for Vanora's birthday, and make sure Pa didn't overdo so he'd heal properly. Those were enough things to occupy Kenna.

But she flicked one more glance at Mr. Warley and allowed herself a moment to admire his profile, his breath misting against the backdrop of the flatlands surrounding them.

He was a handsome man in an understated sort of way.

A man from a background way above hers, even coated with the same grime that covered them all, even working just as hard as everyone else on the drive, and even if he sometimes looked at her in a way that made her mouth go dry. He was still a Galvanized Yankee.

He wasn't to be trusted.

She needed to keep telling herself that.

Even if she didn't believe it anymore.

CHAPTER 18

T HE HORSES' GAUNT BODIES, even more than their restiveness, showed their need for water. Ben was glad Squirrel had rationed some of the barrel water the evening before. Each horse had been given a couple of cups. Not enough to satisfy their need, but enough to keep them going.

There was nothing to be done for the cattle. The barrels were half empty already. At least the weather had stayed cool. If it'd been the full heat of summer, they'd be in a worse situation, especially since a watering hole Squirrel had counted on had dried up since he'd last been through. The trail boss had scouted ahead more than an hour ago, looking for another.

Movement on the horizon caught Ben's eye, too much for one man on a horse. If only he could see better into the distance.

"Suh?"

George's voice reached him, but Ben didn't take his eyes off the approaching dust cloud.

"What do you see, George?"

"Indians approaching on spotted horses, suh."

Alarm raised the hairs on the back of Ben's neck. "Stop the horses. I'll alert the wagons."

Ben wheeled the pinto mare around and raced for the chuckwagon.

"I see them." Gus had his mules already at a trot. "I'll drive inside the remuda."

"I'll tell Miss McCrea to pull up beside you, as close as she can."

Gus nodded.

Miss Elva was on the far side of the McCrea wagon, searching for dried cow dung.

"Come, Miss Elva." Ben held his hand down for her. "Drop those."

"But we need—"

"Hurry." It was all he said, but it was enough. She grabbed his hand, and he whisked her to the back of the wagon and all but tossed her over the tailgate. "Stay out of sight, you hear?"

"Yes, Mr. Warley."

"Good girl." He rode along the wagon next to Miss McCrea.

"I see them. Thanks for collecting Elva."

So like her pa. The same grim voice and determined spirit. How he wished she were back in San Antonio. "Gus will stop the chuckwagon in the middle of the remuda. Pull up as close as you can. George and I will move the horses around you for added protection."

Squirrel had devised the plan for when—not if—they'd need it. According to him, every herd traveling north had been approached by Indians at some point. They wanted whiskey, guns, and bullets, but most could be bought off with a few head of cattle to feed their families.

Ben wished the trail boss was there—and hoped he was right.

Both wagons stopped, and Ben helped George move the horses to surround them. It wasn't much protection, but something was better than nothing. Gus and Miss McCrea had rifles stowed at their feet and orders to keep them out of sight unless needed.

Ben fervently hoped they wouldn't be needed.

The bawling cattle grew louder as they closed the gap with the stopped wagons and horses. Charlie was the acting trail boss in Squirrel's absence, and he galloped toward Ben, bringing his horse to a sliding stop.

"Like old times, ain't it?" Charlie kept his eyes on the Indians.

"We've faced them together before." But that was with an entire cavalry unit, not a handful of cowboys, wagons full of women, and two thousand head of thirsty cattle.

"Squirrel said to offer them two beasts and to cut out the weakest of the herd. If they press, we'll offer them four." Charlie twisted to look at the herd, then back to watch the Indians' approach. "But between you and me, we got at least half a dozen that won't make another day if Squirrel doesn't find water."

"Stick to the plan." Ben glanced at Charlie. "You know some of their sign language. That can't hurt."

Charlie shrugged. "If they use the same as those northwest of here."

The Indians had slowed until the dust settled enough to count ten men in the group. Were they being cautious? Or were they dissembling before an attack?

The skin on the back of Ben's neck itched.

The two front riders cantered forward, the rest of the group hanging back.

This was it.

Charlie rode out to meet them, and Ben spurred his mare to keep pace. They stopped a short distance from the remuda and waited.

The Indians halted their ponies, and there followed a few tense moments of sizing each other up. The Indians held long lances, but no rifles or pistols in sight. Both wore leather hunting pants with long knives strapped to their belts. Neither wore a shirt despite the chill in the air.

The shorter Indian raised his hand and garbled out some kind of words. The taller one, who looked much younger, then spoke, "You cross our land, you pay."

Oh good, one spoke English.

"What's your price?" Charlie asked.

The younger splayed his hand. "Five rifles, five whiskey, five horses, five cows."

Charlie snorted and shook his head. "Two cows. Our choice." He made some sort of sign language move. "No more."

The older Indian's eyes narrowed.

Ben's stomach tightened. Did the older man speak English or understand Charlie's signs?

"Our women and children hungry," the younger said.

"Rifles and whiskey won't feed your women and children." Charlie held up three fingers. "Three cows."

The younger pointed to the group waiting. One horse separated from the group. It carried two riders halfway to where their negotiations were taking place. "We need horse and five cows."

Ben urged the mare forward a step. "You tell us where to find water, and we'll give you one horse—of my choice—and four cows."

Charlie stiffened beside him. Nowhere in the plan was there a negotiation of horses.

The two Indians exchanged glances. The older one shook his head. So he did understand English.

"One horse, five cows for water," the younger said.

Ben wanted to agree, but he'd butted in once already, and Charlie had the authority. Charlie let the moment draw out. He'd had a lot more dealings with Indians than Ben had, so Ben followed his lead and relaxed in his saddle. The cattle were almost on their heels before Charlie nodded.

"One horse and five cows. Where is the water?"

The younger one waved, and the horse carrying double came forward. Both riders were barely more than boys. More words garbled back and forth before the speaker turned back to them.

"Give horse to Painted Tree. He take to water."

Ben hollered back to George. "Bring up Squirrel's bay with the stockings." The horse had a quarter crack on one back hoof that Ben had discovered that morning. Not enough to make him lame, but he wasn't fit for hard riding, or wouldn't be before they reached Abilene.

Charlie cocked an eyebrow at him, then twisted in his saddle and called out for five steers. He wouldn't have to tell them to pick the weaker beasts. Everyone knew the plan.

Squirrel had prepared them for everything except his absence.

One of the young Indians slid off the pony and slipped a bridle on the bay George brought forward. Then he vaulted on the horse bareback, raised his lance, and warbled some sort of shout.

Too loudly.

The thirsty cattle broke into a run.

Kenna had no idea what tribe they might be. So many had been pushed together by the government on too little land. Barren, dry land for the most part. Land they were crossing with their cattle. These Indians were short and stocky, bare to the waist, long hair braided and tied with leather at the ends.

And the cattle drive was trespassing across their land.

Elva rustled behind her.

"Stay out of sight."

"I'm afraid."

Kenna couldn't turn around. It might alert the Indians to her sister's presence. "Me too. But the men know what to do. They'll keep us safe." Mr. Warley had promised he'd stay close and protect them.

But those were Indians.

Sweat broke across Kenna's brow despite the wind's chilly breath.

The men spoke a little, then watched each other across no more than a wagon's length. Why did they have to be so close to those wicked-looking lances?

Perversely, she wished she were close enough to hear their words.

Then George looped a rope over one of the horses and led it to where the others waited. They were giving up a horse? Mr. Brinkmann would not be pleased. How many times had she heard him lecture a tired cowboy about caring for his mount before himself? About how the drive would succeed or fail on the backs of the remuda?

The lead cattle were even with the men when one of the Indians shouted.

Then the thundering of hooves shook the ground and wagon.

"What is it, Kenna?" Elva wailed.

"Stampede!" The shout from numerous throats almost drowned out Elva's cry.

The remuda milled around her mules, heads high, nostrils flared. George caught the lead mare with a loop of his lariat and turned her to circle around the wagons. Pa's "Whoa!" beside her broke through the noise and swirling dust.

"Whoa!" Kenna tightened the reins of her mules. Jack and Hobbs were tossing their heads but held their position. It was Tanny causing trouble. The right-hand swing mule was the skittish one of the bunch, which is why he was paired with Cigar, the most placid. But even Cigar's nip of correction didn't help. Tanny started side-kicking at the milling horses who got too close.

"Bring his head around," Pa shouted.

Kenna did her best, but the panicking mule kicked Manny, the red wheel mule behind him. Manny then kicked the wagon, hooves connecting with the wood like a gunshot, and the lead mules bolted.

"Hang on, lass!" Pa shouted.

Kenna couldn't do much else. The remuda parted as the mules surged forward. Kenna planted both feet on the kickboard and hauled back on the reins for all she was worth. But it wasn't enough.

The wagon hit a rut, and her backside lifted clear off the seat. She reconnected with a thump. She didn't dare let go of the reins to try and set the brake.

Cattle flowed to their left like a menacing dark horde. Cowboys raced alongside, trying to turn the herd.

Her mules charged blindly, bouncing over ruts and stones, almost unseating Kenna more than once.

"Kenna!" Elva screamed.

"Don't scream." Kenna kept her voice as steady as possible. "The animals are panicked enough already."

"So am I." Her sister's voice was lower but no less frightened.

Then a cowboy on a silver-gray horse broke from the herd and caught up to her lead mules. He got close enough to Jack to grab his harness. And then—in an amazing leap—the man was on Jack's back and hauling the frightened mule to a stop. The cowboy turned and glanced at her.

Leppo.

Kenna's ragged breathing robbed her of speech, but she nodded her thanks even though he'd already turned away, and then set the brake.

Somehow, Leppo had kept hold of his horse's rein through it all. He leaped back into the saddle and took off for the herd once again, several loose horses from the remuda running beside him.

Elva's arms came around Kenna and held fast. Kenna needed the comfort as much as her sister. She kept a firm grip on the reins as Pa pulled the other wagon alongside.

"Ye all right, lassie?" His words were laced with equal parts fear and pain.

She glanced at his leg, a dark stain marking his injury.

"We're fine, but you're bleeding again."

Vanora climbed over the back of the seat waving a handful of cloth. "I have bandages."

"Good thinking, Vanora," Kenna said. "Stop the bleeding. We'll have to check his stitches when we can."

"Dinna worry." Pa wiped his brow with the back of one glove. "Just took a bit of a jolt."

"I thought the chuckwagon was going to flip," Vanora said.

"What do we do now, Pa?"

"The herd is almost past, so we wait and see where they stop. Someone will come back for us."

George rode up on the opposite side of Pa. "Everyone all right, suh?"

"Aye."

"Glad you got your team stopped, miss."

"It wasn't me, it was Leppo."

George cast a glance at the disappearing herd and scratched his unshaven jaw. "Well, ain't that something."

"He jumped from his horse onto Jack and stopped the mules," she explained. "Then he jumped back onto his horse and took off after the herd."

"Ain't nobody better with horses than that Leppo."

"Better than you, George?" Vanora asked.

"Yes, missy. He is." George touched his hat and reined his horse around. "I best be rounding up the scattered remuda." He touched his heels to his horse and cantered off.

By himself? Where was Mr. Warley? The last time Kenna had seen him—

He'd been right in the path of the stampede.

The pinto mare was beginning to falter beneath Ben, white lather covering her neck and shoulders. He'd been riding her since sunup and had intended to change mounts about the time the Indians appeared. If he didn't pull her up soon, he risked her getting injured—or worse. But the herd wasn't turning, and it wasn't slowing. It had veered to the northwest shortly after taking flight, and nothing or nobody was going to stop it. Like the pinto, the cattle were in danger of running themselves into the ground.

They could lose half the herd.

"Water!" came a shout from ahead. "Water!"

The cowboys riding point cheered.

Ben eased the mare up, letting the cattle rush past her. Water would stop them now.

Squirrel rode a barely lathered buckskin alongside of Ben, letting the animal slow to a walk.

"I didn't know you'd returned," Ben said.

"I didn't. You brought the herd to me."

"Not intentionally, I assure you."

"Charlie gave me the gist of it. I'm guessing along with the Indian shouting, the beasts had caught the scent of water."

"We did our best to turn them, but they were having none of it."

Squirrel nodded. "As thirsty as they are, you didn't have a chance."

"I fear we lost a few to exhaustion. I saw two drop out of the herd and hit the ground."

"We did. But the Indians will pick them up." Squirrel leaned over and spit. "What's this I heard about you giving my horse away?"

"It was in exchange for them leading us to water." Ben pointed to the long swampy area ahead of them. "Which it turns out we didn't need."

"Why *my* horse?"

"I found a quarter crack on his near hind hoof this morning. He wouldn't have been fit to work before we reach Abilene."

Squirrel grunted.

"The Indian boy who got him couldn't have weighed a hundred pounds, and with no saddle—"

"He won't hurt the horse by riding it."

"That was my thought."

Squirrel loosened his rope and looked behind them. "Good decision. Now we need fresh horses. We're going to have to pull cattle out of the water."

"Boggy?"

"Yup, but not quicksand. They'll be fine until we can haul them out. How far behind is the remuda?"

"I'm not sure. I was in negotiations with the Indians when everything broke loose. George will have them following, I'm sure." He shot Squirrel a glance. "He's a good man."

"Glad you've come to appreciate him."

There wasn't an answer to that.

"Ride back and find the remuda. Bring them here as fast as you can." Squirrel reined the buckskin toward where the cattle were already wading into the boggy water.

Ben urged the pinto into an easy trot, wishing he could push her faster. George had stayed with the wagons and remuda, but Ben would feel better once he saw the wagons and knew Miss McCrea and her family were safe.

CHAPTER 19

P A HADN'T TORN ANY stitches, but the bleeding worried Kenna. She'd put her foot down and—surprising and worrisome in equal parts—Pa had agreed to stay on the chuckwagon's bunk with his leg elevated. Which left her and the girls to feed the crew again.

Vanora had a pot of buffalo and beans cooking over the fire while Elva was setting out the plates and spoons. Kenna angled her body to shield her activities from Vanora. Sugar was precious on a cattle drive, but it was Vanora's birthday, after all. They were running low on wheat flour, so Kenna mixed a couple of handfuls of cornmeal in with the sugar, lard, and baking powder. It would be better with an egg, but that was something they didn't have. And no icing sugar either, but Pa had stashed away some cinnamon she sprinkled on top with a little more sugar. She had enough to pour two cakes, enough for everyone to get a slice. She assembled the Dutch ovens and then carried them to the fire, sprinkling hot coals around the bases and on top of the lids.

"Cornbread will be good with dinner." Vanora glanced at the chuckwagon and then leaned closer to Kenna. "Don't tell Pa, but I think yours are better than his."

Kenna pressed a finger to her lips, glad her surprise had gone undetected, then returned to their family wagon for Vanora's gift. Best to give it to her before the men came to eat.

Elva appeared at Kenna's elbow. "Is it time?"

"It is, and you've been a dear to keep the secret."

Her youngest sister bounced on her toes, hands clasped. "May I give it to her?"

Kenna handed over the bonnet. "Of course you may, but mind you keep it hidden behind you until we say happy birthday."

"I will."

Pa was laid up and the boys were working, pulling cattle from the muck, but the girls would celebrate quietly anyway.

"Vanora." Elva sashayed to the fire, bonnet gripped behind her skirt.

"Hmm?"

Elva stopped beside Vanora, and Kenna stopped behind her.

"Have you forgotten what day it is?" Kenna asked.

Vanora looked up, face somber. "I know, but I don't expect a fuss during a cattle drive." So young and yet so mature.

"We have something for you," Elva blurted out.

That brought a sparkle to Vanora's eyes.

"Happy birthday," Kenna and Elva said together, and then Elva pulled the bonnet from behind her.

Vanora let go of the spoon and took the bonnet, a vivid green that would look fetching against her dark hair while it kept the sun from her face. It was stylish but still practical. Kenna had trimmed the brim with a strip. of tatted black lace she'd been saving and added dark green ribbons for the tie with an extra bit for a bow at the back above a ruffle to keep the sun and dust from the back of Vanora's neck.

"Oh, it's beautiful." She turned it around, admiring every angle.

Elva hopped like a jackrabbit. "Put it on."

"It's much too pretty to cook in and—"

"Wear it and enjoy it." Kenna held out her hand for the old poke bonnet.

Vanora wasted no time untying and removing the frayed and dust-coated thing.

"Let me tidy your hair." Kenna tucked the old bonnet in her apron and stepped behind her sister. She fluffed the dark locks, securing them with pins, then settled the bonnet on top. She turned Vanora around. "You look lovely." Perhaps too lovely for her thirteen years. Too mature.

Vanora threw her arms around Kenna and squeezed, then giggled. Maybe not too mature after all.

"We best finish the meal. The men must be starving." There'd been no noon break, nothing to fill the bellies of those working since sunup. "Looks like they're bringing the last of the cows across now." They'd found a spot with enough stable bottom to drive the wagons over. Mr. Brinkmann had insisted they push the cattle across before resting for the night.

Carl was the first cowboy to arrive for supper. He took one long look at Vanora, flushed to the roots of his blond hair, and held out his cup for coffee. Elva dipped the drink out. She wasn't strong enough to lift and pour from the huge pot. Then Vanora dished up a plate of buffalo and beans.

"When you bring your plate back, there's cake," Kenna said.

"Cake?" His voice cracked on the word.

Kenna hid the smile that tugged at her lips. Perhaps Vanora wasn't the only one still a child beneath it all. "It's Vanora's birthday."

He wished her a shy happy birthday and then moved on so they could serve the two others who'd come in with him.

"You baked a cake?" Vanora said when they were alone.

"Of course I did." Kenna put her arm around Vanora's shoulders and gave a quick squeeze. "It's your birthday."

Vanora's eyes grew shiny.

"Fix another plate and I'll take it to Pa," Kenna said. "Coffee too, Elva."

Back at the diner, she'd never have left her sisters alone with a bunch of cowboys. They weren't at the diner anymore, though, and among the cowboys were her brothers, Mr. Warley, Mr. Brinkmann, and George to watch over the girls.

Maybe Leppo would too. She didn't know what to think of him, but if he hadn't saved hers and Elva's lives today, he'd at least saved their wagon and probably some of the mules.

With her hands full, Kenna entered the chuckwagon. Pa was still stretched out with his leg on a roll of blankets. He started to move when she climbed in.

"Let's just turn you on your side and keep your leg up. You should be able to eat that way." Kenna pulled a crate near the bunk to set the plate and cup where Pa could reach it.

"I can sit and—"

"And start your leg bleeding again?"

Pa grumped and huffed but with her help got rolled to his side with his leg supported.

"Elva and I gave Vanora her birthday gift. She was pleased."

Pa sighed. "I dinna give it a thought since..." He glanced at his leg with a dark scowl.

"She understands that a birthday on a cattle drive can't be the same as it was at the diner."

He looked at her, brows drawing together. "Do you miss it? The diner?"

"I do." Kenna sighed and sat on the floor while Pa spooned up his dinner. "I suppose I always will. We watched the lads and lassies grow up there."

"Aye, that we did." Pa stared into his coffee for a moment before taking a sip. "We did grand there."

Kenna couldn't keep from asking, "Then why did we leave?"

Pa pushed his half-eaten plate away, but Kenna pushed it back toward him. He needed to eat to heal. He frowned at her, then took another bite, chewing it slowly.

"I wanted to be out from under a roof, away from walls, to have the freedom of the open range." He pushed the plate away again. "Selfish of me, I know. It was too much to watch the lads ride out and feel left behind again."

She inched the plate back toward him. "Finish it, and I'll bring you a slice of birthday cake."

That earned her a halfhearted smile.

"What will we do when we reach Abilene, Pa?"

Pa cleaned his plate and took another sip of coffee before answering. "Start over, I suppose, maybe another diner."

"Will you be happy with that?"

Pa glanced at his leg, then gestured at the cramped confines of the chuckwagon. "Happier than I am with this."

A whoop came from outside, and Kenna caught the word *cake* in the excitement.

"It's a good thing we're a ways from the cattle, or Mr. Brinkmann would be scolding someone out there." Kenna took the empty plate. "I'll bring you some of the cake before it's gone."

She'd have to set aside pieces for Vanora, Elva, and herself too. And an extra-large one for Leppo. Without him, Vanora's birthday may have turned out very differently—perhaps tragically.

The sun had already dropped below the horizon, but colorful layers of yellow, orange, and scarlet still lit the sky. The nights were coming faster and turning colder. Frost would be upon them soon. The herd would cover less ground as the days grew shorter.

And Abilene was still a long, long way north. What else could happen before they reached it? It was a question best left unasked, even to herself.

Coated in muck and drenched to the skin, the men had grumbled a good bit at Squirrel's insistence they cross the creek the evening before. The tired and water-sated cattle hadn't been eager to cross either.

Nobody was complaining that morning.

Ben reined Rusty away from the remuda. The horses were somewhat sheltered by a line of scraggly willows, more bushes than trees. But they broke the wind and driving rain, and the horses were well away from the water.

Last evening's boggy creek had turned into a raging river overnight.

Ben had heard of flash floods during his time riding between Kansas and Colorado with the cavalry, but he'd never seen one. They'd heard it first the night before, and several of the old hands had yelped a warning, but they'd already brought the wagons, cattle, horses, and gear high enough for safety.

Through the deluge, the river surged and boiled like a witch's cauldron. If they hadn't crossed when they did, they'd have been stuck on the other side for days. Squirrel had planned to push on that morning, since the cattle hadn't scattered or run nearly the distance of the last stampede, but even he wasn't keen on moving out in the driving rain. The footing for the animals was poor, and the visibility for the cowboys limited. He'd weighed the risks against the rewards and decided to wait until the rain or wind or hopefully both let up.

Ben headed for the chuckwagon. They'd started a cooking fire under the canvas, where Miss McCrea had coffee hot and ready. He could smell it even through the rain. He pulled his cup from his saddlebag and handed it down, preferring to stay in the saddle to keep it dry, covered as it was by the length of his slicker.

Miss McCrea took the cup and filled it, steam rolling from the coffeepot into the chilled air. "Here you go." She passed it back to him.

He angled Rusty so that the wind was behind them and, after a sip of the scalding brew, held the cup close against his chest where it was shielded from the rain by his hat brim.

"All the stories I heard of the drives were of heat and lack of water." He gestured around them with his cup. "This is the second gully-washer we've endured."

"I thought the same." She pulled her shawl around her shoulders. "But then, I suppose they were like that in the summer."

She was beautiful standing there, smoke from the fire gathering under the canvas in ghostly breaths that moved above her, making her look more spirit than human. She awarded him another of those dazzling smiles despite the wretched weather, and he knew he'd ride through any sort of cold and rain and slop just to see it again.

"The horses and mules are well?" she asked.

It jarred him out of his runaway thoughts. "They're huddled together on the backside of a willow break."

She glanced toward the cattle. "Too bad the men couldn't have a day off and a place to stay dry."

Thinking of her brothers, no doubt.

"But you probably think me silly."

"No, Miss McCrea, that's one thing I'll never think. You have become the backbone of this drive. If you weren't here..." He shrugged and took another sip of the cooling coffee. "I don't know where any of us would be. How is Gus?"

"A little feverish this morning, but it seems to have worn off. He's sleeping now." The worry line on her forehead deepened. "The wound is dry and warm, but not hot. He should be fine."

Was she trying to convince him or herself?

Two slicker-covered cowboys rode to the fire, Lloyd and Tyree.

"How's Pa?" the elder asked.

"I was just telling Mr. Warley he's sleeping now, and the fever is gone."

"Good."

Both boys—men—handed over their cups, electing to stay in the saddle the same as Ben. It was miserable to ride in the rain, but even more miserable to do so with a wet seat.

"Squirrel thinks we'll be able to move on this afternoon." Tyree lifted his cup toward the west. "Says that sky means this'll break in an hour or so."

Ben couldn't see anything different than he'd seen all morning—heavy clouds through a curtain of rain. But he'd learned to trust the tall trail boss. If Squirrel said it'd break, then most likely it would.

Maybe they'd get dried out before evening when the temperature fell with the setting sun.

The boys chatted with their sister until their coffee was gone, then returned to the herd. They'd tap two others to come and warm up, but Ben had a few moments alone with Miss McCrea until then.

He screwed up his courage and took the plunge. "After supper tonight, if the weather clears, would you enjoy a walk?"

She turned her face up to him and blinked her blue-gray eyes. Tendrils of damp hair that had escaped her bonnet curled against the sides of her face.

He held his breath, only then realizing how much he wanted her to agree.

"That would be lovely." She dipped her head, then glanced at the pair of approaching riders. "Weather permitting."

"Until then." Ben touched the dripping brim of his hat, barely noticing the narrow stream of water it released across the back of his glove to soak his sleeve.

She'd said yes.

Kenna had agreed to walk out with Mr. Warley. What had she been thinking? He was a Galvanized Yankee. He was way above her in social standing. His father had owned a plantation—not a diner. He'd grown up with servants at least and possibly slaves. She served in the diner and now from the chuckwagon. She mentally ticked off on her fingers the litany of why it was a poor idea.

In short, they were worlds apart.

It might not look that way while she huddled under the chuck-wagon's canvas fly and watched him ride into the pouring rain, but it was the truth. And they wouldn't be on the drive forever. Once they reached Abilene, they would go their separate ways. She would continue to raise her sisters for as long as they needed her, and Mr. Warley would return to San Antonio to organize the next year's herds for Mr. McCoy.

That would be the end of it.

Yet something inside of Kenna longed to experience that *it* in a way she never had before.

"I can't wait for a man to look at me the way Mr. Warley looks at you."

Kenna almost jumped out of her skin at Vanora's wistful voice.

She turned to face the girl behind her. "Carl has been mooning over you since the beginning of the drive." Kenna couldn't keep the exasperation out of her voice.

Vanora stepped beside her and shrugged. "He's only a boy."

"And you're only a girl."

"For another year or two."

Kenna bit her tongue on the denial posed there. "Ma was seventeen before she married Pa. In case your arithmetic skills are rusting away, that's four years, not two."

Vanora giggled, then clutched Kenna's arm. "You're so easy to tease anymore." With that, she retreated to the fire and started another pot of coffee.

Kenna could almost feel her hair turning gray. That girl would lead to her premature death, she was certain of it. But she had no time to respond as another pair of cowboys arrived for a hot drink.

By the time both coffeepots were empty, the wind had ceased, and the rain had slowed to a misty drizzle. Squirrel shouted orders, and the camp prepared to move.

George hitched Pa's mules while Kenna hitched her team, but when it came time to roll out, Mr. Warley was on the seat of the chuckwagon.

Vanora leaned against Kenna's back as the mules strained against their harnesses and unstuck the wagon from the clinging mud. "You know he's helping Pa because of you, right? And Pa doesn't mind a bit." Then she flopped onto the bunk with Elva, the two of them not bothering to smother their giggles.

Was Kenna the only one who understood the situation? And if she was... why had she agreed to walk out with Mr. Warley?

CHAPTER 20

I T WAS A DRY camp, no water in sight, but they'd been soaked for most of the morning and half the afternoon, so Ben was as close to clean as he could get. He wasn't turned out as he'd have been back in South Carolina going to call on a young lady, and back then, he'd not been half as interested in making a good impression as he was now.

He'd spoken to Gus, and the man had given his consent. Ben was fairly sure it wasn't due to his driving the chuckwagon that day. At least, not totally. He genuinely liked the bearded cook. In fact, he genuinely liked the whole family.

Family. The missing ingredient in Ben's life.

He kept in touch with his sisters via occasional letters, but it wasn't the same. They were busy with their lives, their husbands, and their babies. He'd left a forwarding address in San Antonio to Red's saloon in Abilene. Perhaps a letter would catch up to him there.

When first Peter and then their father had been killed in the war, Ben was devastated. Perhaps part of his reasoning for not running off with Emmet and returning to South Carolina had been because he couldn't face being there—living there—with his brother and father both dead.

Not for the first time, the *why* questions fogged his thinking. Why had he survived and they hadn't? Why had he been captured and not killed? Why had he signed the loyalty oath to the United States of America? Why couldn't things have remained the same? Why had he lost everything—been reduced to a pauper?

He shook his head to clear the circling questions. He'd been down that path too many times. There were no answers—only more questions. After all, he wasn't alone. So many of his fellow soldiers—on both sides—had been uprooted and left destitute.

He brushed the clinging horsehairs from his coat, then combed his hair back before settling his hat in place. It was time to look to the future instead of chewing on the past. As Joseph McCoy's trusted employee, he'd successfully organized and overseen the movement of tens of thousands of head of Texas cattle. He'd proved himself.

He wasn't the failed Confederate soldier anymore.

So why was he more nervous about walking with Miss McCrea than he'd been while facing Yankees, negotiating with Indians, racing a stampede, or swimming a horse across a swift river?

Ben led the saddled liver chestnut gelding from his personal mounts to the picket line and tied it. He might be walking out with a lady, but he still needed to have a horse prepared in case of an emergency.

Lloyd tied his bald-faced black horse next to Ben's, then cleared his throat. "Pa says you're walking out with Kenna this evening."

"With his permission."

Lloyd nodded, glanced at the wagons, then back to Ben. "His permission, but Tyree and I will be nearby."

"You mistrust me?" Ben hadn't considered that. Hadn't he always been proper towards the McCrea women?

Lloyd took his time answering, wearing a groove in one cheek with a gloved finger. "Not exactly. You're a good hand with horses, and you've been good to the girls, but there's your past..."

"And what past is that?" Ben snapped the words, but he couldn't help it. He'd just been through all this in his head. He didn't need to rehash it with Miss McCrea's younger brother.

"A past that says your loyalties can change."

Ben wanted to argue the point, wanted to lash out with words—or maybe a fist—but what would be the point? "How many people know?"

Lloyd shrugged. "Nobody is talking about it, if that's what you mean. I overheard Vernon talking to Kenna while she was tending to him. I haven't said anything to anyone else."

"Not even Tyree?"

"No."

"Why not?"

"Because I've got a feeling you're a better man than most would think if they heard that part of your story."

"If that's true, why are you telling me this now?"

"Because she's my sister."

That deflated the anger building under Ben's ribs. What if Amelia or Pauleen had taken up with a man of questionable character? How would he have reacted?

He gave a soft snort. "I have two sisters of my own."

"Then you understand."

"I do." Ben gripped the younger man's upper arm. "My intentions are honorable. If you ever find them less than that, I expect you to come looking for me."

Lloyd grinned. "I'd have to beat Pa to it."

Ben could picture the barrel-chested cook with the chuckwagon's rifle in his hands, and he didn't have to use much imagination to picture him dressed in a kilt with bagpipe music sounding in the background. He gave Lloyd's arm a shake and let it go. "I'll remember that."

The sun had dipped behind the horizon and the moon had yet to rise, but the cookfire was burning bright, and beside it sat Miss McCrea, bent over her sewing. Ben approached and slicked off his hat.

"Would you like to take that walk, Miss McCrea?"

She'd been expecting Mr. Warley for the past half hour, but she still stammered her answer to his question. "L-let me fetch my shawl." She'd left it hanging over the side of the wagon while sitting near the fire's heat, but she'd need its warmth walking away from the flames. And it gave her a moment to collect herself for what she needed to do.

Because she must make clear to Mr. Warley that this would be their only such evening walk, that it'd been an unwise thing for her to accept his offer, that they were far too different to be considering courting.

But he offered his arm, and her traitorous fingers slid into the crook of his elbow as if they belonged there.

"I wish we had a river or lake to stroll along." His deep voice rumbled near her ear since he wasn't very much taller. "But Squirrel was right. There's no water for miles around."

She let her fingers brush the almost waist-high brush they walked through, its silvery-green foliage visible in the waning light. "At least there is plenty for the cattle to graze." On a cattle drive, small talk around water and grazing seemed safe enough.

He snapped off a twig that hadn't dropped its delicate flowers yet and handed it to her, its subtle scent spicing the evening air.

Kenna ought to get right to the point. But he spoke before she could. "Miss McCrea?"

"Yes?"

"I'd like to know more about you." He paused and faced her, his features shadowed in the darkness. "I've met your whole family—unless there are more I don't know of. I know you raised your brothers and sisters after your mother died, and you ran the diner with your father. I know you're a hard worker and a wonderful cook, and you have a smile that can make a man's throat close up."

Kenna toyed with the flowered twig, twirling it between her fingers in front of her waistband. What should she tell him? What more was there to say? He'd pretty much summed up her life in those few words. "There isn't much more to tell."

"What do you do for enjoyment?" His teeth flashed white and his low chuckle vibrated the air between them. "I recall you don't enjoy fishing."

"It's not that I don't enjoy it." She let her arms drop to her sides, keeping hold of the flower. "But I have so few hours of relaxation, and when I sit beside the river..."

"You fall asleep?"

She nodded, feeling like a schoolgirl caught daydreaming during a lesson.

"Back home, I was known to fall asleep along the riverbank many times."

Curiosity got the better of her. Instead of telling him that they couldn't walk out again, she asked, "Where is your home?"

After a moment, he resumed walking, and she moved with him. "I was born and raised in South Carolina. My father owned property he'd inherited from my grandfather, who'd inherited it from my great-grandfather, who'd carved a working plantation out of the wilderness after my great-great-grandfather fought the British over it."

"That's quite a legacy." How had he turned his back on all of that to join the U.S. Cavalry?

"It should have been Peter's legacy, my brother. But he was killed in the war. He was the eldest son."

"I'm sorry you lost your brother." She spoke from the heart. "I can't imagine losing Lloyd or Tyree."

"I hope you never do." He stopped again and faced her. "It's... it changes you. Or maybe it was because of how I lost him—and our father. We'd been led to believe that we'd whip the Yankees and be home in time to bring the crops in." He snorted. "We were such fools."

"But the North's oppression had to be stopped." After all, she'd heard that repeated for years.

"Did it?" Mr. Warley turned to look back at the camp, the rising moon exposing his strong profile. "Because we didn't stop it, we aggravated it. Instead of pressing us on tariffs and slavery and bills in Congress..." His voice dropped to whisper. "They rolled over us like a plague of locusts and stripped the South down to her bones. Stripped her until she couldn't even feed her people."

It wasn't his words that caught at Kenna's heartstrings as much as the tone of them. The flat finality of them. What had the man seen, perhaps even done, that marked his soul so deeply?

While she had served in the diner and watched over her family... and lost nothing.

Instead of drawing her out, Ben was dumping his sorry past in her lap. Hardly the way to win a young woman's affection. Walking with her beneath the rising moon, he realized how much he wanted to do exactly that. She wasn't a pampered and primped Southern belle—far from it—but she had something none of those ever had.

His full attention.

"Enough about that. I'm concentrating on the future now, not the past." He made a broad gesture to the north. "The country is opening up, and opportunities are there for anyone who wants to build something for himself. My great-grandfather took his opportunity in South Carolina, but my opportunities are here on the prairie."

His great-grandfather hadn't done it alone. Ben's great-grandmother had worked alongside him after the Revolution. Together, they'd created the plantation. Ben was certain he could build his own legacy in the West, but he understood that he'd need someone by his side. He couldn't imagine anyone more suited than Miss McCrea, even if he weren't strongly attracted to her—which he most definitely was.

"My father said something similar." Miss McCrea sighed, the gentle sound blending with the soft prairie breeze. "Why do men crave change so much?"

"I don't know that we all do." He'd have been very content to spend his life in South Carolina on the plantation, working as his brother's overseer. "Some of us have no choice."

"Lloyd and Tyree couldn't wait to shake the dust of San Antonio off their boots and join the cowboys." She gave a halfhearted laugh. "Changing it for the constant dust of a cattle drive, no less."

"I doubt either will stay a cowboy for long."

She stopped and faced him, eyes almost black in the darkness. "Why do you say that?"

"Lloyd is ambitious—not in a bad way—but he wants more than to follow behind a herd of cattle. Tyree is devoted to him, much like I was to Peter. I can see it. He'll follow Lloyd into whatever business venture opens for them."

Her answering smile was a faint twitch of her lips. "You're correct about Lloyd. He'd never have followed Pa in the diner, but he's sharp. He'll make something of himself."

"Peter was that way, too. I think if he'd lived..." There he went again, talking about himself. He cleared his throat. "What about you, Miss McCrea? What do you want to find in Abilene?"

"Safety, Mr. Warley." She spoke without hesitation. "Security for my family. A home to call our own again instead of canvas walls and beds on wheels."

What would she think of the soddies that passed for houses in Abilene? Dirt dwellings with dirt floors and dirt roofs? Although, now that the railroad had arrived, there would be deliveries of board lumber to build with. McCoy was building his fancy hotel, so materials were arriving in the West.

"A noble goal for your family, but what about for *you*?"

Her breath misted between them, and then she turned away, starting back toward camp. They'd walked halfway before she paused and faced him again. "I want what anyone wants, I suppose, a home and family. But I don't know if it will happen for me."

Uh-oh. "Why?"

"Elva is only ten years old. She'll need me for another seven at least. By then, I'll be considered an old maid."

"How old are you?" He wanted the words back as soon as they'd frosted the air.

She frowned at him. "What a question to ask a woman."

He raised one hand, palm toward her. "I know, I apologize. I was brought up better than that. I didn't mean to offend."

Her answering giggle caught him by surprise. "I'm not so easily offended, I assure you. I'm twenty years old, tottering on the brink of spinsterhood as we speak. But..." She cocked her head. "I'm very content here on the edge."

She continued toward the wagons, and if he let her walk away for a moment to enjoy the gentle sway of her skirts, who could blame him? He caught up to her in a few long strides.

"I'll be twenty-five after the first of the year. According to your reckoning, that must make me halfway to ancient."

She glanced at him but kept moving. "I'd have guessed you older than that."

He wasn't surprised. The war had left its mark on his face, lines that hadn't been there before. And he couldn't remember the last time he'd enjoyed a walk with a pretty woman or laughed in the evening air. He'd thought such lighthearted moments a thing of the past.

Before they reached the wagons, Miss McCrea stopped and faced him again, all levity gone from her expression.

"Mr. Warley, I enjoyed our walk. I truly did." She twirled the twig still in her hand while staring at a point beyond his shoulder. "But I don't believe it a good idea to indulge in more of them."

Was the *thunk* he felt his heart hitting the dirt at his feet? "Why?"

She examined the flower, lifting it to her nose for a moment before meeting his eyes. "Nothing can come of it, you know."

"Why?" Had his entire vocabulary been reduced to a single word?

"We come from very different backgrounds, very different families." She sighed, then tucked the twig into the front of his vest. "But thank you for this one walk."

Then she was gone, slipping past the glowing cookfire and into the back of her wagon.

Leaving Ben alone in the darkness with his hopes scattered on the prairie breeze.

CHAPTER 21

B EN WRAPPED RUSTY'S REINS around the horn of his saddle and lifted Squirrel's spyglass to his eye. The landscape before them jumped into view, a startlingly clear view. According to Squirrel, this slight rise in the prairie was smack in the middle of Oklahoma Territory.

Indian country.

He lowered the spyglass, then handed it back to Squirrel. "That's amazing. I could see everything so clearly."

Squirrel gave him a sideways glance. "Ever think about getting fitted for spectacles?"

"I can read and write and keep books just fine. "It's only out there"—Ben swept his hand in an arc—"that everything grows fuzzy."

Squirrel grunted, scanning around them without the aid of the spyglass. "It's unusual that we've only been approached once by Indians. I spoke with other trail bosses on my way back to San Antonio. They all encountered more than one group. I expect our good fortune won't last. This is the perfect place to be overtaken by them."

"How many times did Indians find you with the first herd?"

"Six. All of them wanted the same thing. All of them more or less content to make off with a few head of cattle." Squirrel raised a brow at Ben. "Never with one of my horses."

"It would have been a good trade if only—"

"I know. And I don't begrudge it."

"Hard riding would have lamed him, I have no doubt."

Squirrel shielded his eyes with one hand, still watchful. "I can't fault you for doing what was best for the horse. He's better off where he is, under the circumstances."

The long dark line of cattle crawled across the prairie behind them. From their vantage point, they could see the whole herd, from leaders to stragglers. The wagons and remuda were perhaps a quarter mile ahead. All of them headed toward where Squirrel and Ben waited and watched.

"I hate losing any of the cattle." But Ben wouldn't mind some more meat with their meals if one of the animals needed to be put down. They'd run out of buffalo nearly a week ago, and Squirrel had not allowed any hunting on the tribal lands. No sense in asking for trouble. "These Triple S cattle are good stock. Schmidt deserves to get paid for them."

"He understood we'd have to pay some tribute to appease the Indians and that we'd lose some to accidents and illness, the same as he would on the ranch."

Ben nodded. "How many more rivers will we have to cross? Seems like we've already crossed more on the way north than Timothy and I did on the way south."

"Makes a difference when you've got a herd of beeves, a remuda, and wagons along." Squirrel leaned over and let loose a stream of tobacco juice. "The only rivers to worry us will be the Cimarron and Arkansas until we get almost to Abilene, and then the Smokey Hill River."

Ben stuck his gloved hands in his armpits, trusting Rusty to stand still on his own. He couldn't imagine having to swim a river with it so cold—but they would.

He should be getting used to the cold. For the past week, there'd been frost on the grass, frost on the horses' whiskers in the mornings, and frost curling off Miss McCrea like whittled shavings. No, that wasn't honest. She was still polite and friendly with him, but nothing more.

Ben wanted more. A whole lot more.

"Over there." Squirrel pointed to the northwest.

Even with the midmorning sun to his back, Ben couldn't see anything but vague movement. "Let me have the spyglass." He took the instrument and pointed it in the same direction as Squirrel's finger.

Indians—maybe half a dozen—popped into view as clearly as if they were an arm's length away.

"You predicted it."

Squirrel grunted.

"They must have seen the cattle, but they're riding at an easy trot," Ben said.

"I make out six or seven."

Ben studied them through the glass. "Six." Maybe he should think about a pair of spectacles. He closed the spyglass and returned it to Squirrel. "I'll ride for the wagons and get them in the middle of the remuda."

"Shout at Charlie to join me. I'll make for the Indians."

Ben lifted his reins and touched his heels to Rusty's sides. The mustang sprang forward, and they raced to the wagons. "Indians coming!" Ben yelled to Gus, who'd claimed he was well enough to drive again. "Pull up the wagons. George, gather the remuda around them. I need to find Charlie—"

"He be right behind you, suh," George shouted.

Sure enough, Charlie's mount was leveled out in a full gallop on his way to join Squirrel. The man must have better eyes than Ben.

Ben whirled Rusty around and rode beside Miss McCrea's wagon. "Indians coming in. Are both girls with you?"

"They are." Her voice was tight, but her chin was high, determination in the clean lines of her jaw and neck.

"The same as before, pull up next to the chuckwagon and don't touch that rifle unless you mean to use it."

He fervently hoped that wouldn't happen. And he was very glad Squirrel was with them this time. Not that he didn't think Charlie could handle things, but the trail boss should be the one to make such decisions. Plus it left Ben free to stand guard with the wagons.

To protect Miss McCrea whether she wanted him to or not.

"What do you see, Kenna?" asked Elva from behind in the wagon.

"It looks like six Indians. They are different than the first ones we met." These had short hair down the middle that stuck straight up in the air, while the rest of their heads were shaved to their dark skin. They wore cloth shirts with some sort of a vest over them, breech clouts, and leather leggings. Two carried rifles, the rest lances, and all had knives at their waists.

"Are they very frightening to look at?" Elva's voice was half whisper and half squeak.

"Of course they are," Vanora answered. "But magnificent in a wild sort of way."

Kenna twisted on the seat. Vanora had her finger in a three-corner tear in the canvas, opening it so she could see.

"Stop that before they see your finger."

Vanora huffed, but she did as told, keeping her eye close to the narrower opening. But not too close.

George and Mr. Warley kept the remuda and wagons between them and the Indians, who were now in negotiations with Mr. Brinkmann and Charlie. Funny that she didn't know Charlie's last name. Funnier still that she'd wonder about it in the middle of such a tense situation. She touched the loaded rifle with the toe of her boot to reassure herself it was there.

These natives were taller than the last bunch, and very lean. The shirts they wore didn't hide the bony points of their shoulders. Their faces were pinched and hollow-eyed, and their hair standing on end lacked any gloss. Those not speaking to Mr. Brinkmann eyed the cattle and ignored the horses and wagons altogether.

They were hungry.

The cattle had reached their wagons before negotiations came to a close. Charlie whirled his horse around and barked orders. Within moments, four of the long-horned cattle were walking away, trailed by the Indians on their horses.

How long would those four animals feed the village of the hungry people? How would anyone already so thin survive the coming winter? It wasn't right that the tribes had been pushed onto this barren land, and yet, the savage attacks that left countless pioneers slaughtered on their homesteads weren't right either. Life was messy—not easy—as Pa would say.

"Get 'em going!" Mr. Brinkmann hollered, waving his hat around his head. The cattle had never stopped, of course, but it was time to get the remuda and wagons moving. Vanora and Elva could stay in the back until they crossed or rejoined the established trail with dried dung to collect. They'd left the main trail that morning because it'd been grazed down to the ground.

Kenna released the brake and flicked the reins. "Get up, Jack! Get up, Hobbs!" She looked to her left, where Pa sat on the chuckwagon, but he wasn't moving forward. He was slumped to the side, hanging onto the seat.

"Pa!" She hauled back on the mules' reins and jammed the brake in place before they'd come to a full stop. The wheel team tucked their tails in protest, and Jack pawed the ground. Kenna wrapped the lines and climbed over the side. "Stay in the wagon," she told her sisters, both of them leaning over the seat to see what was going on.

She climbed onto the chuckwagon, almost tripping on her skirt in her haste.

"What's wrong?" Mr. Warley rode between the two wagons, while George stopped on the other side of the chuckwagon.

"Pa?" Kenna said.

His face was pasty white, and his knuckles matched where they gripped the wooden seat.

"Pa, what's wrong?"

"I dinna think I can drive, lass." His words lacked their normal strength and volume.

Kenna pressed her hand to his forehead. He was on fire. Worse yet, his wounded leg had swelled until his britches looked fit to burst.

She looked from Mr. Warley to George and back. "Help me get him into the wagon. He's not fit to drive."

"You hoists him over the edge, suh, and I carry him into the wagon."

The wagon rocked as Mr. Warley climbed aboard. He slid one arm behind Pa and the other under his legs.

Pa gasped, his face contorted in pain.

"I'm sorry, Gus."

"Not your fault. My own." Pa's breath came in short pants. "I knew the leg was acting up last night and again this morning."

"Pa." Kenna did her best to cushion his leg. "Why didn't you say?"

"Let's just get him in the wagon. Hold on, Gus." Mr. Warley lifted Pa up and over the side and into George's arms.

Pa went limp.

"Pa!" Kenna scrambled down the side of the wagon, barely landing on her feet.

"Easy, miss," George said. "He done blacked out from the pain, I 'spect."

"Put him in the family wagon, please," Kenna said. "There's more room in there."

"What's the holdup?" Mr. Brinkmann arrived, his horse sliding to a stop near the chuckwagon.

"Gus has taken ill." Mr. Warley was stripping his horse of saddle and gear before turning it loose with the rest of the remuda. "I'll drive the chuckwagon. Can you spare Lloyd or Tyree?"

Squirrel gave a curt nod. "We won't stop for a noon break. Do what you can for him." Then he rode for the herd.

It would help to have one of her brothers nearby. Kenna hurried around George and got into the wagon first. She shooed her sisters onto the seat and cleaned off her bunk for Pa. "Put him here."

George managed to climb into the wagon without help, arm muscles bulging, and laid Pa out as gently as could be. Such a contrast of strength and gentleness.

Kenna stared at Pa's leg. If anything, it'd swelled even more during the short move. "I'll have to cut through the cloth."

Before she could search out her sewing box and scissors, George pulled a knife from his belt and slit the fabric without leaving a mark on Pa's leg.

The red, angry flesh around the old wound and the smell that rose from it made Kenna's stomach spasm. She pressed her hand over her mouth.

Vanora choked out a hoarse cry as she pulled Elva behind her to shield their sister from the sight.

"That ain't good, missy." George's words pushed against Kenna's ears, but she fought to deny the meaning behind them. "Best to open the wound and drain it, but missy, I don't know..."

He didn't know if Pa would live.

Lloyd and Tyree arrived together at the wagons and stopped their horses in front of Ben.

"What's happened to Pa?" Lloyd asked.

"He's fevered from his wound."

"I thought it was healed." Tyree's brows drew together. "What happened?"

"I don't know. He told us it was acting up since last night."

"Where is he?" Lloyd asked.

"In your wagon, but"—Ben held an arm out to stop him—"I need to know if either of you can drive a six-hitch."

"I haven't done it, but I know the basics," Lloyd said.

Tyree just shook his head.

"All right then, you two drive the remuda." He jerked his head toward the McCrea's wagon. "Five minutes to see your father, then we have to get moving, understood?"

Twin nods of one dark head and one red were his only answer as they spurred their horses past him.

Ben had a bad feeling. He'd caught the odor from Gus's wound. An odor he'd smelled too many times on the battlefield.

Infection—advanced.

With a good doctor, Gus might have a chance. Even then, he'd probably lose his leg. But they were in the middle of Indian territory. There wasn't a town or a doctor for who knew how many miles.

He walked around to the other wagon. The girls were perched on the seat, Miss Elva's face buried in Miss Vanora's shoulder, the older girl's face as white as dandelion fluff, but she had her older sister's look of determination.

"I'm going to move you to the chuckwagon." Ben held his arms out for Miss Elva, who practically fell into them.

"Is Pa going to... die?" Her last word came out in a watery hiccup.

"Only God knows for sure, but we'll do the very best we can. I promise you that, Miss Elva."

A shudder passed through her slight body. "Thank you, Mr. Warley."

He took her to the side opening of the chuckwagon and set her inside. "I'll be right back with your sister. You stay here."

Miss Vanora was halfway down the wagon. He offered his arm, and she took it with a quiet dignity that reminded him of Miss McCrea.

He escorted her to the chuckwagon. "One of us will be back to drive this wagon. Lloyd and Tyree will stay close by with the remuda."

"Thank you, Mr. Warley." Miss Vanora pulled her sister close. "We're much obliged."

He stalked back to the other wagon, teeth clenched in the frustration of helplessness.

Miss McCrea was on the seat gathering the reins.

"George can drive—"

She silenced him with a raised hand. "He knows more about doctoring than I do, so I'll drive." A deep moan came from the wagon, and her face blanched.

Ben nodded and walked to the back, poking his head inside. The smell about knocked him over. It was worse than he'd thought. George raised his eyes to Ben, then dropped them again. Not in submission as he often did, but in defeat.

Lloyd and Tyree both stood behind the big man, hats in their hands.

"Time to move," Ben said.

Tyree scrambled out of the wagon as if it were on fire and jumped on his horse, riding to the back of the remuda.

Lloyd came more slowly, glancing at his father before lowering himself to the ground. "It's not good, is it."

It wasn't a question, but Ben shook his head anyway, wishing he could offer more. He returned to the chuckwagon and climbed onto the seat. He unwrapped the reins and released the brake before flicking the lines. The mules stepped out and passed Miss McCrea in her wagon. She started her mules and fell in line behind him.

The sun wasn't fully overhead yet. They had a long afternoon ahead of them. When they stopped for the evening... would Gus still be with them?

CHAPTER 22

T HE MULES WERE WELL trail-broke and knew to follow the chuck-wagon, which was good because Kenna couldn't concentrate on anything. Pa had awakened when George had pierced the skin to drain the infection. Awakened with a long howl of pain. Kenna was glad Mr. Warley had taken her sisters in the chuckwagon so they couldn't hear it.

George had slid the canvas up on the hoops, hung over the side, and drew enough water from a barrel to cleanse the wound. The odor had dissipated after a while, but Kenna's stomach rebelled at the thought of it. She knew basic doctoring—as any woman who'd raised children would—but she was glad George was working over Pa.

And felt guilty about it.

Though the two men spoke quietly, Kenna caught only a few words from time to time. The one word she wished she hadn't heard made her clench the reins until the thick leather bit into her skin even through her gloves.

Gangrene.

The war hadn't reached San Antonio directly, but she'd seen men who'd returned from battles in the East missing an arm or a leg. It was said doctors in the field hospitals would remove a limb rather than risk gangrene. A man could live without an arm or a leg, but not with gangrene.

"Miss McCrea?"

She jumped at George's soft voice close to her ear.

"I sorry, missy. Didn't mean to frighten you. Your daddy, he wants you to sit with him a spell."

Panic nearly choked her. "I don't know what to do for him." She squeezed out the words in a whisper.

George lowered his voice as well. "Ain't nothing you can do now 'cept be with him."

As if that would be an easy thing? "Whoa, Jack. Whoa, Hobbs." Kenna brought the mules to a stop.

"Just hand me the reins, missy, and I'll hold 'em while you go round back."

Reluctantly, Kenna did as he said. She climbed down from the seat as George stepped over the back and settled himself. She pulled in several long breaths to steady her nerves before climbing over the tailgate.

Pa waved her close, his eyes tight with pain but a smile parting his beard. "Come, lassie. There are things ye must ken before I leave ye."

Her heart pinched—hard—but his steady eyes and deep Scottish burr told her not to argue. Pa was dying, and he knew it.

"Dinna think me too foolish, lass. I knew days ago my leg was going bad, but I wanted to continue on as long as I could." He grasped her hand. "I'm sorry, more sorry than ye can know, for dragging ye and yer sisters onto the prairie again. I canna think what possessed me."

"You wanted to be free of walls again, Pa. I understand." Perhaps not totally, but she understood enough to ease his mind.

"Listen to me, lass. There is money in the chuckwagon from selling the diner, and Squirrel will pay ye my wages at the end of the drive. Dinna worry on that account. He's a fair man."

"I'm not worried." She lied through her teeth.

"Lloyd and Tyree will do their best to take care of ye and the wee lassies." He smiled and then coughed before drawing in another breath. "Vanora isna so wee anymore."

"No, she's not."

"But my wee Elva." Pa coughed again.

"Rest, Pa. Save your strength."

"Nay, I needs must speak now, before the fever steals my wits." He squeezed her hand. "The lads can make their own way. Dinna give them the money. Ye use it to raise the lassies. Lloyd and Tyree will understand. They are men grown now, able to take care of themselves." He took a breath, though it seemed to take much effort. "As it should be."

"As it should be." Kenna blinked back tears. The same words he'd used in the diner when her brothers had signed on for the spring drive.

"But dinna forget about yerself, lass. Find a good man and marry him." His Rs were rolling heavily now. "Start yer own family and raise a brood of bairns. That Benjamin Warley, he has expressed his interest in ye. Dinna let his service to the Union sour ye on him. He's a fine man."

Kenna couldn't speak as Pa's eyes rolled back in his head. She pressed her palm to his forehead, the heat almost branding her.

"George!"

"It be the fever, missy. It take him down fast, but he'll come round again, a few more times maybe."

A few more times. A day? Two? How long until Pa closed his eyes and opened them no more?

Lloyd brought his bay horse beside the chuckwagon and cast a somber look at Ben. "Pa isn't doing well. Kenna is with him. George is driving the wagon."

"I'm sorry about your Pa."

Lloyd looked away, nodded, then faced Ben again. "George thinks it might be a day or two."

Maybe. Ben had seen strong men succumb to gangrene frightfully fast. Gus had been hiding it for a while. He might not have recognized the early signs. He hadn't fought in the war. Hadn't seen the gruesome piles of severed limbs outside of a field hospital. Hadn't lived with the stench of rotting flesh on the wind.

Ben cleared his throat and kept his voice low, even though the girls were quiet and probably sleeping behind him. "I'll watch over your sisters. Squirrel should assign one of you to stay with the remuda."

"I'll ask him. I'd like to stay close."

"You're good with horses."

"Been thinking about that." Lloyd wiped the back of his glove across his nose. "Might be something I can do with horses in Abilene, like work at a livery or dray service."

"There was a livery when I was there in the spring, but it didn't have any horses to sell and didn't appear to be doing much business. Of course, the railroad hadn't arrived yet. I suspect the town will be very different now."

"I'll do whatever needs to be done to take care of my sisters."

"I know you will."

Lloyd touched the brim of his hat and reined his bay toward the remuda that was traveling ahead of the wagons.

He couldn't be more than sixteen, soon to be the man of the family. Ben had been seventeen when he'd joined the Confederate Army. Sometimes, life forced a person to grow up faster than they should. Ben hoped Lloyd made a better job of it than he had.

The miles rolled by beneath the wagon's wheels, and Ben mused over his choices since leaving the plantation. He'd never in his wildest imaginings thought he'd be on a cattle drive in the middle of Indian Territory, driving a six-mule chuckwagon on a cold, windy day. The soft and pampered landowner's younger son, he'd never aspired to anything other than the plantation and working alongside Peter. With slaves to do the actual work, of course. He flexed his callused hands inside their leather gloves, the muscles in his arms pressing against his shirt and coat. His father and Peter wouldn't recognize him.

He barely recognized himself.

Squirrel galloped to the chuckwagon on a lathered horse. "There's water ahead. Not much more than a pond, but we'll set up camp on a rise just beyond it. You can't miss it."

He pointed, and Ben could make out a dark smudge that might be trees. Where there was water, there would be trees.

"How's Gus?"

"Dying." The word slipped out stark and raw, barely more than a whisper. Ben hadn't heard either girl move in a couple of hours, but that didn't mean they weren't awake. He tipped his head toward the back of the wagon, and Squirrel gave a nod of understanding.

"You'll need another hand for the remuda then." Squirrel twisted and frowned in the direction of the herd of horses.

"Lloyd would do well. He's a good hand with horses."

"I'll speak with him while I saddle a fresh mount. I'll see you again on the rise beyond the pond." Squirrel wheeled his horse around and galloped off. The man did everything at top speed, it seemed. But he had a lot resting on his shoulders—and losing a cook was just about the worst thing that could happen on a cattle drive.

Miss McCrea would continue on, of course. She was more than capable of feeding the men with the help of her sisters. She'd once told him that a McCrea could do whatever they'd a mind to. He certainly believed it of her.

But to do it while grieving the loss of her father? That was a grief he knew all too well. The loss of his father and brother had led to his decision to swear loyalty to the United States—the enemy.

Except it didn't feel like the enemy anymore. Hadn't for a long time. If only Miss McCrea could see that. They were still weeks away from Abilene, the days growing shorter and less distance covered each day.

Maybe he had time to redeem himself in her eyes.

"I'm sorry we can't tarry longer, Miss McCrea, girls, but it's just not possible." Mr. Brinkmann stood with his hat in his hands near the foot of Pa's grave. He'd allowed the herd to rest the previous day when it'd been apparent it would be Pa's last.

All the cowboys had been at the burial, every single one. Kenna was touched that Mr. Brinkmann allowed them all to attend. Mr. Warley and George had dug the grave near the pond where the ground was soft enough to break through with a pick and spade but far enough that spring floods wouldn't wash it away. After Pa was laid to rest, Lloyd and Tyree had filled it with dirt. Then, while Jake quoted scriptures, every cowboy had helped to place stones over the freshly turned earth to keep the coyotes from digging. Then they had melted away to pack their gear, hitch the mules, and mount their horses.

Vanora and Elva stood beside Kenna, all three of them at last dry-eyed. Lloyd and Tyree remained across the grave from them. It was their final goodbye to Pa.

"Five minutes." Mr. Brinkmann settled his hat on his head and strode away.

"Reckon I better get to the herd." Tyree shifted his feet but didn't leave.

"I'll see the lassies to the wagons," Lloyd said. "I'm staying with the remuda."

Tyree nodded, then glanced at Kenna.

She opened her arms, and he stepped into them, nearly crushing the breath from her. Lloyd joined his arms around theirs, and the girls managed to squirm into the midst of the group. "We'll take care of you," Lloyd said. "Maybe not as good as Pa could have done, but we will."

Kenna nodded, then let her arms drop to her sides. "We'll do our best to make Pa proud. All of us."

"Me too," Elva said, the first words she'd uttered that morning.

Kenna's heart wrenched yet again.

Lloyd spread his arms and urged them all ahead of him as if he were herding a flock of geese. As if he were taking over for Pa. And wasn't he? After all, she'd stepped in for Ma when she had to, and now it was Lloyd's turn.

"I'll always hate cows." Vanora's voice was crisp and loud in the chilly morning air.

"It wasn't the cow's fault," Tyree said. "It was just an animal running scared. It didn't mean to hurt Pa."

"You don't know that," Vanora said. "You weren't there. Maybe it did mean to gore him. I won't have anything to do with cattle ever again once we reach Abilene."

In the midst of her grief, Kenna spared a glance toward heaven. There was nothing good to come from losing Pa, but perhaps Kenna wouldn't need to worry anymore about Vanora taking up with a cowboy, at least.

George and Mr. Warley had the wagons packed and hitched. George sat on the seat of the chuckwagon, and Kenna took the seat of the family wagon while the girls climbed into the back. Mr. Brinkmann's shout started them off, with George taking the lead and Kenna following.

She wanted to look back at the grave, but she didn't. Pa wasn't there—not really. He was with Ma.

She needed to find what comfort she could in that because her full attention had to be on feeding the men now. Their supplies were running low. They were down to jerked meat, cornmeal, a little wheat flour, dried apples, a few shriveled turnips and carrots, canned peaches, canned milk, and rolled oats.

And they still had a long way to go. Mr. Brinkmann had hoped to reach Abilene on November twenty-third, just nineteen days away. But he'd confided to Kenna that it would likely take at least three and a half weeks. The bottom line was, they didn't have enough food.

Pa would have driven the chuckwagon into the first town they saw once they crossed into Kansas to buy more supplies. Now Kenna would have to do it. He'd told her what to purchase when he'd been lucid enough to speak the evening they'd made camp by the pond. She'd jotted it down on a slip of paper.

But what kind of a town would they find? Would Mr. Brinkmann allow her an escort? Or would Kenna have to do it on her own?

Mr. Warley rode his pinto mare next to her, keeping pace with the mules. "If you need anything, even to rest for a spell, just let me know. Lloyd can handle the remuda for a while so I can drive."

She tried to smile at his offer, but her lips wobbled. "I believe I'll do better if I keep busy."

He nodded. "I understand."

"You do, don't you." She'd forgotten about his loss while going through her own. "You lost your pa during the war."

"I did."

"And a brother too."

"Yes."

"I don't know how you coped, Mr. Warley. Losing one is"—her breath hitched, but she plowed on—"difficult enough."

"I didn't handle it well at all, as it happens, but that's a story for another day." He touched his hat brim and turned his horse around.

What did he mean?

Kenna's mind wasn't steady enough to tackle the puzzling comment, but she spied the familiar dried clumps peppering the prairie to the left of the wagon.

"Vanora, Elva, time to start collecting more fuel." That's what they'd agree to call the dried cattle droppings. *Fuel* sounded better than *dung*, even if it was the same material.

The girls slipped over the tailgate and began their work of gathering the lumps in their aprons and then emptying their aprons into the slings beneath the wagons. It would keep them busy. Keep them from dwelling on their grief.

Maybe.

Three and a half more weeks. They could keep on for three and a half more weeks. It wasn't as if they had a choice.

Pa had thought they'd start a new life in Abilene. And so they would... a life without Pa.

CHAPTER 23

B EN COULDN'T REMEMBER EVER having been so cold. Not even when he'd returned to Fort Dodge from Colorado in a blizzard. They'd awakened to a silver prairie, a crisp white layer of frost that made every step crunchy. He and most of the men had stopped shaving once the weather turned colder, and the whiskers under his nose were coated in his frosty breath.

And then they'd reached the Cimarron River.

He remembered the river from his trip south, but they'd crossed in a different place, where the river had been narrower. Squirrel preferred to take the animals—and especially the wagons—across in the wider, shallower area he'd scouted out. No doubt that was better for the wagons, but it meant longer exposure to the water for everyone else. He'd changed horses for each pass, once with the remuda, and two more times with the wagons, and he was half frozen by the time they got the McCrea wagon across, hitched, and drawn up the riverbank.

He topped the edge and almost groaned in relief at seeing the blazing fires already burning. Two were a distance from the chuck-wagon, surrounded by men changing into dry clothing and warming themselves. Miss McCrea had both coffeepots on the fire blazing near the chuckwagon.

As soon as Rusty had his feet on solid ground, he did his best to shake the water from his coat. Ben hung on when the shake turned into a little crow-hopping.

"Easy, boy." He turned the roan mustang in a tight circle to regain control. "I'm not any happier about it than you are." Then he headed for the chuckwagon, passing the mules pulling the McCrea wagon on the way, George at the reins.

The girls were already in dry clothing, their wet skirts stiffening on a rope stretched outside the chuckwagon from the back to the seat. All three were bundled in coats they'd kept dry in the wagon and woolen shawls pulled up over their heads and tied beneath their chins. Like the cowboys, they'd put their boots in the wagon to keep them dry. Wet feet in such weather would have guaranteed frostbite.

Ben rode to the chuckwagon and collected his dry boots and spare clothing.

"Add more water," Miss McCrea instructed Miss Vanora, who was stirring a pot of something over the fire. "The extra hot liquid will warm the men from the inside... oh." She looked at Ben. "Hello, Mr. Warley. I didn't hear you ride in."

"Your wagon is across. George is bringing it up now."

"We'll have coffee ready in about ten minutes."

"I'll let the men know."

"Thank you, and please tell them that we'll do the best we can for supper." She spread her hands. "I'm afraid our supplies are running very low."

"I'll check with Squirrel, but I think I saw someone pull a cow from the river downstream. It didn't get to its feet. We may have fresh meat."

Her smile was tired and heart-sore, the strain of grief still pulling at the corners of her eyes, but she was soldiering on.

His admiration for her had grown over the past four days since they'd buried Gus. There'd been no question if she'd step into her pa's place as cook, but she'd done it with such quiet dignity and efficiency. All the cowboys had remarked on it, which irked Ben more than a little. He didn't want any of them seeing her the way he did.

"I'll change my clothes and find out about that cow."

He headed for the warming fires. Miss McCrea had kept the chuckwagon between the cowboys and her cooking fire, and the fires were a good distance apart, but it still felt uncomfortable to Ben to strip and change clothing out in the open with women nearby. Not that it took long, his damp hide liked the cold wind even less than it liked the wet fabric. In no time, he was encased in dry clothing and was warming himself by the flames.

"Anyone know if we lost an animal on the swim over?" he asked.

"Leppo dragged one ashore, but I don't know if it survived or not," one of them answered. Several others murmured agreement, most more intent on warmth than their bellies.

Those not warming themselves were circling the herd. Ben scanned the men nearby. Tyree was missing, as were Carl and Leppo. Squirrel was riding toward the fire, holding his dry clothing and boots away from his dripping britches.

"I see the mules are accounted for." Squirrel dismounted and was stripping off his wet clothing almost before his feet hit the dirt. "The remuda make it over?"

"Every one."

"Good. Lost a steer." Squirrel nodded downstream. "Leppo said he knew how to cut it up. He and Tyree and Carl should have it here before long."

"Miss McCrea said we are short of supplies."

Squirrel pulled on his dry shirt and tucked it into his dry britches, then glanced at Ben. "We should hit the Kansas border in four days. There's a trading post not far east of where we'll cross. I'll need to you escort Miss McCrea there to purchase supplies." He shrugged into his coat and stomped into his boots. "I met the man who runs it. Don't trust him an inch. Open every sack, crate, and barrel you buy." He angled his body to shield his words from the other men. "If he has it, buy a barrel of beer. The boys have earned it." Squirrel scratched over his ear. "A small one."

The trail boss started to leave but turned back, keeping his voice low. "Don't take the younger girls. Nobody in that place needs to know about them." His look was too pointed to misinterpret.

"I'll make sure they stay with Lloyd and George."

Squirrel mounted his saddled buckskin and headed for the chuckwagon. For coffee, no doubt.

Ben had stripped Rusty and turned him loose to join the remuda. He hoisted his saddle over his shoulder and followed Squirrel on foot. He could finish warming next to Miss McCrea's fire while he talked to her about the supplies.

They'd be by themselves for a day. That prospect made him smile.

The trading post didn't look like much. There were two buildings made of sod, patchy tufts of grass on their roofs blowing in the wind. A dry, cold wind cut through every layer Kenna had on. If the buffalo hides they hadn't used to patch the barrel weren't stiff as boards, she'd have pulled one around her for added warmth, stink and all.

Kenna drove the chuckwagon with her team of mules. Jack and Hobbs perked their long ears at the dumpy dwellings they approached. The soddies lacked real windows, although they had tall slits covered with boards. Rifle openings, probably. The thought sent a chill through her.

They'd released several more cattle into the hands of Indians before crossing the border into Kansas shortly before stopping last evening. Mr. Brinkmann had warned her and Mr. Warley to keep their eyes open. They were still close to the border of Indian Territory and might be approached by Indians wanting food.

They had precious little to hand over, and after they made their purchases, they'd need to keep as much as they could. Assuming the people in the rundown sod buildings had anything to sell at all. She'd have thought them deserted if not for the laundry whipping from a rope strung between the two.

Mr. Warley rode ahead of her team on the red roan horse he favored. "Hello!" he called as they neared the buildings.

A man wearing a buffalo hide coat opened the door and filled the doorway. His beard was as black and curly as the hair on his coat—and nearly as unkempt. His hair was covered by a red knitted cap, and his britches were tucked into knee-high moccasins topped with some sort of fur. He held a rifle in both hands level with his waist. "What can I do for you folks?"

"Squirrel Brinkmann said we could purchase supplies here." Mr. Warley stayed seated on his horse.

"Can't forget a name like that. He was through here in the summer. Heading to Texas, he said."

"He did. Now he's returning and in need of supplies."

The man's eye shifted to Kenna. They were almost black, or maybe the darkness of his beard reflected in them. "That your woman?"

There was the slightest hesitation, probably not enough for someone who didn't know Mr. Warley to notice. And then he said, "She is."

Kenna wasn't prepared for that answer. Why had he said it? She couldn't very well ask him. And why did his answer make her breath quicken and her heart thump unevenly behind her ribs?

"Step down and come in." The man moved stiffly out of the doorway. "My name's Hatchett, J.B. Hatchett. This is my trading post." His chest puffed beneath the coat as if he were showing off a fairytale castle.

Mr. Warley dismounted, tied his horse to the chuckwagon, then held up his hand to help her climb down.

She set the brake and tied off the reins before accepting it.

He tucked her hand into the crook of his arm and faced Mr. Hatchett. "I'm Ben Warley, and this is Mrs. Warley."

"Come in." The man held the soddy's door open wide.

Kenna stepped through first, greeted by the pungent odors of damp earth, musty hides, smoke from the fireplace, and something savory cooking. The interior was dim, lit by the hearth fire at one end and a lantern at the other. When Mr. Hatchett shut the door, it grew even darker.

An Indian woman turned from the hearth where she'd been tending whatever was in the tin pot. She had long black hair that hung in a single braid drawn across her shoulder and resting on the front of her calico dress. She wore moccasins that matched the man's.

Mr. Hatchett said some words in a language Kenna didn't recognize, but the woman must have. She collected cups and what looked like the makings for tea.

Mr. Hatchett went behind the long bar separating the single room into two halves—the stocked shelves of the trading post on one side, living quarters on the other. Living quarters that included just one bed.

Was the Indian woman his wife? Or...

"What do you need?" Mr. Hatchett asked, eyes fixed on Kenna.

She opened her coat and withdrew the list of supplies Pa had recommended she purchase and handed it over.

He took the paper and studied near the flickering lantern. "You have cash money? Or hides to trade?"

"Some of both," Mr. Warley said.

Kenna didn't like the gleam that came into the other man's eyes.

Mr. Hatchett looked down the list again. "Wheat flour is hard to come by. I have some, but I can substitute barley flour for the rest. No bacon or salt pork, but I have smoked venison. I can let you have three haunches. The rest is easy enough."

"Do you have a small barrel of beer?" Mr. Warley asked.

Kenna tried not to gape at the request, but her shock must have registered on her face.

Mr. Hatchett barked a laugh, bending and slapping his thighs before pointing at Mr. Warley. "I wondered if you were truly married for a bit out there, but I know the face of an indignant wife well enough." He continued to chuckle as he pulled sacks and casks from the shelves behind him.

The woman approached with a tentative smile and handed Kenna a cup of something hot and herbal-smelling. It tasted good, but it was the warmth she needed. She smiled at the woman, who nodded and returned to the hearth.

Mr. Warley checked over the supplies, haggling some on prices. He called her to look at the wheat flour. He plunged his hand in and brought up some from the bottom. It was a different color. The man had layered a quality flour over a poorer milled batch. More haggling ensued until the purchases were all agreed upon. Mr. Warley fetched the two buffalo hides from the wagon, then poured a small sack of coins onto the bar, counting out the correct amount and returning just three coins to the sack.

While the men loaded the purchases, Kenna returned the cup to the woman at the hearth. "Thank you. It was lovely."

The Indian woman nodded and took the cup, but said nothing.

Kenna gathered her coat and shawl close again, bracing herself for the drive back facing the cold wind. She stepped outside and interrupted a fevered conversation between Mr. Warley and Mr. Hatchett.

"What makes you think I'd be willing to transport them?" Ben asked, still reeling from the half-request, half-demand from Hatchett.

"You don't fool me. I know how a cavalryman sits a horse, I done it myself for four long years. And that accent don't fool me either. You're a Southerner."

"The war is over—"

"Not for some of us." Hatchett's eyes took on an almost feral gleam. "I can't ride anymore. Broke my hip in battle, won't let me in a saddle. Them Yankees ruined me." A stiff leg, a limp, but the man was otherwise whole. At least he'd gotten through the war.

Unlike Peter and Father.

"The rifles I've collected need to make it to our fellow soldiers in Mexico in the spring. You'll return for more cattle then. What can be easier than hauling the rifles in a chuckwagon? Nobody'd suspect you, and you'd be doing your country—your real country—a worthy service."

Miss McCrea approached, confusion wrinkling her brow... or was it hope? Had she heard enough to know what was being asked of him? Did she approve? She was a Southerner, too, and she'd made no bones about his service in the U.S. Cavalry being a barrier between them. Maybe not in words, but the distance between them had widened when she learned that he'd served. If he delivered the rifles to Hatchett's contacts at the Mexican border, would she look at him differently?

"I'll think on it." Ben stepped around Hatchett and helped Kenna onto the chuckwagon. He untied Rusty, mounted, and looked down on the other man. "Nothing can be done until spring."

Hatchett grinned, and not in a pleasant way but like a coyote standing guard over its kill. "You'll be back—and the South will rise again."

Ben backed Rusty away from the wagon and gave Miss McCrea a nod. She slapped the reins a little sharper than normal, and the mules jerked the wagon into motion, making a large circle and heading northwest, straight into the wind.

He kept pace with the wagon until the sod buildings were dots in the distance. "Stop the team." Ben dismounted and tied Rusty to the back of the wagon, then pulled his blankets from his bedroll and joined Miss McCrea on the seat.

"I know it's forward of me, at least it would be in other circumstances, but we'll keep a lot warmer with the blankets wrapped around us."

Her lips twitched. "I suppose it can't be too shocking since we're *married*."

"About that..." He cleared his throat and took the reins from her. At least his growing beard hid cheeks that were suddenly far too warm for the weather. "I didn't trust Hatchett, and I didn't want him thinking you were a... that is..."

Her laughter stopped his words. "I was a little miffed at first, I'll admit, but I understand why you made the claim." She settled the blanket across their laps, pulling her side up to her chest to break the wind.

He slapped the reins on the mules, and they set off at a lively trot.

"Especially after he asked you to deliver guns to Mexico for the Confederate holdouts there."

So she'd overheard enough to understand the situation. Did she approve of the idea? Would it redeem him in her eyes?

CHAPTER 24

T HE ADDED RESPONSIBILITIES WERE weighing on Kenna. She barely found the energy to drag herself to her bunk each evening. At least they had enough food for the rest of the drive, even if it wasn't the best quality. She had to sift bugs from the flour before she used it. Some of the cowboys had told her not to bother. They said they'd get used to the extra crunch in their biscuits.

She'd almost lost her breakfast at the thought. And she couldn't afford to. She was already pinning her dresses tighter to make them fit. There was no time to sit and sew anymore, so the pins would have to do.

It was November twenty-third, the day Mr. Brinkmann had hoped to arrive in Abilene, but just that morning he'd estimated they had another seven days to go.

Elva and Vanora were thinner than when they'd left San Antonio too. They walked so much of the day. Little Elva had lost her sparkle since Pa's death, becoming far too serious for her age. Vanora had changed as well, growing more aloof, barely speaking to anyone and ignoring Carl altogether. All the walking kept them warm even as it stole their weight.

Kenna straightened the blanket draped over her lap and blew out a long, frosty breath in the late afternoon air. At least it wasn't raining. After two solid days of rain and drizzle, the weak sun was a blessing. Whoever thought life on the trail was glorious or exciting had lost his mind.

As much as she longed for the cattle drive to be done, what awaited them in Abilene?

Pa had left them enough money to see them through a year if they were careful. Maybe a little longer. Should they return to San

Antonio in the spring with Mr. Warley? They knew people there, and the business owners who'd known Pa would likely hire Kenna if they had an opening.

The wagon's right-hand wheels dropped into a rut and climbed back out, shaking Kenna from side to side. She needed to pay attention, but it was hard when so many thoughts—so many questions—pressed against her. And not just about her family.

Would Mr. Warley take the rifles south in the spring? Would he change sides again?

Did she want him to?

Pa had been sure any chance of the South reorganizing in Mexico had died with Maximilian. Kenna tried to summon her old feelings against the North's oppression, but she couldn't manage it. Her shoulders sagged. She leaned her elbows on her knees, reins still firmly between her fingers. She was too worn out to care anymore.

Elva and Vanora needed her, now more than ever. The South had had its chance... and it had lost. Pa had been right. Their lives hadn't changed with the end of the war. It hadn't changed much when the war started, for that matter. It was the idea of Northern oppression—its similarity to her Scottish ancestors' plight against the English—that had fired her patriotism for the Confederacy. But with Pa gone and her responsibilities doubled, such high-handed ideals didn't matter anymore. It was time to move forward and stop looking back.

Kenna blinked and looked around, taking stock of where they were for the first time in maybe an hour. A river cut through the landscape to the right of them and curved across their path ahead.

The Arkansas River.

Mr. Brinkmann, Mr. Warley, and Charlie sat on their horses overlooking the swiftly moving water. If she held her breath and concentrated, she could hear the river's powerful surge.

A shiver crawled along her back and raised gooseflesh on her arms. The Cimarron River had been hard on everyone, men and beasts alike. On top of it being late in the year, several of the cowboys who knew the area admitted to it being colder than normal. The last creek they'd crossed had been lined with a thin layer of ice along its edges. They'd been able to drive the wagon across the shallow creek.

But they'd have to swim the Arkansas.

It didn't look good. There were no two ways about it. Rain had filled the Arkansas River to its brink. Angry, dirty water frothed and churned between its banks. Ben stroked the muscled neck of the pinto mare. He wouldn't try swimming into that on any other horse.

"I don't like the look of it," Charlie said.

"We're already a week behind." Squirrel spit a stream of tobacco juice with more force than normal.

"You planned to arrive two weeks before the train cars," Ben said.

"Two weeks to let the cattle rest and regain some of their weight."

Ben pointed to the roiling waters. "You'll not get anything for them if they drown before we reach Abilene."

Squirrel shot him a glare.

"He's right." Charlie leaned forward and took a long look upstream. "We need to let this settle down before we try it. The cattle can graze here and rest."

"I know that." Squirrel bit off each word. "But once we're across, we'll have to push the animals even harder."

"Not to mention the women." Ben hadn't missed how wan all three McCrea sisters had become. Grief was a big part of it—but not all of it.

Squirrel settled back in his saddle and glanced at the sky for a long moment before focusing on Ben again. "I know. I feel responsible. I'm the one who talked Gus into coming."

"He knew the risks." Which was true. If he'd lived on the prairie before, he'd known more about the risks that Ben had, and he'd still signed on.

"That doesn't help much." Squirrel reined his horse back toward the herd. "Let's bed 'em down for the night and see what the morning brings."

Ben headed for the chuckwagon and George. "We'll camp on this side tonight and see how the river looks in the morning."

"Yes, suh." George grinned. "Glad to hear it. That water don't look too inviting."

No, if there was one thing it wasn't, it was inviting.

Lloyd cantered his horse to Ben. "We crossing?"

"Not tonight. Let's settle the remuda over there." He pointed to an area where a curve of willows and brush halfway surrounded dried prairie grass and shrubs that would make decent grazing.

Lloyd touched his hat and whirled away.

Ben continued to Miss McCrea's wagon. "We'll be camping on this side for the night."

"Thank goodness." She scanned the river before facing him. "I don't like the thought of crossing this one."

"Me either, but we have no choice. At least we don't have to do it this evening. And we're stopping earlier than normal, so we'll get a full night's sleep."

"That would be lovely." The wistfulness in her voice tugged at him.

He and George were doing their best to shoulder their share of the workload, caring for the mules, hitching and unhitching, toting water, and gathering wood where they found any, which left the girls to tend the fire, cook, and clean.

Ben helped Lloyd settle the remuda before unhitching the mules. He found a tangle of limbs that must have come down in an earlier storm. He roped a large one and dragged it to the cook fire, then sent Lloyd back to drag more to the cowboys' fires. Maybe they'd all stay warm enough tonight.

By the time he got his fresh horse saddled and tied to the picket line, the aroma of coffee led him back to the wagons. He had his cup extended for Miss Elva to fill when someone raised a shout.

"Riders coming in!"

They hadn't seen a soul outside of their crew since leaving Hatchett's trading post a week prior. The skin on the back of Ben's neck prickled. He raised a palm to stop Miss Elva from filling his cup, then tucked it back into this coat's large pocket and strode out to meet the newcomers with Squirrel, Charlie, and Lloyd.

They were riding mustangs and dressed like every other cowboy, but even in the cold weather, their coats were worn drawn back, leaving easy access to the pistols on their hips.

"Don't like the look of them," Squirrel muttered under his breath.

The cowboys not with the herd had all risen, some with long rifles held loosely at their sides. Others opened their coats to expose their sidearms.

There were four strangers, enough alike to be related. Word of outlaw gangs—often consisting of family members—had come to Fort Dodge more than a year ago. They'd been accused of all sorts of crimes, from robbing to kidnapping to murder. It was said some were army deserters—from both North and South.

"Remind you of anything, Charlie?" Ben asked.

"Sure does."

"Care to share before they get any closer?" Squirrel asked.

"We heard of outlaw gangs while in the cavalry," Ben said. "Some of them are made up of families."

Squirrel grunted. "And these boys carry a powerful resemblance."

"I noticed that too," Lloyd said.

The four men halted their horses in front of them. The one with gray in his beard spoke. "We saw your herd. Thought we might find a hot cup of coffee." He made a show of rubbing his hands together as if to warm them even though he wore thick gloves.

The others were watching the cowboys, and then one glanced at the wagons and sat upright, his casual slouch gone.

Ben's stomach dropped.

Squirrel's horse grew restive—a sure sign it was picking up on its rider's tension—shifting its hindquarters until it bumped Ben's liver chestnut. But it gave Ben an excuse to move his gelding over and block the wagons a little more from view.

"We've got coffee, and you're welcome to a cup, but we're short on supplies and running behind schedule."

One of the younger strangers laughed and pointed at the cattle."You got a whole herd to feed your men. Seems you could share some with friendly visitors."

"Those don't belong to me or my men." Squirrel spoke slowly and carefully as if talking to someone of limited intelligence. "We've been hired to deliver them for their owner." He twisted and spit, then leaned back and wiped his chin with the back of his glove. The action left his pistol exposed. "A job we take very seriously."

Graybeard spread his hands. "The boy meant nothing. Coffee is generosity enough."

"Why don't you warm yourself by the double fires." Ben tilted his head to where the cowboys still stood at the ready. "I'll bring the coffee over myself." And keep these men as far from the McCrea sisters as possible.

"Are you sure you don't want me to take the coffee over?" Kenna asked. Ben had been hovering near the cooking fire waiting for a fresh pot to brew ever since the strangers had congregated across the way at the cowboys' fires.

"Very sure." He glared at the other men, arms crossed, hat low and shading his face.

"Who are they?"

"We don't know, but they could be trouble."

Kenna paused, floured hands poised above the biscuit dough in her bread bowl. "Trouble?"

He cut her a quick glance. "Why would four men be here? In the middle of nowhere."

"Why are we?"

"We're trailing a herd to the railhead." He lifted his chin toward the strangers. "They don't have any cattle or other visible need to be here."

That made sense.

"Keep your sisters close to the wagon. Don't let them out of your sight."

Now he had her full attention. "You really think those men are dangerous?"

He shrugged one shoulder, arms still crossed. "Better safe than sorry."

"The coffee should be done." She handed him a rag to wrap around the hot handle. "Thank you." For taking the coffee, for watching over her and her sisters, for... caring.

Kenna had spent the past week pushing all thoughts of Mr. Warley to the back of her mind whenever they cropped up—which was often. Exhaustion made her too introspective. But remembering when he'd claimed her as his wife—even in subterfuge to keep her safe—brought a different kind of shiver to her insides. A kind she'd never felt before, but a kind she knew instinctively would get her into trouble if she didn't rein it in. Hard.

"Who are those men?" Vanora appeared at Kenna's elbow, frowning at the strangers.

"Mr. Warley didn't know, but he said to stay with the wagon, and to stay together."

"They're trouble then." Her sister gave a curt nod. "I figured as much."

George approached. "I done filled the barrels, miss. What else you needs doing?"

Kenna tucked the cut biscuits into the Dutch ovens and dusted off her hands. "We've at least two extra hours tonight since we stopped early. We'll be burning more fuel than usual. Do you think you could drag more branches from that brush near the horses?"

"Sure enough, miss." He strode off.

"What about me, Kenna?" Elva asked. "What do you need me to do?" The poor girl was wilting on her feet.

"You know what I would really like?" Kenna squatted to Elva's level. "I'd love it if you would fetch one of our books, sit by the fire, and read out loud to Vanora and me." Kenna sighed. "I haven't heard a good story in such a long time."

Elva perked up, and the first genuine grin Kenna had seen since burying Pa crossed her sister's face. "Which book should I fetch?"

"You choose. Any one you like."

Elva darted to the tailgate and scrambled into the wagon.

"That was nice of you," Vanora said.

"She's done enough, and we'll all enjoy the story. I wish I could tell you to join her."

Vanora shook her head. "No. My place is to help you as you helped Pa." Her voice wobbled on the last word, but she lifted her chin. "I'm no more tired than you are."

That was probably true. The sister she'd wished wouldn't grow up so fast was the person she must rely on. The irony didn't escape Kenna as she settled the Dutch ovens by the fire and scooped coals onto their lids. The biscuits would bake while she and Vanora finished the beef stew made from the last of the steer that had died crossing the Cimarron.

She glanced at the raging river behind her. How many would they lose crossing that?

Please, Lord, let it be nothing more than cattle.

CHAPTER 25

T HOSE STRANGERS HADN'T LEFT the fire until well after dark, so they couldn't have gone far. But they'd left a bad taste in Ben's mouth.

Ben and George had been bedding down beneath the chuckwagon while Lloyd had taken his father's place, sleeping under the McCrea wagon at night. Tonight, however, Ben couldn't get comfortable with that arrangement.

"I'll join you sleeping under your family wagon tonight, Lloyd."

"You thinking those men might return?"

"Better safe than sorry."

George lifted his bedroll from the chuckwagon and faced them both. "I thinks I should be the one to sleep there, suh."

Ben frowned, then caught himself. He'd learned to trust George. He didn't need to slip back into his old notions about the man. "Why?"

"Them men come back, they be sneaking in. Your light hair and Mr. Lloyd's fair skin, they shine like beacons to them looking close and going careful." He cracked a wide grin and lifted his bedroll made of a nearly black oiled tarp and navy wool blanket. "They won't see me in the dark."

"You can take my rifle," Lloyd said.

"No, suh." George raised a hand as if to ward off the weapon. "Black man can't shoot no white man, not unless he wants to find himself swinging from a tree."

That was true enough.

"But I can holds them until you two get there."

"What do you think, Ben?" Lloyd asked.

"I think he's right. But one man against four?"

George cleared his throat, then glanced over his shoulder and motioned to someone.

Leppo stepped out of the darkness.

Ben hadn't seen him, though he couldn't have been more than five paces away. Lloyd startled beside him, so it wasn't just Ben's eyesight to blame. The dark men were the perfect camouflage for guard duty.

But Leppo...

He'd jumped on Jack and saved Miss McCrea when her mules had bolted, and he'd not said a word about it. In fact, it seemed he'd gone out of his way to avoid the wagons since then. George took him his meals and then sat and ate with him, bringing the plates back to be washed when they were done.

They were an odd combination, the one helpful and kind, the other scowling and silent. The one large and imposing, the other wiry and agile.

"Leppo and me, we both sleep under the wagon. You join us if them men come back, and it be four against four."

More like five against four with George's strength on their side.

Ben nodded. "A good plan." He hoped so, anyway. Lloyd's creased forehead said he had some reservations about the arrangement, but George's reasoning was sound. And Leppo had proved he would protect the women. Maybe because they were the source of his meals, but the reason hardly mattered.

Their protection did.

Cold wind snapped the canvas drawn over the wagon's hoops, but that wasn't what woke Kenna. Snapping canvas had been part of her life for two months and more. No, it was something else. She kept her eyes closed but concentrated on the sounds around her.

The wind, always. The river, distantly. The snort of a horse or mule. The soft breaths of Vanora and Elva.

The jingle of spurs.

Kenna reached under her bunk and touched the rifle she kept there each night. She eased it out, taking care that it didn't drag against the wooden floorboards. She glanced at the other bunk, directly into Vanora's brown eyes.

With one finger pressed to her lips and the other hand clenching the rifle, Kenna scooted into a sitting position facing the tailgate. And waited.

It could be one of the cowboys, but why? They'd never come near the wagon at night before. Whoever it was, he was on foot. Spurs didn't jingle like that from a saddle.

Despite the wind and cold, Kenna broke into a sweat.

Would Lloyd wake up? Should she try to alert him? Or would that merely draw attention to him under the wagon, exposed to whoever was out there?

Indecision clawed at her.

Elva still slept, and Vanora had her arm around their little sister, hand poised to clasp over her mouth if need be. Good thinking. The wee lass would squeal for sure.

Kenna forced herself to breathe deeply. She wouldn't be any good if she got lightheaded from holding her breath.

There. Another jingle.

Was it closer?

Vanora's eyes rounded in the dark. She'd heard it too.

Kenna raised the rifle to her shoulder and pointed it at the closed back opening of the canvas. If anyone came through—

A shout erupted so close to the wagon that Kenna jumped. If she'd had her finger on the trigger, she'd have fired for sure.

Elva squeaked through Vanora's fingers.

A series of thuds and grunts were followed by another shout she recognized.

Lloyd.

Kenna was on her feet and untying the canvas covering. Before she pulled it open, she had the rifle raised to her shoulder... finger on the trigger. If anyone had hurt Lloyd—

She ripped back the canvas.

She looked like Athena stepping out of a Greek tragedy, standing in the back of the wagon, dressed in a white shift that fluttered in the wind, hair escaping her braid and drawing lines across her cheek in the moonlight.

Rifle leveled at the brawling mass of men.

Ben didn't have time for more than a glance as someone swung a fist at his head. Never more thankful for his father's insistence he learn the manly art of fisticuffs, Ben ducked in time and managed a jab to the midsection, which staggered his opponent.

Someone caught the man from behind and secured him by the neck.

"That be the last of them, suh." George's voice carried in the cold air of the wee hours. The dark lump of another man laid unmoving at his feet.

"Lloyd?" Miss McCrea called.

"It's all over, Kenna. Stay in the wagon." There was a new authority in the young man's voice. That and the pounding feet of the cowboys coming to help was enough for her to close the canvas without delay.

"Haul these critters over by the fire. Someone stir it up and toss on a log." Squirrel barked the orders. It didn't surprise Ben to hear the trail boss. Nothing much missed his attention, and Ben half believed the man never slept.

Since his hands were empty, Ben strode to the closest cowboys' fire and stoked it up. Light from the newly kindled flames fell on the faces of the four men who'd ridden out just before sunset.

"What are we going to do with them?" Lloyd asked Squirrel, the new authority adding a steely edge to his voice.

Aside from Squirrel, Tyree, Jake, and Carl had also joined the fight. George held the gray-bearded man, the one who'd done most of the talking earlier, who now had an arm hanging uselessly at his side over an empty holster.

Leppo had the crook of his arm tight around another man's neck.

Lloyd hauled the one off the ground to his feet.

Squirrel held the last man, the one who'd been fighting with Ben, by the collar of his shirt.

"Ain't no law out here that I know of," Squirrel said. "I'm tempted to drown them in the river like the varmints they are and let the water take them out of our way."

Would he... really?

Ben had been through the war and seen men die in more ways than he wanted to remember, but purposefully drowning a man...

"Once we get across the river," Ben said, "they won't be able to follow us without their horses or boots."

"You can't steal our horses—" said the bandit Leppo was holding. The last word ended in a gurgle.

"Let him breathe," Squirrel said. "Ben makes sense. Take their weapons and boots, tie them—tight—and we'll turn 'em loose after we cross."

"How are we supposed to survive out here without horses?" Gray-beard snarled the question.

Squirrel leaned over, spit, and then looked the man in the eye. "That ain't my problem."

"It's over." Kenna squatted by her sisters' bunk and smoothed Elva's hair away from her face. "Lloyd, Mr. Warley, George, and the others have the men in hand. We're safe."

"Are you sure?" Elva's voice trembled.

"Of course she is." Vanora pulled their sister into a hug. "The men have everything in hand, just like Kenna said."

What would they have done without the men who slept nearby? Lloyd couldn't have stopped those outlaws by himself. If he'd tried, he'd have been hurt—if not killed.

And Mr. Warley... Kenna's heart had lodged in her throat when the stranger had swung a punch at his head. The man had towered over Mr. Warley but hadn't laid a finger on him. Mr. Warley had dodged and then—faster than a striking snake—sunk his fist into the man's middle. He'd knocked the man back into Mr. Brinkmann.

There'd be no getting back to sleep, so Kenna dressed as quickly as she could.

"I'm going out to make coffee since the men are awake, but you two see if you can't sleep for another hour or so."

Vanora nodded and pulled the covers over them.

"You'll be close by?" Elva asked.

"I will. And so are Lloyd and the other men."

"Then I will try to sleep." Elva squeezed her eyes shut while Kenna and Vanora exchanged a long glance.

Just one more week to go once they crossed the river. High water or not, Kenna wanted to be over it and moving north. Never again would she live out of a wagon. As her boots hit the ground, a thought jarred as much as the impact.

She wasn't going to back San Antonio. She'd no idea what Abilene had to offer, but if it was nothing more than walls and a roof, it was better than what they had now.

Wrapping her shawl tighter against the wind, she hurried to the chuckwagon and put together one of the coffeepots, then stirred up the fire and set it to brew.

Four men were tied in two pairs, back to back, their stocking-clad feet spread before them. While she hadn't seen them up close, they were obviously the same four who'd come to camp last evening. Lloyd stood near them, rifle cradled in his arms. Mr. Warley also had a rifle in his hands.

"You've got this under control." Mr. Brinkmann turned and called back over his shoulder, "Jake, Tyree, Carl, get what sleep you can before your shift starts."

The other men moved, but Tyree turned toward her as if to reassure himself she and the lassies were safe. She'd have walked over and hugged him, but not in front of the men. He'd not appreciate her for that.

Mr. Warley joined her at the cook fire.

"Thank you for helping Lloyd capture these men," she said. "I don't want to think what might have happened to me and my sisters."

"Thank George and Leppo."

"George and—" She glanced at the two men speaking softly near the prisoners.

"They approached Lloyd and me about sleeping under your wagon." He spread his hands and shrugged. "They made a good case that they are more difficult to detect in the darkness. Those men had no idea they were there until George and Leppo grabbed two of them by the ankles and jerked them off their feet. All Lloyd and I did was help restrain them."

"Well, that was no small thing. I thought the one was going to cave in your head."

He chuckled. "He might be big, but he's slower than cold molasses." There was pride in Ben's voice. The good kind of pride in a job well done, not the vain kind that seeks glory.

She tilted her head toward the tied men. "What will happen to them?"

"After we cross, we'll cut them loose. Without their horses or boots, they won't come after us again."

Kenna rubbed her chilled hands together. She should have donned her gloves. She buried her fingers in the thick wool of her shawl. "Won't they risk frostbitten toes?"

He shot her a startled look. "Why do you care? Do you know what they'd have done to you and your sisters?"

"I'm not a fool, Mr. Warley, but neither am I cruel."

No. She was neither. "I'll get their bedrolls and toss a blanket over them."

"Thank you."

He stomped away, mumbling something it was probably best she didn't hear.

Kenna drew up her courage and approached George and Leppo. George didn't make her nervous, of course, but Leppo... She didn't understand him. And yet, he'd quite likely saved her life—again.

George greeted her, "Everything be all right now, missy."

"Because of you and Leppo." She stood halfway between them, close enough to touch each one's arm. George ducked his head, as he so often did.

Leppo stared at her. It was a hard stare, but it didn't make her fearful. Uncertain, yes, but not fearful. What was behind his dark eyes? He'd never spoken to her, not once, so she was startled when he said, "Can't lose our last cook." And then he did something totally unexpected.

He smiled.

His lips moved hesitantly, as if they weren't used to that position, but the corners of his eyes crinkled, and then a flash of teeth followed.

"If that ain't something," George muttered.

"You're a special man, Leppo. You frightened me at first, and I think you intended to, but then you saved my life—twice—and that of my sisters. I'm in your debt."

The older man sobered, then walked away without another word.

"Why is he like that, George?"

"Leppo had a hard life, missy. We come from the same plantation. We both worked around the house and barns, fixing and tending things there, working the forge." George shook his head. "Leppo wasn't treated well."

"And you? Were you treated well?"

"I be a slave, missy. I did what the massah told me, I went where the massah sent me, I ate what the massah gave me." George shook his head. "I wasn't much different than them cattle over yonder." His voice took on an almost haunting cadence that tightened Kenna's throat.

"Those days are over. You have a different future ahead of you."

"Do I, missy? When Mr. Squirrel come to our camp and asks for workers, I come because I needs work. Wasn't much food, wasn't much of anything in that camp."

"That was San Antonio. Kansas was always a free state." Kenna stopped and pressed her fingers to her lips. She hadn't thought of that before. Kansas had never been part of the Confederacy. It had remained in the Union she'd built so much anger against. But that was over, and those old feelings didn't rush into her again. Instead, she gripped George's arm and gave it a little shake.

"You're a free man now, and you'll find a better life in Kansas."

"Mebbe so, if the Lord wills it."

"Did you leave anyone behind in San Antonio? A wife? A sweetheart?"

George shook his head. "I had me a sweetheart once, but the fever took her."

"I'm sorry."

He patted the hand still holding his sleeve. "The Lord done called her home, missy. Ain't nothing to be sorry about for that."

"George."

"Yes, missy?"

"Pa ran a diner in San Antonio. I think I might want to start a new diner in Abilene. I'll need someone I can trust, someone I can count on. If you stay, I'll hire you if you're agreeable, but I may not be able to pay much at first. Not as much as you'd make with Mr. Brinkmann."

"We'll see how it goes, missy. First, we gots to get the cattle across that river. It ain't going to be easy."

No, it wasn't. It was one more hard thing—in a long line of hard things—they'd have to overcome. But for the first time since Pa died, Kenna felt optimistic about the future. A new town. A new diner. Her family nearby. George watching over them.

And maybe Mr. Warley would frequent it for lunch as he used to in San Antonio. Maybe he'd decide to stay in Abilene.

Maybe it was time she told him she'd changed her mind about walking out with him again some evening.

CHAPTER 26

AT LEAST IT WAS warmer than when they'd arrived, so his breath didn't mist the air in front of him. Ben sat on the pinto mare overlooking the river. While it didn't appear to have lowered much in the three days they'd waited, it lacked its earlier force. It was clean, fast-moving water, not the murky roiling flood it had been.

The mare shifted beneath him, shook her mane, and snorted.

Ben rubbed her neck. "It won't be long now."

Squirrel had given orders. They'd swim the horses and mules over first. Following the horses and mules, they'd push the cattle through, then they'd have the wagons to float across last. Much like the other rivers they'd crossed.

Only deeper, wider, and running faster.

The one plus was that the animals were well-rested, well-fed, well-muscled, and well-practiced crossing rivers now.

Squirrel's shout seemed unnaturally loud with the absence of wind. Lloyd and George started moving the horses and mules. Ben stayed to the rear and made sure none bolted away from the swift water. Swinging his reins to encourage the last one, Miss McCrea's reluctant red mule, into the water, he urged the pinto to follow. Within four strides the mare was swimming.

Cold water encased his feet and legs, making him glad he'd left his boots in the chuckwagon. The horse swam strong and sure, but the current swept them downstream farther than they'd been swept in the other rivers. By the time the pinto's hoofs found purchase in the riverbed again, they were almost three hundred yards from where they'd stepped in.

The three men let the other animals scramble onto the far side but kept their riding horses in the water up to their bellies and waited for the cattle to arrive.

Six cowboys were swimming their horses downstream of the cattle, yelling and slapping their ropes, keeping the animals bunched together and driving them toward the bank.

One beast broke free and drifted downstream.

Ben urged the mare after it while shaking his rope into a loop. On the first throw, he snagged the horns and turned the mare around. She knew what to do, and before long he towed the steer out of the river onto dry land.

Lloyd and George were swimming another pair out, as were two of the other cowboys.

Ben and the pinto pulled three more before he changed horses. He roped Rusty from where the remuda had drifted and led him back to the river. He dismounted, his feet hitting the ground with a soggy splat, his socks the only thing between his toes and the slippery pebbles along the riverbank. The pebbles felt like iron balls against his cold feet.

Lloyd was nearby saddling his second horse. "Did we lose any?"

"Not that I saw." Which was something of a minor miracle. Or maybe it had more to do with the long prayer George had muttered while they'd prepared to cross.

Ben tightened the girth around Rusty and mounted, watching as the long line of cattle fought for footing and then charged up the bank. Several cowboys were towing in stragglers, but Ben and Lloyd weren't needed again. Soon the whole herd was over.

Yips of celebration followed the last beasts ashore.

"No time to waste," Squirrel called. "Lloyd and Tyree, go get your sisters."

Tyree had also changed horses and led another for Miss McCrea. They hit the water together and swam for the opposite shore.

"Everyone else,"—Squirrel waved his hat in the air—"saddle fresh horses and let's float those wagons across."

By the time they crossed back over the river, they had more than a quarter of a mile to backtrack to reach the wagons.

Miss McCrea waited on the seat of her wagon wearing a pair of men's britches, rifle across her knees, a sister looking over each shoulder, the tied men on the ground several yards away.

Ben hadn't liked the idea of leaving the girls behind with the outlaws, but Squirrel had been adamant they needed every hand working the cattle across. And George had the outlaws so trussed up they couldn't move much less stand.

Behind the wagon was tied a horse belonging to one of the outlaws. Squirrel hadn't wanted to leave them with any, but Miss McCrea had insisted. Just as she'd insisted she pack the saddle bag with enough food to last them a few days if they were careful. And she'd gathered all their canteens to hang from the saddle as well. They didn't deserve her kindness, but he admired her for it.

She was a better person than he was—and he wished all the more that he could win her heart.

"It's time, girls." Kenna placed the rifle by her feet, then climbed down as Tyree reached her with his extra horse.

"This one is swift," Tyree said. "Just let the horse follow mine. He's a good swimmer."

"I remember him." Wearing a pair of her brother's britches, Kenna swung aboard the mustang while Vanora climbed up behind Lloyd and Elva behind Tyree.

Mr. Warley stopped his horse beside hers. "Hold on tight."

"I will." She looked back at the wagon. "And you'll see the men have their horse?"

He frowned but nodded. "We'll take the chuckwagon across first, then leave a knife within reach—not too close—so we can get your wagon in the river before they get cut free of their ties."

She met his eyes then, their brown depths holding concern. For her.

"Mr. Warley?"

"Yes?"

"Maybe this evening, when everything has settled down, perhaps you'd escort me for a short walk?"

Gone was the frown. His eyes lit like the first rays of dawn. "I'd like that very much."

Kenna ducked her head and urged her gelding beside Tyree's.

Elva leaned toward her while holding tightly to Tyree's waist. "I like him very much."

"So do I." Tyree grinned at her. "'Bout time you encouraged him. You been mooning over him for weeks."

Kenna straightened in her saddle. "I do not *moon* over anyone."

Lloyd walked his horse past them. "Let's go. We can discuss the finer points of courtship once we all dry out."

Vanora giggled.

Kenna's face flamed hot.

Elva turned and wiggled her fingers, likely at Mr. Warley, but Kenna wasn't about to turn around and see.

The water was shockingly cold. Her horse was one of the larger mustangs, and strong, but even he couldn't keep his back out of the water. Icy current swirled around Kenna's hips, lapping at her waist in places. Chilling her until her teeth rattled by the time they scaled the opposite bank.

She glanced back at the chuckwagon already floating behind them.

"Off you go." Lloyd swung Vanora to the ground.

"I'm so cold." Elva said as Tyree set her beside Vanora.

"Start a fire as soon as the chuckwagon comes across," Lloyd said. "Start all three if you can."

"Come, girls." Kenna led the horse up the bank and tied it to one of the willows lining the river. "Scour the brush for dry wood. Drag it over there for the fires." She pointed to a spot not far from the tree line. "You'll keep warmer if you keep moving."

The soaked britches were better than her full skirts for crossing the river but lacked the warmth, the wet material plastering itself to her legs. She shook them out as best she could for modesty's sake. At least there was no wind, or it would have been much worse. Kenna waited for the chuckwagon, which held the mule harnesses as well as a change of clothing for her and her sisters so they wouldn't need to wait for their wagon to be brought across. Kenna would help harness and hitch the mules to pull the wagons from the river before she changed, but Vanora and Elva could get into dry clothing sooner.

The chuckwagon was already in the middle of the river and drifting fast. It was going to land farther downstream than the horses had, the pull of the water too much for those working the ropes.

Long vines clung to some of the willow trees. Kenna stripped a pair of them and headed for the mules.

"Jack, Hobbs, come on, boys." The two lead mules raised their muzzles from the brown grass they'd been munching. Kenna slipped a loop of vine around each one's neck and led them downstream. As if they were still hitched, Tanny and Cigar followed, with Soulful and Manny bringing up the rear. They reached a depression in the riverbank as the chuckwagon struck bottom.

"Good thinking, Miss McCrea!" Mr. Brinkmann shouted. "Get the harnesses out and hitch the mules."

Cowboys scrambled to do just that, but Tyree reached inside the wagon and pulled the bundle of the girls' dry clothing out, holding it well away from his wet horse and clothing. He rode beside Kenna and handed her the bundle.

"Let's get you and our sisters into dry clothing."

"I should help hitch—"

"There are plenty of men to do that." He gave her a pointed look. "Men who don't need to see my sister's legs outlined in wet britches."

She stopped arguing and accepted his hand, her wet backside meeting the wet horse behind the saddle. The horse must not have appreciated it. It gave a couple of sideways hops before Tyree got it under control.

"He's not used to carrying double." He grinned over his shoulder at her. "At least not someone as heavy as you. Elva hardly weighs a thing."

If her teeth hadn't been chattering so hard, she'd have given him a good dressing down. As it was, all she wanted was her dry clothes and the beginnings of a fire. She'd tucked the fire-starter material inside their clothing before they'd left to keep it dry and ready.

Vanora and Elva had three piles of brush collected when they arrived. Vanora grabbed the dry bundle from Tyree as Kenna slid from the horse. Her feet were barely on the ground before Tyree galloped back to the chuckwagon.

"There's a private place this way." Vanora led them to a tangle of willow and vines where they unrolled the bundle, used the towel to dry off, and then dressed in their blessedly dry clothing. They'd spread their wet things over the bushes and were almost to where the fires were laid when their wagon came into view in the river.

It lurched and swayed in the current, flowing past them to where the chuckwagon had come aground.

Behind them, the outlaws had managed to free themselves. They were on their feet, one of them shaking a raised fist. Voices carried across the still air, but Kenna couldn't make out the words. That was just as well. They likely weren't fit to be heard.

"Let's get the fires going." Kenna turned from the river. "Everyone will be half-frozen by the time they get here."

"Elva and I can do that if you want to drive our wagon up," Vanora said.

It didn't take all three of them to make fires, so Kenna started walking downstream. She hadn't crossed half the distance when shouts broke out from the river. Kenna ran to the next opening in the willows and brush, memories of her almost capsizing on the wagon during the first river crossing making her heart beat faster than her feet.

The shouting increased, Mr. Brinkmann's orders coming fast and furious, an ominous groaning of wood, and the labored breathing of the horses reached her before she could get a clear view of what was going on.

And then she saw it.

Their wagon was on its side, two wheels spinning in the air, the canvas hoops filling with water, tilting it even more dangerously into the river. A horse floundered beside it, black head submerging and then reemerging from the water, nostrils flared and fighting for breath.

Its rider was missing.

Then George was beside the horse, loosening the rope around its saddle's horn, grabbing the bridle and pulling it alongside his.

Where was the rider?

Who was the rider?

Kenna tried to make out the cowboys still in the river, but with their clothing soaked and dark, their hats pulled low over their brows, they looked too much alike. Then she saw Tyree spur his horse into the water from the riverbank. She wanted to yell at him to go back, but what if he could save whoever was in trouble?

Then a red horse pulled itself onto the riverbank. The animal shook, spraying water and revealing its roan coat.

Mr. Warley's horse.

But where was Mr. Warley?

She'd never felt so helpless.

Carl's horse had been pulled under when the wagon toppled. It surfaced—without Carl.

Ben had slid from Rusty's back and dove under the water, dodging the flailing hooves of the other horses beneath the surface. The water was murky, stirred by all the action, but Ben could make out the submerged wheels. If Carl were caught, it'd be on a wheel.

Despite the water, the chaos of the scene sent Ben back to the war—the same way the buffalo stampede had. The gray shirt ahead of him was a brother soldier, pinned down by enemy fire. The muffled thump of hooves against water was the distance charge of the opposing cavalry.

Ben pushed harder against the cold, clinging darkness. His hand connected with cloth. He grabbed a fistful and jerked, but nothing gave. Lungs burning, he walked his hands down the clothing and connected with a foot, a foot stuck between the broken spokes of a wagon wheel. One quick twist and the foot was free.

Ben laced his arm around his fellow soldier's chest and, with a mighty kick, shot for the surface. Before he broke into the light and air, something collided with the side of his head and his shoulder, sending shards of pain screaming clear to his fingertips.

He managed to surface and grab a lungful of air.

Someone grabbed the soldier he'd carried.

Ben sank again, his wounded arm cradled against his chest. He was bumped from behind, then hauled to the surface again by the neck of his shirt. He gasped, sputtered, then fought the one holding him.

"Stop fighting. I gots you." The voice was rough but vaguely familiar, the accent Southern.

A great deal of shouting surrounded him, but his ears were full of water, and his eyes were filled with grit from the river.

What was he doing in a river?

"Ben?" His name cut through the chaos. "Ben, are you all right?" He knew that voice. It was musical. Feminine. He pictured it surrounded by unruly red hair.

Kenna—Miss McCrea.

What was *she* doing in the war?

CHAPTER 27

KENNA RUSHED TO THE riverbank where the cowboys were coming ashore. George brought the loose horse out, followed by Charlie on his mount with Carl draped stomach-down across his thighs, retching river water.

Leppo swam next to his horse, hanging onto the horn of his saddle, his other arm wrapped around Mr. Warley.

"Ben! Ben, are you all right?" She stopped at the water's edge and waited while Leppo got his feet under him and hauled Mr. Warley ashore.

"Roll him onto his stomach," Charlie said.

Leppo heaved him over, and Mr. Warley groaned.

He was alive. Relief nearly took Kenna's knees out from under her. She pressed her hand to her chest and breathed deeply before kneeling beside Mr. Warley.

His eyes were shut, but he mumbled something.

She leaned closer to catch the words, "She shouldn't be here. Not here."

"Mr. Warley?" Had she called him Ben before? "Mr. Warley, where are you hurt?"

He groaned again, attempted to roll onto his side, then gasped.

"Mr. Warley, what hurts?" Flashes of Pa raced through her mind, gored in the stampede, the infection, his last lucid moments... encouraging her to marry the man now facing a similar fate.

Brown eyes blinked up at her as if trying to focus. "Miss McCrea?"

"I'm here."

"Why? Why are you here?"

What could she say? That she was falling in love with him? That she wanted a future with him? That she didn't want him to be injured... or worse?

George came and stood over them before she could utter a word. "Let's have a look at him. 'Scuse me, missy."

Kenna scooted back on the damp sand and pebbles.

George poked and prodded, earning another gasp when he touched Mr. Warley's shoulder and a groan when probing his skull. "You gots a lump the size of a duck's egg on your head, suh, and I 'spect your shoulder done come out."

"Is that bad?" Kenna asked.

"No, missy, not terrible bad, but he'll be laid up for a week or so."

Mr. Brinkmann joined them. "Miss McCrea, I'm sorry about your wagon." He shook his head. "Lloyd dove to the bottom. Both left-hand wheels are broken. Even if we could draw it out, there's no way to repair or replace both wheels."

She glanced up. "I understand." It hardly mattered with Mr. Warley lying there injured. And Carl, who would be dead had Mr. Warley not saved him. The wagon was just a... a thing. Something that could be replaced.

Unlike Mr. Warley.

"Your brother is fetching what he can carry to the surface."

Kenna nodded, realization sinking in. Most of their worldly possessions were in that wagon. Ma's dishes, their spare clothing and linens, her sewing box, everything except for the money. That was still with Pa's things in the chuckwagon. And so was the food.

"If you could lend me a hand, suh." George spoke to Mr. Brinkmann. "We can fix his shoulder right quick."

"Popped it out, did he?"

"I 'spect a horse done it for him, suh." George faced her. "Why don't you gets a place ready for him in the chuckwagon, missy? He going to need to lie still for a couple of days."

Then where would her sisters sleep? On the ground? Of course on the ground. On the cold ground exposed to the elements—but there was no help for it. She rose. "Of course."

Understanding of her predicament and approval at her acceptance warmed his dark eyes, then he turned back to Mr. Warley.

Kenna hurried away, but not fast enough to escape the long wail of agony from the patient. She arrived at the chuckwagon out of breath.

"The wagon?" Vanora's forehead creased with her question.

"Wrecked beyond saving." Kenna stopped with a hand on the wagon before entering, her heart squeezing at the loss of Ma's dishes. "I need to ready Pa's bunk for Mr. Warley. He was hurt in the crossing."

"Will he die like Pa?" Elva's eyes were wide and terrified.

How was Kenna supposed to answer that? She opened her arms and gathered Elva close, resting her chin on the girl's hair, bonnet hanging by its ribbons down her back. "We'll do everything we can for him. You and Vanora and me. George too. He seems to know a great deal about injuries." Then she straightened and settled Elva's bonnet on her head. "You can help me ready the bunk. Vanora, Lloyd is retrieving what he can of our belongings. When he brings them here, spread out whatever needs drying. Afterward, you can help me find places for them in the chuckwagon."

"Kenna?" Elva paused at the wagon's door. "I don't want Mr. Warley to die."

"I don't either, sweetheart. I don't either."

The bed beneath Ben lurched to the left. He flailed his arms and yowled in pain.

"Mr. Warley?" An elfin face, dusted with freckles and framed by red curls, appeared next to him. "Are you awake now?"

Miss Elva... that was her name. Ben tried to work enough moisture into his mouth to answer, but another face came into view, this one serious, with brown eyes and dark hair. He should know her name too.

"Let me raise your head enough so you can sip some water." The older girl placed a canteen to his lips, and he sucked down as much as he could before she pulled it away.

"George says to drink, but not too much all at once." There was an odd maturity in her voice that didn't quite match the youth of her face. What was her name? "I'll let Kenna know you're awake."

Kenna?

That name he knew. Miss McCrea. Of course, the dark girl was Vanora. Why hadn't Ben remembered that? Maybe because his head hurt too much. He rubbed the grit from his eyes and took in his surroundings. He was in the chuckwagon. Why? He tried to sit up.

"George says for you to lie still." Miss Elva pushed on his chest. "He says your shoulder needs time to settle or you might pop it out again." Then she leaned closer. "I don't know what that means, but I think it hurts. A lot."

It did hurt. A lot. Almost as much as his head, which pounded like a blacksmith on an anvil.

The wagon stopped, then jostled, then Miss McCrea appeared beside him. Her hair was untidy—as it usually was—escaping wisps curling around the front of her bonnet. Her blue-gray eyes were creased in the corners, her cheeks dulled with a fine coat of dust.

She was beautiful.

"You're finally awake." She smoothed a tendril of hair away from her forehead. "I was beginning to worry."

"How long have I been sleeping?"

"Two days."

"Two days?" He tried to sit again, but she firmly restrained him, being careful of his painful shoulder. Or maybe it wasn't so firmly. Maybe he was just that weak. "Why am I in the chuckwagon?"

"How much do you remember?"

"We were crossing the river, and then there were Yankees." He pressed his finger and thumb against his eyes. He did remember that, but it made no sense.

"George warned us that you might be a little muddled when you awoke." Her voice was full of tender understanding. "It's common, he said, when someone takes such a hard blow to the head."

"What hit me?" Shrapnel would have cut him, but he didn't feel any cuts, just a lump on the side of his head. A lump that told him to stop touching it.

"George thinks a horse struck you when you pulled Carl from the river."

He'd pulled Carl from the river? "I don't... I don't remember that."

She laid a cool palm against his brow. "You've no fever, and that's a blessing. Your memory should return in time."

"Carl?"

She shook her head, but with a one-sided grin. "He was back in the saddle the next day, working the cattle. He's got a cough, but that's the extent of it." She sobered. "He would have drowned if you hadn't gone after him. He couldn't get free of the broken wagon wheel."

A fraction of a memory surfaced. A leg caught between broken spokes. It was gone in an instant.

"I think I remember..." He rubbed the bridge of his nose. "It was your wagon." He looked around them. "Is that why we're in the chuck-wagon?" He tried to rise again, but she definitely pushed him back this time. "Your wagon was wrecked. Where are you and your sisters sleeping?"

"We're sleeping on the ground," Elva answered, but with a wide smile. "I get to sleep between Kenna and Lloyd under the wagon. Lloyd puts his rope on the ground around me so that no snakes will bother me. We can see the stars because there's no canvas covering the sides."

"Elva is finding it quite the adventure," Miss McCrea said.

But Miss McCrea—Kenna—wasn't. She'd never wanted life on the trail. She wanted a home, security, and her family around her.

Another memory returned—Miss McCrea saying she'd like to walk out with him again. But what would he do after the cattle drive? Would McCoy send him back to San Antonio? And if he didn't, where would that leave Ben?

Without security, a home, or a chance of a family with Miss McCrea.

The morning broke clear and cold with the prairie wind whipping the frozen grass until it rattled. Kenna rolled out from under the blankets, shivering as she left the comfortable heat of her sisters. They all slept in their clothing now, as many layers as they could dress in. Thank goodness Lloyd had been able to retrieve their clothing from the sunken wagon. And more importantly, Ma's dishes. If it had come down to rescuing clothing or dishes, she'd gladly have shivered a little more to keep their last line to Ma with them.

She pulled the canvas sling open, revealing the dried dung. They had to unhook it from the wagon each night now that they were all sleeping underneath it. Not that Mr. Warley was happy about that. But George and Mr. Brinkmann were both adamant that he stay in the wagon and protect his shoulder. The chuckwagon wasn't large enough for her and her sisters anyway, and they preferred to sleep together.

Once she had the fire blazing, she started the coffee—always the first chore. She should have roused Vanora to help, but the girl was as worn out as Kenna and needed her sleep. She and Elva walked all day picking up fuel. They hadn't passed a river or woodlot since crossing the Arkansas.

Kenna stifled a yawn with the back of her hand, then mixed together the cornbread. It was too cold for biscuit batter to rise overnight anymore.

Mr. Brinkmann rode his horse toward her, a smile gleaming in the pre-dawn light. "Good news, Miss McCrea."

"I could use some good news about now."

"From that rise"—he turned and used his spyglass to point—"I can make out a line of trees to our north. Unless I miss my guess, that'll be the Smokey Hill River. Abilene is just on the other side."

"Abilene?" She pressed her hand to her chest, uncaring of leaving a handprint of cornmeal.

"Yes, miss." He took off his hat, rubbed the back of his neck, and then resettled the almost shapeless felt on his head. "I can't tell you how sorry I am that your pa isn't here to see it."

"It wasn't your fault, Mr. Brinkmann. Pa wanted to come."

"But I—"

"If it hadn't been you, he'd have come with someone else. Pa was happiest out on the drive. He bought and ran the diner to honor Ma's dying wish." Kenna's eyes were dry. She'd made peace with Pa's passing. "He kept his word as long as he needed to. He's with her now, and that's not something I can be sad about."

"You are a remarkable young woman, Miss McCrea. I believe you will do well whatever you decide to do from here. But if you wish to return to San Antonio, I'd be more than happy to escort you and your sisters—without a single cow in sight."

"That's very nice of you, but I believe we'll stay in Kansas, if not in Abilene."

He looked out at the eastern glow then back at her. "Abilene will be a rough town, miss. You might do well to move farther east to a town more settled."

"I'll keep that in mind." She wiped her hands and grabbed a towel. "Ready for the first cup of coffee?"

"I was born ready."

She filled his cup and watched him ride off, balancing the scalding hot brew while he rode. How they didn't spill it all down their britches or the side of the horse, she'd no idea, but those cowboys never wasted a drop of coffee.

"You should have poked me awake." Vanora washed her hands in the bucket, wincing. "It's like ice."

"It was iced over until I broke the top open."

"What do we have to go with the cornbread this morning?"

"Hope. We have hope."

Vanora tilted her head and waited.

"Mr. Brinkmann was just here. He spotted a river in the distance. The last river before Abilene."

"So we're almost there? It's almost over?"

Kenna nodded. "By tomorrow we should be there."

Vanora threw her arms around Kenna and squeezed. With a giggle, she stepped back and opened one of the barrels of salted beef, filled after they'd lost two steers to the Arkansas crossing. She leaned over and pulled steaks from the bottom. "I guess we can cook up the last of these then. Looks like enough for this morning and tonight."

Kenna put the cornbread on the coals.

What would she cook on once they reached Abilene? How would she feed her family? Where would they live with their wagon at the bottom of the Arkansas? So many questions she couldn't answer, but there was no time to linger over them. She poured two cups of coffee and headed for the chuckwagon.

Mr. Warley was seated on the edge of the bunk, his arm in a sling Kenna had rigged from one of Pa's old shirts. His face had lost its ghastly white shade, and his eyes seemed clearer. He said he remembered everything, but she suspected he said that to appease her. She handed him one of the cups before gathering her skirts and climbing aboard.

"How's your head this morning?" For all they'd worried about his shoulder, it'd been his head wound that held him back from working.

He still needed to hold onto something when he walked or he wobbled like a newborn foal. But it was getting better. He hadn't been able to walk at all without help for the first two days after waking up five days before.

"Better, thank you." He sipped the hot brew.

"Mr. Brinkmann says we'll reach the Smokey Hill River today."

He closed his eyes and leaned back against the side of the wagon. When he opened them again, they were filled with an odd expression. Was it sadness?

"Don't you want to reach Abilene?"

"Of course I do, but..." He took another drink and grimaced. "I wish I knew what to expect once we get there."

"I feel the same way. I want to be off this drive, but I have no idea what the future will hold."

"If your father had lived—"

"But he didn't." She took a drink of her coffee, surprised at how quickly it had cooled in the frigid temperatures. "And we have to carry on. We have to provide for our little sisters, Lloyd, Tyree, and me." She turned to leave, but he caught her sleeve.

"I'm sorry we weren't able to walk out on the prairie in the evening. I would have enjoyed that, very much."

"So would I, Mr. Warley." Her face heated at the boldness of her words, but she meant them. Meant them from her heart.

CHAPTER 28

K ENNA HAD CONTINUED CROSSING off the days on Pa's calendar. That
morning, she'd not only crossed off the fourth of December, but
she'd circled the fifth. The day they'd arrive in Abilene.

And what an arrival they made.

Dozens of cowboys had come charging from the town, lariats
swinging, ready to push the cattle across the last river between them
and Abilene. It wasn't a river like the Arkansas. It twisted and turned,
more shallow and changeable than the powerful waters they'd already
crossed. And muddier.

Even though the local cowboys had escorted her to a bridge of
sorts—a combination of logs and branches paved over with sod—the
wheels of the chuckwagon were still clogged with mud.

But none of that mattered as she drove the chuckwagon into town.

"I wouldn't have recognized it." Mr. Warley sat beside her on the
narrow seat.

Kenna scanned the buildings, many of them still in the process of
being built. The sharp scent of sawdust hung in the air. "So many new
buildings."

"Made of wood."

She cast him a glance.

"When I was here at the beginning of May, there were more sod
buildings than wood because the train hadn't reached here yet."

And there were no trees to use for building. The prairie surrounding
the town was as flat as the tables in Pa's diner, broken by rows of
willows outlining creeks that broke off of the Smokey Hill River. But
willow was poor wood for building, being too twisted for most uses
and too soft to last.

They rolled past a few soddies, squat little buildings made of dirt that looked dreary and worn. Living in those must be like living in a cave. Kenna suppressed a shudder. With their wagon gone and no place to call home, would Lloyd and Tyree need to build them such a shelter for the winter?

"Look there." Mr. Warley pointed to a building three stories tall, windows marching in shining rows on each floor, a covered porch running the full length its front. It stood out alone and aloof on the edge of town. "That has to be Drovers Cottage, Mr. McCoy's inn, and the stockyards beyond. That's where Squirrel will drive the cattle."

"Right through town?" She could only imagine the havoc that would cause.

"I hear that's how they do it."

Surely they'd move the cattle to the south and swing wide of the buildings. Kenna twisted on her high seat, looking over the heads of Vanora and Elva, who stood behind her. There were the cattle, in their long row, snaking toward the town proper. She shook her head and faced front. "The shop owners must protest this practice."

Mr. Warley rubbed his jaw—was that to hide his amusement? "If you look closely, you'll see most of the shops are taverns. They'll be hoping the cowboys see them and return with haste once the cattle are penned."

Sure enough, Kenna took stock of the businesses they passed, not that there were many. A barber, a tobacconist, a large square general store, a grocery, the steaming pots of a laundry glimpsed between buildings, a livery stable, and a saddlery with all sorts of leatherworks displayed behind its large window. She hoped its glass would survive the cattle behind her. The other buildings, every single one that sported a sign, were taverns of some sort. Several two stories high with upper balconies from which scantily clad women watched their arrival.

When one called an indecent suggestion to Mr. Warley, Kenna said over her shoulder, "Why don't you girls sit on the bunk until we reach the livery stable?

Elva made a squeak of protest, but Vanora must have taken her in hand.

"Don't worry." Mr. Warley's words were soft, his deep voice vibrating the air between them. "She wouldn't tempt me even if you weren't sitting beside me. I fear all other women will forever pale in comparison to you."

"Mr. Warley..."

"Back on the riverbank, when Leppo pulled me ashore, you called me Ben."

Fancy him remembering that detail. "I was so afraid. I wasn't thinking."

"I liked hearing it, my name on your lips."

A dog shot out from between two buildings, barking and nipping at the mules. Manny, the red wheel mule, pinned his long ears and side-kicked the hound. The dog somersaulted, yipped, and then raced back in the direction it'd come from.

"Hey! Watch your mule!" yelled a man running down the street. "That's my kid's dog."

"I'm sorry," Kenna said. "The dog nipped my mule. The poor beast was only protecting himself."

"If that dog has been injured—"

"Mister, judging by the way he skedaddled out of here, he's just fine," Mr. Warley—Ben—said. "And he learned a good lesson—don't mess with mules."

"I don't know who you think you are—"

"I'm Ben Warley, Mr. McCoy's agent from San Antonio." A hush followed Ben's words. People who'd been staring at the fuss over the dog were suddenly examining Ben. Several pointed and whispered to those nearby.

"I'm sorry, mister." The obnoxious man actually removed his hat. "I didn't realize. I'll see to the dog. He won't bother you again." And then he hustled down the street.

What had just happened?

Kenna had always known that Ben—Mr. Warley—was far above her in social standing, but having it displayed so vividly in the street of Abilene was like a smack in the face. He was *somebody* here. He was important. He mattered. Men took their hats off for him and nodded when he passed.

Kenna McCrea was nobody.

"Don't let it worry you." Ben leaned closer to Miss McCrea and dropped his voice. "The dog will be fine. It couldn't have run like that if your mule had seriously injured it."

She didn't make eye contact with him. If anything, she looked more uncomfortable than when the woman had yelled her suggestive comments from the balcony.

"Miss McCrea." He cleared his throat. "May I call you Kenna?"

She nodded, face still forward.

What had changed? Ben clicked back through the scene that had just played out, but he couldn't connect what happened to her apparent avoidance of him. Their legs might be touching on the narrow seat, but she had somehow pulled away from him in the space of a few minutes.

Ben didn't claim to have any in-depth understanding of women, but something had derailed their camaraderie of moments before. And he hadn't a clue what. Nor, it appeared, did he have time to find out.

Kenna halted the chuckwagon in front of Drovers Cottage, and Joseph McCoy burst through the front door.

"Ben!" McCoy stopped short and pointed to the sling stabilizing Ben's arm. "What happened?"

"A bit of bad luck."

"That's no matter." McCoy spread his arms. "What matters is that you're here. But I don't mind telling you, you cut it very close. Very close indeed. The train cars should arrive sometime tomorrow night, and they depart the following day."

They'd made it. They'd lost a lot along the way—too much—but they'd made it.

"Come on down, let me buy you a drink." McCoy turned his attention to Kenna. "And who is this?"

"Miss McCrea, meet Mr. McCoy. Mr. McCoy, Miss McCrea took over our chuckwagon duties when her father died on the journey."

McCoy removed his hat and held it against his chest. "I am truly sorry for your loss, Miss McCrea. If there is anything I can do for you while you're here, you need only ask."

"Thank you, Mr. McCoy." Kenna's words were subdued, and she barely flicked a glance at the man. "Where can I park the chuckwagon and stable my mules?"

Ben climbed down while McCoy explained where to find the company barn and corrals. Company barn? Things hadn't just grown since Ben had been in Abilene, they'd exploded.

Ben's heels hit the dirt, and he dusted off his coat. "McCoy, she'll need an escort, I'll be happy to speak with you once—"

"Nonsense." McCoy waved over a man dressed in clean clothing, not trail-weary garb, a pistol riding on his hip. "Adams here will see her there and back here to the Drovers, won't you, Adams?"

"Yes, sir, Mr. McCoy."

Ben glanced up at Kenna, but she chirped to the mules and left him standing in the dust.

"Is this where we're going to live now?" Elva gawked from the entrance of the large barn at the acres and acres of corrals that flanked it.

"This is Abilene." Kenna gathered her shawl around her shoulders. Not to shut out the cold so much as to feel its woolen comfort. Mr. Adams had shown her where to park the chuckwagon and helped her unhitch and tend the mules before turning them into a small corral behind.

Her mules. She'd become attached to them during the trip, learning their personalities and depending on their strength and steadfastness. She hated the thought of selling them—mostly because Pa had chosen them for her—but she couldn't afford to keep them. Mr. McCoy might purchase them, although he owned the team Pa had driven. That team was inside a larger corral with the remuda.

The end of the line of cattle plodded down the main street. Cowboys worked gates, opening and filling one corral before opening and filling the next. The corrals stood like square boxes lining the north side of the railroad tracks.

"What do we do now?" Vanora asked.

What indeed? "We wait for Lloyd and Tyree." Whatever they did from that point on, they'd do as a family. It was just the five of them now. She was twenty years old, and Lloyd would soon be seventeen. They'd keep the family together.

Her heart twisted in a painful thump. Oh, why had Pa ever mentioned the idea of marrying Be—Mr. Warley? She'd known from the start, or almost from the start, that they weren't suited. She could overlook his service in the U.S. Cavalry, in fact, she already had, but there was no overlooking their different social positions.

George and Leppo rode by, trailing the end of the cattle. George touched his hat brim when their eyes met. Leppo ignored her and her sisters.

The war had changed many things—but not everything.

Mr. Warley had a future with Mr. McCoy's enterprise. Kenna hadn't thought much about what they'd find in Abilene, but she'd never imagined a sprawling, prosperous business that reeked of newness, success, and money.

Lots of money.

Kenna was sure Mr. Brinkmann would pay her Pa's wages, but he wasn't bound to reimburse her for the loss of their wagon. Most of their belongings had been salvaged from the wreck in the river—including the half of Ma's Sunday dishes—thanks to the cowboys who'd assisted her brothers. Those belongings were still in the chuckwagon since she had nowhere to unload them. Mr. Adams had assured her Mr. McCoy wouldn't mind if they stayed in the chuckwagon until spring. The vehicle would remain parked in the barn until it was fitted out again for the spring drives.

Mr. Adams had said they could wait for Lloyd and Tyree at Drovers Cottage, but Kenna had gotten a peek inside when Mr. McCoy had come through the door. It wasn't a place for someone like her. Especially not when she was covered in trail dust and sorely in need of a bath and clean clothing.

Vanora's stomach rumbled, and she pressed her hand over it.

"I'm hungry too," Elva said.

They hadn't stopped for lunch, the cowboys as eager to reach Abilene as Kenna was. Which was good, because she didn't think she had enough cornmeal for another batch of cornbread, and they'd run out of beans two days back. The chuckwagon was as close to empty as it could get.

"I'll fetch the last of the jerked meat." Vanora returned to the chuckwagon and emerged with a cloth-wrapped bundle. "I set it aside this morning." She opened the cloth to a dozen thin strips.

"We'd better be satisfied with two each." Kenna took hers. "The lads will need the rest."

"What will we eat tomorrow?" Elva asked around a mouthful of the tough meat.

If only Kenna had the answer. "We'll see."

There were barrels stacked along the barn wall, and after a while, they seated themselves there to keep watch for their brothers. It felt so good to sit on something that wasn't moving, with the sunshine streaming in the wide barn door and the wind blocked by its wooden sides. Elva soon slumped against Kenna, her eyes closed and her breath coming deep and even.

"We haven't talked about what would happen once we arrived." Vanora kept her voice soft.

"There wasn't time." Kenna leaned against the barn wall and stifled a yawn. "I'm weary to the bone."

"We worked so hard to get here, it was hard to imagine what *here* would be like. Or what we'd do once we arrived." Vanora wiped at a dirty spot on her skirt. "All I really want now is a bath and a soft bed and a full day to sleep."

"That sounds heavenly." Kenna fought to keep her eyes open, Elva's warmth along with the sunshine pulling her toward sleep. She cleared her throat and sat as straight as she could without disturbing her sister. "We'll see what Lloyd has in mind when he joins us."

"Won't he have to stay with the cattle?"

"I don't think so. He and Tyree will be paid, at which point they'll no longer employees of Mr. McCoy. At least, not unless they sign on for another drive." And please—*please*—let them not do that again.

Kenna didn't want to be left alone in Abilene.

CHAPTER 29

"**D**O YOU KNOW HOW many cattle we've brought north? Thirty-five thousand head." McCoy thumped his beer mug on the table near the window in his private office inside Drovers Cottage, satisfaction oozing from his voice. "More than I thought we could in the first year, but I plan on doubling that next year with an earlier start and more herds."

Ben took a drink from his mug and let that number roll over him. They'd lost thirty-two on the drive to Indians, rivers, stampedes, and injuries. But what was thirty-two compared to a number that huge? It'd be like trying to find a copper penny in a spittoon full of silver dollars.

McCoy had a right to be satisfied. He'd been the one to see the rewards above the risks, the visionary who'd pulled Texas ranching back from the brink. How many Texans would keep their land, keep their breeding stock, feed and clothe their families, and maybe even send a son off to college because of what Mr. McCoy had accomplished?

Yet what about those who would never see their families again? Like Gus. Or were laid up in some remote town relying on sympathetic strangers to nurse them back to health? Like Vernon with his broken leg. What about those who'd lost their provider? Like Miss McCrea.

Where was she? Why hadn't she joined them yet?

McCoy was still talking, but Ben couldn't concentrate. He itched to get back outside and see what was going on. And his shoulder ached. He rubbed it.

"That's another thing." McCoy pointed at him. "You need to see Doc Merrill."

"There's a doctor here in Abilene?"

"Oh." McCoy waved a hand dismissively. "He's more horse doctor than anything, but he should look at that shoulder anyway. Can't hurt."

An excuse to get out of Drovers Cottage. "Where's his office?"

McCoy gave him the information, then told him to visit the barber for a bath and a shave and to charge it to him.

Ben drained his drink and left, but he wasn't looking for the doctor or the barber yet. The cowboy called Adams was hanging around the front of the inn, apparently on call should McCoy need him.

"Where are the women from the chuckwagon?" Ben asked.

"They stayed in the barn." Adams pointed to the large building between the inn and the corrals. "Said they'd wait for their brothers."

Ben nodded his thanks and stepped off the porch. The street was packed dirt, partially frozen and rutted, but at least it kept the dust down. The sun was weak but shining and would have been warming if not for the wind. Always the wind. It'd been like that at Fort Dodge too.

If there was one thing Ben missed the most about South Carolina, it was the warmth and stillness. How much his priorities had changed. Once he'd missed Lucy's cooking, idling beside the river, and walking out with a pretty young woman on his arm. None of that mattered now.

That was his past.

This was his future.

He wanted Kenna beside him to share it. If the town had a doctor—even a half-baked one—it must have a preacher.

Ben slowed and examined his filthy clothing and worn-out boots. He removed his hat and ran his fingers through his greasy hair. No wonder McCoy had mentioned the trip to the barber. He was a mess.

A man couldn't propose to a woman looking like he did.

He almost pivoted back toward town when another thought struck him.

Miss McCrea wouldn't appreciate him showing up all spit-and-polish while she was still coated in trail grime. That wouldn't work.

He ground his teeth together, then continued toward the barn. He'd check on Kenna and the girls, see what their plans were, see if they needed anything, and then he'd find the doctor and the barber, and then maybe... he sighed.

Maybe he'd be able to propose the next day.

"There you are."

Lloyd's voice jerked Kenna fully awake. She hadn't been sleeping exactly, but dozing at least. Her motion woke Elva, who sat up and rubbed her eyes.

"I'm starving," said Tyree. "Anything to left to eat?"

"The last of the jerky." Vanora unwrapped the cloth she'd kept beside her.

The lads each grabbed three strips.

"So what do we do now?" Kenna asked.

Lloyd paused, fishing a stringy piece of meat from between his teeth. "Squirrel says us men can visit the barber for a bath and shave, compliments of Mr. McCoy." He dried his hands on the front of his vest. "I suppose we best register you and the girls at Drovers Cottage."

"Where will you and Tyree stay?"

Lloyd shrugged. "Under the stars I suppose. It's not like we aren't used to it."

Kenna grasped his sleeve. "I don't want to be separated."

"I don't either." Elva's eyes were huge and damp, her dirty red curls clinging to her cheeks. "Don't leave us."

Lloyd squatted in front of her. "We won't be far. I can promise you that."

"But we can't stay at the inn very long." Kenna lowered her voice. "The money Pa left will only stretch so far."

"I know." Lloyd rubbed the back of his neck, then examined his fingers. "Let's all get cleaned up, eat a good meal, have a full night's sleep, and take stock of everything in the morning."

It was sound advice.

Kenna and the girls were gathering their bundled belongings from the chuckwagon when a deep voice reached her.

"Lloyd, Tyree, good to see you."

A flutter started in Kenna's middle and rose to warm her cheeks. She took a deep breath and pushed the feeling away. There was no time for daydreams. Her sisters—and her brothers—needed her clear-headed and logical.

"Where are you putting up, Ben?" Tyree asked.

"At the inn. McCoy booked me a room."

Mr. Warley would have a room there—all arranged for him—of course. That's what being part of the upper class did for a person. He still looked like one of them, but they all knew he wasn't.

"We're about to get the girls settled there, then head for the barber's," said Tyree. "Never looked forward to a bath so much in my life."

"Even on your last drive?" Mr. Warley asked.

Tyree shook his head "On the last drive, we all washed off in the river before entering town."

Which of course they hadn't done this time due to the cold.

"If you boys want to head to the barber, I can see your sisters to the inn."

Lloyd cut a look at Kenna, and she froze. Part of her wanted to signal him to stay and see them to the inn. Part of her wanted a few last minutes with Mr. Warley before he stepped out of the position of wrangler and into something much grander.

Ben had to work to keep his focus on Kenna's brothers.

"If you're sure, I wouldn't mind heading straight for the barber." Tyree grinned at Ben, but Lloyd took one last look at his sister.

Ben held his breath, half expecting her to shake her head, and he didn't release it until Lloyd followed his brother. Then he offered Kenna his arm before offering Miss Vanora the other one.

"I'm sorry, Miss Elva, but I only have two arms."

The youngest McCrea giggled and grabbed Miss Vanora's other sleeve. All three sisters carried a bundle of what probably constituted their worldly possessions.

"Are you glad the drive is over?" Ben asked.

"I am," Miss Vanora stated firmly. "And I will never live out of a wagon again."

"Me either," said Miss Elva.

Ben glanced at Kenna—he couldn't really think of her any other way anymore.

She turned her face away from him, her profile stark against the low December sun. Her chin was level, her nose straight, her lips... he probably shouldn't be thinking about those with her younger sisters on his other side. She turned her blue-gray eyes back to him, and the seriousness in them, with a measure of sadness, stirred something protective deep in his chest.

"I'd be much happier if Pa were here." Her words were barely more than a whisper. Then she looked straight ahead toward the inn and said louder. "I agree with my sisters. Abilene appears to be a growing town. I'm sure we'll find a place for ourselves here. A new start in a new place." Determination was back in her voice. She'd once told him that a McCrea could do anything they set their mind to, and he didn't doubt it.

He just hoped she'd set her mind on him—and soon.

They entered the front door of Drovers Cottage and walked to the registration desk. The furnishings were splendid, with plenty of gleaming mahogany giving off the scent of beeswax, rich burgundy draperies, and thick woolen carpets under a crystal chandelier. The desk itself was long and ornate, waist-high, and topped with a guest ledger. Behind it hung an impressive row of room keys. The clerk at the desk was tall and lean with graying whiskers and a thin layer of matching hair combed over the top of his head.

"These ladies require a room," Ben said.

"For how many nights?"

"One," said Kenna.

Ben shot her a glance. "A week, while we sort things out."

"Mr. Warley,"—she leaned close to him and said in a furious whisper—"thank you, but I can handle my family's affairs."

He raised a finger to indicate that they needed a moment, then drew Kenna away from the desk. "I know you can. It's one of the things I admire most about you. But one night is not enough. Look at your sisters." He pulled them closer to his other side. "They are all but dead on their feet. They need a few days to sleep and rest and get the bounce back in their steps."

She studied the girls, lips flattening in what he assumed would be a solid denial, but then Miss Elva blinked at her and wiped her nose with the back of her hand. With the dirt on her face and the condition of her clothing, it tugged at Ben's heart. It must be ripping Kenna's in two.

"I'll see if Mr. McCoy will foot the bill since you lost your—"

"We do not take charity." His words stuffed the iron right through her backbone.

Ben wanted to kick himself for a fool. "Of course not, but your wagon was lost in the effort to deliver his cattle. He owes you something for that."

"Mr. Brinkmann will see that we receive Pa's wages. That was the agreement. We will live by it as Pa would have."

"Then use some of those wages to stay here for a week. You all need to rest. You'll make better decisions afterward, I'm sure." Please, let one of those be a decision that included him.

Kenna gave a curt nod. "Three nights, but that's all."

Better than one, and he was in no real position to negotiate, so he escorted them back to the desk. This time, he kept his mouth shut and let Kenna register herself and her sisters.

She had her key in hand when she turned back to him. "Thank you, Mr. Warley, for everything."

That sounded far too much like goodbye. "Why don't we meet in the inn's dining room for breakfast tomorrow morning?"

"I'm sure you have much more important matters to attend with Mr. McCoy." She guided her sisters toward the stairs. "Perhaps we'll see you about town before you return to San Antonio."

As she herded the girls upstairs, Miss Elva peeked around and wiggled her fingers at him.

He raised his hand in response and hoped against hope it wasn't for the last time.

By the time the girls were bathed and fed—sandwiches delivered to their room, of all things—Kenna was ready for bed. But knuckles rapped on their door.

Kenna drew her wrapper tight and cracked it open. Tyree's grin greeted her, his cheeks shaved and red hair trimmed and smoothed like a well-curried mustang. Lloyd's dark hair was just as clean and sleek as a thoroughbred, but he'd kept his mustache, which completely hid his upper lip.

She opened the door wide. "Come in."

They spilled into the room, and it was like old times, talking over one another, Elva's squeals from Tyree's tickling, laughter—the first she'd heard in a long time—and then a comfortable silence.

"Why don't you lads stay here in our room?" Kenna asked. "The floor can't be any harder than the ground outside."

"We have a room on the top floor." Tyree pulled a key from his pocket and showed it off. "For two nights, courtesy of Mr. McCoy."

Kenna stiffened.

Lloyd squeezed her shoulder. "All the cowboys were given a room for two nights, not just us."

Not charity then. "And after two nights?"

"Tomorrow, Tyree and I will see what kind of work can be had in Abilene and if there are any houses to rent." He cleared his throat. "But you should know, anything we find is likely to be... well... a soddy."

One of those cave-like dwellings they'd passed. She suppressed a shudder. Better to have a soddy they could rent than a wagon open to the elements.

Wasn't it?

"What's a soddy?" Elva asked.

"Sort of like the adobe buildings back home," Tyree said, "but made of dirt and sod, not... adobe."

"Are there snakes?" Elva asked.

Kenna skewered Tyree with her best I-will-thrash-you-if-you-do look, and he grinned. "Not this time of year, silly. They stay underground when it's this cold."

An adamant *no* would have been better, but their sister was mollified, at least. She pelted Tyree with a flurry of new questions, which led to more laughter.

Kenna leaned closer to Lloyd. "What if you can't find work?"

"Dinna worry yerself, lassie." He poured out Pa's thickest Scottish brogue. "We'll take it a day at a time."

"You salvaged Pa's pots and pans." She ignored the twinge in her chest as a memory of Pa in the diner flashed across her mind. "If there's a building in town where we could start a diner—"

"You know Tyree and I aren't cooks."

"I am."

Lloyd stroked the drooping corners of his mustache. "But you can't run a diner and take care of the lassies all by yourself."

"You'll be here." She pulled away slightly and searched his face. "Won't you?"

Another peal of laughter filled the room as Tyree let Elva push him off the bed.

Lloyd caught her eye but then glanced away. "Winter jobs may be hard to find. Tyree and I might wind up working for the railroad."

"But you'd be here, wouldn't you?" Her voice pitched higher, but she couldn't help it.

He shook his head. "The railroad work won't be here in town. It'll be at the end of the line where they are laying new tracks."

"Then, the girls and I... we'd be here by ourselves?" Stuck in a town where they knew nobody?

"There is another solution." He didn't quite meet her eyes. "You could do as Pa suggested and marry Ben."

If only it were that simple. But it wasn't. Why couldn't Lloyd see that?

CHAPTER 30

I F BEN HAD THOUGHT he'd earned some time off once he reached Abilene, he was set straight early the next morning. McCoy had him at a desk outside his office writing letters to the Union Pacific Railway, Samuel C. Pomeroy, the U.S. Senator from Kansas, and Samuel Crawford, the Governor of Kansas.

As the broker for the venture, the railroad had initially agreed to pay McCoy five dollars for each railroad car filled with cattle that left Abilene. So far, he hadn't seen a dime. The cost of the buildings, corrals, equipment, and wages was staggering. The railroad claimed their verbal agreement had been "improvidently" made. McCoy was lobbying for a written contract from the Union Pacific that would honor their verbal agreement.

According to McCoy, after testing him that morning, Ben had the best handwriting in town. McCoy was convinced it would help press his case if the letters arrived looking professional. And he was probably correct.

Father had been a firm believer that ignorance was the bane of society. He'd seen that Ben, Peter, and their sisters were well-educated.

Voices raised from behind the closed door of McCoy's office. Squirrel had entered with George and Leppo moments before. Squirrel's voice all but rattled the door on its hinges.

Ben shot out of his chair and flung open the door.

Squirrel had both fists on McCoy's desk, leaning on his knuckles, looking like he might spit a stream of tobacco juice in their employer's face.

George and Leppo stood behind him with their backs against the wall, expressions blank.

"What's the problem?" Ben caught the flash of relief in McCoy's eyes.

Squirrel whirled and faced him, as fierce as Ben had ever seen him. "Your boss"—he jabbed a finger at McCoy—"says he won't pay these men their full share of wages."

One glance at McCoy and Ben knew he was expected to toe the line. After all, nobody paid a freed slave as much as they paid a white man. Not even the U.S. Army had done that. It was completely unheard of.

But Ben had given Squirrel his word.

And if there was one thing he'd lost on the trip north, it was his misconception of—his outright prejudice against—the freed slaves. His entire life he'd been taught they were an inferior race, childlike in their thinking, needing constant supervision, unable to think or act on their own, and unable to take care of themselves.

These two men had proved him wrong.

Ben squared his shoulders and faced Mr. McCoy. "We couldn't have brought the herd north without these men. They worked the same hours, under the same conditions, ate the same food, and suffered the same hardships as everyone else. They deserve the same pay. I gave my word to Squirrel before we left San Antonio that they'd get it."

"You gave *your* word?" McCoy's voice rose.

"Yes, sir. I did." Ben didn't flinch under McCoy's glare. "You charged me with getting the herds here any way I could, including this last herd—even knowing it was too late in the season and too dangerous an undertaking. Well, sir, we did it. And these men deserve to be paid what they're owed."

"And if I don't agree to pay them the same as the cowboys?"

Ben knew what he needed to do, but a cold sweat broke out along his hairline and prickled between his shoulders. If he took a stand, if it became his hilltop to die on, he'd be unemployed again. He'd wash out on another job, another mission, another chance to make something of himself.

He'd fail.

But he'd given his word. He'd backed out of his word once before when he'd disavowed the Confederacy.

He wasn't going to do it again.

"They *are* cowboys." Ben folded his arms across his chest. "And if they don't get their full pay, my work here is done."

George's "Mmm-hmm" was quiet enough that McCoy probably didn't hear it. And he realized the big man's approval meant more to him than McCoy's did.

What would Ben's father think of that?

It was high time Ben stopped worrying about what his father would or wouldn't have thought. His father had lived in a different time, a different place, and been raised to see the world in a different way.

Ben was seeing the truth now. Living it now.

It was a bit of a shock to realize he liked this new way better. Despite its hardships and uncertainty, he'd never felt more alive than he did at that moment. Nor had he ever felt more strongly that he was doing the right thing—not simply the thing expected of him because of who his family was or where he lived. The *right* thing.

"So you'd quit"—McCoy snapped his fingers—"just like that?"

"I don't want to, but yes." He cleared his throat. "I don't remember where it is, but I know from Sunday preaching that the Bible says a workman is worthy of his hire. I hired these men, under your authority, and they have given their all to get the job done and done well. They deserve to be paid."

"I paid them three-quarters of a cowboy's wage." McCoy ground out the words. "That's the going rate for the railroad hiring freed slaves." McCoy looked like a man backed into a corner, held there by social norms and a railroad that had so far reneged on its financial obligations.

"Then I'll be leaving your employ, Mr. McCoy, and I'm sorry it's come to this."

"Fine." McCoy rose and pulled a bag from his desk drawer. He counted out the difference in silver dollars and then handed them to Squirrel. "This is the only time." He jabbed a finger at Ben. "So don't agree to a penny more in the future."

Ben nodded and then returned to his desk to finish the letters, satisfied that he'd made sure his word had been honored.

George followed him out the door, then Leppo and Squirrel.

Squirrel divided the money between the two cowboys, nodded at Ben, and headed out of the inn with Leppo on his heels.

George stopped at Ben's desk. "That was mighty fine, suh. Leppo and me be obliged to you."

Ben glanced at Leppo disappearing through the doorway.

George chuckled. "He don't talk much, but don't mean he ain't feeling the same, suh." The big man shrugged. "Life been hard on Leppo. Some folks—black or white I 'spect—comes into the world with a fighting spirit. That be Leppo."

"Maybe that's not a bad thing." If Ben had been born with more of a fighting spirit, it might have made him a better soldier. Or perhaps he wouldn't have joined the army at all. Maybe he'd have had the courage to strike out on his own and make a life for himself instead of living the life his father had prepared for him.

Maybe if he had more fighting spirit, he'd have put Mr. McCoy off for the day, pressed his case with Kenna, and gotten that matter settled once and for all.

He dipped his pen in the ink and hunched over the letters again. He'd given his word to finish them, and he couldn't get finished fast enough.

It was a squat hump of earth with a wooden door and oiled hide covering its window openings.

It embodied Kenna's worst fears. She'd found a bulletin board in the general store with a note tacked on it about a house for rent.

House.

She couldn't quite connect the derelict soddy in front of them with the word. Elva squeezed her hand, and Vanora grabbed her opposite elbow.

"We aren't going to have to live in there, are we?" Elva asked.

"It's nothing but a root cellar." Vanora sniffed. "Surely we can find something better."

Could they? Part of Kenna wanted to open the door and see if it was more promising inside. After all, they couldn't afford to stay at the inn for long.

You could do as Pa suggested and marry Ben.

Lloyd's parting words from the night before had cost her a good night's sleep, soured her stomach, and still wouldn't leave her alone. They'd struck a dissonant chord between her longing and her reality.

What would it be like to see Abilene through the eyes of a young bride? To rent a building and start a diner—or another type of business—with the dream of running it beside her husband. To see the bountiful possibilities of a life built from the ground up. A life together. With a husband who'd love and care for her as much as she'd love and care for him. With a gaggle of children added through the years. And then grandchildren.

But while he'd flirted with her, always within the bounds of respectability, and hinted at his regard for her, Ben Warley had never suggested anything beyond the cattle drive. And he'd be heading back to San Antonio with the spring thaw, perhaps carrying rifles for the Confederates in Mexico.

She hoped he didn't. Kenna didn't trust that trader, Mr. Hatchett. Mr. Warley hadn't seemed to trust him either, but—

"Kenna!" Tyree's voice pulled her out of her musings. He and Lloyd jogged toward them. "We got hired." The younger brother grinned.

Lloyd was more somber, as he generally was, but there was a shadow of worry in his dark eyes. "What are you doing out here?" he asked.

Vanora pointed at the soddy. "This is for rent."

Lloyd backed up a step, then shot a glance at Kenna. "You can't stay in that."

"We may not have a choice."

Elva whimpered.

Lloyd scooped her up. "We'll find something else, I promise." But when his eyes met Kenna's, the shadow was still there.

"Tell us about your new jobs," Kenna said.

"With the railroad." Tyree puffed out his chest. "We'll be laying tracks clear to Fort Dodge by spring."

Fort Dodge? So far to the west? She glanced at Lloyd, but he tipped his chin toward Elva, still in his arms. They'd have to talk later. She had a feeling she wasn't going to like what he said.

"Let's find something for lunch," Lloyd said, "and then we'll see what else is available for rent here in town."

It felt good to have him take over for the moment. To have someone else shoulder the burden. But if he was heading west with the railroad, Kenna would be on her own with the girls. Unless...

You could do as Pa suggested and marry Ben.

Red's bar had been transformed in the months Ben had been gone. Wood replaced the previously sod walls and an upper story had been erected. It was no longer dark and dingy. The place had an air of respectability. The long bar still gleamed with polish, and the red-haired brute behind still held the stub of a cigar between his teeth.

"Ben!" Red waved him over to the bar. "I've been hearin' good things about ye." He drew a mug of beer and slid it in front of Ben. "On the house."

"I can pay my tab—"

"Not this time." Red spread his arms and looked around his establishment. "I have ye to thank for all of this." He slapped the bar with a meaty paw. "Ye brung business to Abilene."

"Mr. McCoy gets the credit for that."

"Did himself go to San Antonio in search of the cattle herds?"

"Well, no, but—"

"Then in my book, boyo, we have Ben Warley to thank." Red's grin split his grizzled red beard. He leaned one elbow on the bar. "So what happens now? Ye be headin' back south with the spring thaw?"

Ben studied the white foam ringing the top of his mug. "I don't know."

"Ah, yer at a crossroads again, eh? Like the last time ye stopped in." He cocked his head. "But not about employment, I'm thinkin', so maybe..." He winked. "A woman."

Ben didn't bother to deny it. If the warmth was any indication, his face was telling the truth anyway.

"And what pretty colleen has caught yer eye, if I can be askin'?"

"Her father was the chuckwagon cook, but he died on the drive. She and her sisters took over and fed the crew until we arrived."

Red rubbed his jaw, nails scraping against his beard. "She's here in Abilene then?"

"With her two younger sisters, yes."

"And ye say she can cook." Red leaned closer. "She any good?"

"None better."

"And ye say her father departed on the journey?"

Ben nodded.

Two cowboys entered the bar, and Red stepped away to wait on them. Ben took the time to examine all the changes, not only in building materials, but the new tables and chairs, the mirror behind the bar, and several paintings—landscapes he'd bet resembled Ireland—hanging on the walls. There was a potbellied stove in the center of the room resting on a square of bricks, a bucket of coal with a pair of tongs sticking out beside it. Another improvement brought by rail, burning coal instead of sod or dung.

Red returned and pinned Ben with a narrow-eyed look.

"What?"

"Did ye happen to notice I built me a proper upstairs?"

"I did."

"Five rooms to let, and none of them for the doxies down the street, ye understand." Red shook his head. "I can't compete with McCoy's grand inn, but I ain't settlin' for a low-class saloon neither." He poked his thumb toward the mirror. "On the other side of that wall, there be a new buildin' goin' up. Been thinkin' of openin' an eatery so my overnight guests—and others—could eat right here on this side of town."

Ben straightened on his stool. "And you need a cook."

Red slapped the bar again. "Indeed I do. But a respectable cook, ye understand. I am to serve a clientele between McCoy's grand inn and the brothels down the street. Seems to me, the town needs somethin' in between."

It did, indeed. While the saloons and brothels appeared to be doing a brisk business—their noise spilling into the street—there were many who wouldn't frequent them but couldn't afford McCoy's prices.

"The thing is." Red crossed his arms and surveyed his customers for a moment. "I'll be needin' a partner to make a proper go of it." He raised a brow at Ben.

"I don't know anything about running a—"

"Hear me out." Red raised a hand. "'Tisn't the runnin' that's at issue, but the financin'. The renovations of this place set me back a pretty penny, I can assure ye. And workers be harder to find than snowflakes in July."

There'd been plenty of men out in the street, cowboys mostly, but men who'd need work for the winter months. Ben glanced at the door as a couple of rowdies wandered past, their voices carrying through the closed doors.

"Not them." Red snorted. "I need men who can build and fix and make things work, not men who sit a saddle all day."

Ben tapped his fingertips on the bar. "I think I know the two men."

"Do ye now?"

"The thing is, they're former slaves."

Red didn't even blink. "But they have skills, yer sayin'"

"Both of them. One is larger than you and can run a forge."

"Glory be." Red rubbed his hands together. "And they be here, in Abilene?"

"They are. They worked the drive north with me."

"Ah, boyo, I need to meet these two men, and yer pretty colleen. Methinks we can work out an arrangement."

Ben finished his beer and plunked the mug on the bar. "When and where would you like to meet them?" He couldn't very well bring Kenna into the bar—George or Leppo either.

"Tomorrow mornin', early." Red jerked his head toward where the new building was going up. "Right over there."

Ben left with a little more spring in his step. A partner in an establishment in Abilene. Employment for Kenna—and he'd barter for living quarters above.

Now all he needed was for Kenna to agree to marry him.

CHAPTER 31

"**B**EN GAVE YOU NO clue?" Lloyd shrugged into his coat outside Kenna's room at the inn while she closed the door softly behind her sisters.

If only he had, she might have slept better. Kenna pressed the back of her hand over her yawn. "No. He was very... abrupt." Weak morning light barely lit the hallway from its one window.

"Well then, let's go see." Lloyd moved aside for her and the girls to lead the way down the stairs, Tyree falling into step behind them.

Mr. Warley waited for them at the bottom, dressed in new clothes with a new hat in his hands. "Good morning."

"What's this all about?" Lloyd asked.

"You'll see." Mr. Warley stepped aside to let them pass.

Kenna wanted answers, not riddles, but the man ushered her and her siblings down the street into Abilene, the inn resting on the outer edge of town with its smelly stockyards downwind of the businesses.

The morning was bright and crisp, the sun warming their backs, a sparkle of frost glinting off the grass. It was beautiful. The air was fresh and clean. No dust stirred as the town had yet to come alive. It reminded Kenna of waking early to start a day at the diner—although colder than she was used to.

What she wouldn't give to be back in San Antonio with Pa stoking the stove and her starting the biscuits or kneading yeast bread dough. She released a long plume of breath into the air. Wishing time would turn back never fixed anything.

"Just down there." Mr. Warley pointed to a partially finished building, where George and Leppo waited. They stopped there, and a large man came out of the saloon next door, rubbing his hands together and looking pleased. Very pleased.

"Red O'Callaghan," Ben said, "I'd like to you meet Miss McCrea and her brothers, Lloyd and Tyree, and her sisters, Miss Vanora and Miss Elva."

"'Tis a pleasure." Red doffed his hat with a short bow.

"My friend Red is building this eatery." Mr. Warley pointed to the unfinished building. "And he's in need of a cook."

Kenna took hold of Lloyd's arm, and he placed his hand over hers. Could it be the answer to their problem? Best not to get her hopes up. "Nice to meet you, Mr. O'Callaghan," she said. The others greeted him as well.

"Just call me Red. Everyone does."

"And these men are George and Leppo." Mr. Warley continued the introductions. "You'll not find a handier pair of workers if you search all day."

The two freed slaves glanced at each other. Obviously, Mr. Warley hadn't given them the reason for the meeting either.

"Let's go inside, shall we?" Red opened the door and led them into the shell of the structure. "Ben has recommended ye, and I trust his judgment, so if yer interested, here be me proposition."

Kenna wished there'd been somewhere to sit as Red rolled through his plans for the eatery—complete with living quarters upstairs for the cook's family—including having everything open and functioning shortly after Christmas. Just three weeks away.

Her knees about gave out at the rush of relief that flowed over her.

Lloyd must have felt it, for he slipped an arm around behind her.

"Miss McCrea, ye'll have to share a room with yer sisters above the saloon until those in this buildin' are livable. Then there'll be two bedrooms and a sittin' room. Ye'll use the kitchen below, of course."

Lloyd's arm tightened. "Until then, they'll live above the saloon?"

"My saloon is not a bawdy house." Red shook his head. "And meself will be just down the hall to protect them."

"How soon before the living quarters here would be ready?" Lloyd asked.

Red turned to George and Leppo. "Can ye start right away?"

"Yes, suh." George answered.

Leppo shot him a side glance, then gave a curt nod of agreement.

"How soon can ye get the quarters ready?" Red asked.

George walked the length of the building, tested the ladder set up as temporary stairs, and climbed high enough to have a look around. "If you gots the materials, suh, then I think we do it in ten days, give or take."

"Where have ye been livin'?" Red asked George.

"We been bunking in Mr. McCoy's barn."

Of course, the black men wouldn't be allowed in the inn, even though the rest of the cowboys had been given rooms. Kenna's fingers curled into fists. It wasn't fair.

"Behind me saloon is a room. It's big enough for two. I lived there meself while me upstairs was gettin' built. Ye can use it."

With George nearby, Kenna would feel even safer. She'd come to rely on him during the cattle drive and trusted him with her sisters' lives—as well as her own. Leppo? She'd gotten used to him.

Mr. Warley? Well... he'd soon be gone.

Ben's head was spinning from how quickly everything had come together, not only for himself and Kenna and her sisters but even George and Leppo. Red had surprised him with the extent of his generosity. At least it was a good surprise. Something was going in the right direction for a change.

But before he could speak with Kenna, he needed to talk to Lloyd. He followed the brothers from Red's new building, catching up with them in front of the barber's shop.

"Do you have a minute?" he asked.

"Not much more." Lloyd pulled a pocket watch from his vest—Gus's old watch. "Our train leaves in ten minutes, if it's on time."

Tyree looked at Ben and grinned, then said to Lloyd, "I'll grab our gear and meet you at the station." He loped off in the direction of the inn.

Ben cleared his throat, matching strides with Lloyd. "As you know, Gus approved me courting your sister."

"He did." Lloyd raised an eyebrow at him. "But did Kenna?"

That was the question, of course. "Before I got hurt"—he touched the sling that still supported his arm—"she'd agreed to walk out with me again."

Lloyd hummed, whether in agreement or not, it was difficult to say.

"I'd like to approach her on the matter, but I feel like I should have your permission first."

Lloyd stopped at the edge of the street, and a wagon rumbled past, its driver huddled under a buffalo hide coat. "Will you be returning to San Antonio in the spring?"

"I'm not sure." Ben glanced back at the unfinished building they'd just left. "A lot depends on your sister."

"You mean you'd leave Mr. McCoy's employment to please Kenna?" The words were delivered lightly, but Ben sensed the intensity underneath them.

"I would."

"Then how would you support her?"

Ben rubbed the back of his neck. "I've been thinking about that, and what I keep coming back to is horses. It's what I know the best. But I wonder if you'd be interested in joining me in a dray service? Your mules to get us started—if you haven't sold them already."

"They're Kenna's mules. Pa bought them for her."

"But I'd still need a good man or two to help with a dray business. With the railroad continuing on and the town growing by leaps and bounds, it's a service people and businesses will need—someone to haul freight from the trains to businesses, homes, and ranches."

Lloyd grinned. "I'd had the same idea myself." Then he sobered. "I have nothing but my cowboy pay to put toward it until I finish with the railroad in the spring. I'll save every penny and join you then—whether or not Kenna agrees to marry you."

Ben offered his hand, and Lloyd grasped it.

"Then we're in business." He tipped his head back toward where they'd been. "I just have to convince your sister to rent me her mules."

"That's *all?*"

Ben's neck and cheeks heated despite the cold wind blowing down the street. "I want to marry her if she'll have me."

Lloyd glanced at his pocket watch again. "I have to leave." He met Ben's eyes. "I don't know if she'll have you or not. Kenna's got a mind of her own. But if she agrees, and if you feel you need it after Pa's blessing, you have mine as well."

This time, it was Lloyd who offered his hand and Ben who grasped it.

"Good luck. We'll see you in the spring." Lloyd jogged off toward the station.

Kenna's got a mind of her own.

Ben swallowed, hard, then turned around. The misses McCrea were nowhere in sight. Maybe it was just as well. Maybe he should get his thoughts more firmly together before he faced her. Maybe she needed a little time to consider everything already offered to her that morning.

And maybe Ben needed some time to work up the courage to approach her. If there was one thing he didn't want to fail at—one thing too important to fail at—it was winning her over.

"And we won't have to sleep in that awful soddy." Elva held Kenna's hand and skipped down the street beside her.

Kenna had led them through an alley to the back street—obviously a new addition to the town, as none of the buildings was completed yet—and they were heading to the inn to collect their things. She breathed a sigh of relief that they'd only needed to spend the money for a single night there.

Of course, living above a saloon wasn't exactly what she'd had in mind, but since it was only temporary, since Red was a trusted friend of Mr. Warley, and since George would be nearby, they could stay there until the new quarters were ready.

"Kenna, what will you do with your mules?" Vanora asked.

What indeed? Perhaps Mr. McCoy would purchase them. Yet that thought left her feeling hollow inside. They were mules—not pets. She needed to get over her attachment to them. Needed to stop seeing them as the last gift from Pa.

She blinked back dampness she didn't have time for.

"I'm not sure, but there's time to make that decision." Not much time. Mr. McCoy wouldn't feed and house them forever. Kenna could only imagine the expense of stabling them at the livery. Although, maybe the livery would rent them out for her?

They climbed the stairs at the inn and packed their belongings. She wished her brothers were there to carry some of the bundles, but they'd said their goodbyes at the new diner and hurried to meet the train. She wouldn't see them again until spring.

She and the girls were truly on their own.

The dampness snuck up on her, and she had to dab her eyes with her sleeve when the girls weren't looking. What was wrong with her? She'd traveled over seven hundred miles with her family in tow along with the cowboys, two thousand head of cattle, a remuda of horses, and two full hitches of mules. Why was she getting dewy-eyed now that she had employment, a roof over their heads, and a plan to provide for herself and her sisters?

Because she'd never wanted to do it alone.

She moved the lacy curtain away from the window and took in the street below the inn. Even from a distance, she recognized Mr. Warley's figure as he approached. The sun had risen high enough to draw his shadow on the ground. It made him look larger than life from her vantage point.

Part of her wanted to hurry down the stairs and thank him for what he'd arranged. The other part wanted to fling herself into his arms.

Best to keep her distance.

"I'm hungry," Elva said.

They'd all missed breakfast, scurrying off on Mr. Warley's word that he had something to show them at the break of dawn.

And then, after everything had been settled, he'd left on her brothers' heels without another word. As if he were glad to have his hands washed of her and her sisters. After all, he'd promised Pa to watch over them, protect them, and he'd more than fulfilled that promise after procuring their livelihood and living space.

Vanora stepped closer, her brows drawn together. "I'm hungry too."

"Of course." Kenna pressed the last of her belongings into one of the canvas sacks they'd taken from the chuckwagon. "We'll eat in the inn's dining room this morning and come back for our things after." Then perhaps Mr. Red would be able to suggest a more affordable eating establishment until the new kitchen was ready.

They descended the stairs.

Waiting at the bottom was Mr. Warley.

Kenna pressed a hand to her chest and willed her heart to stop fluttering. The last thing she needed was to disgrace herself in the bustling inn. If not for her hungry sisters, she'd have kept walking, but she'd already promised them a meal.

"Mr. Warley, how nice to see you again so soon." She summoned a smile. "I didn't have the chance to properly thank you for introducing us to Mr. Red."

Vanora shot her a funny look. Maybe her greeting had been a touch too formal.

Mr. Warley turned his new hat in his hand. "If you haven't breakfasted yet, I was just on my way to the dining room. Would you care to join me?"

"We would," Elva said—loudly. "I'm terribly hungry and so is Vanora."

"Then you must be my guests." Mr. Warley cocked his elbow, and Elva slipped her hand inside of it, turning an ear-to-ear grin at Kenna.

"Mr. Warley, we can afford—" Kenna cut off her sentence when Vanora pinched her, hard.

"Thank you, Mr. Warley." Vanora took his other arm. "That's very sweet of you."

Feeling as though she had lost control of the situation—because she obviously had—Kenna trailed them into the dining room.

The younger girls provided most of the chatter, which was fine with Ben, and tucked away an amazing amount of food.

Kenna, on the other hand, picked at her meal of poached eggs and toast, adding very little to the conversation.

Ben responded to the girls, ate a breakfast he never tasted, and did his best not to gawk at the beautiful woman across the table from him.

She'd gathered her red curls into an orderly array and donned a lovely day dress that hadn't seen the rigors of the trail.

Once they were down to sipping coffee, he cleared his throat. "I spoke to Lloyd about your mules."

That brought her eyes up to meet his. He could drown in their blue-gray depths if she'd let him.

"My mules? What about them?"

He set his cup down. It rattled on the saucer until he steadied it. "He and I, we're planning on starting a dray service in the spring. Together. As partners."

She laid her napkin beside her plate and leaned forward. "But aren't you going to be partners with Mr. Red at the new diner?"

Red would hate that mister part—but he'd have to deal with it. Ben wasn't about to correct her. "I think it would be wise to diversify, to have my interests divided into two or maybe even three businesses here in Abilene."

"In Abilene?" She blinked those incredible eyes at him again.

Vanora covered her mouth with her napkin, but not before Ben caught the smile. Elva didn't bother to hide her pixie grin.

"But..." Kenna dropped her voice to a near whisper. "Who will look after your interests when you return to San Antonio?"

When he returned to... Was that what had kept them at arm's length these past weeks?

CHAPTER 32

"I HAVE NO PLANS to return to San Antonio." It wasn't ideal, walking with Kenna down the street through dust kicked up by hooves and wheels as the business district came alive, three of the canvas sacks the girls had packed riding on his good shoulder. But Ben had stopped   waiting   for i   d   e   -al.

Kenna glanced at him, a wrinkle creasing her brow, two more canvas sacks hanging from each hand. "But what of your employment with Mr. McCoy?"

Ben shrugged as best he could with the weight on his shoulder. "If he doesn't have work for me to do here in Abilene, I expect we'll part company."

Kenna stopped, the younger girls moving on ahead of them. "I don't know as much about business as you do, Mr. Warley—"

"I wish you'd call me Ben again."

She glanced toward the girls, who'd stopped and waited a few yards away. "Very well, Ben. I don't know business as you do, but even I know that a partial interest in a dray service and a partial interest in a diner won't give you the financial or social status that being one of Mr. McCoy's men would."

"You're right. But they would give me something more important."

The crease in her brow deepened—adorably.

"What would that be?"

"Time to court you, Kenna, if you'll let me."

Her eyes filled with something he couldn't quite define. But he was fairly certain it wasn't dread or disgust, so he plunged on.

"I want to start over in this new town with new people and new ways." He gestured toward a train puffing along the tracks heading for the station. "I want to put the war and all my past failures behind me once and for all." He swallowed and straightened. "And I want to do that with you by my side."

"Mr.—Ben." She practically breathed his name as she scanned the busy, dusty, blustery street around them. "Perhaps we could speak of this again later this evening? I need to see my sisters settled."

He was such an idiot.

He'd all but proposed to her on a public street in broad daylight. What would his father have... no.

He was done worrying about that. He shifted his bundles to a more secure position.

"I look forward to that. I need to report to Mr. McCoy, but I'll come by after supper."

He escorted her to the back of Red's saloon, where there was a private set of stairs across from the room George and Leppo would be using. The girls wouldn't need to enter the saloon itself to reach or leave their room.

Not ideal—again—but temporary.

And if their evening walk went well, maybe very temporary.

"Promise me you'll stay right here in our room." Kenna laced her fingers together and unlaced them for at least the tenth time. "You'll lock the door and not open it for anyone other than me."

"Of course." Vanora gave her a slanted glance as if to say they weren't stupid.

They weren't. She wasn't honestly concerned about that. About everything else—yes—but not about that. Concerned that Ben was not thinking things through clearly. Concerned that he might have changed his mind since morning. After all, it was well past dinner, and where was he?

"He'll be here," Vanora said, for all the world as if she'd read Kenna's thoughts.

The piano below plinked out a rollicking tune that jarred Kenna's nerves even more. How were they supposed to sleep through that?

The knock at the door made her jump. Elva giggled and Vanora rolled her eyes before heading to the door.

"I'll get it." Kenna had to get control of the situation—as well as herself. She slung her shawl around her shoulders and pulled it open.

Ben waited in the narrow hallway, hat in his hands, looking as cool and collected as she felt flustered and disoriented. It wasn't fair, and her temper simmered, but she raised her chin and nodded her greeting. "Good evening, Ben. Would you like to step in?"

His cool exterior slipped a notch. "I thought we'd"—he made a vague gesture toward the stairs—"take our walk. The evening is cool, but the wind has tapered off."

Vanora pushed Kenna into the hall. "Have a good walk. I'm locking the door now." The door shut and a metallic click followed.

Kenna could have choked her.

Ben hadn't taken a step back, so they were practically nose to nose in the dimly lit hallway. His brown eyes darkened, but he cleared his throat and moved toward the stairs before the moment grew too awkward. He stepped aside and let her descend first.

George and Leppo were entering the back door when they reached it. George grinned and nodded. Leppo raised an eyebrow and entered their room.

Thankful for the low lighting, Kenna swept past them into the evening and let the cool air calm her heated cheeks.

"I'm sorry I'm late." Ben closed the door behind them. "McCoy and I talked things over. It took longer than I'd planned." He put on his hat. "The good news is, he agreed to hire Squirrel as my replacement in San Antonio. Squirrel's a good judge of character, and he'll hire the best men for future drives. Even more important, the ranchers trust him."

"I'm happy for Mr. Brinkmann. He and Pa were good friends for many years." Would Pa still be alive if Mr. Brinkmann hadn't... no. She couldn't think like that. And she didn't really. Pa had done what he wanted to do. None of it was Mr. Brinkmann's fault.

Kenna hadn't mentioned to anyone the extra dollars he'd slipped in with Pa's wages she'd been given, even though she suspected they'd come from Mr. Brinkmann's own pocket. If it made him feel better, who was she to object? He'd done what he wanted to do too.

They walked toward the river, a three-quarter moon casting its silvery light across the prairie, the silence stretching between them like a living thing.

Ben stopped by the edge of the water. "I feel like we got off on the wrong foot months ago." He rubbed his palms against the sides of his hips as if drying them. "But I hold you in very high regard, and I had your father's permission to walk with you on the cattle drive."

She nodded and waited.

And waited.

"The thing is, Kenna, as I said earlier, I want to start over. I want to leave all my past failures behind. And I want to start over with you."

"What failures?"

He groaned, a sound so low it was almost a growl. "I used to think the worst was turning my back on the Confederacy and swearing allegiance to the Union, but to tell you the truth, I think my first failure was joining the Confederacy at all. I was swept along with everyone else of my acquaintance. We were all going to whip the Yankees and be home for the harvest." He shook his head. "We were fools."

"You fought against Northern oppression." But even in her own ears, Kenna's words lacked the conviction they'd once held.

"We fought for our way of life, yes." He looked at her, the moon casting shadows on his face. "But what kind of a life was it? We kept people in bondage who did the hard work while we did practically nothing." He spread his hands and then let them drop to his sides. "I never thought about it growing up. Slavery just... was. It was as much a part of my life as breathing."

"I never thought about it much either. Slaves followed their masters along the street and waited outside the diner while they ate." Guilt pinched at Kenna. "They were just there, a part of everyday life."

"That's it, exactly." Ben sighed. "They were a huge part of my life, and I didn't even realize it. I never saw them as... people."

"And that changed when you signed your oath to the Union?"

"No. I signed that oath to get out of a prison I would most likely have died in. The war was over for me. Father had sunk every last penny into the war before he died. Peter was gone. Even if our place hadn't been burned to the ground, there was no money for taxes. No money to live on. Nothing. Everything I'd ever known was gone."

"So what changed your mind about slavery?"

"George." He shrugged. "And even Leppo. Working with them, actually *with* them, not ordering them around but getting my hands dirty beside them, made me see them for who they are." He pinched the bridge of his nose between a thumb and forefinger.

Kenna touched his sleeve. "It was the same with me."

He lowered his hand and captured hers in the process. "I'm glad we agree on that now."

"We do." And that bit of common ground allowed hope to enter her. A hope that almost stole her breath.

Or maybe it was the warmth in his eyes.

Ben's breath hitched as Kenna laced her fingers with his, but he needed to get the rest of his story out, so she'd know exactly what he was leaving behind. That was only fair. Hard, but fair.

"I knew nothing of hard work before the war. I was the spoiled younger son of a small plantation owner. I amused myself and occasionally listened as Father instructed Peter in the running of our estate. But I knew my place in life was secure. I'd be Peter's overseer, a job without merit, earning an income from the estate to support myself and a family someday." He sighed, twin plumes feathering the air between them. "And I was content with that." He shook his head. "Content to not amount to anything."

"But you joined the Confederate Army."

"Only because it was expected of me."

"And then you served in the U.S. Cavalry."

"I did. And I didn't run away like my cousin did. By then I'd gained enough self-respect to know I needed to follow through with something—even a loyalty oath to my former sworn enemy." He paused, letting the cold air between them grow still. "But they weren't, you know."

"They weren't your enemy?"

"No. They were just men—like all men—doing what they thought was right. Men like Charlie, Jake, and Vernon who brought the cattle north with us."

Kenna nodded. "It took me a long time to see that. Pa tried to tell me back in San Antonio, but I wouldn't listen. After working with them—and you—day after day, I realized the same thing. They're good men." She squeezed his hand. "You're a good man."

His heart did all sorts of strange contortions at her touch. "But when we visited that trader..."

"Mr. Hatchett?"

"Him." Ben closed his eyes for a moment, and then met her gaze through the darkness. "I was tempted to do what he asked."

"Because it brought back your loyalty to the Confederacy?"

"No. I thought if I took the rifles south, then maybe you'd—" He dropped her hand and scrubbed his jaw, the rasp of a day's growth of whiskers loud in the stillness. "I thought it might win your approval."

"Because of my dislike of Yankees?"

"Yes."

"You're not going to take the rifles." It wasn't a question, just a soft assurance.

"No. The war is over and—I have to say it—I believe that the right side won."

She grasped his hand again, and he stole another look at her.

She smiled, the same smile he'd fallen in love with back in San Antonio. The smile that came not from her lips or her eyes or anything so earthly. A smile that came from her soul. The smile that touched his.

"I agree."

Her words loosened the bands around his chest, allowing air to enter fully for the first time in... hours? Days? Weeks? It didn't matter.

He cupped her face between his palms, gently, giving her every opportunity to escape as he lowered his lips to hers.

She didn't.

The next few moments were lost in a rush of something pure and honest and beautiful.

Then she pulled back, only far enough to look into his eyes, their noses almost touching. "If you choose me, you'll never have the social standing you were born to. And you'll never earn the amount of gold you would with Mr. McCoy. He's building a new kind of empire. In his employment, you could be a powerful figure in Abilene or San Antonio or maybe even Chicago. Are you sure you want to turn all that down?"

He had to concentrate on her words—her silly words—when all he wanted to do was kiss her again. But the sincerity in her eyes said she needed his answer.

"I guess I could have taken his offer and earned myself a pile of gold." Maybe even his late father's approval. He pulled her closer, enjoying the feel of her pressed against him even through their thick winter clothing. "But social standing and all the Yankee gold in the world isn't as enticing as life on these silver prairies with you by my side."

She melted against him, head pressed to his chest, and he rested his chin on her hair, looking out over the frosty prairie surrounding them. They'd work hard and they'd sacrifice, but they'd build a good life here.

With Kenna by his side, nothing was impossible.

AUTHOR'S HISTORICAL NOTES

The fall cattle drive depicted in this novel is completely fictional. The drives started in the early spring and went through the summer months. Conditions in the fall and winter were too harsh and feed too scarce to safely move the vast numbers of cattle, horses, and men. I took liberties with the history because it made for a good "what if" scenario.

Joseph McCoy was a visionary from Chicago whose idea of driving nearly worthless cattle up from Texas to meet the railheads in Kansas and ship to the eastern markets was a huge success that benefited the country in a time of deep need and financial crisis. That first year, 1867, saw 35,000 head of cattle moved north. It wasn't all smooth sailing. McCoy had to do a fair share of politicking to make it happen, and in the end, he had to take the railroad to court to get paid, but the nation was grateful.

The route mapped out by surveyor Timothy Hersey would come to be known in later years as the Chisholm Trail.

The Menger Hotel was opened in 1859 by William Menger as a result of his successful brewery. It was said that he brought beer to San Antonio. During the Civil War, he shut down the hotel's guest rooms and housed Confederate personnel, also giving space to care for wounded soldiers. After the war, the hotel once again resumed its full operation. It's still a working hotel today.

One of the fun facts I discovered while researching for this book is that San Antonio—which was the largest city in Texas at that time—had a large German population, including William Menger who owned the famous hotel. Some seven thousand Germans settled there from 1847 to 1861. German was a common language heard along its streets.

Water sources for San Antonio were open air canals that served as both water and sewer. In 1836, the San Pedro canal was designated for drinking and cooking only. There were stiff penalties if caught using it for bathing or sewage. A severe cholera outbreak in 1866 forced the city to find another way to provide water to its residents.

Ferdinand Maximilian Joseph, Archduke of Austria, was crowned Emperor of Mexico in 1864—backed by the French army—and ruled there until 1867, when he was executed by the native Mexican forces. After the American Civil War, there was a movement of some Confederate troops to join with Maximilian in the hopes that he would assist them in another attempt to rekindle the Confederacy, but it never happened.

The remuda's wrangler was a very important position in the cattle drive. It took a lot of horses to move cattle. Ten mounts per cowboy was normal. The men would overwork themselves—but rarely the horses. Success, even survival, depended on the animals they rode.

In the late 1860s, the great buffalo herds still roamed the prairies. They weren't hunted to almost extinction until later in the 1880s. A constant danger to the cattle drives—one of many—were these massive herds. They spooked the cattle as well as the horses, and even the steady mules were known to run in fear at the sight and smell of those big shaggies.

Another danger on the trail was boggy ground, generally riverbeds and creeks that had low water levels. Thirsty cattle would wade in for a drink and get stuck. It could take cowboys the better part of a day to rope and drag the heavy beasts through the depth of clinging mud and back to safe footing. I read one account where the mud was so deep and so thick that in the process of dragging out a steer, it was separated from one of its legs, which remained behind in the mire.

In some of the boggy places, the cowboys had to construct "bridges" of fallen trees, fresh-cut branches, and brush that they paved over with sod cut from the prairie. As the reader can imagine, such structures were far from solid footing, the green branches bending and giving with each step while still allowing water to flow through them beneath the sod. It could take the cowboys a full day to force the lead horses and cattle across such a bridge, but once they did, the rest would follow. The bridges were built wide enough to allow the chuckwagon to cross, so they were quite the undertaking and only built when absolutely necessary.

Joseph McCoy's Drovers Cottage (spelled without an apostrophe) was built in the summer of 1867, and enough was finished to welcome the cattlemen when the drives reached Abilene. It consisted of thirty bedrooms and was lavishly furnished. McCoy went bankrupt in 1870 (due to the railroad defaulting on its promises of payment) and the new owners expanded it. It stayed a landmark until 1871, when the cattle drives moved farther west and Abilene became a quiet prairie town. It's believed that Jesse & Frank James and others of the James Gang hid out there sometime in 1871.

The cattle drives proved to be very successful, with the following numbers coming into Abilene:

1867   35,000
1868   75,000
1869   150,000
1870   300,000
1871   600,000

Cattle were moved farther south and west as the railroad expanded, including the towns of Wichita, Ellsworth, and Dodge City. It was a tremendous undertaking that created a whole new class of Americans—the cowboys—and fueled stories in print, on radio, and eventually on the silver screen that are still entertaining people to this day.

REVIEWS ARE GOLDEN

Reviews are the lifeblood of authors. Leaving a review on **Amazon, Goodreads**, and/or **BookBub** means that more readers will find our books! Reviews can be long or short - your honest opinion of the book. Shout-outs on any social media platforms also help!

About Pegg Thomas

Pegg Thomas lives in Michigan's Upper Peninsula with Michael, her husband of *mumble* years. She creates American stories with real history and fictional characters inspired by her ancestors who immigrated here in the early 1600s.

Pegg won the 2019 FHL Readers' Choice Award for novellas, was a double-finalist for the 2019 ACFW Carol Award for novellas, and a finalist for the 2019 ACFW Editor of the Year. She was a finalist in the 2021 FHL Readers' Choice Award for novellas. Pegg won the 2022 Selah Award for historical romance and placed 2nd with her second entry. She was a finalist for the 2023 FHL Selah Award, placed 2nd in the 2024 Selah Award, and won the 2024 Will Rogers Silver AND Bronze Medallion Awards. Pegg spent 3 ½ years as the managing editor of Smitten Historical Romance.

PeggThomas.com
Facebook
Goodreads
BookBub
Amazon
Newsletter signup